# To Reach For
# The Stars

## Ray Burston

© 2016

During the darkest days of the Second World War, Eileen Kimberley – a pretty teenage girl from the backstreets of Birmingham – makes her bid to escape a claustrophobic home life by enlisting in Britain's Women's Auxiliary Air Force.

What follows proves to be not just the adventure of a lifetime, playing her part in her country's desperate war in the skies over Germany; but also a painful voyage of self-discovery in which a tragic past impels this gifted young woman to seek out that special someone with whom she can share her crazy dreams.

*'Per Ardua Ad Astra'*

Dedicated to the memory of my mother,
Hilda Eileen Jones…


…who – like a quarter of a million other remarkable young
women – served her country during wartime in the
Women's Auxiliary Air Force.

10% of the royalties from the sale of this book will be donated to the Royal Air Force Benevolent Fund and its ongoing work amongst veterans of all ages – men and women – who have served in the RAF.

**For more information, visit rafbf.org.**

## *Table of equivalent ranks*

| Royal Air Force | Women's Auxiliary Air Force | United States Army Air Force |
|---|---|---|
| Marshal of the RAF | | General of the Army |
| Air Chief Marshal | | General |
| Air Marshal | | Lieutenant General |
| Air Vice-Marshal | Air Chief Commandant | Major General |
| Air Commodore | Air Commandant | Brigadier General |
| Group Captain | Group Officer | Colonel |
| Wing Commander | Wing Officer | Lieutenant Colonel |
| Squadron Leader | Squadron Officer | Major |
| Flight Lieutenant | Flight Officer | Captain |
| Flying Officer | Section Officer | First Lieutenant |
| Pilot Officer | Assistant Section Officer | Second Lieutenant |
| Warrant Officer | Warrant Officer | Warrant Officer |
| Flight Sergeant | Flight Sergeant | Master Sergeant |
| Sergeant | Sergeant | Technical Sergeant |
| Corporal | Corporal | Staff Sergeant |
| Leading Aircraftman | Leading Aircraftwoman | Corporal |
| Aircraftman First Class | Aircraftwoman First Class | Private First Class |
| Aircraftman Second Class | Aircraftwoman Second Class | Private Second Class |

# *Glossary*

All terms refer to British usage unless otherwise stated.

Ack-ack – anti-aircraft guns (also known as flak)
ACW – Aircraftwoman
AOC – Air Officer Commanding
AWOL – Absent Without Leave
ARP – Air Raid Precautions warden
ATS – Army Territorial Service (women's branch of the British Army)
Base bludger –administration personnel (Australian term)
Battle-dress blues – heavy, woollen RAF uniform.
Best blues – RAF parade uniform
Biscuits – Standard issue straw mattress units
Blower – telephone
Boffin – scientist or inventor
Brass hats – senior officers
Brylcreem boys – RAF airmen (after the hair gel many of them used)
Bumf – RAF forms and paperwork
Chain Home – a network of coastal early warning radar stations.
Civvies – civilian clothes
Civvy Street – civilian life after leaving the service
CO – Commanding Officer
Combat box – bombers flying in a tight defensive formation (US term)
Contrails – vapour trails produced by aircraft when flying at high altitude
Corkscrew – a twisting dive designed to shake off enemy fighters
Darkie – A plane in distress looking for somewhere to land
Demob – termination of military service at war's end (demobilisation)
Dicey-do – air operation encountering stiff opposition
Drop-tanks – external fuel tanks that can be jettisoned when emptied
ENSA – Entertainments National Service Association
Erk – nickname for an ordinary airmen
Feathering – trimming a propeller's blades to reduce drag
FFI – 'Free from infections' (especially of the sexually-transmitted variety)
Fifty – a bomber's .50 calibre machine gun (US term)
Five shilling meals – restricted portions in restaurants due to food rationing
Flak – anti-aircraft guns (from German *fliegabwehrkanone*)
FMU – Field Maintenance Unit
'For the chop' – a premonition of impending death
'48' – a pass granting forty-eight hours leave
FUBAR – 'F***ed up beyond all recognition' (derogatory US term)
GI – US serviceman (ironic acronym of 'Government Issue' equipment)
GI Jane – US servicewoman
Greenhouse – the cockpit of a bomber (US term)
Gremlins – inexplicable mechanical or electrical faults afflicting aircraft
Hallybag – Nickname for a Handley Page Halifax bomber

Hang-ups – bombs that fail to release from the bomb bay

Intercom – internal radio system aboard a bomber

Interphone – internal radio system aboard a bomber (US term)

Jankers – menial punishment duties

Jerry – Germans

Jinking – sharp evasive flying manoeuvres (US term)

Kite – affectionate term for a heavy bomber

Krauts – Germans (US term)

LACW – Leading Aircraftwoman

Land Army – women enlisted to work on the farms

*Luftwaffe* – the German air force

Mae West – lifejacket (supposedly resembling the actress's ample cleavage)

Milk Run – an operation encountering little, if any opposition (US term)

MO – Medical Officer

MQ – Married quarters

NAAFI – Navy, Army & Air Force Institute (armed forces social club)

Ninety Day Wonder – US officer commissioned directly from civilian life

NCO – non-commissioned officer (warrant officers, sergeants and corporals)

Nuffields – sanitary towels issued to British servicewomen

Odd-bod – someone who has lost or become separated from his fellow aircrew

Ops – flying operations and missions

Pass – authorisation granted to be absent from camp

Pea-souper – Thick fog that prevents flying

Pusser – sailor (Australian term)

Queen – Nickname for a Boeing B17 Flying Fortress bomber (US term)

POW – Prisoner of war

PX – Post Exchange (armed forces post office and trading store – US term)

R & R – leave ('rest and recuperation' – US term)

Rooinek –an English person (Rhodesian term)

Second dickey – co-pilot

Spam Can – Nickname for a North American P51 Mustang fighter

Spiv – a black market trader

Sprog – a new, inexperienced member of aircrew

Squaddie – nickname for an ordinary British soldier

Square-bashing – drill, marching and parading

Sugar Report – love letter (US term)

Tabbies – servicewomen (Australian term)

Tail-end Charlie – nickname for rear turret gunners

USO – United Service Organisation (US military entertainment service)

W/O – Wireless Operator

W/T – Wireless transmitter (radio)

WAAF – member of the Women's Auxiliary Air Force

Wimpy – nickname for a Vickers Wellington bomber

WingCo – Wing Commander

Wren – member of the WRNS (Women's Royal Naval Service)

WO – Warrant Officer

*"We are all in the gutter.*
*But some of us are looking up at the stars."*

*Oscar Wilde*

# 1

Snip… snip… snip.

It was a drastic, if grievous price to pay. However, with the brisk, resolute wielding of those scissors Eileen Kathleen Kimberley was at last beginning to leave her old life behind. Besides, the regulations stated her hair must be off the collar, so off the collar it had to be.

Snip… snip… snip…

And so it was that a head of flowing sable curls had been reduced to a more modest barnet. Upon which, the job of transformation complete, she now alighted from the barber's chair and moved aside for the next recipient to seat herself down. Then it was off to the quartermaster's store to collect her smart new uniform, as well as the other bits of standard issue kit that would become her possessions for the duration of the war.

Eileen adored those gorgeous flowing locks. So why had this happy-go-lucky eighteen year-old consented to this? Of course, there was the stirring of the patriotism that dwells in the bosom of any self-respecting Englishwoman; of wanting to defend her plucky little island home from those evil Nazi hordes. There was the tinge of excitement mixed with apprehension at being away from home for the first time. However, there was also an inward yearning to be free from a home life that, while cushioned by familial love, had also been proving more suffocating with each passing day.

To be sure, many young women of Eileen's age were also answering their country's call, whether in the women's branches of the armed forces; or in the Land Army helping out on the farms; or in the factories that had been emptied of young men also answering the call to arms. So why the Royal Air Force? Well, apart from that smart blue uniform and the thrill of being around aeroplanes, there was something about the motto that had captured the imagination of this bright young lass from Birmingham: *'Per Ardua Ad Astra'* – 'to reach for the stars'. Yes, that too spoke eloquently of the free spirit within her that yearned to soar without limits.

For now though, freedom and 'soaring without limits' were the last things on offer. As she permitted herself a momentary glance in the mirror to survey how that uniform became her, like her fellow recruits to the Women's Auxiliary Air Force – or WAAFs, as the female branch of the RAF had been promptly nicknamed – she was conscious that henceforth she was a woman under orders.

In the first instance, those orders had been to report for induction and basic training at RAF Innsworth outside Gloucester, where she would now spend the next few weeks learning how to comport herself as an a servicewoman. And if she survived all that, then she would in due course 'pass out' and set off elsewhere to learn the 'trade' that would be her modest contribution to the victory that Mr Churchill was confident her country would yet achieve.

\* \* \* \* \*

"Not exactly the height of fashion, are they? I can see why the guys called them 'black-outs'!" one of new recruits scoffed, holding the pair of giant navy blue bloomers aloft and examining them in dismay.

Eileen raised a smile as she sat on the bunk examining her own pair. Drape anything in a pair of those and Jerry would have a hard time spotting it from ten thousand feet at night! However, they were regulation issue and so she gathered them together to stow away with the rest of the kit she had acquired, and which included: 'irons' (RAF slang for an unpretentious cutlery set), a 'housewife' (ditto, your needle-and-thread clothes repair kit), 'Nuffields' (ditto, what every woman needs at a certain time of the month – so named after the aristocratic benefactor who had kindly made it his calling to finance their provision to every servicewomen!), two bras, two vests, two pairs of the aforementioned 'black-outs', two pairs of more appealing knickers (more hopefully termed 'knock-outs!), two pairs of thick lisle stockings (once again, definitely not the height of fashion!), two pairs of suspender belts to hold them up, two pairs of standard black lace-up Oxford shoes, a pair of striped flannelette pyjamas, a greatcoat, a gas mask and tin hat (and woe betide any WAAF who didn't have them to hand at all times) and your '1250' regulation ID card. Upon receipt of these, it was goodbye to your civilian clothes (which would be posted home). Throw in a few injections to guard against this or that, a declaration form stating you were 'FFI' (free from infections – especially of the sexual variety!), and behold – it was hello Aircraftswoman Second Class 2090088 Kimberley, Eileen K.!

Grumbles there were aplenty amongst the assorted intake of girls who now staked their claims to bunks within the draughty Nissen huts that would be their home for the next few weeks. Hailing from all parts of the British Isles, and all manner of different backgrounds, they certainly made for an entertaining human soup. There were prim, middle-class girls from good homes for whom descent into this Spartan existence would surely come as one almighty shock. Conversely, there were rough-and-ready lasses for whom enlistment was almost a step up, the three-meals-a-day and the opportunities to travel and to learn a useful trade more than compensating for the rigours of structured service life.

Though Eileen assured herself that everything would be fine, inwardly she too was prone to wonder what she had let herself in for. Though she was no stranger to hardship, for the first time in her life she felt quaintly attached to the things she had left behind in Birmingham. She certainly missed her mother, though she was glad that the grounding she had given her in the school-of-hard-knocks might just see her through the next few challenging weeks.

When the time came for lights-out she curled up beneath the sheets on the hard straw 'biscuits' that formed the mattress of her rough wooden bunk, pondering these things. In particular, once again she questioned how her yearning for freedom could be squared with the regime of duty and discipline that she had just signed up for. As was the habit of this good Catholic girl, she closed her eyes and quietly said her prayers, trusting that the Good Lord Himself would make everything plain in His own good time.

It was while she was whispering her way through the final petitioning to 'God bless Mum, God bless Frank, God bless Auntie Kathleen, God bless Granny… And God bless Dad – wherever he may be' that, amongst the voluble snoring going on within the darkened hut, she thought she could hear sniffling. Cocking open an eye, as well as craning an ear to the bunk above her, she could indeed make out the sound of its occupant weeping. Never one to pass up the obligation of charity towards a fellow human being, Eileen discreetly slithered out of her bunk and stood up to behold the source of such tearful solicitude.

"Shhh. You'll be okay," she counselled laying her hand upon her shoulder.

"I'm so scared. I've never been away from home before," the girl whispered, dabbing away those tears before they wet the hard, stuffed pillow-roll her head was nestled upon.

"Me neither. It is scary, I know. But… well… I guess we're all just going to have to learn to be strong."

Such exhortation seemed of little comfort, the girl closing her eyes in a further bout of muffled sobbing. Anxious lest it wake the others, Eileen could tell that something more specific was needed.

"I'm Eileen. Eileen Kimberley. From Birmingham. What's your name?"

"Ruth. Ruth Owen. From Buckinghamshire."

"Well, Ruth. If I can be your friend, you can be mine. You stick by me and *together* we will help *each other* to be strong."

It seemed to work. Eileen watched as a smile reluctantly broke upon tear-streaked cheeks and a hand popped up from beneath the sheets to take hold of her own in a comradely grip.

Yes, together they would do this. Together they would show what the women of the September 1941 intake could do.

\* \* \* \* \*

This was it: she was all alone and this was destined to be the first test of whether she could get it right. Let's see: three bars on his arm – wing commander. Or were those the bars that signified a squadron leader? Eileen frantically interrogated herself. Yet it was too late to trawl through what she had learned so far and be certain. Instead, here he was, heading her way – even as she was making for the NAAFI, otherwise minding her own business. Here goes. Nervously she made 'eyes right', yanked her right arm up rigidly until her forefingers touched her cap and… oops!

The officer glanced her way and saluted also, Eileen catching the trajectory of his eyes and the slight wince on his face that surely spoke of despair at observing this callow, bumbling recruit almost trip over herself in her anxiety to get it right. However, all too soon they had passed each other by and it was over. She had survived the encounter with an officer.

'If it moves, salute it; if it doesn't, paint it', some navy lads had sought to educate her during the train journey down. She cursed herself. Next time she would get it right.

\* \* \* \* \*

"Left… left… left, right, left…"

Someone was flat-footed. Someone was out-of-step. Someone was surely about to be…

"Owen, have you got two left feet? Or are you completely incapable of counting time?" the corporal shrieked, the wayward recruit in question trying that bit harder to keep up.

The squad was duly halted outside the block and marked time until the order was given to turn about and face the wicked harridan with the 'stripes' who had been assigned to knock this particular cohort into shape.

"Squad, halt… Stand at ease!"

They duly stood themselves at ease. Or so they had thought.

"Good grief! That sounded like a ruddy machine gun rattling off. So we will do it again. Only this time I want to hear those feet snap in unison… Squad, attention…! That's better… Stand at ease…!"

There was a wary look on the corporal's face as she wandered up and down the lines and scowled at each of them in turn.

"Eyes front, Aircraftwoman Owen… I have eyes in the back of my head. So if I catch yours following my arse again…"

Ruth's eyeballs duly shot forward in their sockets, a rapid turn of the corporal's head quickly extinguishing any nascent tittering in the ranks. Then satisfied they knew who was in charge, she stood at their head once more and briefed them about the morning's activities. Then she brought them to attention one more time (in unison, she was pleased to hear) before dismissing them to head inside the mess hall.

\* \* \* \* \*

"That corporal certainly has it in for you," someone guffawed as they all sat down to partake of the cook's idea of a solid, if unappetising square meal.

"Mind you, by now, Owen, you really should know your left foot from your right!" Aircraftwoman Harris added wearily.

"Yes, and unless you do, sooner or later we'll all end up doing 'jankers'!" Aircraftwoman Cove snarled by way of a reminder, glancing around the table at the others, who nonetheless tried as best they could to hide their embarrassment that sadly there was much truth in her observation.

While Eileen couldn't wholly deny the assessment of Harris and Cove regarding her mishap-making new friend, she even so despised the mocking, condescending spirit of which it was borne (though she bit her tongue and said nothing).

Instead she surmised that in every cohort of recruits – male or female; Army, Navy or Air Force – there are cocky, domineering ones like Harris who like to think they are setting the pace; sly, sycophantic ones like Cove who mask their own insecurities and inadequacies by enthusiastically pointing out the foibles of others; and accident-prone loners like Ruth Owen who invariably attract the enraged ire of the NCOs. And maybe (she hoped) generous souls like Eileen too, who, whilst proud of what they had mastered so far, could nonetheless still find within themselves the patience and charity to keep on coaching the no-hopers in the hope that they would finally 'get it right' – whether 'getting it right' entailed turning out smartly, or presenting their kit correctly, or being able to drill with consistent efficiency.

From the look of dejection upon Ruth's cherubic face she could see that the hope was fast fading from this particular 'no-hoper'. As the rest of their squad gathered at table rose to get ready to present themselves on parade once more, Eileen therefore reached her hand across to squeeze Ruth's own and assure her one more time that '*together* we will help *each other* to be strong'.

\* \* \* \* \*

The burly MPs tried to be as gentle as the restraining of a diminutive young lady demanded, but in the end there was no escaping the fact that at least some man-handing would be required to transport the tearful, grovelling WAAF from the back of the van and into the CO's office, where she was about to discover her fate.

Observing the return to camp of Aircraftwoman Owen in this way, Eileen desperately wanted to race in and say something in mitigation for her hapless colleague. However, she knew it was probably too late. Ruth had clearly been at the end of her tether emotionally and had confided in her only 'friend' on the camp about her yearning to 'get out and go home'. Eileen, in turn, had done her best to talk her out of such nonsense and tried one last time to fire her up with the knowledge that '*together* we will help *each other* to be strong'.

However, in the end it had been no use. Whilst she and the others had promptly returned to camp after their afternoon leave in town, Ruth had not. Her absence had been noted, the authorities informed, and in due course the RAF Military Police had caught up with her. If she was lucky she would be charged with being AWOL and put on humiliating, but hopefully bearable jankers duties around the camp. If not, then something altogether more ominous would be prescribed. The fact that Ruth had been apprehended on Gloucester railway station about to board a train for London led Eileen to fear that the latter option would regrettably prevail.

"Serves her right," sneered the butch, unsmiling Aircraftwoman Harris, who had meanwhile sidled up alongside Eileen to observe the MPs frog-march her inside. "She should have stuck it out. Then again, some people are born to succeed and some people are born to fail. That's just how it is."

Eileen turned her head. Though once again she said nothing, this time the harsh glare in brown eyes must have told Harris that she considered such a remark wholly out of order. Instead, Harris glared back dismissively before wandering back to their quarters.

\* \* \* \* \*

This was it – the big day. The band was playing. Even the Air Commodore had put in an appearance.

Eileen couldn't decide whether his presence on the parade ground made the girls more nervous or just more determined to put on a good show. Either way, the weeks of relentless drilling and being barked at by the NCOs – plus the privations and the aching attention to spit-and-polish – had finally paid off. Even their Corporal couldn't believe how well-oiled the 'machine gun' now was, each ordered turn, halt and quick march executed without fault. Then, at last, the music ceased. They were brought to attention and their officer drew up to the Air Commodore, saluting and presenting them for review. She then escorted him as he paced along the silent ranks of recruits.

Eyes fixed rigidly forward, Aircraftwoman Kimberley thrust her chest out proudly and waited anxiously as the portly chief passed her by, the periphery of her forward gaze just catching him briefly cast his eyes over her uniform before moving on. It occasioned a blink on her part that she hoped he had not noticed. Then a few moments later she sensed him pass behind her to review the second line of WAAFs.

It had certainly been a gruelling few weeks. Recalling it left her remorseful that she had not been able to do more to persuade her friend Ruth Owen to see things through to the pass out parade. However, she had not been the only one to fall by the wayside: Aircraftwoman Cove was also not present today, having no longer been able to hide the 'bun in the oven' that had been growing inside her. The discovery that she was pregnant by persons unknown had abruptly brought to an end her hopes of a career in the Royal Air Force.

The band striking up abruptly snapped Eileen out of her fretting. Then the corporal turned the squad about and marched them off the parade ground. The deed done, she eventually stood them at ease. Upon which their squadron officer dug her fists into her hips and moved in to address them.

"Well done, girls. You'll be pleased to know that, with immediate effect, you are now all fully-fledged members of the Women's Auxiliary Air Force. These last few weeks have been testing, I know; but you have been tested and you have not been found wanting. As such, you will shortly be advised of your new postings, where you will begin the next leg of your journey in the RAF.

"Remember, you may not be paid as much as the men alongside whom you will serve. Neither, I fear, will you ever receive the glory that attends those who soar above you in their Spitfires and their Hurricanes. But without your work, lowly and often unsung though it may be, we cannot win this war. And because that work is so vital, I want you never to think that your contribution is worth any less than that of an airman. I am immensely proud of you. I believe, in the fullness of time, your country will be immensely proud of you too. Don't let them down.

"Finally, you will be pleased to know that once you have received your postings you will be granted forty-eight hours leave in order to relay this good news to your families. That is all. You may dismiss them, Corporal," the officer instructed, turning to the NCO – both of them saluting, both of them sporting a smile of satisfaction at a job well done.

"Squad, attention…! Squad, dismiss."

The moment formalities ceased there was hugging and rejoicing in the ranks. They had done it! And now they wasted no time readying themselves for the chance to seize their first real taste of freedom for a long while.

# 2

The locomotive wheezed and hissed on its passage into New Street Station, its rake of carriages trundling and squealing to a halt behind it. Then, joining the throngs of other assorted service personnel stepping down to either head off on leave (if they were lucky) or change trains en route to other postings (if they weren't), there disembarked the proudest girl in all of Birmingham at that very moment: Aircraftswoman Second Class Eileen Kimberley – resplendent in her smart blue uniform (even though its resplendence owed more to the martial bearing with which she now comported herself than the opportunity it afforded her to show off her undeniable feminine allure!).

In many respects it was as if Eileen had never been away. The streets of Birmingham had certainly not changed. The buildings damaged by the last big air raids in April still stood defiant, their hollowed out shells looking all the more gaunt as the dull, autumnal drizzle enveloped them in its gloom. Mercifully, with old Adolf's gaze now turned towards Russia the attention of the *Luftwaffe* had turned with it, meaning that it had been a long while since any serious air raids had been experienced in the city.

Even the suburbs had not been spared. The tram ride along the Bristol Road to her Selly Oak home quickly revealed a spread of damaged or destroyed properties that had presumably been the result of near misses as the Germans had sought to knock out the 'battery' works at the back of where she lived (or maybe even the Austin Motor Works at Longbridge, the Spitfire factory at Castle Bromwich, or one of the many other important war industries located in this, Britain's second city and 'workshop of the world').

Eventually, stepping down from the tram and making her way up the street she was relieved to discover that the little terraced house in which she had grown up was still there, and which once more evoked memories – both good and bad. And yet before she had had chance to trawl back into that quiver of memories, a face at the parlour window had spied her passage and the front door opened. For a brief moment no words passed between them until pent-up emotion drove both of them to launch arms around each other.

"Mum!" Eileen wept.

To be sure, her mother, Mary Kimberley, was also well-acquainted with the school-of-hard-knocks that she had so diligently coached her daughter through. A rare tear glistening in her eye spoke touchingly of how she had perhaps never realised just how much she would miss her 'little girl'.

"Bab!" came the reply as, tears hastily shoved aside, she eventually released her embrace in order to usher her inside.

"Look who's finally returned!" she then announced, bidding her daughter remove her damp greatcoat and locate a spot next to the roaring coal fire.

It was a most welcome spot too, and Eileen wasted no time drawing up a chair and holding her dainty hands out to it to soak up its warmth.

"There was no need to worry, Mum. I'm a big girl now. And though it's been hard, I really feel like I've achieved something," she enthused, rubbing those hands together.

"Your mother was right to worry, Eileen," noted the other familiar figure in her life, and who was sat at the kitchen table observing the homecoming with a rejoicing in her heart that promptly lifted her to feet to also embrace Eileen – even as she couldn't resist adding, "A young girl away from home on an airfield full of young men. She had every right to worry."

"It was not that bad, Auntie Kathleen. They don't call it No.2 WAAF Depot for nothing!" the wanderer assured them both. "Most of the folk on the camp are women. I overheard someone say that this year over eighty thousand girls have volunteered to join the Air Force – four thousand in one week alone. I tell you, we women are going to win this war. After all, without us doing the vital jobs on the ground there would be no fighters or bombers taking to the skies to sock it to Hitler. I'm told the telephonist trade that I've applied for is becoming exclusively the preserve of women."

It was a confident boast which rendered Auntie Kathleen alternately sceptical and slightly horrified. But then, in so many ways, Mary and Kathleen were so unalike that it was hard to believe they were sisters. Whereas Eileen's mother was feisty, plain-speaking, and unashamed of her working-class pedigree, Auntie Kathleen was pious, well-spoken and demure.

It seldom took long for Auntie Kathleen's demonstrative piety to make itself apparent. As Eileen turned her gaze from the glowing hearth, she spotted her mother set down upon the kitchen table a plate of sandwiches that had been put together from whatever the weekly rations had enabled her to bring home. In the time it took Mary to swivel about and retrieve the teapot from off the stove Eileen also noticed Auntie Kathleen discreetly make the sign of the Cross, glancing at Eileen as if to affirm that it was the only correct response to God's goodness to this otherwise impecunious household.

Conversely, when her mother sat down and urged Eileen to drew her own chair back around the table, Mary crossed herself in such perfunctory fashion that it clearly alluded to the fact that her own Roman Catholic faith was, to put it generously, merely surface deep – the inevitable veneer of their shared Irish roots which needn't be allowed to unduly intrude upon what few worldly pleasures life tossed her way.

"I thought you might like to know that someone else is home of leave this weekend," her mother then noted, hoping that the tantalising hint would evoke a response.

"Who? You mean...?"

"Yes. He's home. Frank is back from sea. And he can't wait to see you."

There was certainly a glow in Eileen's eyes at the thought that her childhood sweetheart was at that moment standing barely a few streets away from them. However, the more discerning Kathleen could see that it was a glint that was tinged with a certain unsettling ambiguity.

"He's a nice lad, is young Frank," she affirmed for her niece's benefit.

That Eileen didn't doubt. She had known him long enough to appreciate her aunt's inference that, once this wretched war was over, he would make a superb husband. Solid and dependable, the boy positively doted on her. He was a good Catholic too. Surely she would never find a better match.

"I took the liberty of telling him you would see him tonight," her mother proffered.

Eileen sighed contentedly and nestled her hands around the warm cup of tea that had been poured. "Yes, why not," she concurred, sipping on the brew. Otherwise, the moment of shared refreshment gave her the opportunity to marvel at what a peculiar family she possessed.

For a start, its most notable aspect was the absence of a strong male figure. Mary herself had married young and given birth to Eileen when she was only eighteen. For the first few years, Eileen had vague infant memories of domestic bliss. Then – inexplicably (certainly in the eyes of a small girl) – her parents had separated. All too soon, the promise of happiness in an aspiring middle-class home vanished, replaced instead by life apart from her father in this more insalubrious abode in the backstreets of Selly Oak. Though civil divorce had been made easier in recent years, it was still a taboo subject outside of the effete world of high society. As such, it remained impossible to escape the stigma and shame of it – especially in a close-knit working-class Catholic community. This applied as much to Eileen as an unfortunate casualty of her parents' separation as it did to Mary herself as the co-instigator of it. Maybe one day things would look up and they would all move into one of those opulent new houses being built in Quinton and Northfield. For now though, straightened circumstance was to be her mother's lot. And without the opening that her newfound vocation in the Royal Air Force had availed her, Eileen had feared such would have been her lot too.

Meanwhile, Auntie Kathleen's life had been no less tragic. She had conversely married late; and, in the year that King Edward and Mrs Simpson had scandalised polite society (as well as occasioning a constitutional crisis), had borne a daughter of her own – Monica. Alas, this little girl was also now destined to grow up with only the vaguest recollections of her father, who had been killed in an industrial accident when she was just an infant.

Ordinarily, such tragedy might have invoked a certain cynicism in a hapless widow. However, in Auntie Kathleen's case it had instead compelled her to cast herself upon her faith with ever greater earnestness and intensity. Unable to pursue the frustrated calling of her teenage years to be a nun, it was almost as if, as some kind of prophylactic to her loss, she had sublimated her love into charity towards those around her, and to exhorting them – Eileen included – to greater faith in the ultimate beneficence of the Almighty.

"Frank said he would come round for you at six," her mother observed, breaking from the delightful unspoken communion of having the two most important people in her life gathered back around the family dining table.

"I better get ready then," Eileen replied, glancing at the clock on the mantelpiece. "I'll change out of uniform and make myself look like a woman again!"

"Yes, why not. You're such an attractive girl, Eileen. And you always looked so smart," her mother replied.

"Mind you be careful if you're going up town," Auntie Kathleen cautioned, still not quite able to accept that her favourite niece was not just possessed of stunning movie star good looks, but was a big girl now – a big girl for whom the 'Black Out' held no fear.

Still, her exhortations had not been entirely in vain. They had instilled in Eileen a residual faith that had been a source of strength to her so far and – she remained confident – would continue to be so in the exciting days that lay ahead. It was this faith that was enabling her to face the future increasingly confident of her God-given destiny.

\* \* \* \* \*

There was the obligatory shuffling aside of legs, as well as the impatient interrupting of snatched canoodles. Frank and Eileen were apologetic and hastily slithered their way past until they arrived at the empty seats in the middle of the row, into which they slotted themselves down. Making themselves at home, they then stared out through the fug of cigarette smoke at the images of titanic struggle now raging across the enormous screen in front of them, thankful that the cinema's main programme had yet to commence.

*"In what may yet prove to be one of the most decisive battles of war so far, Hitler has launched German troops upon an all-out assault to capture Moscow,"* the clipped tones of the newsreel commentator dramatically announced. *"However, he will not take this courageous city without a fight... Over a quarter of a million Muscovites have been hard at work, braving the cold to dig trenches and build fortifications to make sure the hated Hun shall not pass..."*

Eileen marvelled that Russian women too were busy doing their bit to defend their motherland. At least it was good to know that Britain was no longer fighting this war 'alone'. However, from her own cursory knowledge of events she knew things were not going at all well for the Russians. The fear remained that should they submit then it would not be long before German bombers would return to drop their nightly cargoes upon Britain instead.

"So how long are you home on leave, Frank?" she whispered, her eyes still fixed on the screen.

"We have been ordered to report for duty no later than Thursday. How about you?" Frank whispered too, his gaze likewise transfixed.

"I report for duty on Monday. So tonight and tomorrow are all we'll have together I'm afraid."

*"...Meanwhile, events in the Atlantic have taken a dramatic turn with the news that a German U-boat has brazenly fired upon an American warship patrolling off Iceland. Several torpedoes were reportedly launched at the USS Greer, although the destroyer managed to successfully evade them..."*

"That's where we went to: America... Well, Canada actually. Well, some bay off the coast."

"Yes, you said," replied Eileen, a distinct paucity of awe in her tone.

"We had Mr Churchill himself aboard" Frank reminded her, again aware that he might have already told her about his modest part in helping bring the Prime Minister of Great Britain and the President of the United States together for their historic meeting off Newfoundland, and from which had come forth the Atlantic Charter binding both their countries closer together in the struggle against aggression.

*"...Addressing the American people afterwards, President Roosevelt condemned what he called this "an act of piracy" and ordered the United States Navy to "shoot on sight" any more Nazi submarines caught shadowing American warships... One wonders how much longer it will be before America finds itself forced into this war, which is creeping ever closer to its shores with each passing day..."*

"About bloody time too!" someone called out from the back of the cinema.

"Shhhh!" came the collective response from all around him.

Indeed, her boyfriend's home afloat – the brand new battleship *HMS Prince of Wales* – had certainly seen more than its fair share of action since Frank had set off with her on her maiden voyage. As he had unburdened to her on the journey into town, it was from her decks that he had witnessed the appalling loss of *HMS Hood* off Greenland on May 24th, the mighty and iconic battlecruiser blasted apart by gunfire from the German battleship *Bismarck*.

"So where are you off to when you get back?" was Eileen's next enquiry. For the first time, Frank broke his gaze to look at her in astonishment.

"Come on, girl, you know better than to ask a silly question like that. Besides, they never tell us where we're heading next," he insisted, though from the unenthusiastic glint in his eye she could guess he was probably off to the insufferable bleakness of Scapa Flow once more.

"Shhhh!" came the collective response from their neighbouring cinema-goers, prompting them both to fix their gaze back on the news.

*"...Finally, the defence of Malaya and Singapore continues to looms large. With the Japanese blustering in the Far East, British and Indian troops there remain at full readiness... Whatever Johnny Jap's intentions, it's good to know that British Empire forces stand ready and able to give him a bloody nose should he try anything silly..."*

Eventually, the real entertainment got underway. Both of them nestled down into their seats, Frank running his fingers through Eileen's hair, trying to come to terms with those more modest locks. He also stole a crafty nibble of an exposed ear own as he did so.

"Ah, Frank. Look. *'It's Turned Out Nice Again'*..." she pointed up, abruptly terminating such amorous contemplations. "I'm told it's really funny, this one."

Frank reluctantly accepted that he would be unlikely to win back the attention of his girlfriend this side of the interlude. Therefore, conscious he might as well get his two shilling's worth out of the admission price, he too settled into the film, gazing out through the tobacco fug and joining in the periodic laughter at George Formby playing a hapless underwear salesman desperately trying to please both his go-getting wife and his over-bearing mother.

He could empathise with the bit about the go-getting wife alright. Though call-up in the Royal Navy had interrupted Frank's dreams of domestic bliss, he had still not given up hope that Eileen would one day marry him. However, though they had been courting since she was sixteen and he seventeen, of late he had noticed that she had developed a markedly more independent streak – of which her sudden desire to sign up with the Royal Air Force had been a symptom rather than the cause. Gone was the chirpy, uncomplicated soul he had first taken a shine to as a boy living in the next street. In had come a bolder, more assertive Eileen, who he feared was not going to be content to just sit out the war and await his return from distant oceans. Furthermore, since she had enlisted she had even taken up smoking – something her Auntie Kathleen would definitely have a thing or two to say about were she to find out!

Still, at least her family remained incurably fond of him. He had even managed to retain a place in the affections of Eileen's perennially irascible grandmother. Never one to hold her tongue or fail to venture an opinion of anyone she thought might be 'leading her grand-daughter astray', to have remained in the good books of old Bridie O'Leary was no mean achievement. Perhaps there was hope yet that things would indeed 'turn out nice again'!

"Oh look, Frank. *'The Road to Singapore'*. This is another good one: Bing Crosby, Bob Hope and Dorothy Lamour."

And so, after just the briefest of kisses and cuddles during the interlude, it looked like what Frank was failing to pocket in accomplished ardour he would again have to make up for by way of value for money from his admission ticket.

Eileen was mindful of not deliberately wanting to leave him disappointed. However, he ought to know by now that if there was one thing that was sure to arrest her attention then it was Hollywood glamour. Ever since she was a little girl she had been in awe of its screen idols and goddesses and the portrait they sketched of America itself: the great big 'Land of Opportunity'. Enormous cars rolling down endless freeways, towering skyscrapers reaching up to touch vivid skies, and larger-than-life heroes juxtaposed against breath-taking landscapes. No wonder she had oft times found herself lost in dreams of being a 1930s Hollywood starlet in the way of Katharine Hepburn, Bette Davis, Rita Hayworth or Jean Harlow, swooning into the embrace of an achingly-handsome Clark Gable, Cary Grant or Humphrey Bogart. Or better still, like the gorgeous and talented Ginger Rogers, to be found gliding effortless in the arms of an ever-graceful and debonair Fred Astaire in unforgettable movies like *'The Gay Divorcee'* and *'Swing Time'*.

Alas, it had been another dream that had remained just that: a dream. Having had to abandon the dancing classes in which she had shown such promise during her early teenage years, the closest she had ever come to fulfilling such ambitions since had been to show off her terpsichorean talent to the neighbours in brew house yard. And all that remained of her love of singing had been appearances in the church choir. Yet she would not be despondent. Neither would she surrender her dreams of one day making something of her life in a place like America. And who could say: one day she might indeed get to dance in the arms of some tall, heroic American.

\* \* \* \* \*

"You know, Eileen, I'm convinced that as long as I live I'll never find another girl like you."

"Oh, Frank. You say the sweetest things. You really do."

"No, it's true," he insisted as they walked home arm-in-arm through a city that was trying to go about its business as normal – even if so many of its frontages were either missing or had been reduced to tidied-up mounds of rubble. Meanwhile, Eileen resolved to make the most of this brief moment of 'normality' – despite sensing what was coming next.

"I still think we should get married," Frank ventured again. Perhaps, based on his experience of similar probing expeditions, he too sensed what was coming next. "I love you, Eileen," he therefore added, the better to sugar the pill and lay upon her that stifling sense of obligation. Upon which, Eileen drew breath and sighed deeply.

"I love you too, Frank," she replied, prevarication redolent in her manner even as she uttered those awkward few words. "Maybe when the war is over, and there's no more uncertainty about what tomorrow may bring."

"But isn't that all the more reason to tie the knot now," he pleaded expectantly.

"Maybe. I don't know," she shrugged her shoulders before squeezing his waist in an attempt to head off the melancholy that always descended upon him whenever he had been subjected to another of her gentle rebuffs.

She knew that such evasion was no longer working. Her longsuffering, love-struck boyfriend could by now see through it. All during the tram journey home they sat in silence, Eileen peering out through the gauze of the blacked-out windows, even though there was no more chance of her making out anything distinctive amongst the jumble of shapes that was her city than there was of likewise discerning a safe and easy path through the fraught landscape that had become her tangled personal life.

One thing she had decided though. As profound as was her admiration for (and gratitude towards) Able Seaman Frank Rossiter – and for all that her family kept reminding her that he would make a superb husband and an excellent father – she would never be his wife; and the children he would one day proudly sire would never be hers either. She had made up her mind that she could not marry him. The hard – and regrettably once more postponed – part was how to tell him in a way that would not devastate a gentle, well-meaning soul for whom she cared deeply.

Frank represented a life that, for all their good times together, was tainted with an ambiguity that she was desperate to leave behind. Indeed, Frank's very closeness to her family (and the affection in which they held him) was almost certainly his Achilles Heel as far as Eileen was concerned. For all that he could enthuse about his new life at sea, as well as the places he'd been and the people (including Mr Churchill) that he'd met, she knew that above all he represented the sort of staid domesticity that she was so eager to eschew. She was yearning to escape the prospect of a hum-drum existence in the city she had grown up in (but which felt like it had become too small for her ever-expanding horizons), and was instead looking forward to embracing the adventures that her promised new role in Britain's war effort had now opened up.

"Dawlish Road," the conductor meanwhile called along the tram, prompting Frank to escort her from her seat and then – ever the gentleman that he was – hold her hand by her gloved fingertips as she stepped down onto the moonlit streets.

"Next week I might be back at sea again. Then who knows how long it will be before I'll be home. Or even if I ever will see 'home' again."

"Don't talk like that, Frank," she counselled as they strolled the last few hundred yards to her home, genuinely anguished that she had once again left him in limbo. "You will be back. And in the meantime, maybe they will post you somewhere exciting. Singapore sounds wonderful – perhaps you'll be sailing there. Just think of all those swaying palm trees and those golden beaches," she mused, recalling the magical scenes in the newsreel and the eponymous movie they had enjoyed together.

"That's you all over, Eileen: always yearning after faraway places. Always wanting something more than what you already have."

"There's nothing wrong with wanting better," she chided him playfully.

They halted a few doors away. Then, having gazed wistfully into her eyes, she obligingly formed her lips ready for him to offer his customary, prolonged goodnight kiss. It had become a ritual only broken by the long absences that their respective service to their country had necessitated.

"Your grandmother's right, Eileen. You sometimes think you're too good for us ordinary folk," Frank added poignantly.

She said nothing. It was a charge she had faced on other diverse occasions, more and more so of late – and especially from Granny O'Leary, who was never one to mince words. Yet somehow it hurt to hear those words tumble from Frank's lips, with its implicit accusation that she regarded him as not 'good' enough, and therefore 'wanted better'. She stared down guiltily at the darkened pavement, though once more inwardly annoyed that Frank was trying to play the 'family' card to make her feel guiltier still.

"Just remember, Eileen. Like me, this war may take you to some unfamiliar places. You may meet and befriend many different people too – in all kinds of bizarre circumstances. But never forget where you come from; nor the people in your life who have been there for you. In the end, they are the only ones who will really care about you. They are the only ones who will be there for you when this war is over and all the others have moved on."

Just then searchlight beams reached up into the chill night sky, the familiar wail of the sirens gathering pace as those beams anxiously scanned hither and thither for evidence of enemy planes.

"It's probably a false alarm," Eileen noted, their eyes scanning the skies too. "It's been ages since the bombers have been over."

"Yes, you're probably right. That full moon has got the look-outs all on edge. Still, we best take no chances. You get yourself inside the shelter."

She nodded dutifully. Then, totally unexpectedly, she seized Frank by the cheeks and hurriedly stole one final, passionate kiss before breaking and heading for the front door.

"You better be off too. Before the ARPs start bawling at you. Goodnight, Frank. And take care," she waved.

He acknowledged her concern, drew up the collar of his coat, and lingering just long enough to witness her disappear inside. Then he turned to head home, quickening his pace. Yet soon he found himself dispensing with the haste, slowing instead to a careless, disinterested amble. After all, even if the air raid warning was for real, what were a few bombs! One of them might even have his name proverbially scrawled upon it. If, as he feared with each day that passed, he could not have the hand in marriage of the only girl he had ever loved then he would even be tempted to count it a blessing.

# 3

Another train, another station. This time, it was hissing to a halt in the delightful North Yorkshire spa town of Harrogate, disgorging throngs of young men and women – some already in uniform whilst others (judging by their demeanours of anxiety and apprehension) probably soon would be. Amongst their number, and hauling her kit back down onto the platform, was Eileen Kimberley, girding herself up for the next chapter of her adventure with the Women's Auxiliary Air Force.

At the exits from the platform there had already gathered a phalanx of NCOs from the different branches ready to tick off those young passengers arriving today. WRNS NCOs had already corralled up a posse of their new arrivals. Air Force corporals were likewise spying out their new intakes to whisk off to the WAAF depot in the town.

"Aircraftwoman Second Class 2090088 Kimberley, reporting for duty," she announced, the WAAF corporal scanning down her list.

"Ah yes, Kimberley… You're with the group for telephonist training. In which case, go report to the warrant officer who's waiting opposite the hotel. You'll find transport there to take you to your billet."

This Eileen duly did, reporting to her and then being waved towards a canvas-topped lorry that was waiting on the street nearby.

"Room for a little one?" she enquired of a solitary girl with blond-curls protruding around her cap who had been eagerly eyeing Eileen's arrival from the back of the truck.

"I'll say. Welcome aboard. I'm glad someone has shown up. I was getting rather lonely sat here all on my own," she joked, helping Eileen to haul her kit bag up over the lip of the lorry's rear end before instructing her to make use of the knotted rope suspended from its canopy frame to haul herself inside.

"I'm Nancy. Nancy King. From Hampshire," she then announced in a well-spoken accent, offering Eileen the dainty paw of her friendship. Eileen sat down on the hard side-facing bench opposite and gratefully accepted it.

"Eileen Kimberley. From Birmingham."

"Gosh! I'd never have guessed," Nancy chuckled, her new friend taking it as a compliment to how well she could mask her humble Midlands background when the occasion demanded.

Not that there seemed any need for heirs-and-graces. Nancy was such a vivacious and witty soul that she was soon making light of their new situation, indifferent to the obvious imbalance in their backgrounds.

"I'm told we're to be billeted in a guest house on the outskirts of town. It's not that far from where we are to be sent for training. Mind you, it's got to be better than where these poor girls are heading. I'm told it gets quite nippy up on the moors in December!" she joked, both of them gazing out at the ranks of ATS girls being marched away to board the line of army trucks that were parked further up the street.

In due course, a few more stragglers found their way to the warrant officer and were herded aboard the RAF truck. Then, having established that everyone was present and correct, the WO hopped into the front and ordered its driver to make haste to their new quarters. In no time at all, they were chugging along elegant streets where the sandbags that clad its fine Victorian buildings and the ack-ack guns mounted on its manicured lawns were a salutary reminder that this was a town at war.

"Apparently, there's quite a substantial Air Ministry presence in Harrogate," Nancy called across above the painful crashing of the gearbox. "Many of the big and famous hotels have been requisitioned for all the staff relocated from London."

Indeed, the place did seem to be buzzing with top-brass. Furthermore, its streets were frequented by plenty of folk attired in air force blue. Eileen had heard that there was a reception centre in the town for new flight crews. The Royal Canadian Air Force's No. 6 Bomber Group was also based outside the town. Elsewhere, a secret Royal Navy 'Y-station' had been established to monitor German signals traffic. No wonder the *Luftwaffe* had taken quite an active interest in what was going on here.

Eventually, the truck pulled up outside a modest little suburban dwelling and the girls were ordered to fall in on the street outside.

"Right," the warrant officer read out, checking against her list once more, "Collins and Crossman, you're on the first floor, Room 10... Edgeley and Shipman, Room 12 also on the first floor... King and Kimberley, I'm afraid you're up with the gods on the top floor, Room 18... Dinner is a six-thirty prompt; lights out at ten-thirty prompt. And make sure you all report to the GPO telephone exchange on Gladstone Street on the dot at 0-800 hours tomorrow morning. So don't get any ideas about sneaking out to visit the pub tonight. Oh, and make sure there are no lights showing because if the ARPs report to me otherwise, you'll all be on a charge. Understood?

"Yes, Warrant Officer," was the collective reply.

"So make yourself at home, girls... and sleep tight!"

With that admonition still ringing in their ears, they fell out and began the process of hauling their bulky kit bags up the flights of steep stairs to what was to be their new home for the next few weeks.

"Goodness, the WO wasn't joking when she said we were up with the gods!" Nancy groaned as she finally dragged over the threshold the regulation issue canvas bag that contained her worldly possessions. She huffed wearily and slumped down exhausted upon one of the lumpy, iron-framed single beds that – along with the single wooden wardrobe in which it was intended they should store it all – virtually filled the pokey little loft.

"Well, at least the view is better from up here. You can see for miles. Is that Leeds over there?" Eileen quizzed her new room mate, pointing excitedly through the small dormer window to a town in the distance.

"I doubt it – unless you have exceptionally good eyesight. Leeds is over thirty miles away!"

Ah, well: good guess. Nancy seemed so much more knowledgeable about such things, Eileen marvelled – the product she didn't doubt of a private education that befitted her middle-class upbringing.

"You see, one of my aunties lives not too far away. That's how I know about this place. I used to visit Harrogate in the summers before war broke out. That's when I wasn't holidaying with my grandfather, who lives in Torquay. How about you, Eileen? Have you travelled much?"

"Not really," Nancy observed her reluctantly confess. In fact – aside from an odd bank holiday excursion in the charabanc to the seaside, Eileen had never really ventured much further than the limits of the Birmingham Corporation tram network. Scenic as they were – and treasured as childhood picnics upon them had been – the Lickey Hills didn't seem in quite the same league as the North Yorkshire Moors or the Devon Riviera.

"Then you'll enjoy Harrogate, I'm sure," Nancy counselled, draping a comradely arm across her shoulder and smiling warmly. "While we're here you can come with me to my auntie's cottage if we get the chance. I like you, Eileen. You're genuine. I can see we're going to be good friends."

Then she dispensed with what little formality had so far existed between these two new chums and squeezed her tight in a big, girlish hug. Yes, they would be good friends indeed, Eileen felt herself rejoicing.

"Gosh! He's a handsome chap. Your boyfriend?" Nancy enthused, by-and-by taking the liberty of carefully lifting up and examining a small, framed portrait of a dapper man with a moustache, movie star good looks, seductive eyes and a beguiling smile ensconced beneath his tilted trilby.

Eileen smiled feebly. "It's actually my father… when he was a lot younger."

"Goodness! I can see where the daughter gets her stunning looks from then," Nancy glanced up at her mischievously.

"It's one of the few pictures I have of him. I carry it with me everywhere; to remind me of the most important man who was ever in my life. Perhaps the most important man who will forever be in my heart"

"Was?" Nancy glanced up again mystified. "Is he dead then?" she added, trying to sound as gently empathetic as she could upon beholding her colleague blink exaggeratedly, as if to force back a stray tear or two.

"No. But sometimes it feels that way. He and Mum separated when I was only young. I have such happy memories of him though; of him holding my tiny hand as we'd walk and chat together in Cannon Hill Park; of him proudly smiling at me singing and dancing in my first school play. But it's been many years since I've seen him. I don't even know where is – except that he has moved away from Birmingham. I still miss him so much though. Maybe one day I shall catch up with him again; to see him beaming proudly that I have made something out of my life."

"I'm sorry," was all Nancy could think to say, hiding her awkwardness by staring again at the treasured image of another era. Then she gently placed it back down and cast her arms around her again, hugging her close.

"He will be proud of you, Eileen. I know he will," she assured her.

Meanwhile, as Eileen gripped her new friend in turn, she glanced down over her shoulder at the man whose legacy of love had been this crazy quest to 'reach for the stars' – however distant and far away.

* * * * *

'Telephonist' sounded like an interesting job. It had a distinct aura of technology and all things modern about it – in like manner to how the RAF itself symbolised technology and its relentless application to the winning of the war. It certainly sounded more interesting than the shop work that Eileen had been engaged in since she had left school. However, that noble thought was of only modest comfort to her – and to her new colleagues too – as they found themselves gazing awestruck at the colossal wall of flashing lights and trailing wires that now confronted them.

"Right, pay attention, girls. This is similar to the switchboard you'll soon be working... Over here, this is your 'home' section. When a subscriber's light appears on the 'home' section, you take a lead and insert it into the jack beneath the light... like so. Then you say 'Number, please'," said the instructor as they gathered around a section of the huge exchange board, watching the operator with her headphones and voice trumpet taking hold of the lead and demonstrating for their benefit.

"Then this section over here is your 'multiple' section. Once your caller has given the number they wish to be connected to – and if that number is located on the same exchange – then you connect this end of the lead into that jack and then the other end to the appropriate jack, pressing the bell to alert the recipient that they have a call."

Again, rapidly jotting down the number, almost as if by intuition the operator reached across, inserted the cable into the jack, and crisply announced who was on the line. Call connected.

"If, however, the caller is requesting to be put through to a number on a different exchange, then you insert the lead into this 'junction' and announce to its operator who the caller is and where they wish to be connected."

So much to learn. And yet the operator seemed to perform all this without a second thought, swiftly connecting and disconnecting calls without ever elbowing her colleagues who were working the adjacent boards. However, even she seemed to manifest a glint of trepidation when suddenly taking an incoming call and buzzing the number of a commanding officer.

"Group Captain, I have Air Marshal Craddock on the line for you... Thank you... Go ahead, Air Marshal, you are connected," she replied, a discernable mien of relief again manifest as she vacated the line and left the Group Captain to discover whatever grave matter it was he was about to be told.

"Yes, woe betide anyone who misdirects or accidentally cuts off a 'brass-hat'," the instructor turned and cautioned them all, thereby not noticing the operator also glance away from the flashing board to offer them that brief, yet knowing look that spoke of having found out herself at some point during her telephonist's career. Furthermore, the supervisors hovering over the backs of the girls elsewhere along the exchange would be only to ready to come down hard on anyone who similarly made a boo-boo!

Then it was time for the practical. Each of them took turns to relieve the operator of her headset and try their own hand at plugging, announcing and unplugging, the instructor coaching them to employ the sort of polite, yet firm tone of voice required to conduct each call briskly and efficiently. After all, on a typical shift they could be handling hundreds of such calls.

Deftness, tone, and verbal clarity were the requisite skills of this particular trade. Indeed – like Nancy – most of the girls gathered around to observe how it was done were free of the pronounced regional accents that many of Eileen's fellow cohort of recruits had possessed. Presumably, that's why those who weren't been had been assigned instead to learn clerking, cooking, packing parachutes, manning barrage balloons, or any one of the hundred or more trades that were open to women enrolled with the RAF – jobs that involved doing rather than speaking.

Meanwhile, the efforts Eileen had made during her teen years to iron out her own mild Brummie ling – and so speak with the sort of polished voice she remembered her father possessing – had paid off sufficient that she too could now take the seat and don the headset to practice connecting caller with recipient. After the initial hesitation and inevitable fumbling over which jacks were to be poked where on the board, she was soon getting into the swing of things. Then the instructor watched as she took an incoming call and seemed to freeze for just the briefest of moments before mental agility (as well as the imbibing of what she had learned so far) kicked back in.

"Yes sir, please hold the line…" she requested in the best Queen's English she could muster, trailing the cable across and searching out the jack that would connect it up to the Group Captain's telephone.

"I have Air Marshal Craddock on the line for you again, sir… Thank you… Go ahead, Air Marshal, you are connected."

The others looked at Eileen with relief that they had not been in the 'hot seat' when the dreaded return call had come through, mixed in with admiration that she had handled it with aplomb – and on her first outing on a real switchboard too! Her turn complete, she then alighted from the seat when ordered and tremulously passed the headset back to its owner.

"Well done, Kimberley," the instructor nodded before turning to the others.

"Just remember: Air Marshal Craddock is God," she reminded them. "When he is on the line then, regardless of who the officer is talking to, you need to break into the call, announce the Air Marshal's presence, and then connect him. Unless, that is, the Group Captain is perchance speaking to the Air Chief Marshal. In which case, Air Marshal Craddock will just have to wait his turn like the rest of them. You do not cut off the Air Chief Marshal – ever. He is Very God!"

\* \* \* \* \*

As the weeks passed, Eileen came to appreciate that they had probably bagged one of the RAF's more pleasant postings. The guest house where they were staying was little more than twenty minutes walk from Harrogate town centre, where there were cinemas, theatres, parks to stroll through, and wonderful majestic hotels – all thronging with dashing servicemen hailing from all corners of the Empire. It was certainly better than being marooned on a windswept airfield where there might only be one bus a day into town and back, and where ablutions huts located away from the main billets involved a sprint across chilly parade grounds in order to reach them. Meanwhile, Eileen, Nancy and their little *côterie* enjoyed access to an indoor bath and toilet, and three hearty meals a day served up with a finesse that would have been lost on an RAF cookhouse! There was also a roaring fire in the sitting room in which one could browse through a well-stocked library and a daily horde of newspapers. It was from one of these that Eileen learned that Churchill had despatched the battleships *HMS Prince of Wales* and *HMS Repulse* to Singapore as a deterrent to Japan meddling with Britain's resource-rich colonies in the Far East. So Frank would indeed be gone for some time, though she hoped even this incurable 'home bird' would appreciate how preferable it was to swap a Christmas at anchor at cold, windswept Scapa Flow for one moored up in this bustling isle in the tropics!

It seemed they had both landed plum postings after all. Eileen was certainly determined to enjoy hers. In the company of Nancy and the girls it would certainly not be an arduous undertaking! Nancy, in particular, was as daring as she was vivacious. It was therefore her idea that they chance popping in for a festive drink or two at one of the more exclusive hotels that was known to be a haunt of similarly fun-loving aviators. Already the management had acquired and decorated a Christmas tree in tinsel and baubles, the delightful seasonal accoutrements twinkling in the glow of a roaring log fire in the opulent, tall-ceilinged lounge. It reminded Eileen of those glorious old country houses that she had seen in films, but had never been privileged to actually step inside.

"You sure we're supposed to be here?" one of the girls quizzed Nancy from behind anxious, darting eyes.

"Look, we're young women. These guys are young men. They probably haven't clapped eyes on a girl all week. We'll be okay, you'll see. If anyone asks, just say our section officer gave us permission to be here as a thank-you for the invaluable top-secret war work we've just completed.

"What top-secret war work?" another girl wondered naively.

"Shhhh! We mustn't talk about such things. After all, 'walls have ears' and all that!" Nancy insisted with a wicked wink.

Like the others, Eileen giggled obligingly. She had really come to like Nancy. She was so much a breathe of fresh air after the stuffiness of her own devout Irish-Catholic upbringing – as exemplified by the fact that she had absolutely no inhibitions at all about stripping off when getting ready for bed (unlike Eileen herself, who had not entirely forsaken the need to show modesty in the presence of other girls!). Likewise, with no sweetheart of her own waiting patiently for war's end, Nancy had no scruples at all about milking male attention for all it was worth, craftily tweaking her battle dress blues to rid them of some of the frumpiness, as well as coquettishly glancing over her shoulder to smile back whenever airmen whistled the two of them as they strolled back home to their lodging each night. Eileen could see she had a lot to learn when it came to such things.

Just then the lassitude of the establishment was rudely disturbed by the entrance of a rather excitable troop of uniformed aircrew, who – as Nancy had correctly predicted – were not going to waste this opportunity to swap the austerity of a rain-lashed bomber station for a draught of ale and cosy chair drawn up around that roaring fire. Especially if seated upon some of those chairs were shapely feminine bottoms.

"Gee, you sheilas look like you've made yourselves at home," one of the airmen ventured in a broad, yet unfamiliar accent.

"And you lads sound like you're an awful long way from home," Nancy riposted quick-as-a-flash.

"Sure. But if the fire's aglow and the company's amenable, I guess we can live with that. What say ya', Digger?" he sighed, gripping a fellow airman by the shoulder and giving it a matey squeeze.

"Oh, I'm thinking I could happily be a base bludger any day if this is the company we get to keep." Digger crowed, gazing down in awe at Nancy.

"Wow! Tabbies! Where did they come from?" another exuberant young flyer gawped. Having been ordered to get the rounds in, he now rejoined his comrades to cast an approving eye over these exquisite 'decorations' gathered about the Christmas tree!

"Oh, wakey-wakey, Joey. If you spot Messerschmitts with all the alacrity that you spot 'bandits' of the female variety then no wonder our trusty old kite's always limping home with its arse chewed!"

With the back of his hand, Digger swished away the cap of his tail-gunner, ruffling his tuft of curly blond hair while hilarity erupted amongst both Australian aviators and British WAAF telephonists alike. It was therefore the most natural thing in the world for these big, bluff antipodeans to summarily slot themselves down in the remaining chairs around the fire. All, that was, except for Joey, whose alacrity failed him once again when he discovered that there was nowhere left upon which to perch his own much shot-at arse. Gentleman-like, he begged to perch it instead upon the arm of Eileen's chair. She shuffled aside obligingly.

"Thank you, lady. You're very kind," he grinned in his rich Queensland drawl, repaying the favour by offering her one of his cigarettes.

"Carrots," she replied to his obvious puzzlement before taking it and permitting him to light it for her. Once she had drawn on it, the imprint of the cherry-red theatrical grease paint the girls had learned to use in place of rationed lipstick was visible on its tip. "Apparently if you eat plenty of carrots you can see better in the dark. Like rabbits can. Then you will better be able to spot those Germans on your tail."

"Oh, I see," Joey frowned, none the wiser. "I guess that must be why you Pommies are so good at finding your way around town in the dark," he then smiled at her.

"How 'bout we just plonk a bloody rabbit in the rear turret. After all, the little blighter surely couldn't be any worse at spottin' night fighters than young Joey 'ere!" Digger roared.

There were belly laughs all round. Once more Joey felt his blond quiff being playfully tussled.

"Pommies?" exclaimed Eileen, mystified.

"It's what these Australians call us English," Nancy enlightened her.

"You're from Australia?" she marvelled, the penny having finally dropped and her epiphany greeted by further hilarity on the part of the airmen present.

"Anyway, don't you get too friendly with young Eileen here. She has a boyfriend, you know. He's away in the Royal Navy," one of the girl cautioned.

"Never mind, Joey lad," a fellow airman meanwhile comforted the plainly besotted young Aussie. "You wouldn't want be coming between this good lady and the pusser she's dating."

It was almost as if these 'cousins' from Down Under were speaking another language. However, their informality was refreshing. As the banter progressed, it all made for a welcome opportunity to unwind from the cares of the war – to say nothing of the ongoing challenge of mastering a switchboard.

"My boyfriend's been posted to Singapore," Eileen elaborated in a further reluctant signal to Joey not to build his hopes up. Meanwhile, from the corner of her eye as she exchanged pleasantries with him, she could see that one or two of her colleagues were under no such inhibitions with regards to familiarising themselves with his comrades.

"I really envy him. I saw Malaya in a newsreel a few weeks back. It looks so wonderful. Wouldn't you have liked to have been posted somewhere like that – with palm trees, beautiful beaches and warm, tropical seas?" she meanwhile enquired of her new friend.

Joey smiled again. "Lady, they got plenty of palm trees, beautiful beaches and warm, tropical seas where I come from."

"Really?"

"Sure. I'm from Queensland. Up north. The hot bit," he explained.

"I thought all of Australia was hot."

"I kinda' guess it must seem like that to you Brits, what with the way that icy north wind blows around these parts. But where I come from is… well, one day you'll have to visit Queensland yourself and find out."

"I'd love to. I've always wanted to travel. Do they have kangaroos in Queensland?"

"Oh, I'm sure I could find a kangaroo just for you."

Joey was clearly falling head over heels for this cute and adorable girl with every innocent and excited question she asked. Once again, he responded with a touching grin, disappointed that she was 'spoken for' – but maybe subconsciously trying his luck anyway.

Eileen was tempted to succumb to his boyish charm. After all, there was a war on. Who could say whether a subsequent encounter with a Messerschmitt over the night skies of Germany would end in something more awful than further ribaldry about Joey's supposedly poor eyesight. What's more, he seemed so desperately young to be a flight sergeant. What kind of madness had now wrenched him from his parent's sun-kissed sugar plantation ten thousand miles away – and Eileen from her backstreet abode in industrial Birmingham –

and thrown them both together on this cold, damp evening in Yorkshire. The reflected glow from the fire danced in each of their eyes as they both longed to cast off propriety and snatch what little joy they might have left before the devil took tomorrow.

"Anyway, much as we have enjoyed your company, gentleman, I'm afraid we have to be back in our lodgings by 22-30 hours. Otherwise, we'll be having our tails chewed as well!" Nancy regretfully reminded the boys.

It was the cue for the happy ensemble to bid their reluctant farewells. Eileen too rose to her feet and squared up to Joey, who had lifted himself from the arm of her chair.

"Thank you. It really has been lovely to talk to you," she smiled.

"No. Thank you, lady. The pleasure has been all mine. I hope I've explained a bit more about Australia. You really will have to come and visit. Failing that, who knows – maybe we will bump into each other again one day."

Then, totally unexpected, the hand that she had offered for him to shake he now lifted up to his lips, kissing it tenderly before helping her into the smothering embrace of her greatcoat.

Before they set off though, Eileen needed to make one final port of call. Thus she strolled off by herself to find the correct door along the hallway. It was always chore having to undo and haul down all those infernal contraptions that held the show together, so to speak. Added to which, Eileen was afflicted with a lifelong aversion to large spiders. She had no doubt that the local arachnoids were as partial to the toilets of these posh hotels in Harrogate as their cousins were to the draughty outhouse latrines of Selly Oak. Therefore, she was glad that, penny spent, she could haul the whole lot back up and make haste for the wash basin.

As she stood there, tucking her hair back under her cap and admiring herself in the mirror, she thought she could hear voices in the drayman's yard outside. Placing an ear against the painted-out glass she could make out the sound of breathlessness too – like the exertions of someone try to lift some huge heavy weight. What's more, the two voices were distinctly male and female – and by the sound of things it was the woman who was doing most of the lifting!

Curiosity caused her to risk the censure of the ARPs by stealthily undoing the latch of the window, craning herself up to peer out into the gloom – though it was not so gloomy that she couldn't make out the trails of exhaled breath rising into the cold night sky. Then she spotted uniforms; and bodies grinding rhythmically together between a lowered pair of trousers and a hitched-up skirt. And on such a cold night too!

She drew away in horror, pulling the window shut. Then she scurried back out into the long hallway that led to the hotel lobby and to the street outside, where her colleagues were waiting.

"Ah, there you are," Nancy fretted, trying to spy out the hour on her delicate wristwatch and becoming ever more agitated that one of their number was still missing.

"I don't suppose you've seen that infernal Mabel Shipman on your travels, have you?" she enquired, thumping her chest to keep warm.

Eileen shook her head speciously.

"Oh, where is she? That girl really is going to have us all drummed out of the service at this rate... Ah, there she is!" Nancy breathed a sigh of relief, Eileen locking arms with her as together they all headed off at a brisk rate of knots in order to avert the dreaded wrath of the warrant officer.

"Get lost on the way back from ladies' room?" Nancy called back to chide their tardy comrade, Eileen also availing herself of a quick glance over her shoulder to spot the incorrigible Aircraftwoman Shipman still twitching to straighten her dishevelled uniform, culpability pervading her return stare.

"You know, Eileen, it sounds almost cruel in the circumstances. But I think we are both going to enjoy this war," Nancy mused. "What's more, I'm told it's going to be Bomber Command where most of the fun is to be had – certainly if you're a WAAF. I'm hoping that's where we'll be assigned. Just remember though not to spread your womanly favours around too liberally – unlike young Shipman back there," she whispered.

They were sage words. Whilst Eileen was an ingénue in so many respects (and Nancy was not averse to teasing her about it), by way of hints and allusions her Auntie Kathleen had bequeathed her sufficient knowledge of the ways of men to make her aware of where liberally bestowing such 'womanly favours' could lead a girl. Countering that, however, was the ever-present, over-idealised notion of the opposite sex that both her beloved father and those matinee screen idols had bequeathed her. It meant that, while that little three-letter-word-ending-in-x was something of a taboo subject, love, romance and chivalry certainly weren't. Perhaps that was why she had found herself strangely warming to Joey. Unlike his more forward (and, in Mabel Shipman's case, very forward) comrades, he seemed almost as naïve to the ways of the flesh as she was. In that sense, he was not unlike Frank. As onward she and her friends strolled, all merrily swapping tales about the evening, she tried to imagine her boyfriend at that very moment taking in the sights of Singapore, spending his shore leave buying up souvenirs to bring home for her while his more lusty shipmates were buying up the services of those ladies who probably hawked themselves in its more shady quarters.

"Greetings, Mrs Braithwaite. I told you we'd all be back for half-ten," Nancy announced, employing her cheeky charm to pacify their landlady, who from the matronly furrows rippling across her forehead was clearly agitated about something. Hopefully, it was not a gaggle of giggling WAAFs traipsing through her hallway in high spirit that was about to occasion from her a stern lecture as she scurried out of her parlour to square up to them.

"Yes, we're really sorry, Mrs B. You see, we met these lovely Australian airmen up town and… well…"

"So tha' hasn't heard yet?" the old girl expressed surprise.

"Heard what, Mrs B?" the others petitioned, their own foreheads furrowing to match.

"It's just come through on t' radio. Apparently t' Japanese have attacked and sunk American ships in Hawaii. There are reports they're also attacking Malaya and Hong Kong too!"

All of a sudden, the carnival gaiety of the evening evaporated – not least because the others could see that the startling news that the Japs were training their fury upon the British in the Far East had cast a pall of anxiety over Eileen. It was barely lifted by the assurance of one of the girls that – as the Prime Minister had promised – with two of the Royal Navy's mightiest battleships guarding the gateway to Singapore there was no way the avaricious schemes of these dastardly little yellow men were going to prevail.

Eventually, the girls retired to their beds. With the lights out, Nancy performed the nightly ritual of hauling aside the black-out drapes so that they could both gaze out of their little dormer window at the clouds lifting to give way to a clear night sky. The two girls often found themselves gazing up at the stars from their window – especially if sleep had been disturbed by the wailing of the air raid siren and another false alarm had sent them racing from their beds into Mrs Braithwaite's pokey little air raid shelter.

Tonight, however, Eileen's was clearly concerned about her boyfriend's whereabouts on this night when it seemed the whole world was in turmoil. Such concern was also patently troubling her friend too. Eventually, Nancy could bear it no longer and rose from her bed, sitting herself down on Eileen's and reaching a sisterly arm across to her.

"Don't cry. Things will be okay. If nothing else, maybe what has happened will finally bring the Americans into this war," she whispered tenderly. "With the Yanks on our side, it will only be a matter of time before we see off Hitler, Mussolini – and those bloody Japs too."

* * * * *

It transpired that the happy gathering around the fire that night in Harrogate was to be symbolic of the only merriment to be had during that dark, dismal Christmas of 1941 – for both Eileen and the beleaguered Allies. Although (as Nancy had correctly predicted) President Roosevelt had committed his country to join Britain's war against Germany, hard on the heels of this welcome fillip had come truly terrible news. Having sallied forth to intercept a Japanese invasion, in the absence of adequate air cover both the *Prince of Wales* and the *Repulse* had been quickly despatched to the bottom of the Gulf of Siam by Japanese bombers operating out of French Indo-China.

There was now nothing to stop the Japanese army landing and racing down the Malay Peninsula to seize the island citadel of Singapore at its tip, which duly capitulated on February 15th 1942 – along with more than one hundred thousand British and Empire troops that had retreated there. It was the greatest military defeat Britain had ever suffered. Thereafter, the all-conquering Japanese had captured the Dutch East Indies, holed up the beleaguered American garrison in the Philippines, and were now advancing into Burma and threatening Australia. Elsewhere, Rommel's *Afrika Korps* had recaptured Benghazi from the British; while the German battlecruisers *Scharnhorst* and *Gneisenau* had successfully given the Royal Navy the slip and dashed through the English Channel back to Germany.

The only good news amidst this litany of unrelenting woe was that German panzers had been halted and routed outside Moscow. However, though Hitler's colossal army in the Soviet Union had been left licking its wounds for now, it would surely be back again in the spring once the ferocious Russian snows had melted.

# 4

It was as bleak as bleak could be. To be sure, the leaden winter skies that held the promise of yet more rain (or maybe even snow – it was certainly cold enough!) didn't exactly enhance the vista of flat, endless fens – mile after mile of boring nothingness broken only by the occasional isolated hamlet.

As the two new telephonists bounced about in the back of the truck ferrying them from the railway station to their new posting, Eileen stared across at Nancy as if to remind her of her little gem about Bomber Command being the place where the 'fun' was to be had. They were certainly in 'Bomber Command country' now. Ever since the British Expeditionary Force had been unceremoniously plucked from the sands of Dunkirk – and hitting back from the air had been the only means left for Britain to take the war to Germany – it seemed as if the whole east side of England had been transformed into one gigantic bomber base (although, in reality, it was an archipelago of scores of bases and satellite facilities dotted from Suffolk in the south to Yorkshire in the north). As if to remind them both of this, a large bomber in camouflage markings as drab as the landscape it was traversing flew low overhead, its twin engines droning Doppler-like as it headed away into the distance.

"That's a Stirling, isn't it?" said Eileen, peering out of the back of the lorry.

"Wellington, I think. Stirlings have four engines," Nancy replied.

"Spot on, darlin'. You've been studying the ol' recognition manuals!" commended one of the half dozen RAF ground crew personnel who had also cadged a lift with them.

Yes, they had certainly been posted to Bomber Command alright: No. 3 Group, to be precise, where they were about to get their first taste of life on a real operational air station. RAF Feltwell in Norfolk – located a dozen miles north-west of Thetford – would be their new home for the next few months. It was a home they would be sharing with the lads of No. 75 Squadron. It was one of their Vickers Wellington machines that they had indeed just spotted making an approach to land.

"The aircrew call them 'Wimpeys', don't they," Nancy called across to the guys in the truck.

"That's right. You can tell them by their distinctive fabric-covered latticework fuselages. Mind you, they're not a patch on the new Lancaster four-engine bombers that are being introduced."

Eileen raised a smile at her friend's erudition. Nancy had certainly lost none of her coquettishness. Indeed, as with this impromptu display of aviation expertise, her lively blonde companion could also shamelessly play at being one-of-the-boys when the mood took her. Eileen was so glad that they would now remain together as best friends, rising to the challenge of being WAAFs billeted on a camp comprised predominantly of men. Surely this was Auntie Kathleen's worst nightmare, she chuckled to herself. As the truck trundled up to the front gates, and the sentries checked the driver's papers and waved them through, she could only too well imagine her devout godmother spluttering 'Hail Marys' like billy-ho whilst imploring the Virgin Mother to shield the girls from all the temptations they were about to be subjected to. However, temptation was the last thing on the cards as they dismounted with their trusty kit bags, reported for duty, and were detailed to their quarters.

"Bloody hell, this place is draughty," Nancy announced, peering through the glass door of the little stove roaring away in the middle of the billet (and which was attempting without much success to banish the distinct nip in the air). Meanwhile, a similar mien of despondency was apparent upon Eileen's face too as she dropped her kit bag down upon her bunk.

"So where are the facilities around here?" she wondered aloud, scanning each of the four corners of the block in turn.

"Ah, you must those two telephonist girls from Harrogate they said were arriving this morning," one of the existing residents noted with a wry smile.

"That's right. I'm Eileen. And this is my friend, Nancy."

"Good to meet you. I'm Doreen. And that's Joan over there. We're plotters. Meanwhile, Jennie over in that corner is a telephonist too… while Daisy and Queenie over there are parachute packers," she replied, the girls acknowledging each other in turn.

"In answer to your question though, it looks like the RAF really have spoiled you. I'm afraid you'll find none of your posh indoor plumbing here. The 'facilities' – as you call them – are outside; turn left, past huts seven and eight and across the way. So make sure you have everything with you before you set out. It's a long walk back if you discover you've forgotten the soap!"

"Oh, and make sure you're decent when you emerge. Those fitters over in No.4 Hangar are a right lecherous bunch!" Daisy scowled.

"Gosh! Welcome to RAF Feltwell," Nancy huffed again, more despondent than ever.

"The good news is that the guys on the base are great fun and really do look after us. You'll probably find that most of the aircrew are from New Zealand. Apparently they were over here training when war broke out. Rather than ship them home, the RAF decided to just absorb them into No. 75 Squadron. They've been here ever since."

"I've heard about New Zealand. It's another one of those faraway places I'd love to travel to," Eileen meanwhile enthused, once more betraying her penchant for alluring destinations she had seen in newsreels – the distant dominion being another one of those red-coloured bits on the map of the world that she remembered adorning the classroom wall at school.

"Guess we'll just have to make sure they look after us too then," Nancy beamed, the focus of her own enthusing directed more towards the allure of homesick New Zealanders than the land they had left behind.

"I'm afraid you'll have to join the queue behind Daisy and Queenie if you're looking to date them," Joan announced, playfully alerting them to the notion that "the aircrew always take extra special 'care' of the parachute girls. After all, if your life depended on a few strings and a sheet of silk being folded and packed correctly, wouldn't you!"

They all laughed heartily. In particular, Nancy was pleased to see Eileen's big, broad grin suggest that she was at last emerging from the dark trough she had sunken into over the loss of her boyfriend. Three months or more had passed and there was still no news of his whereabouts. The realisation had to be faced that he had probably perished along with the hundreds of other British sailors who had gone down with the two doomed warships. It was immensely sad; but that was war. Almost everyone in the country had by now lost someone dear as a consequence of it.

* * * * *

That first night Eileen and Nancy reacquainted themselves with just how uncomfortable RAF issue 'biscuit' mattresses and coarse blankets could be. Neither was that little stove much good at heating the billets. Indeed, Daisy had waggishly remarked that the reason the RAF had given them metal lockers to store their things in was to prevent the WAAFs breaking up wooden furniture to feed the damn thing! Had it not been for the exhaustion induced by a long, overnight train journey from Yorkshire they would both have been hard-pressed to snatch any sleep at all.

The two girls soon settled into the more austere regime at Feltwell, slotting themselves into the small, close-knit team manning the switchboards on rostered shifts. Although the day shift gave them the opportunity to avail themselves of an evening pass with which to visit the nearest town, they also enjoyed the greater informality of the night duties. With fewer calls and less onerous supervision, sometimes the chance arose to engage in a spot of flirtatious banter with the guys calling from other air stations. This was especially so when poor weather halted flying operations. However, at dusk when the familiar drone of bombers could be heard heading down the runway things would be remain quiet only until around three o'clock in the small hours. Then a steady stream of calls would light up the boards as airfields filed reports back and forth concerning which planes had returned, which had been diverted because they were damaged or out of fuel, and – more ominously – which ones nothing had been heard of.

At daybreak, Eileen and Nancy would often find themselves taking calls from wives and sweethearts also awaiting the return of their men. Furthermore, the fellow WAAFs amongst that anxious number hoped that their inside rapport with the girls on the boards would coax them to put their minds at ease. However, procedure dictated that all they do was parrot the official line that there was 'no news yet' – though they knew that, even as they spoke, an officer somewhere on the camp was struggling to put together a form of words to explain that their husband or fiancé had offered up the ultimate sacrifice for his country. Sometimes it was the little things that brought home the true cost of the war they were all fighting.

\* \* \* \* \*

*"Bless 'em all, bless 'em all,*
*The long and the short and the tall.*
*Bless all the sergeants and WO1s,*
*Bless all the corporal and their blinkin' sons,*
*'Cause we're saying goodbye to them all,*
*As back to their billets they crawl.*
*You'll get no promotion this side of the ocean,*
*So cheer up, my lads, bless 'em all..."*

In common with their male colleagues, if the rigours and privations of wartime service had taught the girls of the Women's Auxiliary Air Force one thing it was that, for the sake of ones sanity, it was as important to play hard as it was to work hard. Consequently, they soon learned to never pass up an opportunity for fun, however it presented itself. And a midnight pass, combined with an invitation to a dance at a village hall surely spelt fun in anybody's book.

Thus it was that this warm, pleasant spring evening found Eileen, Nancy and the other girls laughing, singing, and dingling the bells on their bicycles as they pedalled down quiet country lanes, the fast-fading sun casting their shadows long across the fields and hedgerows.

The brass hats at No. 3 Group were eager to placate the locals. Perhaps they were never entirely sure whether wartime solidarity would completely reconcile them to the presence in their midst of thousands of air force personnel; or whether the jingling of the tills from those play-hard service personnel spending their pay packets with the pub landlord and the village shopkeeper outweighed the irking of local farmhands about all that extra competition for their womenfolk, to say nothing of low-flying bombers constantly spooking the farmers' best-laying hens.

The WAAF girls were determined to play their part in the fostering of good relations too, and so propped their bikes up and wandered inside brimming with excitement about what the evening had in store. However, it was apparent that the event they had been invited to had yet to fully warm up. For company so far they had just a handful of locals and some singer who was crooning *'Hang Out The Washing On The Siegfried Line'* on a stage draped with Union Jack bunting. Meanwhile, the advance party of a pair of senior RAF officers was attempting to do their bit by chatting to the Mayor and his wife around a table in the far corner. Elsewhere, some Home Guard lads had bagged a table not far away, but seemed more taken by the beer than the arrival of this posse of attractive WAAFs.

"Golly, I hope this isn't going to be a damp squib," muttered Eileen, taking a sip of the brandy she had ordered from the bar and joining the others at a spare table (of which there seems an alarming number!). Meanwhile, she smiled politely but otherwise feigned not to notice the suggestive glances of the local farm lads hugging the far wall.

"Give it time. It looks like our boys haven't turned up yet. They'll soon liven the place up," Nancy countered, ever the optimist amongst them.

"Here, Eileen, I think that lad quite fancies you," one of the other girls meanwhile nudged her, doffing her head in the requisite direction. Again, Eileen feigned not to notice.

"Makes one wonder what excuse they've concocted to avoid being called up," Nancy wondered aloud, having plainly caught the eye of his mate as well. "'Reserved occupation', my arse!"

"Let's just hope 'our boys' turn up soon. This do is so tedious it could bore the propeller off a Spitfire!" Eileen sighed, wondering how long she could make the brandy last before the lad still eyeing her up would pluck up the courage to wander over and offer to refill it.

At last, salvation arrived in the form of the first wave of Bomber boys in RAF blue. Then more of their colleagues began to file in, quickly filling the room with their banter and japing. Neither did they waste a moment gathering around to introduce themselves to Eileen, Nancy and their companions. The local lads meanwhile wisely accepted *force majeure* – their brief window of opportunity for chancing romance clearly having passed.

Indeed, the tempo of the evening was picking up too. Once the Mayor had offered his official greeting on behalf of the townsfolk (as well as a plug for the sale of few more war bonds), the band and its vocalist took his place on the stage, the cue for people to start drifting onto the dance floor. Inevitably, it wasn't long before the two prettiest girls in the room also found themselves being invited to partake of the proceedings.

"You dance well – very graceful," Eileen's partner felt moved to complement her as they swayed together arm-in-arm.

"Thank you."

"You're Eileen, aren't you?" he then thought to remark.

"That's right. Or Aircraftwoman 2090088 Kimberley, as the RAF would prefer us to address each other."

He smiled. "In which case, I guess that makes me Flight Sergeant 1978651 Graham... Gerald John... But if you prefer you can call me 'Spanners'... It's my nickname amongst the lads... Apparently, they insist, because I'm so mechanically-minded that I can fix almost any problem aboard the plane!"

It was Eileen's turn to smile – a coy, yet impish ripple across her comely face that spoke of how she was touched by his modesty and good humour.

"So how do you know me then?" she was curious to discover.

"Oh, I've seen you about. In fact, I think I might also have spoken to you once or twice... Through the switchboard, that is.... It's the voice, you know. For a moment I thought I was speaking to a duchess..."

"Thank you. But not quite!" she chuckled.

"But you are a lady though... There's something about you that makes you stand out from the other girls... I guess that why I made a bee-line for you... If you'll forgive me for being so bold."

Eileen smiled again. She just hoped Gerald hadn't noticed her head begin to swell. If he was correct, then she had certainly travelled a long way – physically and metaphorically – from those humble roots in a two-up-two-down terraced house at the back of the 'battery' works in Selly Oak.

"And what about you? You're aircrew, aren't you," she ventured as the band meanwhile eased the happy revellers into another melody.

"Oh, I've been known to tag along for the ride!" he replied self-effacingly. "Seriously though, I'm a flight engineer... I watch the engines and gauges... to make sure the old bird is purring along nicely."

Gerald was such a sweet young man – handsome too, with an angular Roman nose and lush obsidian eyes. As they traded backgrounds and sashayed around the dance floor, it was not hard to imagine this mild-mannered country boy from Herefordshire being the quietest, most unassuming member of a flight crew which he informed her was otherwise comprised of raucous antipodeans (including, bizarrely, a solitary South African who worked the W/T). Although nominally an RAF outfit, No. 75 Squadron was to all intents and purposes the preserve of those New Zealanders, one or two of whom took the opportunity of bumping into the couple on the floor to cheekily commend their flight engineer over his choice of dance partner.

"Thank you very much. I have so enjoyed that," Eileen insisted as the band struck up a different tune.

"No, Eileen. The pleasure has been all mine, I assure you," Gerald was most emphatic. However, being overly forward was not his way. In its absence he permitted Eileen to smile one final time and rejoin her friends, who were now being cheekily assailed by the other New Zealand lads, who had possessed the foresight to furnish them all with another round of drinks.

Therefore, he could only glance across from time to time as Eileen, Nancy and their comrades savoured the Kiwis' wit and charm, his own presence on the dance floor having meanwhile been requested by a very forward (and rather plump) local girl who, goaded on by her equally rotund best friend, was most determined to grab a dance with a dashing aviator. The loss of their remaining womenfolk to the clutches of the aircrews was just one more reason for those beer-supping farm boys to glance across the dance floor with sullen eyes.

It went without saying that Eileen was once again indulging her penchant for teasing out of young men from faraway places titbits about their 'exciting' distant lands. It turned out that the two guys with whom she found herself chatting had enlisted together, hailing from a little sea port on the southern-most tip of South Island (next stop the South Pole!). They assured her there was nothing remotely 'exciting' about where they lived – unless one was into oyster farming and quaint timber-framed houses. Meanwhile, Gerald's flagging heart rallied upon observing that Eileen did occasionally glance his way, not entirely oblivious to his patent interest in her. Once again, they found themselves exchanging a passing smile or two before they were lost once more in the swathe of couples revolving around the floor.

Finally, at eleven o'clock sharp, the music stopped and it was time to head back out into the night. Full of excitement (and perhaps a beer too many), the New Zealanders all noisily piled into the battered old dispersal van they had commandeered – and from which they now bade the WAAFs farewell, hanging on any-which-way as the overloaded beast laboured past the girls, who were busy rounding up their bikes.

"Awfully sorry there's no room, ladies!" they called out.

They weren't joking either! Even the addition aboard of the lithest of young feminine bottoms would have surely proved the straw that broke the camel's cruelly-burdened back axle!

"Next time you find yourself in Bluff, give me a call!" added one of the two young Kiwis who had been offering Eileen that rough-and-ready geography lesson. Meanwhile, his friend blew her a kiss.

"I will," she called back, blowing both lads a kiss back in response.

"Eileen, you are such a dreamer, you really are" Queenie marvelled. "When are you ever likely to go to New Zealand?"

"I might. One day," she riposted chirpily, perching her own pert little bottom onto the saddle of her bike and setting off with the others.

"You should know by now, girls: young Eileen here is hopelessly smitten by the Big Wide World," Nancy cheerfully reminded them. "She's already bagged several offers of hospitality in Australia after the war. Goodness knows where she'll be off too once the Yanks start arriving in England!"

"Grief! What's the matter, Eileen? England not big enough for you," a fellow cyclist joked.

"Or is it English men that are not 'big' enough?" another chided lustily, the other girls laughing.

"I swear I don't know what you're talking about," Eileen scowled, feigning an innocence that was no longer entirely credible.

What other choice did she have? How could she tell them the real reasons why nowadays she found even the wonderful little country she had pledged herself to defend too small for her expanding horizons? In like manner, how could she have explained to her two Kiwi *raconteurs* that it was the very fact that their home town was about as far away from her own as it was possible to be that intrigued her most? Neither was it all a product of an obsession with the glamour of Hollywood. One day she might explain to someone; maybe to Nancy – when the time was right.

"Say girls, these lamps are bloody useless. I can't see a darn thing in front of me," someone complained.

"What do you expect, Roberts? We can't have Jerry finding his way to camp by the glow from your squeaky old bike!"

"Oh, bother," Eileen cussed once they had cycled a little further, halting and peering down at the road through the darkness.

"What's the matter?"

"I think I've got a puncture," she cursed, the tyre wobbling and squelching as she pressed down hard on the handlebars.

"Well, there's no way we can fix it in this gloom. Perhaps we should have chanced our fate with the New Zealanders after all," Nancy opined.

"You do realise that if we're not back by midnight we'll end up on a charge."

"But we can't just leave Eileen here. We're in the middle of nowhere," someone else fretted. It was an invidious choice – comradely solidarity; or jankers with no more midnight passes.

"Look, you lot carry on," said Nancy, seizing the initiative. "I'll stay with Eileen and we'll walk our bikes back. If we get a move on we might just make it before the MPs are ordered out to round us up."

It seemed a reasonable compromise. Therefore, off the others set, reluctantly leaving the two friends alone with only a galaxy of stars to guide their way and keep them company.

"So tell me, what are your hopes and plans for when this war is over?" Eileen enquired. It was a question she realised that neither of them had ever properly broached before now. The quiescence of just the two of them pushing their bikes back along this lonely country by-way seemed as good a place as any to commence the task of finding out.

"Oh, I don't know. But I suspect I'll probably end up marrying and settling down in middle-class bliss somewhere: raise a family; bake cakes; and have my husband's tea waiting for him each evening."

"You? Bake cakes and all that? Nonsense! You're too much of a free spirit to ever be satisfied with a life as conventional as that," Eileen shook her head in disbelief.

"Somehow I don't think this war will be like the last one," she then continued. "People won't settle for the lives they had before – least of all us women in uniform. I can't see many of us wanting to swap the excitement of what we are doing now for life behind a kitchen sink. You know, many people look down on us. They think we only enlisted to get a man – preferably an officer. Yet I joined up to achieve something more than that. And certainly not the kind of staid domesticity my family think I should be grateful with."

"You're right," Nancy conceded, pondering her friend's observation. "Perhaps, like you, I'll try and find a way to travel; to see the world and experience all kinds of exotic places. If nothing else, being in uniform has certainly widened my horizons."

There was a magical hiatus in the conversation as both girls found themselves wistfully gazing up at the multitude of tiny stars spangling the heavens above them. Then Nancy turned to make out instead the twinkling in her friend's eyes.

"How about you?" she asked.

"What? Marry? Frank always wanted us to marry. I was always the one who fought shy. Why? Because I want to reach for those stars. Especially for the one up there somewhere that has my name on it. I guess I couldn't commit my life to a man who – God bless him, and for all his many virtues – was content merely to stare at his shoes. If you know what I mean."

There was no need for a response. Nancy knew alright. She could empathise with Eileen's seemingly quixotic quest. She was just curious about what had ignited it in this ordinary, working class girl whose horizons ought, by virtue of her meagre education, to have been no broader than any of the other unaspiring pram-and-kitchen-sink fodder in her street. Yet from the furtive way her friend declined to elaborate Nancy sensed that – for all the wondrous communion that existed between them – this particular unburdening of Aircraftwoman Kimberley's restless soul would have to await another occasion.

Just then, the two girls thought they detected footsteps approaching from behind, turning about to make out two shapes advancing along the lane at a brisk pace and in their direction,

"Evening, ladies. Nice night for a stroll," one of them mused, the Norfolk accent and the doffing of his cap hinting that they were probably the local lads who had been eyeing them up without success at the dance earlier on.

"Evening," Nancy and Eileen replied cagily as the two men overtook them and hurried off up the lane.

"Got a problem with your bike?" the other surmised with just a hint of sarcasm in his tone, turning about to address them.

"Yes, it's got a puncture, I'm afraid," Nancy replied on Eileen's behalf.

"Would you like us to take a look at it, love?"

"No, it's okay," Eileen shrugged, "We must get back. I'm sure one of the lads on camp will fix it for us tomorrow."

The two men stopped dead, prompting Nancy and Eileen to do likewise in order to preserve a wary distance between them. For suddenly there was tension in the air – as well as a faint chill breeze soughing across their faces that neither of them had been minded to notice.

"I said do you want us to take a look at your bike," the guy grizzled a second time, lazily advancing forward to rest his rough, throbbing hands upon the handlebars of Eileen's bicycle.

"Yeah. We know a thing or two about bikes, don't we Charlie," his mate informed them. This time there was no mistaking the menace in his tone.

"Look, I don't know what your game is…" Nancy cautioned them.

"Game? Oh, we're not playing games," he sneered, turning to his friend whose snide, toothy grin now left the two girls in no doubt that they were now in a very tight spot indeed.

"You look quite nice in your uniforms," Charlie then complimented them, running the knuckle of his coarse finger along the breast of Eileen's tunic before lifting her tie away, flicking it between his fingers, and then alighting that greasy knuckle upon the outline of her brassiere instead.

"Yeah, no wonder all those lardy-dah 'Brylcreem Boys' just can't wait to get their fingers inside your knickers!" his accomplice leered crudely, the smell of fear animating the predatory feral beast that plainly lurked inside him.

Just then, across the fields, the landscape lit up and what seemed like mile after mile of bright lights banished the dimness around them.

"Look! It's the Military Police. They're coming out to fetch us!" Eileen pointed to the array, Charlie's anxious gaze following the trajectory of her outstretched finger. In the split-second that it did Eileen took hold of her bike and rammed the front wheel hard into the groin of her assailant, who let out a devilish shriek before keeling over in agony.

Quick as a flash, Nancy too squared up to the other fellow, who made as if to grab hold of her. As he reached across, instead he stumbled over her bike, which she had heaved up and thrown into his path. While he was on all fours, disorientated, she spotted her moment. With a well-aimed shot from behind, she hammered the toe of her shoe between his legs. He too now wailed as the forward motion of the merciless kick launched him into the stagnant watery ditch beside the lane, which he sank down into with a ker-plunching great splash.

"Quick! Run for it!" Nancy hollered, her cap flung from head by the velocity of her acceleration, her bushy blonde locks racing free.

Together the two girls took off in the direction of the base, fuelled by the high-octane adrenaline that now coursed through their bodies. They ran and ran and ran until they finally spied the familiar outline of the guard house up ahead, racing up to the sentry out of breath – ready to collapse, but safe at last.

\* \* \* \* \*

"Aircraftwoman King. Aircraftwoman Kimberley. Inside. Now. At the double... left, right, left, right..."

The NCO's brusque order brought the two girls wheeling square on to the Section Officer's desk, where they halted, stood to attention, saluted, and awaited their fate.

The matronly officer sat nonchalantly reading her notes for what seemed like an eternity while Eileen and Nancy gazed rigidly ahead. Then, her exaggerated perusal complete, she deigned to look up at them sternly.

"You know why you are here, airwomen," she sat up and charged.

"Yes, ma'am," was the collective reply.

"Charge number one: failure to report back at the prescribed time. Charge number two: reporting back in a state of dishevelment and with one of you minus her cap. Charge number three: the mislaying of RAF property – namely two bicycles."

"Yes, ma'am."

"Now, as for your excuse that you were 'importuned' on your way back from the village, I am minded to give it credence and pass it to the police for further investigation. However, I have to say your descriptions of your assailants are sketchy, to say the least. Frankly, I don't hold out much hope of the local constabulary being able to follow these allegations up..."

"But it was very dark, Section Officer," Nancy pleaded. "And we daren't have hung about..."

"Silence when the officer is speaking," the corporal barked.

Nice try, Nancy, Eileen desperately wanted to commend her. If ever there was a moment when she admired the fearless spunk of her best friend it was now. It had taken guts to do what she had done the previous evening – what they had both done. No helpless, swooning Hollywood maidens these, timidly waiting rescue by Gary Cooper heroically riding up in the nick of time. Reacting on their wits, instead they had successfully effected their own rescue – aided, it had to be said, by the unexpected switching on of the station's landing lights to guide in an aircraft in distress. Furthermore, if nothing else Nancy had proved that those stout RAF shoes were good for something more than just marching in!

"I'm afraid in the meantime you will be put on camp cleaning duties and have pass privileges withdrawn for the next two weeks. Meanwhile, the cost of the missing bicycles will be deducted from your pay in instalments. Hopefully, this will encourage you to pay more attention to your own personal safety in future. And to take more care of RAF property."

"Yes, ma'am."

"That will be all. Corporal, you may dismiss them," she glanced across at the NCO, who was staring dead ahead beneath the peak of her cap. However, before she could bark instructions for both girls to file back out, the officer's business-like severity eased into a glimmer of a grin instead.

"By the way, girls," she observed, glancing down at her notes, "Assuming your story is true – especially the bit about ramming your bicycle 'where it hurts' and shoving these ruffians into a ditch ... then bloody good show!"

Eileen and Nancy dared to glance at each other for the first time, though not so daring as to grin themselves.

"Er… yes, ma'am."

"Thank you, ma'am," they each stuttered before finally being escorted from her presence.

"… Left, right, left, right, left right…"

# 5

"They're beautiful!" she swooned, admiring the vivid colours of the huge bouquet, and taking in the sweet scent with which it filled the ward.

Two weeks of scrubbing latrines and sweeping out the mess hall soon passed. In Eileen's case, it passed even quicker when she was forced to hobble to the sick bay with an inflamed bunion – the result of trying to squeeze those tender young feet into silly pointed shoes, a condition that had since been exacerbated by having to march (and run!) in those RAF Oxford shoes. The MO promptly signed her off punishment duties and within a few days she found herself being packed off to the hospital at nearby RAF Ely to undergo a corrective operation. This, in turn, took her off all duties for the next few weeks. Apparently, an awful lot of WAAFs had trod (or limped!) the same path before her – again, the result of having been slaves to teenage footwear fashions prior to enlisting.

Nancy and the girls took turns to visit her and try and leaven the boredom of having ones foot bound in plaster, which Eileen appreciated. However, today she was receiving the most surprise visitor of all: Flight Sergeant Gerald Graham with his thoughtful little gift (well, quite a large gift actually).

"I heard about your little escapade on the way back from the dance. Then before I could grab the chance to see you, they told me you'd been packed off here," he explained, examining the plaster-cast foot before returning to offer his whole-hearted attention to its owner.

"You know, you really should have said. I'm sure at a push the lads could have squeezed you into Jock's car with us," he berated her as gently as his chivalrous concern for her welfare would permit. "We could even have swapped places and I'd have ridden your ruddy bike back to camp!"

"But you couldn't possibly have squeezed all six of us in. Anyway, what's done is done. Hopefully, I should be up and walking in the next few days. Well, hobbling at least!"

"Yes, well, my girl. You make sure you don't go 'hobbling' home from any more dances alone," he berated her again. Then the avuncular tone dissolved and he stared into her bright brown eyes hopefully. "In fact, you will not be going to any more such events alone. From now, I'd... well... I'd be honoured if I could be the one who, er... escorts you to the dance," he finally mumbled, gazing down at the floor apologetically as he uttered the fraught admission.

"Are you perchance asking me for a date?" Eileen sank back into her pillow and smiled.

While that smile lingered, Gerald looked into her eyes again before confessing that "Yes, I would very much like to go on a date with you. Lots of dates, in fact – if that's okay with you."

She propped herself up on her elbows and positively beamed from ear to ear. "This time it's my turn to be honoured and privileged. Of course I will."

With that, he leant forward and kissed her tenderly on the lips. Then, the brief deed done, he glanced down at his watch.

"Better go. We're off somewhere 'interesting' again tonight. Can't say where, you understand. But let's just say Jerry won't be dancing by the time we've finished with him!" he winked knowingly. Then, glancing at the plaster-covered foot a final time, he took a pen from the pocket of his tunic and leant across to scribble a few words upon it, rounding the message off with a dash and a dot to fashion an exaggerated exclamation mark.

"Take care, Eileen," he whispered as he rose to his feet and headed for the exit. "I'll try and pop by again."

"You take care too – over Ger... where ever you're off to tonight!" she corrected herself, covering her mouth impishly. Then he was gone.

Seeing that the patient was desperately craning her heed to read whatever it was someone had scribbled on her plaster-cast, the nursing sister halted as she was passing by on her peregrinations around the ward and glanced down to make out the text.

"It says 'Here's to my love, Eileen. Wishing you a swift recovery... Spanners'" she obliged. Then she squinted to make out the rest of the message, reading it out verbatim. "'...P.S. – all you amorous Kiwis... Leave well alone... This is my girl!'"

* * * * *

"You really don't need to fuss, Mum," Eileen insisted, curling her forefinger through the handle, taking a sip from the cup and closing her eyes with bliss.

One further perk of her convalescence was that towards its end she was granted a few days leave. Thus it was that she now found herself back in Birmingham, enjoying a nice cup of tea the way only her mother could brew it – along with a chat and a wicked exchange of gossip. Therefore, it required no great sacrifice to indulge her mother's fussing, which was infinitely preferable to another telling-off from Auntie Kathleen about the perils of wearing fashionable, if ill-fitting shoes. However, having said her piece, Auntie Kathleen sipped from her own cup and returned to stony-faced silence.

"I hear German bombers were over again the other night," noted Eileen, determined to coax Auntie Kathleen out of a censorious dismay borne of the realisation that her beloved niece and god-daughter was no longer the sweet little girl in pig-tails who used to skip alongside her hand-in-hand as they would make their way to church. Indeed, Auntie Kathleen looked as if she was sore tempted to enquire whether Eileen was still dutifully attending Mass and Confession now she had been posted away from home. Instead her beloved aunt decided to answer the matter in hand.

"Yes, the first time this year. Ladywood, Edgbaston, Harborne, Kings Norton – they were all hit," she tutted.

"If it's any consolation our boys are giving Jerry a right pasting. Now the weather's picked up they're off almost every night on missions," Eileen continued. Then her jingoism gave way to a sudden melancholy.

"The terrible thing is though they are paying such a heavy cost. I remember the first occasion when Nancy and I strolled into the village pub. We asked the landlord what all the tankards were for that he had hung up behind the bar. He explained that each of the aircrew kept their own personally-inscribed one there for use whenever they popped by. Then he took us out the back and showed us the shelves on which he kept all the tankards whose owners were either captured, dead or missing. Each time we called in there were new tankards hanging up; but also more and more of them gathering dust on those shelves out the back – including two belonging those young New Zealanders that Nancy and I were quite friendly with."

Auntie Kathleen declined to comment about the way her niece seemed to be 'quite friendly' with a lot of young men of late. Instead she sighed as if to express her regret and condolence. Eileen knew she, of all people, could emphasise with tragedy and loss; and brush aside petty moral qualms to summon up the Christian charity that such gaping forfeiture demanded.

"Anyway, who's this new man in your life that you wrote and told me about in your letter," her mother was keen to discover, changing the subject.

"You mean Gerald. Yes, you'd like him, Mum. He's an absolute gentleman. He came to see me almost every day when I was in hospital. Well, as often as he was able to sweet-talk the WingCo into authorising a pass."

"Good. It's so nice to see you happy again. Everyone has the right to be happy. After all, we've all experienced far too much heartache these last few years."

With her mother's word still ringing in her ears, Eileen was surprised to catch the sound of the merry whistling of some bloke strolling up the back passage, and who then tapped briskly on the back door and let himself in.

"Aw'right, ladies. Still tea in the pot for another thirsty soul?" he begged in a Brummie accent that was even flatter than her mother's. Mum herself reached over and shook the teapot.

"Aren't you the lucky man," she replied.

"Good. Then you sure you don't mind if I join you, like?" he not so much asked as informed them, diving into the empty place around the table and permitting Mary to fill a cup and place it before him.

"Anyway, who's this delightful young thing?" he then grinned at Eileen, revealing a set of crooked, tobacco-stained teeth that complimented the weathered appearance of his grubby work apparel.

"Stan, this is Eileen. She's a WAAF. And she's home on leave... Eileen, this is Stan Smith – a good friend of mine,"

"Pleased to meet ya', like... Eileen," Stan enthused, sitting up, wiping the palm of his chunky hand against his jacket, and then thrusting it in her direction, along with another crooked grin to match. Eileen hesitated for a split second before reluctantly slipping her smoother, cleaner and more delicate paw inside it to be heartily shaken as only a straight-as-a-dye son of toil would do.

"Eileen's my... my younger sister."

Eileen looked up at her mother. Straight away an iron scowl banished the angelic countenance that this happy-go-lucky teenager invariably presented to the world.

"You didn't tell me you had another sister, Mary," Stan marvelled, slurping on his tea and thereby remaining oblivious to the set of blazing brown eyes alternately shifting their gaze between her mother and this 'new man', whoever he was. Perhaps he didn't think it strange, nor the age gap particularly intriguing. After all, these Irish families do go in for children in a big way; and little 'accidents' late in life can happen to the best of good Catholics.

"So what brings you this way so early in the day?" Mary was anxious to know, though not unpleasantly surprised judging by the fuss she was now lavishing upon their visitor, delving into the cupboard and emerging with a slice of freshly-baked cake she must have been saving especially for him.

"We've been up town helping clear up the damage from that raid the other night. Apparently, the buggers were after the BSA factory again. Anyway, I was in the lorry, so I'd thought I'd pop by, like."

"We still on for tonight then?" Mary was equally anxious to know.

"You bet, love. You just give me half-hour when I clock off and I'll be home, out of this clobber and dressed up like a dog's dinner!" Stan boasted, munching on the cake before resting back into his chair. There he deftly swished the crumbs from his palms before propping up his forearms and inter-locked fingers on the beer belly that emerged as his jacket slid open.

All this time he failed to notice that the 'little sister' was becoming ever more unsettled by the déjà vu he had unwittingly stirred inside her, preferring instead to speculate aloud on where he might take Mary tonight that would impress her with his favour and generosity. Otherwise, Auntie Kathleen too had donned a look that spoke of appalled incredulity mixed in with prescience concerning the trouble another 'new man' spreading favours and generosity might occasion in the Kimberley household. She discreetly swapped glances with Eileen, both of them praying that history would not be repeating itself.

"Anyway, that was much appreciated, Mrs K. You're a good woman. And a good woman is hard to find these day. I best be off though before I have the gaffer on me' case... I'll see you later," he assured her, winking as he whipped his cap from his back pocket and slapped it back on his furrowed head. Then he disappeared out of the door as suddenly as he had breezed in, once more whistling merrily as he made his way back down the passage.

"Well, what are you two gawping at?" Mary squawked, gathering up the crocks. "Don't I have a right to happiness too?"

\* \* \* \* \*

Eileen couldn't sleep. Forcing away another tear lest it add to an already dampened pillow, she closed her eyes and slithered her face back beneath the shielding of the bed sheet, praying a bit harder that the bad memories might go away. Once more she felt her mother was metaphorically a million miles away from her just when the closeness they had always enjoyed had been returning again to their relationship. As such, she had resolved that she would not hang around to witness the playing out of its denial again. Her case was packed and her uniform hung up ready. Tomorrow at the crack of dawn she would be up and off to board the train that would enable her to return instead to the new relationships she had made, and to the new life she had been busy fashioning.

Just then her angry self-absorption was interrupted by the familiar wail of the air raid sirens. Lifting herself from her bed she hauled the black-out drapes away to observe the first searchlights reaching out into the night sky. Grabbing her dressing gown she strode out onto the landing and opened the door to her mother's bedroom. There was no sign of her. Neither did her bed appear to have been slept in.

Instead, Eileen made her way down the stairs alone and out of the front door, racing across to Auntie Kathleen's house a few doors up the street. Bursting in through the back door she beheld her aunt steadying Granny O'Leary as together they descended the last few stairs before making for the back door too. Behind her, with her favourite teddy clutched to her chest, was Kathleen's six year-old daughter, Monica. Eileen had often helped to babysit and care for her little cousin. Quite a close bond had therefore developed between them, and she cast a protective arm around her to reassure her and hurry her along.

"Ah, the little blighters are back, they are. And there was I thinking I'd seen the last of them."

"It may only be a false alarm, Granny," Eileen countered, although her assurance was rudely punctured by the distant crump of anti-aircraft batteries opening up.

It was the prompt for Granny – assisted by Eileen and her aunt (and with Monica in tow) – to hobble a little faster in the direction of the Anderson shelter that had been erected and partially-buried on waste ground out the back. Already one or two neighbouring families had nestled themselves up the corner and had lit a candle or two to add illumination. This assisted Auntie Kathleen to help Granny down the step and inside. Meanwhile, Eileen glanced behind and allowed her eyes to follow the powerful beam of a searchlight that had picked out a Heinkel 111 commencing its run over the city, several strands of tracer fire heading up in its direction through the night sky. For a split second she froze in terror. Then, regaining her wits, she instead ushered Monica inside. Shutting the door behind them, together they joined the others now sealed within the shelter's gloom.

"They're after the BSA factory at Small Heath again," someone noted sardonically. Meanwhile, his wife was rocking their baby, who was fast asleep and blissfully oblivious to the drama going on all around.

"Cheer up, everyone. It'll soon be over," Eileen smiled, feeling it incumbent upon her as a servicewoman to do something to lift morale. Raids at this time of year were never quite as bad. Apart from the fact that it was warm tonight, the short nights meant that the enemy planes would have a smaller window of darkness in which to deliver their attack and head home. Even so, as she remembered was the custom in their shelter, the time passed quicker if they attempted to forget what was going on above their heads and make their own entertainment instead.

"Run rabbit, run rabbit, run, run, run..." she thus began to sing.

BANG!

Alas, it was not 'the farmer's gun' that shook the ground beneath them. Instead, a loud explosion filled ears quickly covered by hands raised to shield them. Over in the corner the neighbour's infant began to cry, its mother desperately cradling it in her arms. Meanwhile, Monica and her teddy snuggled even tighter into the protective carapace of Eileen's own enveloping arms. A faint trace of dust sprinkled them lightly.

"Blimey. That was close," someone commented, exhaling exaggeratedly.

"False alarm, my arse!" Granny O'Leary snorted in her broad Connemara accent, seemingly more annoyed than fazed by it all. "And will yer' stop yer' snivellin', child. It's damp enough in here already, it is. It's no good fer' me' bones!"

Her blunt aside was intended as wit, but its effect was to force Monica to bury her moist, cherubic face even deeper into Eileen's bosom. Granny had what might be euphemistically termed a 'dry' sense of humour – never more so than in times of crisis like these. During the height of the Blitz their times spent in the shelter had often been leavened by it, as well as by the regurgitating of all those tales about the family from long ago. She would wax lyrical about the hard times in the remote, rural west of Ireland at the close of the nineteenth century, and which had driven one impoverished son to emigrate to America, and the other – Eileen's deceased grandfather – to settle with his young wife in Birmingham. Tonight, however, Granny seemed in no mood for nostalgia or reflection. The contorted scowl she wore Eileen had witnessed before – angry, embittered and spiked with recrimination. Indeed, Granny O'Leary's unpredictable mood swings seemed to personify everything that was topsy-turvy and bittersweet about Eileen's family life. Trying not to notice the agitation in her manner, the teenager instead rested her cheek upon Monica's little head, rocking her gently and continuing to sing *sotto voce* in her ear.

"Kiss me goodnight, Sergeant Major. Tuck me in my little wooden bed..."

"Agh! Away wit'ya, girl," Granny snorted again upon overhearing Eileen's gorgeous mellow voice. "And talkin' of beds, I don't suppose we'll be seeing that mother of yours any time tonight."

"Mary's gone up town with a friend. They've probably taken shelter somewhere on the way back," Auntie Kathleen, explained, evincing either a startling innocence or (Eileen preferred to think) a willingness to paint the most benign picture of her sister's nocturnal whereabouts.

"Oh, she'll be sheltering alright. And with this 'friend', I shouldn't wonder. Any port in a storm, as they say. And pray tell us who this 'friend' might be now. Although, second thoughts, I can guess. Probably another useless wastrel like the ne'er-do-well I caught her with the other day.

"…And what might you be gawping at, girl?" Granny then suddenly exclaimed, catching Eileen eyes locking onto her as she pondered whether to join Auntie Kathleen in defending her mother's honour or to concur with her grandmother's not-entirely inaccurate judgement upon Mary's preference in men. Therefore, she said nothing and returned to cradling her cousin, shielding her ears as much from the scandalous invective as from the rumble of bombs and flak still going on outside.

"Mind you, you want to be watching you don't turn out like her," Granny continued pontificating, fixing her beady eye upon her grand-daughter. "…All those fancy ideas of yours about 'doing ya' bit fer' ya' country'. My arse! You'll be chasing men too, I shouldn't wonder. Tis' a disgrace, it is. And without a second thought as to whether that poor fellah who was good to you is either dead or alive!"

It was a barb the inference of which Eileen was in no doubt. "It's not like that at all, Granny," she protested gingerly.

"Isn't it? Isn't it now? Is that why yer' felt this sudden urge to go join the Air Force? And why all these years you've been learning to talk like all those British officer fellahs – puttin' on ya' heirs an' graces, y'are? So was a decent Catholic lad from the next street not good enough for you then?"

"Come on, mother. That is not true," Auntie Kathleen waded in. "Eileen is a good girl. You should be proud that she is attempting to make something of her life."

"Proud? Proud of what, pray tell us?" Granny fired back, her eyes opened wide in exclamation. "Well, you're right, I s'pose. We should all be grateful that she has bit better taste in men than her mother!"

"Granny!" Eileen cried out appalled, pressing Monica's delicate ears ever tighter.

"Agh! Away with yer', Kathleen! All yer' prayin' to Our Lady on yer' knees is wasted on this one, for sure. All this gallivanting with airmen! She's a dreamer, she is – mark my words. Just like all that talk of being a singer or a dancer – tis' all dreamin', it is. But then that trait she definitely gets from her father. He had his head up in the clouds too, he did. He thought he was too good for us all. She'll turn out just like him at this rate, you see if I'm not wrong."

"STOP IT!!!" Eileen screeched and stood to her feet, the draught from her sudden movement almost extinguishing the candles that illuminated the faces of neighbours who had throughout been watching with mounting alarm this suppurating of familial poison. Meanwhile, the baby in the corner began to cry even louder.

"I will not have you talk about my father like that!" she cried.

The mention of his name had struck the rawest nerve within her and she now flung open the door and raced out of the shelter.

"Eileen! Eileen!" she heard the voice of little Monica cry out behind her. However, she had taken off and did not look back. Instead, it was left to Kathleen to grab the startled youngster as she was about to chase after her and pull her back inside the shelter just as bomb impacted somewhere on the far side of the Bristol Road.

With a deafening burst, it lit up the skyline, illuminating Eileen's passage as she ran the short distance back to the house. Racing up the stairs, she quickly divested her night clothes and began to throw on her uniform, straightening her skirt and her tie and slotting her arms into her tunic.

"PUT THAT RUDDY LIGHT OUT!" she heard a voice shriek from the street below. She poked her head out of the window to observe the local air raid warden hands-on-hips staring up at her, his face aglow as much from indignation as the reflected aura of the city burning all around them.

Minded to give the jumped-up little jobs-worth an earful, she cursed under her breath and withdrew her head back inside. She extinguished the bedroom light and instead availed herself of that same rippling aura to tie up her hair and set her cap in place. Then she grabbed her case, slung over her shoulder the little khaki bag containing her gas mask, and rushed back down the stairs onto the street. She once more turned her face away from the old life she had known and which she knew could never heal its scars or hold out the promise of the freedom and self-betterment she craved.

Eventually reaching the main road – and guessing that the trams had all been halted – she wiped away a stray tear and settled into a brisk, yet purposeful walk in the direction of town, all the time the continuing 'crump-crump' of the ack-ack batteries carrying on around her. She had not been going long when above her she thought she could make out a faint, yet eerie swishing noise that grew louder as its source accelerated towards the Earth. Instinctively, she threw herself to the ground. She closed her eyes tight and prayed. This is it, she thought. Otherwise, in a moment that seemed to play out in agonising slow motion, all those terrible things Granny had accused her of – along with the memory of every other thing she had ever done in her life, good or bad – raced through her head as she waited for 'the end' to finally arrive. If she had indeed fallen so far – from a good and devout Catholic girl to a heartless, snobbish, self-seeking hussy – then, like some latter-day Mary Magdalene, there was surely no other recourse left to her now than to cast herself upon the mercy of the Blessed Saviour whose forgiveness Auntie Kathleen had taught her to seek.

The swishing stopped at the very instant that a small metal object impacted onto the roof of a house nearby. She looked up to behold this diminutive, cylindrical canister smash several tiles before rolling off the roof to clang to halt on the street a few yards from her.

She froze. Then suddenly the object ignited and glowed white as lightning, burning furiously as she frantically lifted herself to her feet and stumbled backwards away from it.

"Get back, Miss! Go on, get out of here," she turned to observe two police officers sprint up to her as if from nowhere.

One of them removed his tunic and began to flail at the sizzling phosphorus bomb. His colleague – more attuned to what it would take to deal with the device – instead spread his own tunic out and smothered it, the other officer likewise heeding his example and casting his tunic upon it too, both of them stamping on their uniforms until the canister billowed smoke, but was otherwise extinguished.

Meanwhile, Eileen nervously shuffled away, her gaze still captivated by its smouldering remains. Then, snapping out of her daze, she rushed back in to grab her cap and her case and hurry back away again. Positioning her cap back upon her head, she continued on her journey – albeit with a renewed sense of determination. Finally, she looked up to the heavens from where the device had come and crossed herself vigorously, her hand trembling as she drew on a cigarette she then lit with a heart humbled by thanksgiving.

# 6

There was so much unspoken yearning abroad amongst everyone present. They were being reacquainted again with those tremendous, uplifting words of hope bound up in *'The White Cliffs of Dover'* that the concert party's talented young songstress was crying out. Perhaps it was for this reason that Eileen had become suddenly misty-eyed and trance-like in the arms of her gallant new boyfriend as they swayed together cheek-to-cheek. Meanwhile, a six-piece ENSA ensemble was playing along softly, whilst outside glistening stars filled the warm evening sky, commencing their distant nocturnal vigil – such that the war and all its horror really did seem a million miles away too. Breaking from her thoughts, Eileen glanced around at them and smiled, as if lost in the romance of it all.

"You look contented," Gerald smiled too, craning his head away just sufficiently to be able to observe more fully her serene countenance.

"Maybe I am," was her soft, tantalising response.

She carried on starring up at those stars for a moment or two longer before turning to behold instead the sparkle in her sweetheart's dark, seductive eyes. Surely God in His Heaven was smiling down on this magical evening that He had created especially for the two of them.

"You know, I was just thinking," Gerald continued. "When this wretched war is over, maybe I shall try something new... Put all the skills I've learned in the RAF to good use.... There's going to be a need for good engineers to service all the motor cars that people will want to buy, and which will no longer be the exclusive preserve of the rich, you know... Maybe I'll even open my own garage somewhere... What do you think?"

"That sounds like a super idea," she nodded, her gaze otherwise once more transfixed by the stars.

"And, of course, a good garage will certainly need a good receptionist: someone with a perfect telephone manner and that reassurance in her voice that will leave the customer in no doubt that his pride-and-joy is about to be entrusted to good hands."

Why did she get the impression that Flight Sergeant Gerald 'Spanners' Graham had just the person in mind to lavish that reassurance upon his prospective customers! She smiled serenely at him once more – Gerald taking it she was not averse to what he had in mind. Thereafter, he held her tight again as their feet and bodies synchronised perfectly with the wistful melody reaching its reprise. Amongst the other happy couples who were also serenely gliding around the impromptu dance floor of the cavernous aircraft hangar there were also lovers gazing into each other's eyes and charily broaching plans for a shared future. Indeed, it seemed a night made for such dreamy deliberations.

\* \* \* \* \*

*"Is your journey really necessary?"* she recalled the official poster on Cambridge railway station cautioning.

Staring out of the window of the crowded passenger train, Eileen observed the verdant countryside of Hertfordshire give way to the factories and tenements of north London that were flashing past. Though not without much soul-searching, she had wrestled with the thing she was about to do and was satisfied she could answer that question in the affirmative. It was 'necessary' that she spend this weekend's '48' in the capital resolving something that had been weighing heavily on her mind.

In the late summer of 1942, No. 75 Squadron had vacated RAF Feltwell to commence training elsewhere on the more powerful Short Stirling bombers it was to receive. Gerald had promised to write to her every day – and so far had been as good as his word. Indeed, to read his beautifully-crafted letters to her was to behold a man who would unhesitatingly pay any price in order to make her happy.

Yet much as she loved her job manning an RAF switchboard, Eileen was not entirely smitten with the thought of spending the rest of her life answering telephones behind the reception counter of a garage – even as she reluctantly accepted that Nancy was right: she was unlikely to ever find another man who would love her with such unflinching devotion as Gerald.

"King's Cross! King's Cross! All change!" the stout little guard bawled as he wandered through the emptying carriage.

"King's Cross, miss. This train has terminated here," he then popped his head inside the deserted compartment to gently counsel the attractive young WAAF who was still sat there all by herself, as if in a daydream.

She acknowledged him and rose to lift her small night case down from the rack above her head, making her way out onto the platform. Having saved up to purchase the rail warrant, she was brimming with a most feverish longing; and yet a longing tinged with trepidation – so much so as to be tempted to jump back on a train heading in the other direction. For she was about to spend her weekend leave in the company of another gentleman whom she loved, and whose existence Gerald was only vaguely aware of.

* * * * *

She had never been to London before. Notwithstanding the terrible devastation that had been wrought by the Blitz, the capital seemed to have lost none of its legendary bustle and excitement – far more bustle than anything Birmingham's pre-war provincial gaiety had mustered.

Attempting to orientate herself and make sense of the instructions she had written down, it seemed like every other soul amongst the crowds racing past her was – like her – a man or woman in uniform. As well as coming or going to and from leave or postings, many of them had presumably come to see the sights too – Leicester Square and the West End theatres; music and entertainment in the capital's many clubs and restaurants; or maybe even the legendary prostitutes that thronged these venues (and which waggish servicemen dubbed the 'Piccadilly Commandoes'!). Failing that, they could instead savour those traditional attractions that reminded the British people of their unique way of life and of the long and glorious heritage of law and liberty that they were fighting to uphold – St Paul's Cathedral, Westminster Abbey, Big Ben and the House of Parliament, Buckingham Palace.

By-and-by, having availed herself of the kindness and helpfulness of strangers along the way, she managed to piece together a journey by bus that brought her just a short walk from a large terraced town house in Notting Hill – one of many that had somehow miraculously escaped the depredations of the *Luftwaffe*. Alternately staring up at it and at the address in the letter, it seemed to correspond to the details she had been given. Therefore, summoning up the courage, and praying that she was doing the right thing, she mounted the wide flight of white-washed stone steps and rang the bell. There was no response. Therefore, she rang it again, this time rapping the knocker lustily to make sure that her presence had been noted. It worked. After hearing the sound of voices inside, the door partially opened and Eileen was surprised to discover a child's face appear around it: a young girl with freckles and pretty amber pony-tails who she surmised could have been no older than six years of age.

"Oh... Hello. I'm Eileen," she announced, jauntily donning her best beaming smile and a manner calculated to put a wary child at ease.

"My name is Maureen," the little girl replied in a conversely sheepish, adult-wary voice, her winsome eyes squinting in the September sun.

"I'm looking for George. I'm told he lives at this address."

The child took a moment to shield her eyes, the better to conduct one final survey of this mysterious visitor in the smart blue uniform. Then she disappeared back behind the door, leaving Eileen to listen whilst her little leaden feet clumped up the stairs. It momentarily reminded her of her cousin, Monica, and how she too seemed incapable of scampering about Auntie Kathleen's house without pounding the boards like a troop of elephants!

"Mummy…. There's a lady downstairs. I think she's looking for Daddy."

The muffled announcement left Eileen bewildered. Had she heard correct? Perhaps she didn't have the right address after all. She anxiously scanned Auntie Kathleen's letter once more to be certain.

Just then her straining at the handwriting was interrupted by another jolt of the imposing front door, this time a tall, elegantly-attired woman (who she guessed to be in her early thirties) looking her up and down in curiosity.

"Hello, I'm Eileen. I'm looking for George."

"Oh really," the woman leered, again studying this attractive young WAAF most attentively.

"Yes, George Kimberley. I'm told he lives at this address. This is 139A Rochester Terrace?"

"That's right," the woman confirmed, her austere, punctilious gaze never faltering. "…And yes, George Kimberley does indeed reside here," she continued in her frightfully refined tones.

"Good… And may I see him?" Eileen pressed, her host offering the impression that she was not going to be at all forthcoming of her own volition.

"I'm afraid he's not in. He has been away on business this week. He's not due back home until late. Very late, I would imagine."

"Oh… I see," said Eileen again, disappointment abroad in both her laconic reply and her doleful eyes. Then, after an agonising silence that, once again, her host was not minded to relieve, she added "I could call again tomorrow… when he's back."

"Well… I suppose, if you insist," her host conceded, a tad rude and grudgingly Eileen thought. "But you'd best make it in the afternoon. No doubt he'll be tired after his journey and will want to keep the morning to himself. Otherwise, I'm afraid we have an engagement tomorrow evening."

"Okay. Shall I call at one o'clock?"

"Yes. That should be alright. Who shall I tell him to expect? What was your name again?"

"Eileen. Eileen Kimberley. I'm his daughter," the visitor cheerfully smiled.

"Oh… I see."

It was the turn of the lady of the house to offer a laconic exclamation, her face turning ghostly as she did. Eileen could detect that that portentous eight-letter word had not been received at all auspiciously.

"Well, like I said: one o'clock. Try not to make it any later."

With that the door was closed and the visiting airwoman was left alone on the doorstep once more – unacquainted with, and frankly unwelcomed by whoever this woman (and her little child) might be. Meanwhile, her anxious introspection was punctured by the excited cries of children playing further up street. Dejected, she turned about and descended the steps. As she walked back towards the bus stop her forlorn self-reproach gave way to the realisation that it was time to urgently put together a wholly unexpected Plan B for her weekend sojourn in the capital: where to stay tonight.

* * * * *

As promised, Eileen returned to the elegant town house the following day at one o'clock on the dot, having managed to overnight in a cheap boarding house she had been directed to that was not too far away.

Therefore, she remounted the white-washed steps and rung the bell, rapping hard on the door knocker for good measure. However, she was once again confronted by an ominous stillness that was broken only by the distant screams and giggles of those same children playing further up the street. She waited and tried again. There was no response.

Perhaps they had popped out that morning and were late returning, for she felt sure her father would be overjoyed at the prospect of meeting his long lost daughter again – the same irrepressible joy that had impelled that daughter to then dissemble to her boyfriend why she could not be with him on this otherwise gorgeous late summer weekend. Therefore, descending the steps again and perching her bottom upon the stone wall outside, she resolved to await his return, removing her cap. She took a moment to locate the mirror in her bag in order to make herself more presentable upon his return.

Time passed by, and while it was no great burden to feel the caressing of the warm sun upon her face, still there was no sign of his return. Even so, looking at her little watch she decided to quickly pop along and re-victual herself at the tea room she had spotted earlier on the main road.

In no time at all, she was back outside the house again, where she once more propped herself up on the wall outside to resume her anxious vigil. There she waited. And waited. And waited.

Eventually, thinking he may have returned and disappeared back inside during the brief interlude while she had been away, she remounted the steps again and gave the door a hearty tap. Then another tap just to be sure.

Her resolute knocking must surely have been heard because in due course the next door neighbour appeared on her doorstep, the diminutive woman in a patterned pinafore and head scarf peering around the colonnade to make her presence known to the source of the disturbance.

"Hello," Eileen called across to greet her. "I'm looking for George Kimberley. I was told he would be in this afternoon."

"You'll be lucky, Miss. He went out with his wife and daughter this morning – at about eleven o'clock, if I recall." she tutted, leaning on the broom that she was gripping and studying this attractive young lass in the smart blue uniform.

"Oh... Do you know what time they will be back?"

"I'm afraid I haven't a clue. Judging by the things they had packed in the car with them when they left I'd say they've probably gone out for whole day."

"Oh... Thank you," Eileen grinned feebly, unable to mask her disappointment.

"Shall I tell him someone called?"

Eileen offered the old lady another forlorn smile. "No, it's okay. Thank you anyway. Perhaps I'll catch up with him on another occasion."

With that, Eileen slowly descended the steps, turning to survey the house from the street one final time as she did. She also felt it incumbent to nod a parting acknowledgement to the neighbour, who now busied herself sweeping the step. In reality though, she was glancing up and subtly endeavouring to fathom out this beautiful, if mysterious young female visitor that she had been discreetly spying from behind her curtain all afternoon, and who had waited so patiently to confront the respectable family man who lived next door.

* * * * *

The sound of the bed springs squeaking finally subsided – along with the panting and moaning of the woman in the next room. It was followed by the sound of the door closing a few minutes later. Much like the previous evening, this unseemly ritual was rounded off by the heavy clump of boots hurriedly descending the stairs and the emergence of yet another satisfied squaddie back onto the street outside to make the most of what was left of his leave.

Goodness knows what else people got up to in this boarding house, but Eileen could stand sitting alone in her dingy little room no longer. The night was young and so she made up her mind that, if only for an hour or two, she would leave the woman next door to her noisy and sordid enterprises and instead find somewhere more edifying to while away her final evening in London. Grabbing her gas mask case from off the bed on which she was sitting, she too elected to make for the stairs and the street outside.

"'Ere, darlin'. Are you Doreen? I'm told I can find her 'ere."

She felt the miasma of booze-laced breath wafting across her face as she tried to brush past the beefy, bull-necked sailor who attempted to waylay her on her passage through the front door.

"Er, no. I think you'll find she's up on the second floor... first room on the left," she insisted, shuddering at the prospect of what the establishment's most sought-after guest was about to entertain.

"Oh, that's a shame, in'it! You look like you could take care of a man who's been at sea too long," he called after her, doffing his matelot's cap whilst studying the rhythmic swaying of Eileen's posterior as she made haste up the street without daring to turn and thank him for the dubious compliment.

It was not supposed to turn out like this. She had earnestly prayed that she might savour an exciting reunion with her father that might even have extended to a willing offer of weekend hospitality on his part. During that time she had hoped they could avail themselves of such opportunity to catch up with the things each of them had been up to since they had last had chance to enjoy the other's company – almost eight years earlier.

Yet could she not have guessed from the outset that it was a foolhardy project? Of attempting to get in touch with her father after all this time; during which he had clearly moved on and found someone new in his life with whom he could perhaps create afresh the sort of happy family home he had once enjoyed in Birmingham. And was Maureen – that little girl she had spoken to yesterday – really the half-sister she never knew she had? More alarming still, the dejected WAAF was left wondering whether her father ever wanted to see her again, and that he had conspired to be elsewhere when alerted to the news that she was planning to call by. Perhaps, like some of the darker memories from her own childhood, she was just another awful ghost from a past that he would rather now forget.

Eventually, her crestfallen jaywalking around the bomb-scarred streets of west London again brought her past the window of that inviting little tea shop that she had discovered earlier. What's more, it was mercifully free of the more voluble company thronging the capital's pubs. Instead, inside there was just some little old man engrossed in a newspaper that he had folded open next to his cup. At his feet, a little white dog was tilting its head this way and that, weighing up the intentions of the establishment's other customer – an air force officer making eyes at it before electing to discreetly toss it a morsel from his plate. He broke to glance up briefly at Eileen as she drifted in past him and sat herself down at a table on the opposite side of the room.

Once the waiter had brought her order, she sank into an introspection disturbed only by the periodical lifting of her own cup up to the cherry red lips of her small, pensive mouth – bequeathing a cherry red imprint on the cup as she set it down again to wallow in her preoccupations once more. In particular, whilst she felt guilty about leaving home without saying goodbye, if nothing else the circumstances of her sudden departure had confirmed why she had been right to grasp the nettle firmly with both hands and enlist in the Royal Air Force. For all that she loved her maternal family she simply had to break free if she was ever to journey to the rainbow's end – however arduous and meandering the quest to find it might be.

Rainbows? Stars? Why did so many of the metaphors that she had chosen to describe all those yearnings within her have a celestial quality about them? Was the Earth really not big enough to contain the dreams of this silly nineteen year-old? To whom could she confide such things? Who would ever understand what it felt like to sense that you were born for the universe, and yet had somehow been burdened with an upbringing that offered few openings for realising that destiny? A destiny that those she loved – her grandmother especially – either scoffed at or scorned as being above her station in life?

It was at moments like this that she missed her father. He would have understood. Maybe Granny was right: she was her father's child after all. In the end, provincial Birmingham had proved too small for him too. Yet this gifted and gregarious man would surely succeed at whatever he did. She had never really understood, or been told, precisely why her parents' marriage hadn't worked out. However, somewhere buried away in the past she wondered whether it too revolved around that same tension between aspirant horizons and settled ones. Like his stargazing seed, it almost seemed preordained that George Wilfred Kimberley would turn out to be one of those restless souls who could never be satisfied with mediocrity. Yet despite it all, she refused to countenance that he could have completely forgotten about her; or blotted out from his memory the wonderful communion that had once existed between proud daddy and adoring daughter.

"If you don't mind me saying, Miss, you look like a young lady who's carrying an awful lot of cares around with her."

She looked up from her daydream. The old man and his dog must have shuffled out of the shop without her even noticing, leaving behind just this handsome, rugged officer with a lyrical North American drawl who was now addressing her across the empty salon.

"Oh, I know," he added, taking advantage of her sudden perplexity to observe that "there's a war on. Therefore, we all have such cares on account of friends, family… I guess you know what I'm trying to say."

Eileen's air of insularity lifted just a little. "If you don't mind me saying, you sound as if you're an awful long way away from your family."

He shrugged. "I guess you could say that. Regina, Saskatchewan – to be precise."

"American?"

"Canadian," he corrected her, pointing to the patch on the shoulder of his uniform. "But I'll forgive you for that mistake!"

"Thank you. I'm afraid I've never been to Canada."

"You should. It's a great place. Big lakes; open prairies; tall mountains; you'd love it. It's the kinda' place where a guy can go off and be alone with his thoughts – like you were just," her fellow patron noted.

"So what brings you to London?" she asked, intrigued enough to sit up more fully and engage with this lonely figure who, like her, seemed oddly out of place in the anonymous, heaving metropolis that was the Hub of Empire.

"Well, it's kinda' hard to get leave to go back home," he chuckled wryly. "So I thought I might as well take in the sights while I'm over here. And you?"

"I'm down for the weekend. I came intending to meet up with someone I once knew. But… unfortunately I wasn't able to find him."

"That's sad. And I'm guessing from that look in your eyes that he is someone who means an awful lot to you."

Eileen nodded obligingly.

"Like I said, I guess some of us have more than our fair share of cares."

There was a long, pregnant silence as both WAAF airwoman and Royal Canadian Air Force officer (a flight lieutenant, she observed, from the stripes on his sleeves) smiled awkwardly at each other before retreating into the succour of what was left of their refreshments.

"Say, Miss, would you like another tea?" he then offered.

Eileen looked down at her watch. Not wanting to linger too long now that dusk was advancing, she politely declined. "I'm afraid I really ought to be going," she advised, drinking down her own, and feeling just a tad cruel for wanting to hurry from his hospitality this way.

"That's okay. A man can get mighty lonely in a city like this. That's why it's been kinda' good to talk to you. Anyway, what's your name?"

"Eileen. Eileen Kimberley."

"Well, Eileen, I'm Alastair. Alastair Manley," he enlightened her, wandering across to shake her hand as she too rose from her table. "Maybe one day we'll get to talk a bit more. Then you can tell me all about this guy who you were so anxious to meet."

"Yes. And you can tell me all about Saskatchewan. And those lakes, prairies and mountains," she grinned, her spirits lifted sufficiently by their brief conversation to be leaving the little tea shop in a better frame of mind than when she had wandered in (notwithstanding her foreboding about who else might mistake her for the ever-munificent Doreen when she arrived back at the boarding house).

\* \* \* \* \*

That summer of 1942 was to witness the war reach its pivotal moment. In June, the Japanese and American fleets clashed at the Battle of Midway, where US planes succeeded in despatching four Japanese carriers to the bottom, effectively halting Japan's lightning dash for hegemony in the Pacific. Meanwhile, in July the Germans opened a colossal two-pronged offensive in southern Russia, pushing deep into the Caucasus region and reaching the Volga at Stalingrad in late August, where the Nazi assault quickly bogged down into a bloody, street-by-street contest for this key city.

In the Middle-East, the British Eighth Army had been driven from Libya, finally digging in at an unsung railway halt sixty miles from Cairo that went by the name of El Alamein. Beckoning the German commander, the formidable

General Erwin Rommel, was the prospect of severing Britain's most important artery of Empire – the Suez Canal. However, like his fellow commanders on the Russian front, Rommel's precarious supply line remained dangerously exposed, while the Eighth Army now boasted a charismatic new commander of its own in the person of General Bernard Montgomery.

Finally, the United States Eighth Air Force had arrived to commence its first daytime bombing missions from its new bases in England. Confidence was high that its heavily-armed B17 Flying Fortresses operating in tight formation would be able to see off German fighter opposition and precision bomb targets by day that the Royal Air Force had so far struggled to hit by night.

Otherwise, RAF Bomber Command was newly-headed by the mercurial, yet pugnacious Air Chief Marshal Arthur 'Bomber' Harris. Following on from the success of its 'Thousand Bomber Raids' (in which sheer numbers had been used to overwhelm enemy defences) – and now equipped with more accurate aiming devices and new targeting and navigational aids – he declared defiantly that, having "sowed the wind" with its pitiless and devastating raids on British cities, the Third Reich was now going to "reap the whirlwind". Morale soared amongst aircrews as, for the first time, the gloves came off, and German cities too began to be attacked and levelled with a vengeance.

# 7

"Feltwell 241. Which number do you require please...? Go ahead caller, you're connected."

Sunday mornings were usually quieter than other mornings for obvious reasons – unless, of course, there was something big going on. As the day progressed and more calls lit up the switchboard, Eileen and Nancy got the sense that something big was indeed going on. In the brief gaps between taking and making calls they both looked at each other keenly. The supervisor too appeared agitated, craning her ears to catch the sound.

"Aren't those the bells of the village church?" she wondered aloud.

"They are, sergeant," Nancy attested, lifting her headset away from her ears to be sure. "They're ringing the church bells."

"The Germans – they must have landed!" Eileen fretted – for the peeling of the nation's church bells was the accepted signal to the populace that the dreaded Nazi invasion of Britain was underway.

Just then, an excited NCO burst through the door and, without pausing to catch his breath, screamed "They've done it! The Eighth Army has broken through at El Alamein. That's why all the bells are ringing!"

For a moment all sense of decorum was cast aside. Nancy and Eileen reached across to hug each other, the supervisor joining in before the board lit up and the duty summoned them once again. Either way, it was impossible to overlook the aura of lifted spirits aboard in the room as the girls once more set about answering calls.

"Switchboard, which number do you require...? That's Cambridge 742... Thank you... You're connected."

Eileen loved her job. It had its tedium for sure. But from time to time you got to talk to some interesting people and be party to some memorable events. Nancy had even had the Prime Minister on the line the other day. Now that would be something to one day put in a book about her life!

"Feltwell 241, which number do you require..." she responded again as a light flashed up on the board, trailing a wire up to intercept it.

*"Is that the RAF station?"* the caller enquired in a voice that sounded a tad familiar.

"This is Feltwell 241, caller. Which number do you require?" Eileen replied, aware of the importance of not giving away information that might be of use to an enemy agent.

*"In which case, I'll have extension 952."*

Eileen searched the board anxiously. "I'm sorry, sir. We don't appear to have an extension 952," she noted, her suspicion heightened by such an implausible request.

*"Then I'll settle for the chance to speak to Aircraftwoman Eileen Kimberley?"*

"Wait a moment please, I'll.... Ron!" she suddenly gasped, glancing over her shoulder and hoping the supervisor hadn't heard her.

*"Good God, woman! You're a difficult person to get hold of,"* he meanwhile chortled down the line.

"You shouldn't be calling me. I'm on duty," she whispered, shielding her speaker trumpet as she spoke into it.

*"How else is a man supposed to snatch an opportunity to talk to the woman he adores? If I didn't know better, I'd swear you were avoiding me! Anyway, darling, I'm calling to tell you I've got a spot of leave coming up. So how about you and I spent it together. Then you can give me a proper explanation for why you preferred to pass your last free weekend somewhere else."*

"Okay, but make this quick. Tell me where and when and I'll see if I can get myself a '48'," she gabbled furtively, all the time the supervisor striding about in the background.

Under the guise of scribbling down a number, she jotted down the details, tearing off the snippet of paper and slipping it in her pocket.

"Sorry caller, we have no person of that name on this exchange. Please call back when you have the correct number," she then rattled off a starched apology before yanking out the jack and moving on to answer another call.

The supervisor remained oblivious. However, Nancy had cottoned on. She glanced across at her friend with that knowing look. It was a look that she was to cast her way several more times before the shift was over and she had chance in the mess hall afterwards to accost her for a fuller explanation.

"You know, if you returned his calls more often he wouldn't have to risk both of you being put on a charge by trying to talk on the sly," she maintained. "Besides, I thought you two were madly in love. It was certainly that way when you started going out together."

"We are. Well, I mean… Well…"

"You mean: he is – but you're no longer sure?"

Nancy had a way of getting to the crux of matters. Perhaps she just knew Aircraftwoman First Class Eileen Kimberley well enough by now to be able to brush aside the circumlocution and peer inside her heart.

"Oh, I don't know. Gerald is such a kind and chivalrous young man. It's just that, come the war's end, I'm not sure I am ready to play the dutiful wife of a provincial garage proprietor."

"There are worse callings in life," Nancy noted before again reading Eileen's thoughts. "… Oh, I see. But there are also better ones?"

"I didn't say that," Eileen snapped.

"It's what you're thinking. Eileen, I know the most important thing in life and love is to be happy. But there's an old saying: a bird in the hand is worth two in the bush. You must weigh up whether what you may – but then may possibly not – find tomorrow is better than what you have in your hand now."

"So you think I should settle for happiness now – with Gerald?"

"I can't answer that for you. All I know is the man you have now is an absolute diamond. And a girl doesn't stumble upon one of those every day,"

Nancy could see Eileen was torn, but was minded to accept her wise words even so. She took from her pocket the note she had scribbled down earlier and glanced down at it. Then she looked up across the table at Nancy again. Sensing she had been chastised enough, Nancy smiled softly and changed the subject.

"Listen, I was sorry to hear about your wasted journey to London the other week. It must be a hard thing to have to face – not knowing whether or not your father wants to see you ever again," Nancy opined, consoling her that "At least you've still got your mum though."

"Huh! For how much longer?" Eileen hissed. "She's got another fellah. And every time she finds someone new it means I end up becoming a very distant second place in her thoughts again. In fact, I've suddenly ceased being 'the daughter' and become 'the younger sister' yet again!"

"What?"

"That's right. Mum gets so wound up about appearing burdened with 'baggage' from a previous life that she refuses to acknowledge me as her child in the presence of her men, telling them instead that I'm her 'sister'."

"Really?" Nancy gasped again, incredulous.

"I can't imagine for one moment that these blokes are stupid enough to believe her. There's almost a twenty year age gap, for goodness sake! Yet still she clings to this deception for all its worth – regardless of my feelings."

"Yes, I'm sure you must be very hurt. I certainly would be."

"Added to which it is not unknown for Mum's men 'friends' to try better acquainting themselves with this younger 'sister'. If you know what I mean."

"How terrible!" Nancy frowned aghast.

"It's just one more reason why I have never looked back since I joined the WAAF. I tell you, I can bear the constant wolf-whistles of the fitters from No. 4 hangar any day to the thought of having to face all that again."

\* \* \* \* \*

As autumn turned to winter further joyous news began to filter through on the switchboards of RAF Feltwell. In mid-November the Soviet Red Army smashed through weakly-held flanks along the Volga and Don rivers to successfully trap over a quarter of a million Axis troops in Stalingrad. Beating off a German attempt to relieve the besieged enclave, the Russians then tightened the noose until, on February $2^{nd}$ 1943, what remained of the beleaguered front finally surrendered. An entire German army had been wiped out. Along with the headlong retreat of Rommel's *Afrika Korps* back into Libya, it now meant that for the first time in the war so far the Nazi war machine was on the back foot. With hundreds of thousands of US troops pouring into southern England in readiness for the launching of a second front in Europe, it could only be a matter of time before the victory that Churchill had promised finally became a blessed reality – and with it the prospect of Gerald and Eileen looking forward to cementing their bliss and perhaps opening that little garage together in Herefordshire.

\* \* \* \* \*

*"Bad news, Skipper. I'm afraid Yorkshire's smothered in another pea-souper this morning. Apparently, it's so bad that the station CO can't even see to tie up his boot laces!"*

It was not what Flight Lieutenant Alastair Manley wanted to hear just then. As if dodging German flak and night fighters wasn't tribulation enough, now it looked like the hearty breakfast they were looking forward to upon their return was not going to materialise. Impatiently, he grabbed his dangling rubber oxygen mask and held it to his lips.

*"Great! So where do they suggest we put this old girl down? They do know we've got a rudder half hanging off?"*

*"I've told them, Skipper. Group Control suggests we head for one of the Suffolk air stations. They are liaising with the sector controllers there now."*

*"Okay, Bonzo. Keep me posted. Meanwhile, Navigator…"*

*"Aye, Skipper."*

*"Plot me a course for the Suffolk coast. Once Bonzo comes back with confirmation of where we can land you can adjust our routing accordingly."*

*"Roger, Skipper."*

"Let's just hope the bacon tastes as good in Suffolk as it does up north, eh Skipper!" the flight engineer meanwhile leant across, trying to make light of their predicament. However, the flipside was that, with less flying time to wherever the sector controllers could establish a landing spot, at least they would get to savour it a bit sooner.

\* \* \* \* \*

The drone of heavy bombers had become a familiar sound over the fens of eastern England by now, and so few people gave a second thought to this stray Handley Page Mark III Halifax B from No. 408 Squadron as it bounced down onto the tarmac.

Still, at least its crew were all back safely, albeit with two rather tattered rudders – the result of a German night fighter sneaking up a bit too close. Meanwhile, there was a heartfelt pat on the back for their 'skipper' who had once again earned their respect. Lauded as one of the best bomber pilots the Royal Canadian Air Force had so far produced, his skill and judgement had once more brought *'P for Popsicle'* safely back to England – or, more precisely, to this unfamiliar, if fog-free air station tucked away somewhere on the Norfolk-Suffolk border.

Alighting from the dispersal van sent to retrieve them, they were quickly debriefed before being at liberty to make their way to the officers' mess for that long-awaited hearty feed – on their way passing two saluting WAAFs, one of whom suddenly caught Manley's eye and momentarily banished all thought of breakfast.

"Eileen…? Eileen Kimberley?" he called after her.

The WAAF in question halted with her friend, turning about and wondering who this officer was who had recognised her (and what she might have done that had occasioned his attention – and possibly incurred his wrath).

"I guess you don't recognise me, do you," he surmised with a disarming smile. She offered him a quizzical frown. However, it was that self-effacing grin and mid-west Canadian drawl that finally jogged her memory.

"It's Alastair, isn't it? Flight Lieutenant Manley. Ah, now I remember – that tea shop in London. I didn't realise you had been posted here" she replied.

"Well, actually, I haven't. I guess it's what you English might call a 'flying visit' – literally, in my case. You see, we came in on that Hallybag that was diverted. So I'm afraid it may well be 'hello and goodbye'," he sighed.

"Ah, well, never mind. It's good to see you again. It's good that you remembered my name too."

"And you mine. Let's just say in the short time we spent chatting together we obviously made an impression upon one another."

"And by the way, this is my friend: Aircraftwoman Nancy King."

"Pleased to meet you, Flight Lieutenant."

Manley was delighted to discover another girlish grin being fired in his direction. In fact, Eileen was not oblivious to the electricity suddenly buzzing between her friend and this rugged North American flyer. Once their parting benedictions had been exchanged and Flight Lieutenant Manley had moved off to grab his breakfast (though not without Nancy coyly glancing over her shoulder to catch him pondering what this new acquaintance looked like from behind), she wasted no time debriefing her colleague also.

"Who is that gorgeous dreamboat?" she demanded to know, positively tingling with awestruck feminine curiosity.

"Oh, he's just some Canadian officer I happened to bump into in London," Eileen replied, as surprised as Nancy that this 'dreamboat' had suddenly descended into her world as if out of nowhere.

\* \* \* \* \*

Alas, Flight Lieutenant Alastair Manley was to remain at Feltwell for only a day or two longer while waiting for the fog up north to lift. However, the opportunity was taken for 'P Popsicle' to have its mangled rudders repaired. During that time he became quite a celebrity on the base as news spread that one of No. 6 Group's most audacious flyers was in their midst. With his winsome grey-blue eyes, swept-back tuff of dark hair and quiet, yet authoritative bearing, the thirty year-old Saskatchewan had certainly been noticed by the WAAFs. However, Nancy was determined to elbow aside the competition. With Eileen roped in for moral support, this normally self-assured young lady became like jelly in his presence. So much so that she contrived almost any excuse to place herself (and thus Eileen too) across his path so that, as if by chance, she would remain in his contemplation throughout his brief stay. It seemed to be working. Wandering past No. 4 hangar on their way to the NAAFI she was pleasantly surprised to hear Manley call them across as he stood there chatting to some of his aircrew.

"I'm afraid it's our last day here, ladies," he shrugged his broad shoulders and narrowed his eyebrows regretfully. "We're just waiting to make a quick test flight to make sure our old kite's 'tickety-boo', as you English would say."

"Oh, that's a shame," Nancy sighed, now desperately trawling her head for some scheme to prolong the moment sufficiently to at least tempt an offer of a date out of him.

"Yes, we've enjoyed our time here. Your cook fries up great-tasting bacon," his flight engineer enthused.

"That's Scottie for you: all he ever thinks about during missions is his next meal! Say, you ladies ever sat inside one of these things?" Manley then enquired, pointing out their camouflage-painted bomber parked inside the hangar.

"No," was their collective response, Eileen adding "We didn't think we were allowed."

"Oh, I'm sure they won't mind you just taking a look. Here, follow me," their host beckoned them. Glancing at each other excitedly, they duly obliged.

"Ladies first," Scottie beamed, bidding them mount the few short steps up the embarkation ladder at the rear of the plane, Manley bodging him to resist the temptation to stare up their skirts.

"Gosh! It's a bit gloomy inside," Nancy commented, surveying the austere, cable-strewn innards of the Halifax.

"A bit cramped too," Eileen added, joining her. Staring back down at the rear turret, she thought of her Australian friend, Joey, and what kind of courage it required to spend a six hour flight squashed into such a cold, lonely and claustrophobic little bubble.

"Yes. Now imagine that it's dark, the plane is filling up with smoke, and it's lunging into a steep dive. Meanwhile, you're swaddled in bulky flying suit and cumbersome Mae West whilst trying to strap on a parachute. It kinda' gives you some idea of why it takes a special sorta' guy to volunteer to fly in these things," Manley counselled grimly. "Anyway, if you'll follow me this way I'll lead you up to where me and Scottie sit," he then gestured as they hunched up and made their way forward.

En route Eileen popped her head up into the dome of the roof-mounted mid-turret to admire the view... well, if only of the inside of the hangar! Then, hitching their skirts, both girls clambered as best they could towards the cockpit.

"Wow! You're up really high here," Nancy further enthused as she popped her head up to enjoy the panoramic view across the plane's one hundred foot wing span. "May I?" she then begged.

"Be my guest," Scottie urged.

And so Nancy found herself squatting in the flight engineer's seat (which on a Halifax was next to the pilot – the flight engineer in effect doubling up as the bomber's co-pilot). There she excitedly gripped the controls and marvelled at the bewildering myriad of switches and dials that greeted her. Meanwhile, Manley sat down to her right in his pilot's seat and began to talk his eager new 'second dickey' through which particular switches and levers did what.

For Eileen though, this was a more sobering moment. While Nancy was trying her hand at this control here or fumbling with that knob there, her friend had clambered down into the bomb aimer's forward glass bubble, which was no less cramped for all the fabulous view ahead that it afforded. Then shuffling to her feet and glancing all around her at the primitive conditions inside the plane she felt herself once again shedding an inward tear upon thinking of all those tankards now hidden away in that cupboard in the little village pub. It reminded her once again of the terrible Jekyll-and-Hyde existence of Bomber

Command aircrews – one evening walking hand-in-hand with their sweethearts along tranquil riverbanks; the following evening experiencing unbridled terror at twenty-thousand feet; the next evening still drowning their sorrows around a piano in the local tavern, bawling beer-fuelled out-of-tune ditties with those of their mates who had made it back.

"Flight Lieutenant Manley, sir," they suddenly heard a mechanic poke his head inside the door and call up. "Chief says she's good to go if you want to just give her a quick buzz around the airfield to check she's to your liking."

"Okay… and thanks for all your hard work," he called back down. Then Nancy looked on while he stared at Scottie in that certain way and winked… and Scottie returned the smirk and the wink. What were these guys up to?

"I'm told we're all off for a spin," declared Bonzo, the radio operator, who had meanwhile clambered aboard with his navigator colleague. He then sealed the door and climbed forward.

"We are?" was Nancy's rictus response, her startled blue eyes flitting anxiously from crew member to crew member. Meanwhile, Eileen re-emerged also looking askance.

"If that is what you two ladies would like, I'm sure it can be arranged," Manley looked them in the eye mischievously.

"Isn't that forbidden? We could get into an awful lot of trouble," Eileen countered, aware that regulations forbade WAAFs from taking to the air in all but a handful of prescribed circumstances – and joy-riding aboard a newly-serviceable Halifax bomber was not one of them!

"Trust me, Eileen. Now you two ladies go strap yourself in and leave the rest to us. A quick breeze around the field and we'll have you safely back on the ground in no time at all."

Whatever Eileen's misgivings (thank goodness they weren't due back on watch for another few hours!), Nancy was certainly partial to their kind offer – almost wetting herself with excitement. Eileen meanwhile felt like wetting herself for a different reason. She had never flown before. Yet before she could verbalise those misgivings, the hangar crews were already pushing the colossal craft out towards runway. Then one by one the four giant Bristol Hercules engines spluttered into life, the propellers spinning and their awesome drone filling the ears of the two 'sprog' WAAF aircrew.

"You like it, ladies?" Manley called down to Nancy, who – as instructed – had donned a thick flying jacket, exchanged her WAAF cap for a flying hat and strapped herself into the front gunner's seat. However, she could barely hear him above the din. Therefore, he raised his thumb, to be rewarded by Nancy raising her thumb too – beaming him a smile to match.

Manley released the brakes and opened the engines up, sending the plane hurtling down the runway. Concentrating intensely to keep it straight in the gentle crosswind, he listened out while Scottie began counting off the airspeed at regular intervals. Without a payload of bombs, by 110 knots *'P Popsicle'* was starting to lift, Scottie pressing the throttles hard against the stops as the end of the runway drew closer. Then a distinct whirring mechanism indicated the undercarriage was being stowed. The drone of the engines began to ease as Manley settled her into a gentle ascent.

Eileen was infused with awe and trepidation to be staring down out of the bomb aimer's bubble and observing the verdant Norfolk countryside rushing past beneath her. It was like the most magical of dreams. Meanwhile, Nancy was thrilled to have been granted a panoramic front gunner's view of all those flat fens now spreading out before her as *'P Popsicle'* climbed higher and then banked to set a course for the coast in the distance.

It was incredible! Eileen was tempted to believe that it would be worth a court martial just to have experienced the once-in-a-lifetime exhilaration of being airborne, gazing down below at tiny villages sweeping past, with motor cars flitting in and out of view, as well as a curate on a bicycle. Meanwhile, following the course of a railway line, the trail of white steam ahead of her indicated a train racing to its destination, soon to be overtaken by the speeding bomber and left far behind.

After skimming above the Norfolk Broads they emerged over the sea just north of Great Yarmouth before banking south to hug the coastline for several miles, the waves breaking on the expansive golden sands below. In due course, Eileen looked up and noticed that they were being shadowed by a Spitfire off their port wing, the pilot of the graceful fighter plane waving an acknowledgement before peeling off and disappearing into the sun that swept across the unseasonable clear midday sky, momentarily blinding her.

Then, just as both girls were finally getting the hang of being impromptu crew members, the runway of Feltwell hove into view and Manley lined the bomber up for a perfect touch down.

"Well, Skipper, I think we can confidently say they've fixed the rudder," Scottie chortled, removing his flying cap and straightening his mop of red hair.

"So there you go: now you ladies know what it's like to be aircrew," Manley curled his eyebrows playfully at the still disbelieving WAAF telephonists scrambling back up into the main body of the fuselage, as if in a daze.

There remained just the little matter of how to sweet-talk the driver of the dispersal van sent to retrieve them to make sure that he deposited the two girls somewhere where they wouldn't be spotted (and could wander back to their billet as if nothing had happened). Hopefully, no one would ever know about this unauthorised little jaunt.

"So long, ladies. Until we meet again," Manley called across to them one final time as the vehicle rumbled off, to which Nancy blew him a discreet kiss of gratitude – and upon which he smiled and discreetly blew her one back. Then she glanced down at the address on the page out of the navigator's log he had torn off and discreetly slipped into her hand.

* * * * *

Over a year had now passed since Eileen had enlisted in the Women's Auxiliary Air Force. Not long after their daring joyride over the Norfolk coast, she and Nancy received news that they had each been assigned new postings somewhere in Lincolnshire. Unfortunately those postings would involve them serving on different stations many miles apart. However, before these two firm friends said their goodbyes there was time for Nancy to announce that she had bagged that eagerly-awaited first date with Flight Lieutenant Alastair Manley – who made a special journey to visit her one weekend. Just like Gerald, he seemed determined that, though posted apart, distance (and petrol rationing) would be no object to seeing the woman he had apparently fallen head over heels in love with.

Eileen was pleased that her friend had found love. Regardless of the age difference – and notwithstanding that he was divorcé – Alastair Manley seemed to perfectly complement Nancy's known penchant for excitement and mischief. It therefore amused her to think that whilst she was privileged to arrive at romantic dinners in Gerald's rather staid, if lovingly cared-for Austin Eight motor car, the wind was breezing through Nancy's hair as she tore down country lanes on the back of Manley's Brough Superior motorbike. If Eileen looked set for a life of contentment as a lavishly-pandered sweetheart, Nancy never quite knew whence the next thrill was coming – except that, Manley being nothing if not a hell-raising maverick, come it surely would! If Eileen's fellah was an 'absolute diamond', then Nancy's rugged and unorthodox Canadian flyer was very 'rough diamond' indeed.

* * * * *

It was a terraced Birmingham street like any other. And nothing particularly marked out this house to distinguish it from those hundreds of others nestled there in the shadow of the railway viaduct.

Flight Sergeant Gerald Graham had been passing through on his way back from home leave in his native Herefordshire. Taking an earlier train he had decided that it would be the gentlemanly thing to do to introduce himself to Eileen's parents and put before her father a proposition he had been considering with regard to their daughter.

That said, it always intrigued him why she was so circumspect when talking about her family – in particular, her father. Apart from a name (and that he was a 'businessman' of some sort), that was about as much as she had revealed of him. Meanwhile, her mother (or so Eileen had told him) was a machinist working in the nearby 'battery' factory (but which Gerald had discovered was so named because they 'battered' metal, rather than rolled it. Apparently, it had never made batteries!).

Otherwise, he had been safely disabused of his first presumption that, on account of Eileen's demure and refined tones, she hailed from one of the city's more upmarket suburbs. Not that he considered there to be any shame in that. For whilst Mr Churchill talked about 'freedom' and 'Anglo-Saxon democracy', like most of his fellows in the ranks Gerald was also fighting this war to put an end to the divisions of class that had marked the inter-war years.

Confident that he had the address right, he approached the front door and tapped on the knocker. Then he stood back to take in the sights and sounds of this ordinary street: the women scrubbing their doorsteps, or returning with their shopping, or chatting to neighbours; the children kicking balls or skipping to the chanting of their favourite playground rhymes. It was the quintessential scene of wartime working class Britain.

He knocked again. Still no reply. He gazed up again at the frontage to look for clues as to its occupants' whereabouts. Meanwhile, from the corner of his eye he noticed a neighbour had emerged to pour the dirty water from her mop-and-bucket into the storm drain outside.

"I'm looking for George and Mary Kimberley. I'm told they live at this address. I'm a friend of their daughter, Eileen," he explained, doffing his cap.

"Oh, ya' are, are ya'," the women mused in a lush Dublin brogue, eyeing his smart blue uniform up and down and trying to ascertain what the nature of that 'friendship' might be. "Well, if you've come looking for George yah'll be in fer' a long wait, you will. He cleared off years ago. As for Mary, well, if she's not in yer' might care to try over tha' road at number one-two-seven. That's where her sister lives."

"I see. Thank you very much," he replied, casting a glance over to the equally unsung terraced frontage that she was pointing out. Again, he doffed his cap as a mark of his gratitude.

Hauling up his kit bag, he then ambled across the road and up the street, employing a touch of nifty footwork to halt the runaway ball that the lads had pelted his way.

"'Ere, mate, am yow' one of them Spitfire pilots?" the lad despatched to retrieve it marvelled with an unmistakably more local accent, eyeing up Gerald's polished shoes and smartly-pressed air force uniform.

"Bombers," Gerald was sorry to disappoint him. "I'm a flight engineer."

"Lancasters?"

"Stirlings, actually."

The lad thanked him for the ball and whacked it back up the street to his waiting pals. 'Go and play in your own street,' Gerald meanwhile overheard a disgruntled old woman chide them from her doorstep.

Locating Number 127, Gerald repeated the ritual of knocking and waiting. Again there was no reply. However, on the second attempt, he thought he heard the cussing of someone making haste towards the front door.

"Will you not be patient? I'm coming as fast as me' legs'll carry me."

"Hello," said Gerald as the door was finally inched opened and the face of a wizened old woman appeared in the gap created, a shawl cast around her head so that only odd wisps of grey locks protruded.

"And who might you be?" she leered, eyeing him up and down as forensically as had her neighbour across the street.

"I'm Gerald. Gerald Graham. I'm looking for Mary Kimberley," he smiled, laying down his kit bag and offering her his hand as a prophylactic to the suspicion his presence had clearly aroused. The old lady stared at it, but otherwise maintained her wary vigil hanging on the edge of the front door.

"Oh, ya' are, are ya'. Well, she's not in. On a Saturday afternoon she'll probably be out gallivanting, she will. Unless, of course, you might be another of those men she'll be wanting to go gallivanting with. The whole street knows she likes 'younger' men. But I must say I'm surprised to see she's going after one as young as you!" she scoffed, eyeing him up and down again.

There was a brief pause while Gerald worked his head around both the heavy West Irish ling and the full import of what his interlocutor was implying. Surely not! Anxious to clear up any misunderstanding, he moved to explain who he was and the purpose of his visit – only to be cut off before he could speak by another perverse panegyric from the cynical old hag.

"Oh, let me guess: you'll be coming around sniffing after that daughter of hers. I should have known. The officer's uniform. It's a dead giveaway, it is."

"Oh, I'm sorry. I'm not an officer. I'm only a humble flight sergeant," he excused himself, pointing to his stripes. By now though, he was becoming uneasy about what had prompted all this invective, though he tried to maintain a genial manner even so.

"Is that so now? Well then you'll be a disappointed young man, yer' will. The last fellah who was just like you she dumped. Or should I say he hadn't been long consigned to the bottom of the ocean, God bless his soul, before she was off chasing after other men – just like her mother."

"Oh, I'm sure you don't mean that," Gerald tried to humour her and make light of such a shocking accusation.

"Oh, young man, you'll learn. She only goes after officers now, does our Eileen. Us 'common people' aren't to her liking any more. So unless you're Lord-this or a Sir-that, she won't be wanting to associate with the likes of you – though I'd venture to say that when all these 'Yanks' come marchin' over here she'll be chasin' after them as well. So be off with yer', young man. And thank the good Lord that there are still nice girls out there who'd be grateful to be seen hangin' on the arm of a fine chap like you."

And with that the front door was unceremoniously slammed in his face and he was left alone on the doorstep again. Meanwhile, a battery of eyes was peeping from behind curtains to see what all the commotion was.

"That's old Bridie O'Leary for ya' – whatever's on her heart, she just comes right out with it. Never one to mince her words," another neighbour meanwhile called across the street by way of consolation.

Gerald heaved up his kit bag and made his way back down the street towards the station. What kind of family was this? What kind of neighbourhood? Was there any truth in what the old woman had so contemptuously spat at him? And, if so, might it have any bearing on why his sweetheart had grown so cool towards him of late?

# 8

Having been summoned to see his commanding officer at short notice and informed that he was to be removed from his squadron forthwith, it was not surprising that Flight Lieutenant Alastair Manley's first thought had been that somebody must have found out about that 'joyride' involving Nancy and Eileen. However, in place of the dreaded dressing down (or worse) he had been told to gather up his kit and report immediately to RAF Scampton outside Lincoln. He would receive further instructions upon arrival.

And so here he was: still the quintessential maverick flyer – though undeniably a bloody good one. Along with almost a hundred and fifty other 'bloody good flyers'– most of them barely into their twenties – they had been gathered together in the cavernous crew room to look on while a dapper, pipe-smoking wing commander mounted the stage to address them all.

"You're here to do a special job. You're here as a crack new squadron. You're here to carry out a raid on Germany which, I am told, will have startling results. Some say it may even cut short the war," he opened, getting briskly to the point.

"We'll all drink to that!" someone at the back muttered under his breath, to a repressed ripple of amusement amongst his new colleagues.

"What the target is, I can't tell you. Nor can I tell you where it is. All I can tell you is that you will have to practice low-flying all day and all night until you know how to do it with your eyes shut. If I tell you to fly to a tree in the middle of England, then I will want you to bomb that tree. If I tell you to fly through a hangar, then you will have to go through that hangar – even though your wing-tips might hit either side. Discipline is absolutely essential."

There was an audible collective gasp at the magnitude of what they were being asked to do. For a moment Manley too shuffled uneasily in his seat. However, there remained an awareness that their new no-nonsense, hands-on commander lived by the motto 'If I can do it, you can do it'. Indeed, at just twenty-four years-old, Guy Penrose Gibson was the youngest man ever to hold so high a rank. Having won his renown as one of Bomber Command's most outstanding pilots, he had led the crack No. 106 Squadron on a daring low-level raid on the huge armament works at Le Creusot in occupied France the previous year. He certainly would not ask them to do anything he was not convinced could be done – that was for sure.

"I needn't tell you that we are going to be talked about," he cautioned them. "It is very unusual to have such a crack crowd of boys in one squadron. There are going to be lots of rumours. We've got to say nothing. When you go into pubs at night, you've got to keep your mouths shut. When the other boys ask you what you're doing, just tell them to mind their own business – because, of all the things in this game, security is the greatest factor."

Gibson was not exaggerating. In great haste and even greater secrecy, twenty-one Lancaster bombers had been assembled at Scampton, some of which were in the process of having their bomb bays modified. Like the intended target itself, Manley looked forward to finding out in due course what kind of bombs they were to be equipped with; and what it was they were intended to destroy – although, by the sound of it, his money was on some sort of mission to sink the giant German battleship *Tirpitz*, which was known to be holed up in an impregnable Norwegian fjord.

\* \* \* \* \*

*March 31ˢᵗ 1943*

*My dearest Eileen,*

*This is just another short note to tell you how much I am missing you. It seems that no matter how hard I try we are forever passing each other by. There are times when I am even tempted to wonder whether it is perhaps our fate to be apart. And yet my heart yearns for you each waking moment. I called by on your folks the other day on the off-chance you might be home on leave and had not told me. How silly is that! And yet how telling of the way you have seized my heart like no other girl I have ever met.*

*How I wish you would confide your thoughts to me more. I know you say you love me. Am I really being selfish when I declare that I wish you would say it more often? I would happily keep on penning my love for you until the world ran out of ink and paper – and even then I would carve that love in granite with my bare fingernails if I had to – so deep is the affection in which I hold you, my sweetheart.*

*However, I must go. Thankfully, my tour of duty will be complete soon. Hopefully the ops we are undertaking will hasten the day when this dreadful war is finally over and we can be together and never have to part again. It is only that blissful thought that keeps me going.*

*All my love – always*

                             *xxx    Gerald*

* * * * *

The fitter had been something of a budding artist prior to enlisting. Consequently, the image he had painted on the huge bomber (and from which he now stepped back to admire, brush in hand) was a perfect likeness of the beautiful, vivacious woman in Flight Lieutenant Manley's life. Thus did *"Nancy Helen"* wink down at them both from just below the cockpit on the port side of *'Y for Yellow'*, its skipper well pleased.

Throughout the days and nights of intense training Manley had become as attached to this incredible machine as he had become to its namesake. He had come to know and love her capabilities, as well as her little quirks. After all, the lives of his crew of six – as well as the success of their mission – would depend on her. Ordinarily, pilots would be court-martialled for undertaking the kind of terrifying, treetop-hugging passes that the newly-formed 617 Squadron had been ordered to practice. Indeed, it was not unknown for its planes to return to Scampton with their undersides having acquired leaves, branches and even birds' nests! However, though it took incredible concentration and every ounce of skill he possessed, Manley was now able to consistently fly the Lancaster at a mere one hundred and fifty feet, a height at which there was little, if any margin for pilot error.

Having tipped the fitter for his trouble, Manley was wandering back to the officers' mess when, having saluted a group of WAAFs who had perchance crossed his path, he felt again that sudden uncanny tug of déjà-vu.

"Eileen…? Eileen Kimberley?"

The Saskatchewan drawl was unmistakable. And so, to the equally startled WAAF turning around to behold him, were his rugged features and piercing grey-blue eyes.

"You know, we really will have to stop meeting like this, Flight Lieutenant, sir," she remarked, having dismissed her colleagues with the assurance she would catch up with them shortly.

Alone together, they glanced each other up and down in wonderment. What were the chances of bumping into each other again this way? This time it fell to Eileen to break the spell of surprise.

"I suppose I could ask you what brings you here. However, with the way everyone talks about maintaining security on the camp lately I guess that would be imprudent," she smiled.

"Correct. However, here we are again."

"Like bad pennies?" she suggested coyly. To which he offered her that self-effacing boyish smile that always made her quiver.

"Does Nancy know you are here?" Eileen wondered.

"Sort of. As you say though, the people who have been posted here don't tend to say too much. The less she knows the better, I guess. How about your guy? What's his name?"

"You mean Gerald. Oh, well… same thing. The less he knows – and all that."

Two intriguing answers that prompted two intrigued stares. Manley had certainly been attracted to Eileen from the day he had first observed her sitting alone with her thoughts in that tea shop in London. Though not as boisterous as her bubbly blonde friend, he had by now come to realise that Eileen possessed a depth of character that the more emotionally-transparent Nancy sometimes lacked. What thoughts dwelt inside her head – behind those resolute brown eyes – he pondered? They were eyes that appeared to be begging the same question of the tall, abstruse Canadian too.

"Anyway, your friends will be waiting," he tipped his eyes away in awkwardness. "I guess we'll see each other around these next few weeks. So maybe we can catch up then. And this time no joyrides… I promise!"

\* \* \* \* \*

*"Target area approaching in five minutes, Skipper,"* the navigator checked his maps and calculations and informed the pilot.

Within moments of relaying the news, all hell broke loose around *'Z for Zulu'*. Way down below them the night sky was punched open by scanning searchlights, the flicker of muzzle flashes also indicating that the enemy was alert to the presence of the squadron of lumbering Short Stirlings. After all, this was 'Happy Valley': the ironic name the bomber boys had bestowed upon the heavily-defended Ruhr district – Germany's industrial powerhouse and home to some of its largest armaments factories.

*"Hang on, chaps. This could be a bit of a dicey-do!"* the pilot warned before requesting *"Hello, Engineer. How's she looking?"*

There was a silence that was broken only by the repetitive beating of the engines, as well as the popping of flak bursts frighteningly close by that added illumination. It prompted the pilot to call down again. *"Hello, Engineer... Can you hear me, Spanners?"*

Sat behind and below the pilot and co-pilot, Flight Sergeant Gerald Graham blinked exaggeratedly, as if to banish the fear that was clawing at him. It made his flight suit and his oxygen mask feel hot and clammy – despite the sub-zero ambient temperature inside the high-flying plane.

*"I'm here, Skipper,"* he gathered up his fraying nerves and stuttered. Meanwhile, a 'flaming onion' suddenly lit up the sky, the flak burst jolting the twenty-six ton bomber as if it were a china cup bouncing on a bashed table.

*"I'll try to keep her level and straight,"* the pilot's voice crackled over the intercom. *"Bomb doors open... In your own time, Bomb Aimer..."*

*"Steady... Steady..."* the bomb aimer muttered, concentrating too intently to be overly-concerned by the fear that he too must surely have been wrestling with as more flak bursts rocked the plane.

Instead, he gazed at the city already aglow from the pathfinder flares that had marked the target zone below him. Above him meanwhile, Gerald nervously dabbed his perspiring brow. He had a job to do, he told himself – as he had done on dozens of such missions that he had flown. He must put aside his fear and get on with it – for the sake of his fellow crew members. To this end he stared intently at the small picture of Eileen that he had taped to the control panel in front of him. He would be strong for her too.

*"Bombs going... going... going..."* the bomb aimer called back, the first hint of excitement in his voice as it rose in a corresponding crescendo as each little gift to the Germans from No. 75 Squadron dropped free from the open bomb bay. As he did so, the pilot began adjusting the flight controls to compensate for the tons of weight that the mighty warbird was now being relieved of as its nocturnal cargo began whistling its way earthwards.

For a few seconds – but which seemed like an eternity – the whole plane was suddenly immersed in blinding white light as a searchlight beam locked onto it. Then fortunately it lost its quarry again – though not before it had alerted someone else to the presence of *'Z Zulu'* over the skies of Essen.

*"Bandit at six o'clock, Skipper!"* the rear gunner suddenly screamed to the judder of his Browning machine guns being unleashed.

*"Bombs clear, Skipper!"* the bomb aimer called up.

*"Corkscrew! Starboard! Go!"* the tail-gunner immediately shouted. The cue for a tried-and-tested manoeuvre, the engines screamed as the pilot hauled his steed hard over in an attempt to evade the Messerschmitt 110 now bearing down on their tail.

*"Hold tight, chaps,"* he screeched, flinging the plane into a steep, twisting dive that must surely have stressed the airframe far beyond what it was ever designed to bear.

As the plane tipped up almost vertical, a burst of fire from the 110 ripped chunks out of the fuselage around them. Gerald closed his eyes and prayed like he had never prayed before. His teeth were chattering uncontrollably. At not even twenty-two years of age he felt far too young to die – obscenely so! Therefore, by a sheer act of will, he opened his eyes again. Through the blur of the tears that were filling them, he stared intently at Eileen's picture on the console, his chest quivering as the demented 'yag-yag-yag-yag-yag' of the Stirling's .303 Brownings furiously pummelling his ears.

*"Where's he gone, Rear Gunner? Can you see him...?"*

*"Bloody hell, I've got him! He's on fire, Skipper...! He's going down!"*

*"He's right, Skipper,"* the bomb aimer chipped in, *"the little bugger's just a mass of flames...! He's breaking up...!"*

Even while the Skipper was pulling hard on the stick to return the bomber to level flight, an almighty cheer was resonating throughout the intercom – the glimmer of one small victory drowning out the renewed hammering of flak bursts exploding all around them.

*"Right, chaps. That's enough fun for one night. How about we skedaddle back to Blighty and find out what's for breakfast!"*

*"That's the best suggestion you've made all night, Skipper!"*

\* \* \* \* \*

The beautiful warm spring evening was made for promenading in the historic old quarter of Lincoln. It really was hard to believe the world was at war – notwithstanding that the city was a hub of Bomber Command stations (and its towering cathedral a key navigational landmark). All along the pleasant banks of Brayford Pool happy couples were out snatching what fleeting joy there was to be had. None of them could say where they might be tomorrow. Or indeed, whether they would even live to see another tomorrow. If so, then this constant feeling of impermanence tended to gnaw away at even the most steadfast of souls. In particular, it was hard to maintain moral virtue in the face of a war that had a terrible habit of making its own plans for its participants – whether in uniform or not.

Eventually, Eileen sat herself down upon the wall overlooking the river from where she proceeded to watch the stars commencing their nightly vigil.

"You know they reckon there are billions of those things out there," she heard his haunting voice casually remark.

Manley had decided it was time to start burrowing inside the soul of this woman he had become increasingly fascinated, if not obsessed by during the weeks that he had been observing her. Therefore, drawing up behind her he too lifted his gaze heavenwards.

"When I was a little girl my father used to tell me that there is a special one out there for each of us," she replied wistfully.

"Wise man, your father," Manley mused, otherwise not quite sure what the correct response was to such a whimsical statement. However, perhaps this was the moment to broach something seemingly so trivial by comparison, but which had meantime been weighing on his mind even so.

"I guess I kinda' owe you an apology for the other night."

"I'm sorry?"

"For that incident… you now, when you kinda' caught me..."

"Oh, that!" she giggled. "Perhaps it should be me apologising for strolling around the corner at the wrong moment," she suggested instead. After all, it was not everyday that she bumped into an inebriated Canadian shinning down the drainpipe of the officers' mess in his underwear.

Fortunately, there was a perfectly rational explanation – which, as Manley explained, went something along the lines of it being a right-of-passage for new members of Gibson's squadron to have their trousers summarily removed by the other aircrew. If nothing else, the hard work that Wing Commander Gibson had set them to was matched on days-off with some equally bibulous and outlandish hard play as well. Gibson meanwhile would shake his head paternally at their high jinks, preferring the company of his pipe and of Nigger – his ever-faithful black Labrador.

"It was my father I was visiting that day we first met," Eileen then proffered, returning to the subject of her stargazing. His apology accepted and his embarrassment assuaged, Manley permitted her to elaborate.

"However, I never did get to meet him. Maybe that's why I like looking up at stars. I keep imagining that, like that special star that is supposed to symbolise our destinies, he too is out there – somewhere – if only I will keep on searching for him."

"I have no wish to pry," he shrugged, not entirely truthfully, "but do I take it your folks are... divorced?"

There was an awkward hiatus as she contemplated that terrible, loaded word before pursing her lips regretfully and nodding in the affirmative. Meanwhile, Manley felt sufficiently in her confidence by now to be able to sit down on the wall beside her, drawing out a cigarette and offering her one, which she accepted. Their eyes briefly met as he lit it for her. She felt a tingle run down her spine.

"I know what it must feel like. I'm divorced myself," he confessed, no less crablike in his painful admission. "Things kinda' didn't work out. How is it that you can love someone with unquenchable passion one minute; and then the next you blink; something has happened; and you find you no longer love each other any more? Of course, you're still young, Eileen. You're probably still idealistic enough to think that love is forever. Or at least it should be. And maybe it will... with that guy you're seeing, I mean."

How could he know? How could she tell him? Instead she guided their conversation back onto the philosophical aspects of love and away from the crumbling edifice that was her own untenable facsimile of it.

"Nothing is ever 'forever'" she sighed. "If there's one thing that my parents' separation has taught me it is that the joy you have today can be snatched away tomorrow. Maybe that's why this war holds no fear for me in that respect. My whole life has been one long preparation for watching opportunities vanish; and for being reminded that you may be destined to be disappointed. And yet still I just cannot get out of my head that you have to cling to the hope of something better eventually turning up. People call me a dreamer because I think that way. I believe that one day I will find that special star – even if I have to search for it my whole life long."

"That strikes me as one incredibly optimistic statement!" he commended her. Then, with his gaze fixed dead ahead, he drew on his cigarette and offered her a confession of his own.

"You know, don't be too hard on your dad. I have a son somewhere back home. I haven't seen him in almost four years. But I always think about him. Maybe when this war is over and I can go back, then I'll get the opportunity to seek him out again. I just hope he remembers me."

"Trust me, Alastair. You never forget your father," she replied.

"Then trust me: your father will never forget you," he added. It prompted another period of quiet reflection on both their parts.

"Anyway, have you told Nancy about him: your son, that is?" she wondered.

Eileen had learned by now that her friend possessed an almost moth-to-the-flame weakness for characters that lived life on the edge, or who so defied convention as to shock her prim, middle-class parents – if only they knew. And dating a hell-raising aviator, who was also much older than her – a divorced loner who had found himself exiled from his child on the wrong side of the Atlantic Ocean – must rate as a most shocking and unconventional act in any anxious parents' book!

"She knows I have a past," was all he would say, clearly uncomfortable at her line of questioning.

Her concern had been occasioned not so much lest Nancy get hurt, but also by her own indwelling sense of Catholic morality. The war had liberated her in so many ways; and yet she had not entirely abandoned the faith of her childhood. In this regard – and as the two of them sat there together on the wall wondering what to say next – it was Eileen who felt herself at risk of getting hurt; and of disregarding the teachings of her faith.

She had fallen for this guy. She realised now that she had done so that first occasion she had set eyes on Manley in that sleepy little tea shop. She reluctantly accepted that this might just be the real reason she had felt her love for Gerald cooling during the weeks they had been apart? To be sure, a journey to the stars is dangerous – far more perilous than keeping ones feet firmly planted on the Earth. Was it because Manley was dangerous that she had felt impelled to suppress every cry of both faith and reason in order to be 'found' in his company – as she was tonight? That he was the lover of her best friend only fuelled the guilt she was wrestling with. However, she felt what resolve she still possessed to fight these feelings was faltering. Like some huge, weakening dam that was also about to break and release its pent-up waters, she sensed there was a terrible inevitability about what was about to happen next.

He moved first, turning to her and locking his hypnotic eyes onto hers. His gaze caused her to close her own eyes as his mouth inched closer. She felt his lips softly impact upon hers and then their penetrating tongues became the conduit by which the searching of their souls might continue unabashed.

* * * * *

That final mission had badly shaken up Flight Sergeant Gerald Graham. Never before had he come so close to losing it – fearing he might be branded 'lacking in moral fibre' (as the RAF euphemism deemed those of its flyers who cracked under the pressure). Yet by the grace of God he had come through. With that, his long and arduous tour of duty was completed. He could finally look forward to a decent spell of leave, after which he would return to a Heavy Conversion Unit and – flying accidents aside – to the less perilous life of training and instructing other new aircrews.

Therefore, with a spring in his step from a heart brimming with thanksgiving, he determined that that little jeweller's shop in Cambridge would be his very first port of call. It was whilst browsing there that he alighted upon a beautiful three-stone diamond cross-over engagement ring. It was not cheap. Yet having emptied a savings account he had been keeping aside he had managed to afford the asking price. Anyway, what was mere money when this was to be his gift of betrothal to the beautiful woman he adored.

As was often the way, attempting to arrange leave together with her would probably prove frustrating. And attempting to seek her father's permission had definitely proved frustrating! Therefore, he determined that he would simply surprise Eileen instead. The purchase complete, he would drive up to Lincoln to deliver the ring in person; and to ask its intended recipient for the superlative honour of having her hand in marriage. The thought of this moment had been all that had kept him going during those many occasions when he thought he had sensed the chill breath of mortality breezing through the claustrophobic innards of that plane. It was this thought that animated him as he jumped back into his little car and set off north with the sparkling jewel safely tucked away in the glove compartment.

# 9

Like the rest of the camp personnel who had spotted them the previous day, Eileen Kimberley had no idea what the huge, drum-like devices were that had been hauled through the main gate on the backs of a convoy of low-loaders. Shrouded in tarpaulin, they had been immediately whisked away to the bomb dump to be hidden from view.

Indeed, everything about Scampton these last few weeks had been swathed in all-pervading secrecy. Though she couldn't be sure, Eileen had her suspicions that her switchboard was being bugged – if not by enemy agents then almost certainly by intelligence personnel anxious to determine whether anyone was inadvertently talking more than they should. All of which pointed to something big about to take place – and probably within the next few days.

Therefore, the Saturday night pass and the get-together in the garden of the local village pub with the girls should have been a welcome chance for her to unwind from both the tension on the camp and the added tension created by her foolish dalliance with Alastair Manley. What had she been thinking? What had they both been thinking? This was absolute madness. Yet still she couldn't get him out of her mind. As such, she found herself not really listening to what was being said, merely nodding and smiling at what seemed like appropriate points so as not to arouse the suspicions of her colleagues.

To be sure, the aircrew present were on fine form. The beer might be warm and flat, but it was being downed in copious quantities. Meanwhile, hilarity there was aplenty – and once again the 'mattress' (as aircrew had a habit of lewdly referring to any gathering of WAAFs!) found themselves the butt of bawdy jokes, which they took in characteristic good humour. Yet, for all the japery – and despite the fact that no one was giving anything away – it was impossible not to sense that there might indeed be some ominous finality about the antics these young men were partaking in.

Clearly, Eileen was not the only person with weighty thoughts on her mind. Sitting inside at the bar as if to also give no hint of the dangerous liaison they had enjoyed, Flight Lieutenant Manley still could not resist the urge to periodically glance in her direction through the open windows; and with that certain look that spoke of sharing a mutual secret that was plainly torturing him too.

"Here, Manley old chap. No need to look so glum," one of the other officers called inside from the beer garden.

"Yes, Flight. You not joining us?" someone else turned about and urged, swivelling about the WAAF who was perched upon his knee as he did so.

"Manley said nothing, preferring to decline the offer with a wan smile and a dismissive wave of the hand."

"You mean not even the beautiful Eileen here can tempt you outside?" one of the WAAF radio operators chided him with a suggestive smile.

"He knows he can't have her. She's spoken for," her colleague piped up, prompting mirth from the others and a visible flush of embarrassment on Eileen's part, which she tried to laugh off.

"Skipper, you can have any woman you want tonight, you great big handsome beast!" one of his fellow aircrew raucously sought to console him.

"Except Eileen. Poor Skipper – he's simply not her type!"

By now Eileen was laughing it off so insincerely that she was certain it must show. Therefore, she pleaded the need to repair to the ladies' room and excused herself.

The gaiety continued, with more of the WAAFs becoming the target of the aircrews' collective innuendoes. Therefore, no one noticed that Eileen had been gone quite a while. However, Manley had. And a sixth sense told him just where to find her. Knocking back what was left of his pint, he slipped unnoticed from the bar stool and made his way out of the pub and across the village green to where a bench was located overlooking a pleasant pond that reflected the twilight sky. From the vacant stare she cast upon the moonlit water he could tell that she was absorbed in painful self-examination.

She said nothing when Manley slipped quietly onto the bench next to her. She knew whatever she said was liable to misinterpretation. If she denied her feelings toward him, she would be mouthing a falsehood. If she openly proclaimed them then who could say what a cauldron of emotional complications she would be lifting the lid upon. Instead, she just carried on gazing at the reflections shimmering upon the surface of the pond.

"Look, Eileen, I'm sorry if I've kinda' messed up your head. It's just right now mine's pretty messed up too. I can't say too much but... Well, you know we've been training quite a lot lately and... well, whatever it is they want us do, I... I don't know.... I just sense I may not be coming back from this one."

Eileen turned and observed that his eyes really did speak of being 'for the chop'. However, while they both sat there haunted by the numbing prospect that one of them could possibly be passing their last weekend on this Earth, they failed to notice a car pull up outside the pub, the merriment of their colleagues in the beer garden still filling the sultry evening air and drowning out the sound of its arrival. Meanwhile, the engine extinguished, its driver sat back in his seat, breathed deeply, and closed his eyes in a momentary attempt to summon up courage. This was make-or-break time, he knew. Hence, opening them, he reached inside the glove compartment and took out the tiny velvet box that symbolised the purpose of the day's long sojourn. Then, alighting from the car, he looked the pub up and down and ventured inside.

"Hello," said Gerald, gingerly approaching the barman, who was busy restocking glasses on the shelves behind. "I'm looking for Eileen Kimberley. She's a WAAF stationed at the local airfield. I'm told she frequents this place."

"You should try asking outside. They're all from the camp around the corner. They might know her," he replied, continuing to line the glasses up.

"Thanks," Gerald nodded, anxiously spying out the party of boys and girls in uniform still laughing and frolicking in the garden. Clutching the ring box in his hand, he strolled off in their direction.

"I'm afraid if you're looking for flight engineers' vacancies, we're full!" one of the pilots roared, spotting the new arrival's 'Flying E' shoulder badge.

"Yes, sorry to disappoint you, old chap. Try Waddington down the road. They might have need of an odd-bod!" another guffawed, the other aircrew joining in.

"Actually, I'm looking for Eileen Kimberley. She's a WAAF. I don't suppose you know where I can find her."

"Eileen? Oh, yes. Why, she was here a moment ago," one of the girls replied, glancing about them.

"Here, are you Gerald, by any chance?" her friend asked, thinking she recognised the face from the photograph she recalled Eileen had showed her.

"Well, yes. I am actually. I'm her fiancé... I mean, her boyfriend," the object of their curiosity replied, remembering that he had yet to place the ring on the finger that would render her such.

"Gosh! Isn't she the lucky lady," one of the other WAAFs then teased, her womanly nose for such things having spied the little velvet box in his hand.

"More a case of 'aren't you the lucky guy', I would have thought," an NCO corrected her, explaining that "Why, not even our over-sexed Saskatchewan skipper can get his hands inside her black-outs! Not for the want of trying though!"

An abrupt nudge in the ribs and a clip around the ear from colleagues halted the tipsy sergeant in his tracks, silencing the assembled revellers. Then one of the girls broke that awkward silence and explained that "She was with us. But we haven't seen her for some time. She disappeared to the powder room and hasn't come back. Perhaps she's made her way back to camp on her own."

"I see. Well, thanks anyway. Maybe if she does return, you'll tell her I called by," Gerald shuffled to hide his own awkwardness, edging himself away from the crowd and returning back inside the pub.

"No joy finding her?" the barman enquired, busying himself polishing more glasses.

Gerald ignored him and breezed past as if in a trance, wandering back outside to his car. Hopping inside, he tossed the velvet box onto the seat next to him. It was as he was about to restart the engine that something across the way suddenly caught his attention. For there – on the village green on a bench overlooking the pond – was an officer and his girl locked in a long, amorous embrace. He knew the RAF frowned upon officers and ranks fraternising in such manner when in uniform. Yet here they were – and he had just caught them *in flagrante*! Then suddenly the thought hit him: perhaps that throw-away remark about a 'big, over-sexed Saskatchewan skipper' wasn't just the alcohol speaking after all.

Surely it wasn't so… no! Stepping from the car, during the first few paces he took he was clearly in denial – after all, plenty of WAAFs wore their dark, curly locks in that same style. If so, then maybe this particular WAAF could at least tell him where he could find his elusive…

"Eileen!"

She turned. Upon recognising him, she froze.

"Gerald. What are you doing…?"

It was one of those terrible moments when words were simply superfluous. He looked at her. Then he looked at the officer who was now hurriedly sliding himself to the far corner of the bench. Then he stared back at Eileen.

"So your grandmother was right about you after all!" he shook his head, appalled at the infamy that he had just witnessed. "You really do chase after officers. And 'Yanks'!" he turned, staring at Manley and his 'Canada' shoulder badge, spitting out the epithet as a calculated insult.

"Look, fellah, I'm sorry if there seems to be some kinda' misunderstanding going on here," the tall North American rose to plead.

"Oh, there's no misunderstanding, mate. She's a tramp. You're a shit. And you're welcome to each other," he sneered. Then he turned and marched off back towards the car.

"No! Gerald! Please! It's not how it appears!" Eileen cried out, at first charging after him, but then – realising he was not even going to deign to turn and face her – she slowed and halted, the tears gushing from her eyes as she sank to her knees and beheld him jump into the car, start it up and speed off, the tyres squealing as he raced out of her life.

"Dear God! No!" was all she could plead in vain.

Though his demeanour had been one of angry indifference, the realisation that the object of all these months of yearning had been sharing another's charms now caused tears to well up in Gerald's eyes too – tears of hurt mingling with tears of despair. Otherwise, he elected to make the motor car the conduit of his mounting anger. He hit the accelerator with a vengeance and braked hard into bends as it made its way down the peaceful country lanes, eventually passing the main gate of the nearby air station (where he had earlier enquired after Eileen). So caught up was he in lover's fury that it was only at the last minute that he spotted a small black shape race past the guard house and out in front him. Though he braked and swerved, the dull thud of bone upon metalwork was a sure sign that the poor creature never stood a chance.

There was a hurried sound of boots running upon asphalt, the duty NCO arriving on the scene just in time to observe the tail lights of the speeding car disappearing into the night. Instead, he crouched down to stroke the pitiful Labrador whimpering as if to acknowledge that its fate was hopeless.

"Oh, no! Nigger, old boy!" the corporal wept.

* * * * *

Dusk was already well advanced when, at 2130 hours, the chocks were released, the runway controller's red Aldis lamp was swapped for green, and the first of 617 Squadron's modified Lancasters took off from Scampton's grassy strip, those strange cylindrical devices protruding from their bellies. Several more planes followed in rapid succession, Eileen looking on as each one strained to take to the sky under the huge weight of its mysterious bomb.

However, she had a job to do. As she waved them off and watched them disappear over the darkening horizon she could only pray that Alastair was wrong: that he would return from whatever it was they were off to do – though it didn't seem a particularly good omen that Wing Commander Gibson's dog (the Squadron's mascot) had been killed the night before. Finally she wandered off to the exchange for what she knew was going to be an anxious night.

"You okay, Kimberley?" the supervisor enquired, sensing that one of her telephonists seemed unusually preoccupied. That said, the NCO knew a lot of the girls on station would be worrying tonight and so said nothing more. Meanwhile, having nodded dutifully, Eileen answered a call.

Whilst she was connecting the call, she was unaware that behind her a dour figure with a clipped moustache and an awful lot of braid had wandered into the room and was casting his eye upon proceedings. The WAAF sergeant supervising the girls saluted stiffly. For several long seconds he then watched Eileen and her colleague at work before acknowledging the sergeant and wandering back out.

"I thought you might like to know, girls. That was Air Chief Marshal 'Bomber' Harris," she confirmed once they were both off their calls.

The two telephonists stared at each other. Now they knew something big was definitely afoot.

\* \* \* \* \*

*"Dutch coast approaching in five minutes."*

So far the flight had been uneventful. However, with that snippet of news Flight Lieutenant Manley knew the real fun was about to begin. Skimming the waves at two hundred knots *'Y for Yellow'* zoomed across the beach to arrive over enemy territory.

*"Now follow the line of that canal, Skipper."*

Manley duly heeded his navigator's instruction, the hair-raising flight such that the bomb aimer up front felt he could almost reach down and grab the bridges and dwellings that were whizzing beneath him at frightening speed. Then suddenly, gazing ahead, he was gripped by a sight he had not been expecting. Neither had it been marked on the map the navigator was anxiously scouring.

*"Bloody hell, Skipper – it's an airfield!"* he cried into his mask.

Indeed it was. All at once it was as if every anti-aircraft battery for miles around had a fix and was hammering away at them with shells and tracer fire. Fortunately, *'Y Yellow'* was flying too low and too fast for the searchlight operators to train their beams on them. Neither would the fighters parked up on the field have time to scramble before had the intruder had overflown the strip.

Eventually, the flak quietened down, permitting Manley to check his instruments. Racing over more trees and buildings, he set a final course for their objective: the huge Möhne dam that supplied vital water and electricity to the Ruhr Valley – Germany's industrial heartland.

Altimeters were as good as useless at this height, and it was now that all those weeks of intense training came into its own. However, even with a full moon illuminating their path, it was difficult to pick out the one hazard that was most likely to imperil their dangerous, ground-hugging mission. Consequently, it was not until the last moment that the eagle-eyed bomb aimer spotted its miniscule profile looming up ahead.

*"Skipper! Climb!"* he screamed, his eyes agape in terror.

It was too late. Though Manley pulled on the stick for all he was worth, there was a brilliant flash as the power lines arced and the steel lattice-work of the high-tension electricity pylon sheared the starboard wing from the fuselage, simultaneously igniting over a thousand gallons of escaping aviation spirit. Within seconds *'Y Yellow'* was consumed in a monstrous fireball that lit up the night sky, the Lancaster's myriad pieces of burning remains flaying out and splattering themselves across the fields below.

\* \* \* \* \*

Silence reigned in the Operations Room back at Scampton. No phones rang. Nobody spoke either. Not the ops girls sat twiddling their thumbs around the plotting table – some of whom were sweethearts of the men of whom news was now anxiously awaited; not the radio operator listening out for the merest hint of a message over the airwaves – of which nothing had been heard since he had intercepted warnings of heavy flak over the Dutch coast being relayed back to the mission's second and third waves; nor too the squadron adjutant trying desperately not to nod off. Then, all of a sudden, something stirred on the radio set and the operator began scribbling, animating the others in the room to look his way in anticipation.

"Goner, sir" he noted. "From *'G George'*. That's Gibson, sir."

Air Vice-Marshal Cochrane – the Air Officer Commanding – acknowledged him and then looked across at the morose presence that was Air Chief Marshal Harris. Neither one said a word. Instead they both looked across at the nervous pacing up and down of Barnes Wallis, the white-haired scientific genius who had first had the brainwave of bouncing a mine across the surface of the water to evade the torpedo nets that the Germans had strung out in front of their largest dams. If Gibson and his fellow flyers could land their 'bouncing bombs' in just the right spot against the dams' huge walls then the subsequent detonation would breach them. It still seemed an impossibly hare-brained scheme. Indeed, Wallis had had to overcome considerable scepticism on the part of the Air Ministry (to say nothing of Harris too) in order that everything might be put in place to make 'Operation Chastise' come to pass – planes, pilots and those special bombs.

Sensing the brief stir in the room, Wallis broke from his anxious musing to return the stares of Harris and Cochrane.

"Goner, sir," the radio operator repeated for his benefit.

"I had hoped one bomb might do it," the anxious boffin muttered.

"It's probably weakened it," Cochrane felt moved to reassure him.

If nothing else, it had proved it could be done. Wallis tried to hide a wince of self-satisfaction on that count at least, rubbing his hands together discreetly. Harris meanwhile turned even more morose as the minutes ticked by and more calls of 'Goner' were radioed through – from *'P Popsie'*, *'A Apple'* and *'J Johnny'* – each repeating of the code word for a successful pass ramping up the tension still further. Harris, Cochrane and the other officers present looked on concerned as an aura of jittery despair began to envelope Wallis. Finally, another call came through, the operator's face swathed in utter astonishment as this time he relayed a different, more exhilarating code word.

"Nigger, sir... NIGGER! The dam's gone!"

Almost immediately, Harris punched the air with both fists in triumph, setting aside all sense of decorum to dance across the room and grab hold of the excited albino-crowned boffin.

"Wallis, I didn't believe a word you said when you first came to see me. But now you could sell me a pink elephant!" he cried. Cochrane too looked chuffed that the boys of No. 5 Group had done them all proud.

"This'll certain give Churchill something to crow about to the Americans," he declared, shaking his head in disbelief, aware the Prime Minister was in the United States to address Congress and rally support for the war in Europe.

"Cochrane, you're right. I must get a message through to Portal immediately," Harris exclaimed, aware also that his superior, Air Chief Marshal Sir Charles Portal, was at that very moment also in Washington dining with President Roosevelt.

* * * * *

The switchboard had been almost deathly quiet that evening. No doubt it would stay that way until 617 Squadron's aircraft began arriving back in a few hours time. It had afforded Eileen the opportunity to be alone with her thoughts again – which was just as well given the turmoil inside her head following the previous night's terrible encounter.

Just then a buzzer went off and a light on the board came on, breaking her doleful solicitude. She drew up a cable and poked it into the jack.

"Go ahead, caller… Yes, sir… Er, of course, sir… Please hold the line."

The look of bafflement in her eyes at receiving such a bizarre request at this time in the morning alerted the supervisor, who had been concerned all night that Aircraftwoman Kimberley seemed to be in another world and was now unable to comprehend even the simplest instruction she was being given.

"Something wrong, Kimberley?" she scowled warily.

"Er… No, Sergeant. It's Air Chief Marshal Harris on the line. He wants to be put through to the White House," she replied sheepishly.

"Well… Don't just sit there, girl. Put him through to the White House!"

* * * * *

Sunday nights were invariably quiet nights. Most of the servicemen and women who had been granted weekend passes were back on camp and tucked up in bed. Therefore, with the doors to the inn all safely bolted shut, there was just time for the licensee to tidy up a few tables before pouring himself a nightcap. He grabbed a glass and tipped the remains of a bottle of scotch into it, leaning back against the bar to stare at the calendar hanging on the wall, contemplating what the coming week might bring.

Just then his pondering was interrupting by the ringing of the telephone that was mounted on the wall further along the bar. Quickly knocking back the dram, he trudged over and answered it.

"Grantham 683," he mumbled wearily. "…Yes, it is indeed… Oh really…? Well, let me have a look," he offered, reaching over to open up a large tattered desk diary that was sat atop the counter. The name didn't sound familiar, but he perused through the pages even so.

"How are you spelling that…? No, sorry, my friend. We have no one with that name staying here tonight. And definitely not an air chief marshal!" he tittered, certain he would have remembered had such an illustrious guest checked in. However, the caller was most insistent that this mysterious colleague of his be located – this instant!

"Do you know what time it is?" the licensee therefore reminded him, alternately glancing at the clock and then at the calendar he had been studying. Surely April Fools' Day had already passed!

"Listen, are you sure you've got the right 'White House'?" he insisted again, annoyance now evident in his tone. "…No, this is the White House public house – in Grantham… Here, pal, there's no need for that kind of language!"

The licensee slammed the receiver back on its plinth and screwed up his face. Just what he needed at this ungodly hour: a gruff prankster purporting to be 'Bomber Harris' and asking to speak to some air force big-wig in America!

\* \* \* \* \*

Having tossed and turned throughout the previous night, both her cares and the lack of sleep they had occasioned were now catching up on Eileen. Therefore, she came close to falling off her chair when the board lit up a second time, catching her almost napping. Then her face suddenly turned ashen when the caller revealed his identity. This time the supervisor was waiting.

"What's got into you, Kimberley! Will you pull yourself together, woman!" she barked.

"I'm sorry, Sergeant. It's Air Chief Marshal Harris again. It was the White House in Washington DC that he wanted to be put through to!"

\* \* \* \* \*

*All ranks in No. 5 Group join me in congratulating you and all in 617 Squadron on a brilliantly conducted operation. The disaster which you have inflicted on the German war machine was a result of hard work, discipline and courage. The determination not to be beaten in the task, and getting the bombs exactly on the aiming point in spite of opposition, have set an example others will be proud to follow.*

*Congratulatory message to Wing Commander Guy Gibson from Air Vice Marshal, the Honourable R A Cochrane, AOC 5 Group, RAF Bomber Command – May 17th 1943.*

\* \* \* \* \*

Eventually, after an hour or so of frantic effort, Eileen Kimberley was able to successfully put a placated 'Bomber' Harris through to Sir Charles Portal at the White House via a secure line routed through United States Embassy in London. And what Harris had to report was truly staggering. Both the Möhne and the Edersee dams had been breached, causing catastrophic flooding of the Ruhr Valley that would occasion months of disruption to German industry. However, the more difficult-to-attack Sorpe and Ennepe dam had been damaged, but had remained intact. Two vital hydro-electric plants had also been destroyed. When news of the attacks was broken to the British public, morale soared – proof, it ever any were needed, that no target was beyond the abilities of the brave lads of RAF Bomber Command to hit.

However, out of nineteen aircraft that had taken off from Scampton that evening, only eleven would return (two having aborted their missions after inbound flak damage and a low-flying scrape had rendered their machines unserviceable). Meanwhile, the human cost was truly staggering: out of 133 crew members, fifty-three were killed and three captured. Thirteen of those killed were Canadians; two Australians. Barnes Wallis, in particular, was inconsolable over their deaths – blaming himself for a rate of loss unprecedented even by Bomber Command's daunting reputation. Meanwhile, six hundred Germans had perished in the ensuing deluge, as well as a thousand (most Soviet POW) forced labourers who had been trapped by the torrents of water sweeping all before them.

Of those crews who did return safely, Wing Commander Guy Gibson was to be awarded the Victoria Cross, while the men of 617 Squadron were to share five Distinguished Services Orders, ten Distinguished Flying Crosses (four with bars), two Conspicuous Gallantry Medals, and eleven Distinguished Flying Crosses.

Of course, the success of this remarkable mission had depended not only on the courage and professionalism of its aviators, but also on the tireless work of those personnel on the ground who made it possible: the aircraft fitters and electricians, the armourers and fuellers, the dispersal crews, the ops room plotters, the signallers, the meteorologists, the photo-reconnaissance teams, the cooks, the quartermasters, the clerks – and yes, the WAAF telephonists too!

\* \* \* \* \*

The deathly silence inside Lincoln's deserted Catholic church was only disturbed by the sound of a young woman timidly closing the door behind her, and then of her heels echoing upon the hard stone floor as she made her way down the aisle to nestle into a pew a few rows back from the altar. In front of her she looked up at the huge cross upon which was draped the sorrowful corpse of Christ, whilst all around her the sun was bursting in through stained glass windows that depicted the Stations of the Cross.

These familiar vistas of suffering and self-sacrifice always made Eileen Kimberley uneasy – reminding her again of how unlikely it was that she would ever be good enough to be counted amongst the saints whose statuettes inhabited the recesses of the church's colonnades. Instead, imitating them in only way she felt able, she knelt to unburden herself of the penitence that had driven her here. Shortly afterwards, the silence that had returned would thus be disturbed again, this time by the sound of weeping as she called upon her Saviour's mercy and forgiveness once more.

The intervening weeks had been a time of mixed emotions. To the confirmation that *'Y Yellow'* had been observed crashing in flames over occupied Holland – and that Flight Lieutenant Alastair Manley was dead – was added self-reproach at wondering whether, on account of all the complications involved, his loss might actually be some kind of perverted blessing in disguise. At least this way Nancy would never know just how shamefully Eileen had betrayed their friendship. Yet how could she possibly think that way! She contemplated Manley's little boy back in Canada, who would now grow up without ever knowing his father – a tragic fate that Eileen, of all people, could empathise with

Whilst she was deep in prayerful remorse – and the omniscient Good Shepherd on His Cross beheld again this wayward sheep of his flock kneeling in His presence – the church door opened and someone else discreetly made their way down the aisle to take up a place in a pew across from her. Glancing up from her supplication, she observed a callow, gangling figure clutching his folded garrison cap in his hand who, by way of acknowledgement, flashed his eyebrows humbly in her direction before he too went down on his knees, closed his eyes tight, and began to pray.

However, as her peeping eye studied him more closely it was his uniform that Eileen's noticed. A smart, light-weight cotton shirt, with neatly-pressed trousers to match; it was certainly nothing like the thick, scratchy battle-dress blues her own side were kitted out in. Then that peeping eye alighted upon the regimental badge and small Stars-and-Stripes patch on the shoulder. It was an American serviceman – one of those famed 'GI's!

Such a frisson of excitement came over her that she quite forgot about praying. She had never set eyes upon a real in-the-flesh American before. It was not so much that the young man sat opposite her was handsome (though he was, in a boyish kind of way). It was that he did indeed look so young – though probably not that much younger than Eileen herself. And, like all those Aussies, Kiwis and Canadians, he was so far from home – from Alabama, Arizona or Arkansas; or any one of those other evocative places she had come across in Hollywood movies. What's more, he had come to pray – perhaps because he was anxious or uncertain; or just plain scared. Perhaps this was the first time he had ever ventured outside the United States, she imagined – never mind the small town he had probably grown up in. Yet here he was: a solitary and devout token of the thousands of his fellow countrymen who were pouring into the country each week on troopships from across the Atlantic.

Meanwhile, his evident piety – plus remembering the sanctity of the ornate building in which she was seated – made her suddenly self-conscious that it had been a long time since she had been to Confession. Therefore, she elected to offer up her repentance directly to the Saviour instead. Crossing herself in the hope that she might thereby retain His favour, she rose, crossed herself again before the altar, and then turned to face the world once more. Her departing steps echoed in the stillness until she had closed the door behind her and the solitary GI was left alone to seek his own penance.

# *10*

It helped to overcome bad memories that Eileen was offered a change of scenery that summer – or, more precisely, a posting to RAF Dunholme Lodge just down the road. The station was home to the Lancaster heavy bombers of No. 44 (Rhodesia) Squadron – so named because it was comprised mostly of aircrew from this fiercely proud and independent-minded colony in southern Africa. Eileen's stunning looks and pleasing manner soon attracted the attention of this sun-bronzed, hard-drinking, and incorrigibly rule-bending crowd (one thing the less class-bound Empire and Dominion aircrews all had in common was their reluctance to put up with the more irksome manifestations of RAF 'bullshit'). Though enjoying their banter, their riotous antics and their old-fashioned protective chivalry ("our little Rooinek Princess," the Rhodies insisted on calling her), still nursing a fragile heart she was reluctant to be swept too headily into their embrace.

If one of the wonders of RAF life was the making of firm friends, then the flipside was often being abruptly parted from those friends – and then having to make new friends all over again. As well as Pippa West – who worked as a batwoman in the officers' mess, and who had introduced herself to Eileen that first day – she also acquired an additional 'friend' of the most unexpected variety. Even before the reveille had sounded on her first day at Dunholme, Eileen had found her somnolence disturbed by a mysterious scratching noise originating from the floorboards beneath her bunk. Burying her head beneath the sheets to shut out the periodic scraping sound, she eventually slithered out of bed and pressed her ear against the planks to try and identify its source. Then she noticed that a knothole in the board had been poked out, up to which she drew a beady eye to better spot the equally beady-eyed creature staring back at her. Meanwhile, from the adjacent bunk, the flame-haired Pippa had been observing the proceeding with a barely-concealed grin.

"Here, there's a chicken under my bunk," Eileen looked across and exclaimed.

"Aye, pet. It's been there a few weeks now," Pippa roared in her broad Durham accent. "We call her Polly. She must have escaped from one of the neighbouring farms. We didn't have the heart to turn her in. Mind you, she's quite a useless bird, if ever there was. Never laid a ruddy egg in the whole time she's been nesting under there!"

"Too right!" one of the other girls scowled. "Pippa might be a great big soft-heart, but I've a good mind to turn her in to the cookhouse. Perhaps that might be a more rewarding means of 'savouring' her company!"

Eileen buried her head under the blanket once more. Just what I need, she cursed: a useless hen keeping me awake. Trust me to end up with this bunk!

* * * * *

"Hey, sweetheart. Isn't it a bit early in the morning to be walking into town alone?" the gum-chewing driver called out from the cab of a chunky, canvas-topped Studebaker truck that had screeched to a halt beside her.

"Oh, that's okay," Eileen chirped gaily. "I'm not going into town – only for a walk. It's such a beautiful morning!"

"Sure is, toots. A real beautiful morning!" one of the guys hanging out of the back of the truck tunefully concurred.

"Yeah, and you're one beautiful broad," the driver again insisted in his thick drawl. "Now hop in, lady. I'll take you wherever you wanna' go. You wanna' be whisked off to Paradise, then I'll take you to Paradise."

"I think he means Camden, New Jersey, ma'am," a waggish GI interjected from across the passenger seat.

"Hey, Frankhauser. Gimme' a break. When I tell the lady Paradise I mean… Paradise," the driver dismissed such levity, shooing his buddy back over to his own side of the cab. Then he rolled his eyes and threw his hands up in the air to signal that he was reluctantly willing to accept no for an answer from this jaywalking English rose.

"Even Camden, New Jersey would be Paradise if a gorgeous dame like you were waiting there for me!" another GI called out wistfully from the back of the truck as it jerked back into gear and rumbled off. He then employed both hands to blow Eileen a kiss that was far more exaggerated than any a British or Commonwealth serviceman had ever treated her too.

These Americans really were a breed apart, she smiled. Like their superlative country, they were bigger, bolder and brasher in every way. What's more, in a Britain beset by shortages of every kind they hailed from a land of relative plenty – and they had shipped that plenty over with them to stock up their PXs. There need be no more backstreet haggling with spivs if a girl wanted to get her hands on nylon stockings.

Alone again with just birdsong and a warm breeze rustling the hedgerows, Eileen carried on her way, singing *'Elmer's Tune'* to herself as she did. She enjoyed these walks down country lanes on quiet summer mornings – one of the rare opportunities in RAF life when one could enjoy true solitude. She also loved singing – she always had. And now that they were able to pick up the US Armed Forces Radio Network on the wireless in the billet she could add more wonderful melodies to the repertoire of tunes she had been covertly singing to Polly the Hen. Who knows; it might even coax the bird into laying an egg!

So intently was she lost in song that at first she failed to notice the trail of a flare rising up into the sky above her. However, when it burst it stopped her in her tracks and caused her to cup her hand to her eyes and look up. Then over on the south-eastern horizon she noticed the reason for the distress signal: a 'darkie' was heading her way with one of its four engines trailing smoke. As it drew closer she strained to make out a Halifax bomber lining up to put down at the adjacent airfield, its remaining engines spluttering it along on the approach. In fact, it was not going to make it. The starboard wing was ablaze and it was losing height rapidly. Then she watched in horror as it ploughed into the field ahead of her, careering along in the dust, its fuselage shredded and battered by the time it finally twisted to a halt.

A sudden explosion then immersed the forward half of the plane. Though a fierce fire was now raging, without thought of her own safety Eileen hitched up her skirt and hopped over the gate, running across the sun-baked field to search for survivors. However, the rear of the plane was the only part that the intense heat permitted her to get close enough to. There she stumbled upon the mangled rear gun turret.

Remarkably, its occupant was still alive. What's more, he was frantically trying to free himself. Peering through the glass, she spotted this breathless young man desperately trying to manipulate the turret mechanism.

"Joey!" she squealed.

He looked up, as startled as she. "Is it...? Eileen!"

"Are you okay?" she asked – a silly question, she knew, when he had just survived a horrific crash which had killed his fellow crew members. Scanning him up and down she tried to ascertain just how badly Joey was injured. And – more to the point – how on Earth she could get him out of there.

"I think I've broken my arm," he replied in his familiar Queensland twang, his left limb hanging limp and useless as still he tried vainly to claw at the turret mechanism with his blooded right hand.

"Tell me how I can help you!" she called back, her eyes trying to make out what he was attempting to do.

"I need to prise the turret open so it will swing around and let me out. But the impact must have jammed the swivel mechanism and I just can't get any leverage on it," he panted, sensing the heat from the blaze advancing towards him with each weary breath.

Eileen tried employing her two good hands to free him. However, though she was able to squeeze open a small gap, the turret was just too badly buckled to open any further. She cast her gaze about the field for makeshift tools: a decent-sized stone, for example, to employ as a hammer. However, there were none – though, bizarrely, she remembered that the wooden gate she had just hopped over was decidedly rickety.

"Eileen, there's fuel and ammunition and God-knows-what still aboard this kite. You'll never free the mechanism. Now get the hell outta' here before the whole lot goes up!" Joey meanwhile wheezed.

In a moment of seemingly awful finality, Eileen looked into his terrified eyes and watched him grip his languid left arm in pain, distraught to observe him weeping like a little child. What a way to go, she cursed: to be fried alive inside a useless glass bubble!

"Tell Mom and Dad that I love them," he pleaded to her, his dying words just audible above the roaring and crackling of the remorseless flames.

Wrenching herself away, she ran and ran for all she was worth until she reached the road. Then training her furious gaze upon that rickety old gate she seized hold of it. Teeth clenched and hollering like a banshee, she dug a heel against the frame and ripped a cross member clean away from it, collapsing on her arse in the dust, her trophy clutched triumphantly in her hands.

Jumping to her feet, she then ran with the timber back to where the crashed bomber was now billowing black smoke into the morning sky. There she found Joey whimpering in despair after a mother who – ten thousand miles away – might have had only a chilling premonition of the wicked denouement that was about to engulf her treasured little boy (the little boy who she had once carried in her womb and nursed at her breast).

Without even sparing a thought for how her own mother might mourn her about-to-be incinerated daughter, Eileen heaved the timber up above her head and launched it into the tiny gap between turret and fuselage that her bare hands had opened up, pressing and jiggling it in for good measure. Then she pushed hard against it, exerting upon it as much force as her feminine frame could muster, the weathered timber flexing to the point where she feared it must surely snap. However, suddenly it was the mechanism of the turret that snapped with a loud clonk. Pushing against the timber some more, inch by agonising inch the glass bubble was rotated around until the gap at its rear was wide enough to present an escape route out of it.

By now oblivious to the bells and flashing lights of the crash tenders as they careered through what she had left standing of the rickety gate, she poked her arms inside the turret and wrapped them around Joey. Braving the scorching heat and the acrid smoke she fumbled with his harness until he was free and she could finally haul him out. Dragging him away for all she was worth, they had barely made it a dozen yards when there erupted a deafening explosion that blew what was left of the plane skywards. Shielding her head, Eileen threw herself across the crippled gunner to protect him from the debris, her skirt and tunic scorched by burning fragments that cascaded down upon them.

Fortunately, that very instant a cowering fire-fighter was upon her, training his extinguisher upon both WAAF and unconscious Aussie gunner while his colleagues with the foam sprays attempted to tackle what was left of the blazing bomber.

\* \* \* \* \*

"I have to say, Kimberley, that what you did was foolish in the extreme. You recklessly placed your own life at risk."

"Yes, ma'am," she replied, equally appalled by the danger she had indeed put herself in.

"However, it must also rank as one of the most selfless and courageous things I have seen any WAAF do," the Squadron Officer conceded, leaning forward on her desk in order to put aside for a moment the formality of their encounter. "What's more, it saved that young man's life. Tail-end Charlies are suffering a grievous casualty rate – even by aircrew standards. Young Joey Abbott was incredibly lucky to have completed so many missions unscathed. Now, thanks to your quick-thinking, his war is over – and on a happy note too. That's because once the MO has fixed his arm he will be put on a ship back to his parent's sugar plantation in Australia – where I'm sure one day this heroic young man will have some truly amazing stories to tell his grandchildren."

"Yes, ma'am," Eileen again acknowledged.

"As for you, Kimberley, I shall be recommending that your name goes forward to receive proper recognition for what you have done. Otherwise, I think a spot of leave is now in order."

"Thank you, ma'am," she blushed.

"However, before you walk out of those front gates it is my pleasure to inform you that you will be doing so as a 'leading aircraftwoman'. Kimberley, you're being promoted with immediate effect. That is all. You are dismissed."

"Thank you, ma'am," Eileen stood to attention and saluted.

\* \* \* \* \*

There was the usual shuffling and coughing as Eileen and Pippa squeezed past, apologising profusely. There was also the inevitable fug of cigarette smoke to contend with. And there was also the usual newsreel presentation to remind Lincoln's Saturday night cinemagoers that there was still a war on – although thankfully on almost every front there was good news to report.

*"Following the large-scale Allied landings at Salerno, British troops have captured the Italian naval base of Taranto... Mussolini's once formidable fleet has sailed to Malta to surrender... With his demoralised army bowing out of this war, the Italian dictator himself has fled Rome..."*

The joyful cheer was such that the roof was almost lifted clean off the stygian fleapit – its exhilarated audience thereby not catching the sting in the tail: namely, amidst the chaos of surrender German troops had swept down into northern Italy, where – after a daring rescue of him – they had dug in and set *Il Duce* up as the head of a puppet administration there. Despite all the rejoicing tonight, the war in Italy was far from over.

*"...Meanwhile, in the Far East, General Douglas MacArthur's 503rd Parachute Division has successfully landed in New Guinea..."*

This time it was the cue for all the Americans thronging the best seats in the house to let out a raucous cheer...

*"...Where it promptly joined up with the Australian troops that have captured the key port city of Lae..."*

Cue an isolated cheer from the more cash-strapped antipodeans sat up in the circles – theirs animated not just by national rivalry, but also an awareness of the bestial treatment the Japanese army was rumoured to be visiting upon the guys who had been captured during fall of Malaya. Thankfully, the Japs too were in headlong retreat as the mighty American war machine (aided by its dauntless Aussie ally) was powering its way back across the Pacific Ocean.

*"...Finally, we report the remarkable story of Leading Aircraftwoman Eileen Kimberley, the plucky little WAAF of RAF Bomber Command who single-handedly rescued an Australian gunner from a burning plane..."*

"Hey look, pet. There's…!" Pippa couldn't resist the urge to cry out in her tuneful northern ling.

"Shhhh!" the other cinemagoers reprimanded her – especially those Australian aircrews thoroughly engrossed in the account of this act of heroism towards one of their boys. Alas, their hasty shushing meant they might never find out that the object of their affection was not a million miles away from where they were sitting.

*"…This amazing young lady was summoned to London, where she received the George Cross from the King himself at a special ceremony conducted at Buckingham Palace,"* the commentator proudly announced, complete with footage of the bashful Eileen posing with her medal outside the Palace gates. *"…Leading Aircraftwoman Kimberley has therefore become one of only a handful of women ever to have received this – the highest award it is possible to receive for gallantry performed away from direct combat with an enemy…"*

"Gee, I'd sure like to shake that little lady's hand," a broad Australian accent could be heard calling down from the circles.

"Yeah, well yer' can shove off, mate, cuz' I intend to be first in line!" another broad Australian accent proclaimed, to mirth all round.

Pippa was minded to pipe up again, but glanced across at her humbled friend and thought better of it. Even now, Eileen still could not believe what had happened. She – a national heroine, whose pretty face had been splashed all over the newspapers! Instead, both Pippa and Eileen grinned knowingly and snuggled down into their seats to await the start of the main programme.

When it arrived – and as the two of them sat there sucking on the sweets they had purchased during the intermission – neither attractive young WAAF could say they were entirely enamoured by the plot. However, *'Orchestra Wives'* certainly had some catchy little numbers. Pippa soon found her feet being jolted by Eileen's, which were tapping away rhythmically next to hers. Meanwhile – transfixed by Tex Beneke's seductive voice, Marion Hutton's blonde screen presence, as well as by Glenn Miller and his awesome big band sound – she was mouthing along to *'I've Got A Gal In Kalamazoo',* her head rocking from side to side as she did.

"You know, I love Glenn Miller and his music," she observed, her appetite for all things American now well and truly whetted.

"Yes, he's all the rage in the States," Pippa counselled, otherwise concerned that her companion's eager rendition of the popular bandleader's score was starting to annoy the couple behind them, the gruff-looking husband in particular dodging his head about to try and see around the flexing shoulders of the jolly WAAF in front.

Otherwise, Pippa was just pleased that her new friend had finally come out of her shell. Indeed, Eileen had been quite withdrawn when she had first arrived at Dunholme back in June – mournful almost. Yet after a few nights out dancing with the Rhodics, or – like tonight – partaking of a girlish jaunt to the cinema, she had revealed a truly magical, fun-loving personality. Her newfound celebrity status aside, nowadays there was never a dull moment whenever Leading Aircraftwoman Eileen Kimberley GC was around!

* * * * *

6.00 am – reveille. Dreams suitably disturbed, the WAAFs roused themselves in their billet, gathered up the things they needed, and donned their greatcoats. Then they drifted outside to complete the necessary ablutions before breakfast was served in the mess hall.

"Bloody hell! This is a pea-souper!" the first airwoman to tiptoe outside exclaimed.

"Yes. There's going to be no flying done today by the look of it," her friend replied upon being confronted with a fog so dense that within a just a few yards of stepping outside they had lost sight of their billet and were having to navigate their way to the wash block by memory.

Pippa and Eileen also warily stepped outside to behold the murky October greyness, pondering that – for all the strategic advantages of locating air stations on the east coast – the downside was that (especially at this time of year) they were liable to be cloaked in dense fog.

"How is it that those two always seem to so lively this time of the morning?" Eileen slurred somnolently, her ears ringing with the giggles of the advance party storming off into the miasma ahead of them.

"Search me, pet. Still at least they woke up in their own beds this morning," Pippa opined, shielding her lips with the back of her hand. "It's a wonder they ever get any sleep after what I've spied them getting up to in the middle of the night!"

By now Eileen could attest to what her friend was hinting at – the discovery that such shocking things took place yet another milestone on the road to parting company with her teenage innocence.

"Let's just hope the corporal doesn't catch them!" she shuddered.

On such a cold, dismal mornings speed was of the essence when completing ablutions. Within no time at all therefore, the girls were washed, brushed, dressed, and ready to endure the ritual of the corporal inspecting their kit to make sure everything was in its place. Over the past two years Eileen had become too proficient to be caught out that easily, but there was always some new recruit whose kit ended up being tipped out on her bed for resorting.

The ritual over, the girls headed off to the mess hall to sample whatever concoction the cook had thrown together this morning. Bringing up the rear, Eileen paused upon hearing that familiar scratching that signalled Polly the Hen at large beneath the boards. It was a minor irritation that she had since learned to live with. Even so, as she hurried off into the pervading gloom outside, something inexplicable goaded her to halt, turn about, and instead stoop down to peer under the gap to see what the fussing fowl was up to this morning. As she did so, she was in for a pleasant surprise.

"Chuck-chuck-chuck-chuck-chicken, lay a little egg for me," was one of the more appropriate verses Eileen had taken to singing – more in hope than expectation. Day-in-day-out, the stupid bird had refused to oblige. And yet today – on this most miserable of autumnal morns – a nice shiny white egg sat invitingly in the pit in the dust that the brooding hen had fashioned.

Eileen scooped it up, thanking Polly profusely. Then she nipped back inside the billet to squirrel the find away for later.

"Get lost in the fog, Kimberley?" the other girls ribbed her when she eventually showed up in the mess hall.

"More likely on the look-out for more dashing young pilots to rescue!" suggested Vera – one of the station meteorologists – whilst poking her fork in the unappetising splodge of powdered-egg that was draped upon her plate.

Eileen kept her counsel. There had to be some perks to being subjected to Polly's incessant scratching when trying to get some shut-eye.

"Anyway," Pippa reminded them all, "I hope you lot haven't forgotten that Waddington are holding a concert tonight. And, canny lass that I am, I've managed to bag some tickets for this most dazzling occasion!"

"Oh, do we have to go?" one of the girls groaned, her protests quickly echoed by the others gathered round.

"Don't be so ungrateful!" Pippa gasped in jest. "And after all this trouble I've gone to on your behalf! Listen, there's a band laid on; and a comedian. What's more, ENSA are despatching a singer up from London especially."

"Well, you know what they say ENSA stands for?" cried Vera.

"EVERY NIGHT SOMETHING AWFUL!" the WAAFs all chanted in unison, reminding each other of the popular refrain.

"Come on, girls. Stop clartin' around, will ya'!" Pippa refused to be deterred, handing out the tickets. "Just get your arses up to the guard house at seven o'clock tonight. There's transport laid on. For goodness sake, it's got to be better than moping about here all night doing 'domestic' chores!"

\* \* \* \* \*

The rugged old truck sauntered through the main gate of RAF Waddington and deposited its neighbouring air station's gaggle of excited WAAFs outside the NAAFI hall. Bursting inside just as the compère was mounting the stage to welcome everybody, they squeezed themselves into one of the rows still unfilled at the back of the darkened hall. Then the band commenced a few numbers that had some of the keener souls swaying before a comedian was trotted out to assail the audience with jokes old and new. Well, perhaps more old than new – though the pipe-puffing officers seated at the front seemed to derive great amusement from them.

"Gosh, I'm sure I heard all these when I saw this guy perform at Binbrook," Vera frowned wearily.

"How about our aircrew drop him on Berlin? If these excruciating gags don't induce old Adolf to surrender nothing will!" someone else quipped to titters all round.

"Shhh!" the NCOs on the row in front turned about to hush them.

Expressing their collective dismay at the tedium of the proceedings was probably not worth the risk of being stuck on a charge for disrupting the performance. Therefore, some of the girls folded their arms in silent protest and willed the comedian to complete his turn. Even the lads from the airmen's mess seated in the opposite aisles looked numbed beyond endurance. Meanwhile, Pippa covered her eyes to conceal a guilty conscience. Whoever this singer was who was supposed to be on next, she'd better be good.

"Ladies and gentleman, put your hands together for the fabulous Max Goddard!" the compère urged, though the staccato response he received probably told him that the 'Fabulous Max' would not be invited back to 'Waddo' in a hurry. He waited while an expectant hush descended upon the audience before stepping up to the microphone again.

"I know how much all you wonderful folks are looking forward to our next act," he chortled hopefully. "However... I'm afraid I have some bad news I have to break to you..."

"The 'Fabulous Max' is doing a second turn!" one of the wags from the ops room catcalled from up the back. For the first time that evening the laughter was truly heartfelt! The compère smiled, but couldn't possibly comment. Instead, he motioned with his hands for the amusement to desist.

"Unfortunately, a few minutes ago I received a telephone call to say that the train she was travelling up on has been cancelled, and that the lovely Rita Bonnington, who was due to sing tonight, cannot now be with us."

There was a unified murmur of disappointment, the compère shrugging his shoulders and throwing up his hands in a vain attempt at an apology.

"Don't tell us we really have got to listen to that joker do another turn!" an airman cried out.

"Yeah! The ruddy joker who can't tell jokes!" someone else barked.

The compère was plainly at a loss what to do or say when, all of a sudden from the back, one of the WAAFs yelled out "Here, pet! Eileen can sing!"

He cupped his eyes beneath the bright stage lights to spy out from whence this offer of possible deliverance had come. As he did, he spotted Pippa rising to her feet to point out the WAAF sat next to her. Mortified, Eileen began to shake her head and protest.

"She certainly can! I've heard her singing each morning to that confounded chicken that nests beneath our billet!" Vera therefore added, to the eager concurrence of her friends around her – determined that their blushing Brummie comrade would not be permitted to deny her talent.

"Yah, Eileen. You can do it, my lady!" a member of 44 Squadron's aircrew whooped in his lush Rhodesian accent, his mates also demanding that their 'little Rooinek Princess' step up to the mark.

"So that's Eileen Kimberley?" one of the dispersal crews gasped.

"Yeah!" another pointed to her in amazement. "She's the WAAF who rescued that Aussie gunner!"

"What? You're the famous Eileen Kimberley," the compère stared out, sharing the awe of the entire room.

Indeed, a hundred or more pairs of disbelieving eyes now alighted upon this timorous airwoman, knowledge of whose presence tonight more than made up for the non-appearance of the 'lovely' Rita. Conversely, Eileen wished for nothing more at that moment than that the floor beneath her feet would just open up and consume her without trace!

"Come on, pet. You have a beautiful voice," Pippa gripped her tenderly by the arm lest she try to flee. "You wanted so much to burst into song in that cinema the other night. Now a real opportunity to do so has presented itself," she urged.

With those heartfelt words ringing in her ears, Eileen finally put aside her embarrassment and gazed around at the sea of eager faces willing her on. Suitably encouraged, she stepped out of her seat, making her way nervously down the aisle towards the stage. Mounting it in trepidation, she allowed herself to be curled beneath the welcoming arm of the concert's thankful host.

"What are you going to sing for us, Eileen?" one of the Rhodies called up.

For a moment she struggled to think what she could possibly sing. Then she remembered those times during the very worst nights of the Birmingham Blitz when she used to huddle together in the air raid shelter with her little cousin, Monica – and a most delightful tune with which she always used to comfort her. She turned and whispered something into the compère's ear. He turned and mumbled something *sotto voce* to the band leader; who nodded his head and in turn put the suggestion to his ensemble of musicians. Thankfully, it was to have been part of the repertoire of the 'lovely' Rita. Hence they had the music to hand, picking up their instruments in readiness. The entire room fell silent when they commenced the intro. Meanwhile, Eileen swallowed hard and stepped up to the microphone.

Barely had her beautiful mezzo-soprano voice glided through the opening stanzas of Walt Disney's classic *'When You Wish Upon A Star'* than every single one of those hundred or more pairs of disbelieving eyes had opened wider still, complemented by mouths also agape in disbelief. Even those fortunate few who had each morning been privileged to catch wind of the crazy Aircraftwoman Kimberley serenading Polly the Hen were left astounded by the breathtakingly rich timbre of such a fine voice. Meanwhile, eyes closed and soaking up the truth conveyed in the lyrics she was singing, it was impossible for Eileen not to let go of meandering tears. It was the first time in many long years that she had stood before an appreciative audience able to loose upon them her incredible vocal dexterity. Nerves resolutely brushed aside, she therefore gave it all she had – the house bristling with awe as she swept to a spine-tingling finale.

There was a fleeting silence in the hall before it erupted in ecstatic foot-stamping and applause – the Rhodies of 44 Squadron, the NCOs, the airmen, the WAAFs, the band leader and his musicians, and the officers present all rising to their feet in a delirious, heartfelt ovation. Eileen drew her slender hands up to face as if to mask from her audience her utter incredulity.

"MORE…! MORE…! MORE…!" they were thundering. So much so that it took several moments before, having raced back onto the stage, the delighted compère could at last restore a hush to the room.

"I think they want you to sing another song, Eileen," he puffed – surely the under-bloody-statement of the entire bloody war so far!

"Yes, come on, Eileen. Sing for us again!" the lads out in the audience implored.

Taking command of her emotions after such a resounding debut, she eventually nodded obligingly and whispered in the compère's ear again.

"Why not!" he grinned and turned to brief the band leader accordingly.

This time, Eileen wasted no time returning to the microphone to announce that "this is a popular little number that I have sung to myself many times during dark moments this year – and to Polly the Hen!" she added, to a ripple knowing laughter. "So if you know the words – and perhaps if you too have experienced dark moments of your own – then sing along with me."

And with that, the band members launched into their introduction and glanced up as Eileen poured out all her frustrations in song – tears again (this time defiant ones) sparkling in her big brown eyes as she belted out the jolly Tommie Connor melody *'Be Like The Kettle And Sing'*.

It was just what was needed. The perfect tonic for a year in which so many of the lads and lasses gathered around her had lost valued comrades and loved ones. They had each learned to get by in the knowledge that they might not live to see the new morn break – none more so that the young aircrews now singing along, one in four of whom would not survive to finish their tour of thirty combat missions. No wonder there was hardly a dry eye in the house when Eileen rallied them one more time to keep alive that flame of hope that one day all this unrelenting grief would surely come to an end.

# *11*

It's always the way that one invariably ends up making the most noise when one is trying ones hardest to be quiet. It was after midnight when the door to the billet inched open and a half-frozen WAAF tiptoed in, hauling her kit bag with her. However, it was while trying to silently locate her bed in the semi-darkness that she stumbled over that kit bag and ended up careering to the floor with a loud clatter – legs akimbo.

"Sorry," she rose to her feet and whispered to those of her somnolent new comrades to whom she had yet to introduce herself, and who glanced up blearily to behold the newcomer before snuggling back under their blankets.

In the blackness Eileen too caught a glimpse of this figure with the blonde curls endeavouring to get undressed and slip into her pyjamas before slithering into a stone cold bed. Having herself only reported for duty at this new posting a few days earlier, she remembered somebody mentioning that another new telephonist was arriving today. Yet from the lateness of her arrival and the clumsiness of her entrance she sounded the sort who would surely attract the ire of her superiors. Eileen rolled over and snuggled under her blankets too.

\* \* \* \* \*

"If you knew what I went through… If you knew how much I loved you… How much I still love you..."

In the half-light of the deserted Moroccan night-spot, barely had those heart-wrenching words tripped from Eileen Kimberley's lips than Humphrey Bogart had embraced her and had pressed his own lips tight against them, her heart palpitating at this final snatched consummation.

Suddenly, the softly-playing strains of *'As Time Goes By'* were replaced by the harsh blast of *'Reveille'*. The dream was over. From balmy Casablanca she had been abruptly transported back to winter-gripped RAF Waterbeach just outside Cambridge – the home of No. 514 Squadron and its Avro Lancasters.

Meanwhile, the sound of that infernal tannoy blaring in her ears was accompanied the sight of two dozen girls slipping out of their beds and into their dressing gowns ready to face the new day.

"Who's the new girl?" one of them pointed to a still-slumbering WAAF buried beneath a jumble of sheets and blankets.

"Search me. But if she doesn't get her arse out of bed sharpish she'll have that new corporal's toe up it!" warned another.

"You're right. I better wake her," Eileen offered, charity towards a fellow human being once again tugging at her heart.

It took a few jolts before that blonde mop and a washed-out face eventually surfaced, the eyes of their owner straining to make sense of her own abrupt exit from the land of dreams.

"Gosh! What's the time? Where am I?"

"Nancy...? It can't be...!"

"Eileen! What are you doing here?"

"I was about to ask you the same question!"

Alas, the lottery that was Royal Air Force posting allocations! But regardless of what chance flourish of a clerk's pen had made it happen, all that mattered at that precious moment was that Eileen Kimberley and Nancy King were back in each others company after almost a year apart. Neither one could quite believe it. The RAF's craziest ever female double act was together again! Whilst the other bemused WAAFs were grabbing their things, this unlikely duo were instead hugging each other tight and sharing a tear-filled moment of rejoicing and thanksgiving.

"Girls, can I introduce you to my very dear friend, Nancy," Eileen crowed once they had rejoined the others in the ablution block.

"Hi, Nancy," a volley of hearty replies echoed from around the wash basins.

"'Wotcha', Nancy. Ah'm Caffy. Caffy Clarke," she found herself being assailed by a pudgy Cockney wench with a gloriously estuarine way of pronouncing the letters 'th'. "'Ere. In't you the new gel' wot' rolled up late last night?" she probed by way of understatement.

"Too right!" Nancy groaned, spreading out her wash kit and hooking up her towel. "I only went and jumped aboard the wrong bloody train at King's Cross. I ended up in Peterborough! Fortunately some American servicemen offered me a lift here – though I still ended up failing to report on time. Now I've lost the opportunity of Christmas leave. They've also stuck me on jankers for the next fortnight cleaning out the washrooms. So don't get stuffing any Nuffields down the pan, ladies. It's Yours Truly here who'll be poking her arm around the bend to fish them out!"

Eileen laughed – as did the other girls. Ever irrepressible, Nancy had lost none of her mischievous ways. Only she could make light of such harsh sanctions – even though it meant mopping floors and unblocking toilets while most of the others would be at home celebrating with their families.

"I reckon yer' must have rubbed that new corporal up the wrong way. 'Er arrived yesterday too. S'pposed to be right cow, 'er is!" Cathy opined, fiddling to hook up a substantial bra that was even so clearly a size or two too small.

"WHAT'S ALL THIS BLOODY RACKET GOING ON HERE THEN?" there suddenly boomed a voice from behind them as the door was thrust open. In strode a brusque and manly NCO to behold the merriment suddenly evaporate as everyone froze to the spot. Glancing around with eagle-eyed curiosity, she then surveyed each scantily-clad airwoman in turn before alighting upon the one sporting that amply-cupped brassiere.

"You. What's your name?" she barked.

"Aircraftwoman First Class 3441042 Clarke… Corporal."

"Well, 'Aircraftwoman First Class whatever-your-number-was'…" she eyeballed the tremulous, rotund Londoner, "Did I perchance hear you casting aspersions upon a certain new NCO on this air station?"

"Er… Wot? Me? No, Corporal," Cathy burbled. "Ah' was just observin' 'ow there seems ter' be a lotta' new girls around 'ere lately."

Stout heels clopped and the eye-balling continued as the feisty corporal strode purposefully about the block, certain that there was a touch of dissembling going on. Otherwise, she was content to observe that Clarke – along with her chastened comrades – had been left in no doubt about who was in charge around here from now on.

"Get ready, you lot. Parade is at 0-800 hours on the dot. For the benefit of those of 'new girls' amongst you who have difficulty telling the time, that's when the big hand is on the twelve and the little hand is on the eight!" she emphasised for effect as she strode past Nancy.

As she strode past Eileen, the new NCO paused for a brief moment.

"Do I know you from somewhere?" she mused, drawing in close to examine that pretty face and those dark locks.

However, the anxious WAAF said nothing and instead carried on staring dead ahead, the obligation to respond removed when the roaming corporal alighted upon the pasty-skinned Aircraftwoman Clarke for a final time.

"And you, Fatso!" she continued, "Put a uniform on over that all that blubber. It's enough to give the poor bloody padre a coronary!"

"Bleedin' cheek!" Cathy grunted once the corporal had strode back out and closed the door behind her.

"Yes, that's the corporal who banged me on a charge last night," Nancy added indignantly.

"Looks like we're in for a thoroughly enjoyable posting them," one of the others surmised.

"Who is that woman anyway?" another WAAF wondered aloud, though the general consensus was that no one had come across her before.

"I know who she is," they were thus surprised to hear Eileen assert, all turning to hear her out. "Harris. That's her name. Muriel Harris. She was on basic training with me at Innsworth. I never liked her then. The bad news is she doesn't suffer fools gladly. The worse news is that she's one of those smug individuals who thinks everyone's a fool – except for her. You may be right, girls. I think we could all be in for an 'interesting' posting."

\* \* \* \* \*

"So why did you never tell anybody that you could sing?"

It seemed a perfectly reasonable question. What's more, huddling together on the back seat of the bus into Cambridge presented Nancy with the perfect opportunity to unravel an enigma that had intrigued her ever since she had first found out on the No. 5 Group grapevine that her best friend had stepped up to a microphone to make such a dazzling, if impromptu showbiz debut.

"I didn't think I could," Eileen replied feebly, staring out of the window.

"But that's silly. People are saying you have an amazing voice. Did you never think about becoming a professional singer?" Nancy probed again. Eileen re-engaged eye contact, but still struggled to verbalise something that was clearly troubling her soul.

"I used to sing when I was a little girl. And yes, once upon a time I dreamed of being a singer... and a dancer. In fact, my Auntie Kathleen paid for me to have dance lessons. I was quite good at them too. However, when Uncle

Michael was killed, and she was forced to work to support herself, it fell to me to look after my cousin Monica. Therefore, I was no longer able to put the time in to attend lessons. Likewise, any hope of ever becoming a singer. And anyway, certain members of my family would not have been enamoured by the thought of me pursuing a career on the stage. Or 'getting ideas above my station', as my grandmother would have called it."

"But surely there was someone who could appreciate what talent you possessed?" Nancy delved.

"My mom was supportive. But then often at the times when I needed her most she had other things on her mind – or, more precisely, other people."

"Yes, I can imagine," her friend sighed, recalling conversations about the matter on previous occasions. Probing further she wondered aloud what Eileen's father would have done had he stuck around, remembering too the photograph of the debonair figure that her comrade still kept beside her bed.

"He would have supported me," was all she would say, resting her head against the window with an air of resignation.

Nancy was no fool. She could read between the lines of a disjointed childhood and an impoverished upbringing that had left her friend without a crucial mentor to encourage her and spur her on towards achieving her dreams. Yet to have observed Eileen gaze up in awe at all those Hollywood movies they had often watched together – scenes much more stirring to the soul, she imagined, than the grimy vista of factories and ramshackle streets that was industrial Birmingham – was to be reminded that those dreams had not been entirely snuffed out. All that would be needed, Nancy remained certain, was a lucky break that would set them ablaze.

"Anyway, I was really sorry that Alistair was... well, you know," Eileen felt minded to mention – another matter that had been burdening her soul.

"I know. I must have cried an ocean that first week I learned he had been killed," Nancy recalled. "But at least he died doing a job he loved and for a cause he believed in. He always told me how he feared growing old. Besides, we were having so much fun racing everywhere on his motorbike that we never gave a second thought to commitment. These days maybe it's better that way. Too many people I have known have given their heart to someone one day only to find that person gone the next. Instead, I have resolved to keep things simple. You do the same, Eileen. Enjoy the good times while they last so that at least you'll be spared the hurt when they're over."

Wise words, Eileen thought – and which increasingly reflected her own outlook with regard to matters of the heart. Although, since that night of jealous rage, Gerald had written to cautiously explore if there was any prospect of them getting back together, she had been resolutely non-committal. Eventually, the letters had stopped and she hoped and prayed that this kind and chivalrous man would soon enough find someone more worthy of his many fine qualities than the flighty young girl from Birmingham who he had had the dubious fortune to surrender his own heart to.

The bus deposited the party of WAAFs in the city centre and the excited throng began to make their way to the appointed venue. One happy outcome of Nancy's misbegotten train adventure the other day was that the Americans with whom she had cadged a lift had told her about a big dance that the United States' 'Mighty Eighth' Air Force had organised to see in the New Year. It hadn't taken Nancy long to wheedle out of them a promise to post some tickets to her. Hence if she had been forced to spend Christmas confined to camp she was determined that the New Year was going to be celebrated in style.

The minute that Eileen, Nancy and the others sauntered through the door it was plain that this was not going to be like any event they had ever been to before. In place of the mawkish stoicism that often characterised British dances and concerts, this particular New Year's Eve bash was positively sizzling with infectious, upbeat optimism. The music too pounded decidedly faster, with a sizeable swing band and a threesome of 'GI Jane' singers belting out *Boogie-Woogie Bugle Boy Of Company B'* – the trio wiggling about on a stage draped with the most enormous Stars-and-Stripes, and in uniforms far more svelte and figure-hugging than anything the WAAFs had ever seen British servicewomen wear. Meanwhile, bunting and decorations trailed from every corner of the cavernous dance hall.

Even the dancing was a world removed from anything that Nancy and Eileen had ever witnessed before. Couples were pulling each other this way and that, waving their arms about, and swinging themselves around at breath-taking speed. The guys were tossing the girls over their shoulders to land on the floor bouncing and spinning, whilst the girls themselves were showing off thighs galore as their skirts swished about with abandon.

Eileen stood there with her pert little mouth open, eyes transfixed with a trepidation that was even so remorselessly surrendering to sheer exhilaration. She had heard about 'jiving' and 'lindy-hopping' before, but had yet to witness either being performed right in front of her very own eyes. She could only too readily imagine Auntie Kathleen swooning at such a spectacle.

"Yes, they don't hang about these Yanks," Nancy enlightened them all above the din. "Whether it's dancing, romancing or chancing their luck with a 'broad' – as they call us women – our Americans cousins seem utterly incapable of doing anything in half-measures. Hold on to your caps, girls. 'Uncle Sam' has come to town. This is going to be one *swell* party!"

"'Ere, look at this pair 'ere. They're goin' at it like the bleedin' clappers!" Cathy meanwhile observed, the poor WAAF's eyeballs darting hither and thither as she watched one particular couple stamping and swirling around the floor at a dizzying pace.

"Hey, you two dames look like you kinda' wanna' join in," suggested a pair of tall, handsome staff sergeants sweeping in to assail Eileen and Nancy.

"Yeah, come on down, ladies. Me and Dick here will show you how it's done," his friend hollered, seizing Eileen by the hand and dragging her onto the dance floor without so much as a by-your-leave. What a contrast to Gerald, who she recalled nervously enquiring if she would mind most awfully accompanying him for their very first dance!

And so the two girls permitted themselves to be coached in all these vigorous, newfangled dance moves, gingerly attempting to master each twist and turn – their partners determined that master them they surely would.

Alas, with each of the other Waterbeach WAAFs also quickly snaffled up by beaming Americans, poor Cathy found herself stood alone watching from the sidelines – a glum frown perhaps confirming every teenage neurosis she must ever have laboured under regarding her less than comely looks and the rather generous proportions of her figure. Imagine then how that downcast demeanour was suddenly transformed upon discovering that those supposedly unlovely qualities might have found favour with someone.

"I say, ma'am. I couldn't help thinkin' that you look kinda' lonely standing there all by yourself," a big, beefy, yet bashful black GI observed in a deep, rumbling voice. Before he had even finished his sentence, it was this coy, coal-coloured chap from Dixie who suddenly found himself being accosted.

"Gawd blimey, mate. Ah' fawt' yer'd never bleedin' ahsk'!" Cathy whooped.

And so too Aircraftwoman Clarke took to the floor, dragging her at first hesitant partner along behind her as together they too launched into an ever more lively interpretation of 'Jumpin' Jive'.

"Wow! One of our girls can certainly move!" Eileen observed.

Exhausted, she and Nancy returned to the periphery to sit the next dance out – fascinated that, in Cathy's case, carrying a few extra pounds around the bust and the waistline was clearly no barrier to niftiness on the dance floor.

"Yes, she's must have been practising all year for this moment. However, studying some of the glowering faces around this place I'm not too sure she was wise in her choice of dance partner."

"What do you mean?"

"I'm told the Yanks don't take too kindly to their Negro countrymen dancing with white girls. And if you're from the Deep South then the kind of things they're getting up to could end up with the poor chap being lynched."

"What do you mean: 'lynched'?" Eileen ventured, rudely disabused of her delightful innocence when Nancy leant over and whispered in her ear.

"What? You mean being hung from a tree? That's terrible!"

"Yes, you wouldn't think we're fighting a war to put an end to that kind of savagery," Nancy scowled, Cathy and her partner still lost in a fury of abandon, oblivious to some of the dismayed glances of their audience.

"Bleedin' 'ell. That geezer dun' arf' know his moves. Wot's more, Ah' fink' ah' got me'self a date. Wilbur's 'is name. Right bleedin' 'an'some, 'e is!" Cathy proudly beamed, puffing and wriggling excitedly as she hauled her tunic back into place, plumping up her voluminous bosom.

It fell to one of the girls from their party to then quietly take her aside and explain to the disappointed young lass why a date with Wilbur might not materialise after all. Meanwhile, it wasn't long before Eileen and Nancy found their company being requested for more dance numbers, each time another pair of dashing GIs showering them with all manner of compliments.

As the night drew on, the three singers retired and in their place a willowy, bespectacled crooner in uniform stepped up to the microphone to offer the happy revellers a selection of slower melodies like *'Imagination'*, *'At Last'* and *'Indian Summer'*. Eileen barely had time to admire his beautiful baritone voice before her company was requested on the dance floor again.

"If I may be so bold, ma'am, I don't think I have ever set eyes on such a beautiful dame as you," her partner complimented her.

She was touched. At least some Americans did old-fashioned chivalry. The young airman held her close and drew in the scent of her perfume (she didn't have the heart to tell him it was only *'Evening In Paris'* – the cheapest and most commonly available smelly water that every WAAF routinely dabbed herself with). Meanwhile, she felt it was time for a little polite confession of her own.

"I love America. It always looks so big and amazing… I'd love to go there one day… Would you mind if I ask where you come from?"

He drew back to glance at her and smile. "Ma'am, I come from a place called Monterey – it's a little town on the Pacific coast of California."

California! Mention of the very name sent a shiver down her spine. How much more American could one get! And so by the time the singer had progressed to the heart-melting *'Serenade In Blue'* – and the clock was ticking away towards the midnight hour – Eileen Kimberley was well and truly lost in a dream. Indeed, not just any old two-dimensional Hollywood celluloid dream. No, it was Friday, December 31st 1943 and this was really happening. At last she was dancing cheek to cheek with a tall, dark, handsome American. And then – much too soon – the music stopped and the bliss was broken.

"TEN… NINE… EIGHT… SEVEN… SIX… FIVE… FOUR… THREE… TWO… ONE… HAPPY NEW YEAR!"

1944 had arrived to a deafening cheer. Everyone quickly linked arms to stomp back and forth in a huge rippling circle as the band launched into a breezy, allegretto rendition of *'Auld Lang Syne'*. Once the music stopped, the mass of revellers then raced about hugging each other. In the melee, Eileen turned to discover that her newfound American admirer was nowhere to be seen – like her swept up by the several hundred delirious souls all shaking hands, kissing, embracing or throwing their caps in the air. Though she searched and searched (and imagined him doing the same) she could not locate him amongst the chopping sea of happy faces. Then suddenly she felt her arm being grabbed from behind.

"Come on, Eileen," Nancy yelled. "It's time to go. We've got just fifteen minutes to make the last bus back to camp!"

Would a spell of jankers really be too high a price to pay for just one last glance at her lofty, sun-bronzed Californian? She would never know. Eager parting kisses rudely interrupted, Nancy had soon corralled Waterbeach's WAAFs together again on the pavement outside for the brisk walk to the bus stop in the cold night air. With everyone safely aboard the bus, there was thus time to blink and remind each other that, yes, the last three-and-a-half hours of inexpressible joy really had happened.

"Oh, my feet ache!" one of them sighed.

"Never mind your ruddy feet. My heart's aching too!" swooned another.

"Yes, wasn't that singer with the fabulous voice just so good looking!"

"It sounds like you girls had a good time then," piped up an acne-speckled airman who had propped his forearms on the back of the seat in front of him. Sat up the back amidst his RAF colleagues, the waft of their breaths and the wooziness in their eyes suggested he and his mates had been drowning their unrequited New Year's Eve sorrows down the local pub.

"Yeah. I suppose you've all been swanning around at that big dance the Yanks organised," surmised another, plainly irritated that invitations to these glitzy occasions seldom extended to any of the men amongst the 'Mighty Eighth's' British allies – and certainly not to the lowly airfield 'erks'.

"No doubt your American buddies have been spinning you all that bullshit about their pilots being able to bomb Jerry better than our boys can!" his mate grunted, reflecting the commonly-held sentiment about their big-spending, big-mouthing and big-schmoozing cousins from across the ocean – overpaid, oversexed... and over here!

"Of course, lads, you know what else the Yanks always say: 'Up with the larks; and to bed with a Wren'," another airman leered. "Trouble is there aren't too many Wrens stationed around Cambridge. So it looks like they're gonna' make do with putting up our WAAFs instead!"

The back end of the bus erupted in ironic laughter that spoke painfully of the hurt and rejection abroad on the faces of these airmen.

"Come on, guys, give us break," Nancy groaned over her shoulder. "We were only dancing with them."

"'Ere, listen, lads. Did you hear that? 'Give us a break'? She's even talking like one of 'em now! What's more, a little bird tells me you WAAFs have also been cavorting with their niggers!"

The acerbic jibe prompted Eileen to turn and behold that the lad who had been leaning on the back of the seat was now burning holes into the back of Cathy's head with eyes ablaze with contempt.

"What? A bloody coon!" he hissed. "Come on, girls. That's not on. It's bad enough you ditching us to go play with the Yanks. But their ruddy wogs?"

"Nah' listen 'ere. Why don't you jealous little pricks just shove off!" Cathy swivelled about on her seat and spat back, her blistering, unladylike turn-of-phrase jolting the other passengers on the crowded bus to stare over their shoulders in disbelief at the porky airwoman. "Wot' duz' it mah'ta where they cahm' from? Or wot' bleedin' colour they are? For Gawd's sake, we're awl' s'posed ter' be fightin' on the same bleedin' side, ain't we!"

She then turned to face the front again and angrily folded her arms for effect before huffing "An' there wuz' me finkin' only Adolf bleedin' 'Itler an' them bleedin' Nahtzi' geezers wuz' s'pose ter' get awl' aerated about stoopid' fings' like that!"

Nancy couldn't resist a wry smile. If not exactly laced with Churchillian prose about 'broad, sunlit uplands' or 'tormented generations' marching forth 'serene and triumphant from hideous epochs' then the blistering rebuke of this unschooled East End lass had not only put the lads firmly in their place, but had captured the essence of the great struggle in which they were contending far more concisely than even the master orator himself could have done.

\* \* \* \* \*

"Waterbeach 848, which number do you require...? Thank you... Go ahead, caller, you're connected..."

"Switchboard... Yes, sir, of course. That's Norwich 1957. Please wait while I try that number for you... Go ahead, Wing Commander, you're connected..."

After two years on the job, Eileen and Nancy could work the switchboards with their eyes shut. Although things could get hectic, and (like all jobs) there were good days and bad days, they loved their work as telephonists. If it was busy and there were important ops going on then the time passed quickly.

After this afternoon's particularly gruelling shift they hung up their headset and made their way to their billet with the self-satisfied glow of having 'done their bit' in the great struggle their country was engaged in. With the pale February sunshine casting long shadows over the Lancasters being readied for yet another mission by the dispersal crews, Eileen pondered aloud the prospect of a nice hot soak in the bath.

"Well make sure you leave some water for me," Nancy ribbed her as they swapped gossip and traded ideas for how they might spend their leave. Nancy reminded Eileen that there was still an open invitation to join her at her parent's delightful cottage deep in the New Forest.

"KIMBERLEY!" they suddenly heard a wearily familiar voice boom out across the airfield. Both girls froze before nervously turning about. Sure enough, their 'favourite' NCO was wearing her usual iron scowl.

"Corporal," Eileen acknowledged anxiously, trying to second guess what minor infraction of King's Regulations she might have committed that had warranted the fierce-tongued Corporal Harris waylaying her

"Where might you be off to, girl?"

"I was going to run a bath, Corporal."

"Well, I'm afraid bath time has been cancelled. The station commander himself wants to see you – immediately."

"Er... Yes, Corporal."

"Well, go on, girl. Off you go and see what he wants," Harris barked.

"Yes, Corporal."

She wandered off in the direction of the admin block, leaving Nancy to worry that whatever her friend had done must be serious if no less a personage than the station commander was requesting her presence at this late hour.

"And what are you gawping at, Aircraftwoman King?"

"Nothing, Corporal."

"Well, the station commander doesn't want to see *you*. So thank your lucky stars, you horrible little reprobate. Now be on your way."

"Yes, Corporal."

Give someone some stripes and see what a monster they become. While Nancy hurried away and prepared to take her bath, Eileen eventually found her way to Group Captain Parker's office and nervously knocked on his door.

"Come in."

"Leading Aircraftwoman Kimberley, sir. You requested to see me," Eileen stood to attention and saluted, fearing the worst – more so when she noticed that the WAAF squadron officer was also standing there alongside him.

"That's right, Kimberley. This won't take long," he bade her, drawing his chair up to his desk more fully and plucking some sheaves of paper from a file that had been dropped on it. He sucked on his pipe and finally found the one was looking for.

"Now, first of all, I'm afraid I've got a spot a bad news to break to you," he opened, tweaking his moustache. "Namely, the leave that is due to you next week will unfortunately have to be cancelled."

Damn! Eileen had been looking forward to meeting Nancy's folks too. However, of more concern to the anxious airwoman who was trying hard not to gulp with apprehension was the reason why she was suddenly to be denied this privilege. Again, she racked her brain trying to recall what misdemeanour Corporal Harris might have reported that had left the station's most senior WAAF officer with little choice but to refer the matter up to be dealt with by the CO himself.

"The good news," Group Captain Parker continued, "is that the RAF will make good that leave at a later date. For now though I have to inform you that the Air Ministry, in its infinite wisdom, has decided that it wants Bomber Command to undertake a little exercise to keep the general public abreast of what we are up to. To this end, they have requested that Group despatch a few of its more high-profile personnel on a tour of some of the towns and cities that play host to important war industries. Talk to the workers, give a few speeches, sign a few autographs – that kind of thing. The intention is that this tour should be a bit of a morale booster.

"Now unfortunately these Air Ministry types don't inhabit the same planet as the rest of us, Kimberley. Therefore, I have had to tell them bluntly that, with operations running at their current levels of intensity, I really can't spare any of my aircrew to go swanning off on jaunts around factories. Therefore, your squadron officer here had the wizard idea that I offer to despatch you in their place. After all, you are one of only a handful of women to have ever been awarded a George Cross for gallantry. And your story about rescuing that Australian gunner should stir the women who work in these industries. Who knows, your example may even help boost the recruitment of a few more WAAFs – or at the very least sell a few more war bonds."

To say Eileen was surprised would not have done justice to the excitement laced with trepidation that was swirling inside her head at that moment. She had never given a speech before. She didn't even know how!

"Of course, it will mean you will be away from Waterbeach for about a fortnight. However, your squadron officer here will fill you in on all the practicalities. Make no mistake, Kimberley, without the work these civilians do our aircrew out there would have no planes to fly or bombs to drop. It is therefore an immense privilege for a young airwoman like you to be chosen to be the public face of the Royal Air Force. I trust therefore that you will at all times comport yourself in a manner worthy of that privilege."

"Er, yes, sir. I will, sir."

"Leading Aircraftwoman Kimberley, you will report to my office at 0-800 hours tomorrow with your kit packed and your uniform smart – and I mean smart!" the squadron officer instructed her. "You will then be handed your itinerary; and transport will be laid on for you as appropriate. Otherwise I suggest you retire early tonight and make preparations for your departure."

"Yes, ma'am."

"Good luck, Kimberley," Group Captain Parker bade her, sinking back into his chair and sucking his pipe through a satisfied grin. "And remember," he removed the pipe, winking and employing it to lecture her indulgently, "don't let the side down."

# 12

The deed had been done. Yet though he had some money in his hand to show for selling back that three-stone diamond cross-over ring it was nowhere near what he had paid for it. But then Flight Sergeant Gerald Graham guessed the little backstreet jeweller in Cambridge from whom he had purchased it wasn't in the business of philanthropy – even towards a hapless young serviceman who had witnessed his high hopes of love dashed so cruelly.

Though he had implored her to change her mind, he had now resigned himself to the fact that Eileen Kimberley was out of his life for good. As such, the ring would never grace the finger of the woman he loved. It was a bitter pill to swallow, made palatable only by the uncanny news that the Canadian pilot he had caught her in the arms of that evening had perished on a mission the very next night. However, Eileen had rebuffed his pleading that they let bygones be bygones and start over again. This was perhaps the most galling aspect of all about their doomed romance. How else could a man take it other than as a damning indictment upon him personally? Or was it really just the case (as the modest flight engineer suspected) that he had never dreamed big enough to capture the heart of this intriguing woman – who, though lowly of birth and circumstance herself, seemed destined to be eternally searching for something more than a prospective provincial garage manager could offer?

Having exited the shop, he sank his hands in his pockets and paused on the street outside. There he stared up at the leaden skies and ached to know if anyone could ever fill the gaping void in his life that Eileen had now left. Eventually, from out of the corner of his eye, he noticed the jeweller open the partition to place the ring back on display in the shop window. Unable to resist, Gerald drifted back over and spent a final moment studying the gorgeous band of gold and pondering what could have been. However, he knew he had to let go of such futile longing – as indeed he had now done of the ring that symbolised it. Therefore, with a heavy heart, he turned and merged back into the throngs of pedestrians and cyclists going about their business. He just hoped that the guy who bought it next would have better luck in love than he had – as would his sweetheart who would finally have the joy of wearing it.

\* \* \* \* \*

After all her trepidation, Eileen Kimberley's two week sojourn touring the factories that built the planes and the munitions works that made the bombs had been a triumphant success. The delegation from RAF Bomber Command had visited the Vickers bomber factory in Blackpool, the Rolls Royce aero-engine works in Derby, the Handley Page factory in Liverpool, and the Stirling bomber factory in Swindon, as well as the great munitions works outside Glasgow. They had been well received by a civilian workforce that was totally committed to fashioning the tools without which the Royal Air Force could not have delivered the war so directly to the enemy.

Meanwhile, Eileen had been content to modestly recount how she had come by the George Cross medal that adorned her uniform, the making of rousing speeches having mercifully fallen to her officer colleagues. Proud of all they had accomplished together on their morale-raising tour, she was heartened that it should be drawing to a close barely a few miles from where she had been born and had grown up.

The Austin Motor Works at Longbridge on the south-western fringes of Birmingham was one of many 'shadow' factories that had been given over to military production upon the outbreak of war. In particular, it had played its part in churning out the Spitfire and Hurricane fighter planes that had won the Battle of Britain in 1940. In late 1942 it had been granted a contract to build one hundred and fifty Avro Lancaster bombers.

The Bomber Command delegation had toured the labyrinth of underground tunnels beneath the factory to meet and talk with those women who laboured day and night to machine the components and put together the sub-assemblies that went into the finished product. They had been privileged too to watch the first aircraft of that delivery roll off the production line (or rather on account of the factory's short runway nearby, the Longbridge Lancasters would roll off in several parts, to be transported across the city to the airfield at Elmdon for the final marriage of wings and fuselage.

At the end of this historic day, the workers found themselves downing tools in order to gather together and listen to a short address by the factory's management – as well as by the Lord Mayor of Birmingham adorned in his civic chains of office, who thanked the Bomber Command delegation on behalf of the city. Not only was the long canteen where the impromptu ceremony took place packed to capacity, but there was great excitement abroad amongst the women piling through the doors in their headscarves and oily overalls that one of their own was amongst them: Leading Aircraftwoman Eileen Kimberley, the plucky little WAAF telephonist from Selly Oak whose exploits they had all read about in the newspapers.

Soon it was time for the members of the delegation to step up to the microphone and say a few words of encouragement. However, after the obligatory applause for the gung-ho speeches of her male officer companions, Eileen was surprised to hear that it was a different voice that the workers really wanted to hear.

"Where's our Eileen?" someone called up from the back.

"Yeah, she's the one we've all come here to hear. And we ay' gooin' back to work until we do!" another woman reminded them.

The worthies on the platform took such cries in the good humour they were intended. Notwithstanding that the object of their fierce admiration was turning a brighter shade of bashful scarlet with each hollered summons from the factory floor, the Lord Mayor and Eileen's officer colleagues beckoned her forward. Feeling unable to resist their calls, she therefore nervously wandered up to the microphone to say something to them – Brummie to Brummie. Yet this humble, working class girl – who prior to enlisting in the WAAF had left school at fourteen and worked as an assistant in a ladies' fashion store – had never made a speech before; and certainly not to an expectant audience that, from staring out across the sea of heads heaving in front of her, she guessed numbered several hundred strong.

"Er... Er..." she fumbled, the microphone oscillating. "Unfortunately... I'm not very good at, er... making speeches. And I don't think I can really add that much to what has already been said," she apologised, painfully aware that such a paucity of eloquence did not exactly constitute much by way of a spur to greater effort in the struggle for victory.

"It doh' matter, bab. Yer' the best little wench ter' come outta' Brum in a long time!" someone assured her.

"Yes, love. We're all proud of yer'!"

Eileen smiled in self-effacement. She felt so unworthy of their esteem.

"Our brother's away in the RAF. He serves on the bombers," she then spotted a young lass suddenly cry out to her workmates. "He tells me Eileen can sing too. He heard her once at a concert," she added for good measure.

It was a revelation that instantly set the canteen afire. From amidst the hubbub of hundreds of excited voices, others began to spot a way that their tongue-tied heroine might assuage their desire that she 'speak' to them.

"Sing for us then, Eileen!"

"Yeah, come on, bab. Give us a song. Gladys here can play the piano for yer' if yer' shy, like!"

"Ar'. 'Er's good too. Doh' need no music. 'Er' can play by ear, like. Yow' tell 'er what yow' wanna' sing, luv, an' 'er'll accompany yer'."

Before Eileen could even think of protesting, the matronly Gladys was bodily heaved all the way from the back of the canteen to the old upright piano at the foot of the stage. There she sat down and smiled up obligingly, placing herself at the willing service of the quivering airwoman – who was at that moment desperately racking her brain for a song, the words to which she had memorised. What's more, one that would strike a chord, so to speak, with these steadfast and determined women whose fathers, husbands and sons were away at the front – whether that front was the one-in-waiting now amassing in southern England, or the ones being valiantly contested in the mountain passes of Italy and the steamy jungles of Burma; whether it be the 'front' that was braving U-boats and mountainous seas in the North Atlantic, or the one over the skies of Germany (where the toil of their very own hands would soon be in action). Then, at last, it came to her. She crouched down to mutter something to the indomitable Gladys, who took a moment to string it together in her head before nodding eagerly. Then Gladys returned to the piano and Eileen returned to the microphone, clearing her throat.

"This is something I'd like to dedicate to all you women; and to your loved ones too – where ever they might be. I pray they will be back with you soon. But until then…" she smiled, trying not to weep.

She need not have bothered. Even as Gladys was tinkling the ivories for an intro Eileen could sense tears beginning to well up in other eyes as her audience fell silent and listened on as she sang out *'We'll Meet Again'*.

The lowly works canteen felt as if its very roof was about to be lifted off – if not by the almost palpable release of tension as hearts wearied by five long years of war and separation warmed again to those stirring words, then certainly on account of the awe in which they beheld them being articulated. For this was the voice of one of their own, from their own fair city; from one of their own ordinary neighbourhoods. As more salty tears streamed from eyes touched by her amazing voice, it gave Eileen the confidence to throw herself body and soul into what she was singing.

"Come on, sing it with me!" she broke to implore them. With no hesitation, this they did – man and woman; worker and manager; air force officer; and even the good old Lord Mayor himself…!

> *"…We'll meet again.*
> *Don't know where, don't know when.*
> *But I know we'll meet again some sunny day!"*

\* \* \* \* \*

"Blimey, Cathy! What's this?"

"This," Waterbeach's Cockney cook explained, her chunky hands heavy-handedly wielding a ladle, "is good ol'-fashioned plain cookin'. Jus' like me' muvva' awlways' served up."

Eileen and Nancy could agree on at least one of those adjectives. As they stared down they could see the breakfast that Aircraftwoman Clarke had unceremoniously dolloped on their mess tray was plain alright.

"Besides, there's a bleedin' war on in case you've forgotten. Wot' wiv' rationin' and awl' that, yer' can't get yer' bleedin' 'ands on fings like yer' used to."

The rationing they understood. The abysmal presentation of the food served up was another matter. However, when Cathy invited them to take it up with her superior, the two girls politely declined. The catering officer was a fearsome enough woman even when she was in good mood!

"I bet they have bigger and better portions than this in the officers' mess," Nancy muttered beneath her breath as they wandered away to locate a table.

"Yes. Come back Polly the Hen, all is forgiven!" Eileen groaned.

"I'm sorry?"

"She was this chicken that used to burrow beneath my billet when I was stationed in Lincolnshire. I discovered that if I sang to her she would lay me an egg. If this is the best the cookhouse can come up with then I can see I'm going to miss that old bird."

"I can understand why. By all accounts, you've had other audiences spellbound with that incredible voice of yours too."

Eileen tried to be more modest, but it was written all over her face. She concurred with the rumours that were circulating around the camp about how well received her recent factory tour had been (though she endeavoured not to sound too pleased with herself as they sat down).

"I think it's safe to say the CO was impressed too," she admitted. "He was full of praise... Offered me promotion to corporal... And a promise that if I'm successful in that role to maybe recommend me for officer training."

"Gosh! That's marvellous news!" Nancy's face lit up. However, it was noticeable that Eileen's hadn't.

"I asked if he would permit me time to think about his kind offer."

"You did what? Oh, Eileen! You'd make a superb NCO… and an officer. Besides, at least then you won't have the likes of that insufferable Corporal Harris on your back every five minutes."

Eileen winced – and not just from rolling another forkful of Cathy's breakfast on her tongue. "I don't think I could. I'm not cut out to give orders to people. It's not what I was born to do. And anyway, you'd make a better one. You have a wonderful knack of organising things and people – like that New Year's Eve dance we so enjoyed."

"Fat chance! With my record of jankers as long as your arm!"

Nancy's tongue also wrestled with something that had surfaced in Cathy's breakfast offering before it was free to respond to Eileen's other observation.

"So what were you *born* to do?"

They had spoken often enough during the last few weeks for Eileen to be sure Nancy had a pretty good idea already. It was redolent in all the many words of encouragement she had offered her friend. Now, at last, Eileen herself finally felt confident enough to articulate that answer for herself.

"This may sound silly. But I believe I was born to sing."

The earnest look in Nancy's big blue eyes told her that she did not consider her reply remotely silly. "You were indeed," she confirmed. "One day the world will realise that. And, believe you me, if there was any power I possessed that would draw forward that day then I wouldn't hesitate to use it."

There was a moment of profound silence between them of the kind that only true friends can ever know. Yet it was over too quickly. Eileen blushed and carried on picking at her unappetising breakfast.

"Anyhow," Nancy continued, "Changing the subject, I have an enormous favour to ask of you. You remember that American guy who gave me a lift when I wound up in Peterborough by mistake?"

"The one who posted you the tickets for the New Year's Eve dance? The one who also had his eye on you the whole night long?"

"That's him. Well, it would appear he is looking to call in his debts. And unfortunately I don't think I can put him off any longer. He is now pestering me for a date. Trouble is, I'm not entirely sure I fancy him. Therefore, knowing you're off this Saturday I have taken the liberty of agreeing to a date – subject to it being a double date."

"And you want me to make up the double date?"

"In a word: yes."

"But you know any Saturday night pass nowadays means 'dancing'?"

"Yes, and I'm sorry," Nancy sighed, aware of how addictive opportunities to swirl about to lively numbers like *'American Patrol'*, *'String of Pearls'* and *'Little Brown Jug'* had become to all those WAAFs like Eileen whose faces would also light up at the mere thought.

"Please, Eileen. I wouldn't ask – except that I desperately need your moral support. Anyway, apparently his friend is a real dish of a guy. A pilot no less. Nicky, he's called: one of the guys skippering those big Flying Fortresses."

Dish – pilot – Nicky – Flying Fortress. Like a prize angler cunningly reeling out a line, Nancy could detect Eileen edging closer to the bait as each titbit of information was fed out. In no time at all she was hooked.

"Okay. Just for you – because you're my best friend," she conceded, as they headed out of the mess hall to their duties,

"Good. I'll give him a bell and ask him to book a table in the city. And no chickening out at the last minute!"

"KIMBERLEY! KING!"

Corporal Harris's gruff bark once again stopped both girls dead in their tracks, turning their heads to observe her come striding towards them. They stood to attention to await revelation of what trouble they might have inadvertently strayed into now.

"Corporal?"

"A word," the burly corporal insisted with ominous laconism, drawing in closer to eyeball them both. "It has come to my attention that certain WAAFs on this station have been arranging little assignations in secluded spots with male personnel from that American fighter base just up the road. You reprobates wouldn't happen to be engaging in such activities, would you?"

The two airwomen looked at each other genuinely mystified. "No, Corporal."

"Neither of us has a boyfriend at the moment," Eileen added truthfully (well, truthfullish: at least up until this coming Saturday night, she hoped!).

Harris scanned them up and down with that familiar beady eye that she reserved for those of her charges who she suspected of dissembling to her. However, perhaps she too could discern that they were telling the truth, for the beady eye relented and she stepped back out of their faces.

"Yes, well. That makes a change. But then I suppose with all this 'singing' you've been doing lately you can't find the time to chase one now, can you," Harris scoffed, confirming Eileen's prognosis that it was envy as much as an arbitrary desire to torment that had of late prompted the nit-picking corporal to constantly upbraid her over petty matters.

"Of course, if you do find out who has been sneaking out to indulge in such reprehensible immorality I trust you will confide that information to me."

"Of course, Corporal."

"Suffice to say, if I do find out that one of my girls has been hitching her skirt in the local woods then she will rue the day she ever set eyes on that sex-starved Yank... and on his willing appendage. Do I make myself clear?"

"Yes, corporal."

"Please, Lord, I pray you will change Eileen's mind about that promotion," Nancy lifted her eyes heavenwards and mumbled once safely out of earshot.

"Oh, and by the way...!" they heard the NCO bawl in parting. Horror-struck, Nancy suddenly feared she might not have been far enough out of earshot of the omnipresent Corporal Harris. They turned about again.

"I almost forgot. I thought you might both want to congratulate me. I have received a letter this morning confirming my promotion to the rank of sergeant," Harris beamed.

It was the first time during their entire posting that either of them had witnessed this wasp-chewing martinet even attempt to smile. Perhaps she had wind! Perhaps Cathy had been serving up that stomach-curdling mish-mash of a breakfast in the NCOs' mess too!

"Congratulations, Corporal," said Nancy, forcing a grin.

"We mean Sergeant," Eileen corrected her.

"Please, Lord, will you change Eileen's mind about applying for that officer training too!" Nancy prayed a second time, this time in deadly earnest and after making sure Corporal, nay Sergeant Harris was definitely out of earshot.

\* \* \* \* \*

Be outside the enchanted little restaurant in Cambridge at seven-thirty, Nancy's date had advised. This the girls had managed just in time, having legged it from the bus stop as fast as their civvy high heels had permitted; on gorgeous legs that had even so received a coating of gravy browning that Cathy had smuggled out of the kitchen. Gently applied – and with a pencil-line painted up the back of their calves – only the brush of a hand would reveal that they were not wearing real stockings. And on a first date they swore an oath that neither of the two American aviators they now met up with would be permitted to brush their hands anywhere down there!

"Wow! Ladies, we are so glad you're able to make it," Nancy's prospective suitor enthused, scanning them both up and down and being permitted instead to land a gentle kiss of greeting upon each of their cheeks.

"It was touch and go, I'll tell you," Nancy puffed. "Our new sergeant is on the warpath for WAAFs who are dating off the camp. She doesn't particularly like men; and she certainly doesn't like American men."

"So we told her we were off to the cinema instead," Eileen chuckled, relieved (like Nancy) to be out of uniform for once – and feeling wonderful and womanly again on account of it.

"Well, now we're all here I guess we better make some introductions. I'm First Lieutenant Fred Garrett," her suitor exclaimed, reaching over to seize Eileen's hand. "...And this is my good buddy, First Lieutenant Nicky Braschetti. We're both 'Ragged Irregulars' with the 322nd Squadron, 91st Bombardment Group. We're based at Bassingbourn, not far from here."

"Pleased to meet you, ma'am," Nicky acknowledged as he leant forward to shake their hands – Nancy's first and then her friend's.

As his hand slipped around Eileen's and lingered, there was a tangible warmth and gentleness to it that matched his voice. He offered her a lush smile.

"I'm Leading Aircraftwoman Nancy King. And this is my best friend, Leading Aircraftwoman Eileen Kimberley," Nancy rounded off the introductions as the waiter breezed in to usher them to their table. She smiled too – a cunning smile discerning that, whatever romantic openings the voluble and persistent Lieutenant Garrett was hoping would accrue from tonight's date, Nicky and Eileen were not going to be disappointed.

"So tell me, ladies. Where are you both from?" Garrett opened.

"I'm from Hampshire: a little village called Nomansland."

"Nomansland? Gee, that sounds like the middle of a war zone," her date exclaimed, intrigued that Americans weren't the only ones who went in for strange or exotic place names.

"Nothing could be further from the truth. Where I live is set deep in the New Forest. Lovely and peaceful – with wild horses roaming on the common. Mind you, last time I was home there were tanks, trucks and field guns everywhere – and GIs! It really did seem like the middle of a war zone. So that's put paid to Mum and Dad's peace and quiet – at least for the duration!"

"On behalf of the United States Department of Defense, I formally apologise," Garrett jovially placated her, liberally refilling both her glass and Eileen's as a sop – and as if wartime 'five shilling meals' had been suspended. In fact, neither girl was indifferent to how dining out with a Yank invariably meant a surfeit of everything. Perhaps they just left larger tips.

"How about you, Eileen?" Nicky enquired across the table. "Where do you come from?"

Aware this was going to sound a terrible anti-climax after the way Nancy had so eloquently described her enchanted rustic abode, she ventured timidly "I come from Birmingham. It's England's second biggest city. Lots of industry; lots of factories. Not many horses though, I'm afraid – apart from the ones belonging to the milkman, the coalman and the rag-and-bone man."

"Then we have things in common, I guess," Nicky looked her in the eye. "I come from Chicago. That's also a very big city – on the Great Lakes. It too has lots of industry; lots of factories. And tell me, what's a 'rag-and-bone man'?" he flashed a mystified smile. These were definitely two people separated by a common language.

"It's like… well, someone who takes away all your old household junk – the things that you no longer want," she tried to explain, her heart fluttering as she spoke – and not just on account of the quirky manner in which these Americans pronounced 'leff-tenant' as 'loo-tenant', or the curious way they handled a knife and fork! Nicky's face seemed somehow familiar too.

"Oh, you mean a scrap collector," Garrett loudly raced in to answer, annoyingly fitting the stereotype of a brash American. No wonder Nancy's face spoke of indulgent annoyance.

Nicky, however, was tender and gracious in every way. Though he was an officer in the United States Army Air Force, and a pilot of one of those famed B17 Flying Fortresses, at no point did he seek to brag about the fact – unlike his colleague who (with dramatic hand movements to match) wasted no time recounting how he had manoeuvred his plane to throw off all those pesky German fighters. Even Nicky's discreet steel-rimmed spectacles seemed to belie his status as a flyer – although a passing reference to the matter prompted him to modestly recount how, though he had passed the sight test during basic training, like many flyers his vision had deteriorated since being posted to England over a year ago. Once again, studying those spectacles reminded Eileen that his face was indeed familiar.

"So what did you do before you enlisted?" she quizzed him eagerly.

"I taught physics in a junior high school. I believe that's equates to teaching fourteen year-olds in your country," he recounted, fourteen being the age at which Eileen had left school – though she considered it meet not to tell him so. She was self-conscious that she found herself again playing at being cultured and educated in order to impress (and once more wondering whether those of her listeners who truly were cultured and educated were ever really fooled).

"So why become a pilot?"

"The science degree helped. And I guess the Draft Board kinda' thought if I could control a class of surly eighth-graders then I must be officer material! Besides, flying sounded kinda' fun – much more fun than marching men across muddy fields, or rolling around the ocean in a destroyer. So in the blink of an eye I progressed from 'Ninety Day Wonder' to skippering a 'Queen' over here on your side of the Pond."

For her part, Eileen was conscious that she could either deflect the conversation whenever it risked her having to expose her humble background and her complicated home situation – as she had sought to do with Gerald – or she could be upfront about it. Yet there was something genuine about Nicky that coaxed her to adopt the latter course. She was rewarded with another of his self-effacing jokes. She chuckled again.

It was a sweet chuckle that Nicky had fallen in love with the first time he had heard it. Unlike her middle class best friend, who had so much to say, Eileen was content to listen as well as talk. Once he had put her at ease that her background was not so different from that of his own immigrant parents on Taylor Street – Chicago's working class 'Little Italy' – she permitted him to elaborate for her benefit, soaking it all up as a flower would the passing rain.

"…So, you see, like you, my parents weren't people of means. In fact, they struggled to put me through college. I kinda' guess it helped that I could sing. Not only did I get to serve in the choir of the Holy Name Cathedral, but it enabled me to land an occasional job in a nightspot to help out."

"You can sing?" she sat up, eyes open wide to expose the fire igniting inside them. Then the penny dropped – Nicky was the vocalist with the gorgeous crooning voice who had rounded off that New Year's Eve dance! All of a sudden, no more was Eileen Kimberley the crablike enquirer willing to be flattered by this tall, handsome twenty-five year-old. Now she really was hanging on his every word.

"Hell, yes! Nick can sing!" Garrett interjected loudly again. "Why between missions this guy's performances are the toast of the 'Mighty Eighth'! I tell you, Eileen, you are looking at the next Frank Sinatra – sitting right here making eyes at you!"

Nicky blushed awkwardly and shrugged yet more self-effacement. However, whilst the others proffered amusement at such untoward modesty, they failed to spot that a fire had been ignited in Nancy's eyes too.

"Gosh! That is a coincidence," she announced, her words oozing opportunistic glee. Spotting and seizing Eileen's moment on her behalf, she added "Eileen can sing too. NAAFI concerts; factory tours. Why, she's the darling of Bomber Command."

All of a sudden, it was Eileen's turn to join Nicky by feigning modesty and spluttering nervous laughter. Then, staring across at each other tentatively, these two prospective lovers wondered whether they might have even more in common than they had first realised.

\* \* \* \* \*

*April 3ʳᵈ 1944.*

*Dear Mum,*

*Thank you for your last letter. I'm sorry to hear than Granny passed away suddenly. I will try my best to obtain a pass to come home for the funeral. I am pleased you and Eric are such good friends. I hope this new guy makes you happy. You have endured so many bad things in your life. As you often say, everybody has the right to be happy. Perhaps Granny's going to be with Our Lord will mark a new chapter in which we can put what is past behind us and both find happiness.*

*Talking of happiness, I simply must tell you about a most amazing man I have met. He is an officer in the United States Army Air Force near where I am stationed. His name is Nicolino Braschetti – though everyone calls him Nicky. His surname is Italian, and is pronounced BRA-SKETTY – though most of his friends pronounce it BRA-SHETTY (and he has given up correcting them!).*

*We have been dating for a few weeks now, and he enjoys many of the things I do. We go to the cinema and dances together. Wherever we go, he never fails to treat me with the utmost respect. He is a true gentleman. And he can sing too! In fact, he's going to see if I can join him and sing at one or two of those fabulous concerts the Yanks are always putting on. He's also a good Catholic – so Auntie Kathleen will be pleased!*

*I am so looking forward to it. I don't think there has ever been a time in my life when I have been more thankful to be alive. All of a sudden so many amazing opportunities are opening up before me. Dare I say, but I think for the first time too I am truly in love with someone. In fact, it must be love – Nicky has even convinced me to give up smoking! Oh Mum, please pray for me. Ask Auntie Kathleen to pray for me too – because I know Our Lady always listens to her. Pray that, at last, my dream of being able to sing might come true; and that I might have found that wonderful special star that Dad used to say belongs to each one of us if only we will find the courage to reach out for it.*

*Your ever-loving daughter,*
*Eileen*

\* \* \* \* \*

In the flat, featureless fens of Cambridgeshire there were few hiding places. Yet here, deep in this isolated forest, a besotted young couple could finally be alone together for a few precious hours.

To be sure, Wilbur's jeep had come in handy for negotiating the rutted trail that wound off the main road, and upon which he and Cathy eventually arrived at the familiar clearing. He extinguished the engine and together these two unlikely lovers slipped out from their seats to savour their solitude for a moment. Staring up around them, they marvelled how once again they had only the birds in the treetops for an audience. Meanwhile, the ground had been baked firm by warm spring sunshine that had been beating down upon it through the opening in the surrounding tall oaks. The days were getting longer too, affording them greater scope for indulging in their illicit pleasure.

"Ah' got summat' to show you, Miss Cathy. An' ah' think you gonna' like it real good," Wilbur chortled in his deep, lyrical Southern drawl. As he loosened his tunic, a wide and wicked albino grin thrust out his ebony cheeks.

He wandered around to the back of the jeep and lifted the cover on the precious cargo he had brought with him, unveiling a small, box-like device that revealed itself to be an air force radio set.

"Oh, Wilbur. Yer' such a darlin', ain't ya'!" Cathy marvelled, ever touched by the thoughtfulness of her gentle giant of a boyfriend.

"Now we no longer have to hum along by ah'selves, Miss Cathy. Ah' reckon we gonna' be able to jitterbug in style – just like all dem' white folks on the dance floor," he proudly announced.

Rigging the device up to a spare truck battery he had also secreted out of the camp, he then switched it on, tuning it until it homed in on a station.

*"...This is the BBC Home Service... Here is the news... After weeks of intense fighting, British and Indian troops have finally broken a determined siege by the Japanese army at Imphal..."*

Cathy wagged a stubby finger disapprovingly. Therefore, Wilbur twiddled with the dial again and alighted upon something more conducive to an afternoon's snatched intimacy, turning up the volume as loud as he dared. While the drummer was busy pounding out a crazy jungle beat, he seized his beloved by the hand and hurried her onto the patch of flat ground that they had cleared on an earlier occasion. Then the brass section of the orchestra wailed like an elephant. Suddenly there was no stopping these two seemingly oddball jitterbuggers as Benny Goodman's electrifying *'Sing Sing Sing'* poured forth from the tinny speaker.

Wilbur pushed her away then pulled her close again, Cathy sliding between his legs to emerge spinning on the other side. Following a wiggle or two of those broad hips that Cathy dug her stubby fists into – as well as a bit more finger-wagging, this time purely for dramatic effect – she then found herself being hauled back again and launched effortlessly up and around his big broad shoulders. Whether it was Artie Shaw, Duke Ellington or Ella Fitzgerald coming through their little makeshift radio, Wilbur and Cathy were confident that their frenetic interpretations of these insane swing rhythms could best those of any other couple on their imaginary dance floor.

If only. Alas, they knew their respective fellow countrymen would never accept their teamwork and proficiency – still less their romantic relationship. However, in this small clearing in deserted ancient woodland, the stout, pale-skinned WAAF cook and the bear-like, black American stores driver were at liberty to indulge in their shared passion for dance – away from the censure of a world that worried too much about 'stoopid fings' like the colour of ones skin. Instead, here were two people gloriously in love, celebrating the music that had first drawn them together and that expressed all the joy in their souls.

Here, if only for a precious hour or two, these two quintessential outsiders could spin merrily around and – by so doing – maybe reach up to seize hold of their own humble star in the heavens.

# 13

Leave had been cancelled. Aircraft were coming and going almost around the clock. Indeed, on this June morning there was a gathering awareness amongst everyone that something big was going on. Little clues were everywhere to be seen: the increased intensity of flying operations; the sudden mass movement of troops and equipment during the preceding days, and which had been clogging up the roads heading south. Then finally, the suspense was over: RAF Waterbeach fell silent and everyone stopped what they were doing as the tannoys crackled into life and the solemn tones of a radio announcer could be heard being broadcast around the camp.

> *"This is the BBC Home Service – and here is a special bulletin... D-Day has come. Early this morning the Allies began the assault on the north-western face of Hitler's European fortress. The first official news came just after half past nine, when the Supreme Headquarters of the Allied Expeditionary Force issued Communique No. 1. This said "Under the command of General Eisenhower, Allied naval forces, supported by strong air forces, began landing Allied armies this morning on the northern coast of France..."*

The news was met with delirious cheering. In the telephone exchange Eileen, Nancy and the other girls on duty leapt up and embraced each other. Truly a spring had been placed in their step for the rest of the day. It also made up for the absence of loved ones over these last few weeks (and probably for a few more weeks to come) as the attention of Allied air forces switched from bombing German cities to relentlessly attacking key targets in France in support of the Normandy landings.

\* \* \* \* \*

"So this is it. It's definitely love."

"Nancy's question-cum-observation occasioned a glow in Eileen's gorgeous brown eyes. She twisted on her heels and nibbled her bottom lip teasingly before nodding in the affirmative.

"So you see: just look at what wonderful things happen when you trust your 'Auntie Nancy' to fix you up with a date," her friend crowed excitedly.

They certainly had. And this overcast spring evening was to witness its first fruits. With a great big hug for luck, Nancy permitted Eileen to disappear backstage to join the concert acts preparing to sally forth in front of the packed audience of USAAF personnel now crowded into the huge hangar. With fighting (and the concomitant air operations) still raging in and over Normandy, this Saturday night stand down could not have been a better tonic to fire everyone up in readiness for the intense days of struggle still to come.

Taking their seats, Nancy and her invited WAAF colleagues suddenly found themselves surrounded by hundreds of exceedingly friendly Americans all eager to know their names and swap addresses with them. Nancy certainly couldn't resist being her usual flirtatious self.

Eventually, an expectant hush descended as the concert got underway, opening with gags from a wise-cracking Brooklyn comedian that soon had the guys splitting their sides. Like ENSA (its British equivalent, only bigger and gliztier), USO had enlisted some of the top names in American showbiz to the cause of rallying the hundreds of thousands of young GIs serving overseas. Bing Crosby, Judy Garland, Marlene Dietrich, Laurel and Hardy, Al Jolson, the Andrews Sisters, Lucille Ball and – mostly famously – that respected, all-American wise-cracker, Bob Hope (though he was actually English by birth!). They had all offered their services to make sure that, whether in Europe or the Pacific, Uncle Sam would not be found wanting on the entertainment front. USO events too were often supplemented by locally-available talent – a point now driven home when the show's host returned to the microphone.

"Ladies and gentlemen, here in the 'Mighty Eighth' we consider ourselves immensely privileged to have a guy who can not only fly but who also has one of the most incredible voices you'll hear this side of the ocean. So won't you put your hands together for our very own Lieutenant Nicky Braschetti!"

The holler eclipsed anything Nancy and the girls had ever heard at an ENSA bash. Meanwhile, in from the wings strode Nicky, looking resplendent in uniform and with his dark wavy hair brushed back. Offering the crowds both a discreet wave and a flash of his heart-melting smile, the holler subsided and the band started up, everyone looking on with baited breath as he sang out the opening bars of 'Fools Rush In (Where Angels Fear To Tread)'.

Nancy was moved almost to tears. So Fred Garrett was right after all: her best friend might just be dating the next Frank Sinatra. The shy teacher-turned-aviator's voice was certainly silky enough to render any girl weak at the knees – as it was clearly doing to the handful of gorgeous 'GI Jane' nurses sitting along the opposite row, whose love-struck eyes were fixed upon him.

Furthermore, Nancy was even tempted to wonder whether Nicky's haunting rendition of the Hoboken crooner's 1940 hit might conceivably work its magic upon the misandrous Sergeant Harris – who was still scheming for ways to frustrate this heady over-infatuation amongst her WAAFs with all things American. Perhaps they should have invited her along. After all, with Cathy absent tonight on home leave they had been left with a ticket to spare.

"Thank you... Ladies and gentlemen, Lieutenant Nicky Braschetti!" their host joined in the applause, returning to the stage in the aftermath of Nicky having offered them additional songs from his repertoire.

He waited for the cheering to die down before announcing "... Now I'm sure while you guys out there have been in England you've been busy making many firm friends amongst all the beautiful girls they have over here..."

There was a wicked innuendo in his observation that induced whooping from the massed ranks of airmen gathered inside the cavernous hangar.

"Hey, bud. This gorgeous dame here won't let me be her 'friend'!" one of them yelled from behind the line of WAAFs, rising to his feet and specifically pointing down at a blushing Nancy nestled in the seat in front of him.

"Sit down, Komalski, you bum. Who the hell would wanna' be your friend!" a colleague scoffed to guffaws all round.

"...Seriously though, you guys, our British allies have been fighting this war for almost five years now. During that time they have been fortunate to have had talented folk of their own who have been helping to keep morale up – in particular, that redoubtable broad, Vera Lynn, whose tireless touring and performing has, so I'm told, made a bigger contribution to Britain's war effort than all the lend-lease Uncle Sam has been shipping over to 'em...!"

The ripple of amusement that greeted his flippant observation hinted that such hyperbole was not entirely without truth.

"...And so tonight it gives me immense pleasure to introduce a delightful young English lady who may not be a big name over here yet, but believe me she soon will be. So, all of you, let's give a great big 'Mighty Eighth' welcome to Eileen Kimberley!"

This time the thunderous delight was testosterone-fuelled as hundreds of applauding flyboys clapped eyes upon Eileen's stunning good looks and evocative figure for the very first time. Nancy too marvelled at how adept the girls had been at effecting subtle tweaks to her WAAF uniform so that, for once, its wearer unashamedly resembled a woman – and an undeniably alluring one too! Meanwhile, Eileen glanced off-stage to where Nicky was standing, proudly admiring her. He discreetly gave her the thumbs-up, the cue for her to fire that glance back at the audience when the orchestra launched into an introduction. Like the incredulity that had greeted her boyfriend barely a few minutes earlier, that audience was once more rendered spellbound as she took a deep breath and moved up to the microphone.

Much as her burgeoning professionalism bade her to address the lyrics of *'You'll Never Know'* to each of the hundreds of pairs of admiring eyes gazing up at her, still she could not resist glancing down at Nicky. She remained indebted for the way he had taken her under his wing and coached the latent talent she possessed, their snatched moments together as much an exploration of the art of making beautiful music as ever they had been of exploring their romantic feelings towards each other. At last, an illusive star that she had been seeking after was perhaps within her grasp.

Even if she had been impervious to the words of encouragement that Nicky, Nancy and her fellow WAAFs had been lavishing upon of her, she could not gainsay the rapturous reception her rendition of this popular song occasioned, and which billowed up into the crimson sunset. Before her very eyes the entire audience was on its feet yelling for more. She gazed out at them and struggled to take in the magnitude of the triumph she had just wrought.

If Uncle Sam's colossal multi-million dollar music industry had given lyrical form to the exuberant optimism of America's cause, then Britain's much smaller music industry continued to express the grittier, unflinching determination of its people to press on to victory. Yet running through so many of the songs it had churned out – including *'After The Rain'*, made famous by that "redoubtable broad" herself, Vera Lynn (and the final song that Eileen was now singing) – there remained a certain sobering melancholy that reflected the terrible price this proud island nation had paid (in both blood and treasure) to wage its war of national survival. For the United States – and notwithstanding the courage of its fighting men and the terrible sacrifices they were offering up – this war was very much a noble crusade fought on other shores. For Eileen and her fellow countrymen however, this war had been a bitter life-and-death struggle, in which only now were the 'grey clouds' dissipating sufficiently that that promise of victory – the 'blue skies after the rain' – could be glimpsed with greater clarity.

Her rendition was another triumph crowned with a frenzied standing ovation. Eileen waved and bowed and blew them all a parting kiss, fighting to hold back tears as she exited the stage into the arms of her waiting mentor.

"Hey, didn't I tell you you'd blow 'em away!" Nicky enthused, clutching her tight. However, despite his warm words and comforting embrace still the tears kept gushing, loud sobs only muffled by a face buried deep in his shoulder as if almost fearful of what she had unleashed.

"Oh, Nicky. I'm so scared," she confirmed. "Every time I have ever had anything good in my life, sooner or later it has been snatched away me. I'm just too frightened to dream any more."

"Hey, come on. Quit the worrying. You're gonna' be just fine. Listen to 'em, honey. They love you; and no one is ever gonna' take that away."

He wished he could assuage her anxiety about something else that was on her mind. Indeed, with a briefing for tomorrow's mission already pencilled in, he knew it would be foolish to promise what was not in his gift to deliver. He could only assure her that the overwhelming Allied air superiority over the skies of France meant he and his men might yet successfully complete their tour of duty in Europe. However, with Air Chief Marshall 'Bomber' Harris itching to resume the targeting of German cities again it would only be a matter of time before the Eighth Air Force would do likewise – with all the punishing losses that would inevitably entail.

\* \* \* \* \*

Spirits were high that night and the songs continued on the journey back to camp. Hence the driver that Nicky had assigned to ensure that Eileen, Nancy and their two WAAF colleagues were returned safely soon found himself the butt not just of their upbeat girlish harmonies, but their tomfoolery too – having suffered his cap to be swiped off his head and cheekily passed around amongst his passengers. Therefore, when he bounced the jeep up into the turning circle outside Waterbeach's guard house, and the girls all jumped out, he thought it opportune to beg a favour in return for his longsuffering.

"Excuse me, Miss Kimberley, but can I trouble you for an autograph?" he petitioned, whipping out of the breast pocket of his tunic both the concert programme and a pen.

"I beg your pardon! You want *my* autograph?" Eileen gasped, taken aback at such an unexpected, if flattering request.

"Sure. Lieutenant Braschetti has been telling all the guys that one day you're gonna' be real famous – even back home in the States. So I kinda' reckoned I'd be the first one to pocket an autograph. As a memento, you understand."

She was touched. "What's your name?" she enquired, locking her big brown eyes onto those of the callow airman.

"Martinez. Private First Class Oscar Martinez. From New Mexico, ma'am."

"To Private… First Class… Oscar… Martinez… All my love… and thank you… for the lift home… Eileen," she then repeated aloud, scribbling it down like so, dating it and handing it back to its grateful owner.

"Thank you, ma'am. And good luck with your singing career," he bade her, pocketing both programme and pen. "Oh… and my cap, ma'am," he then remembered.

Nancy obligingly drew it from behind her back and took the liberty of positioning it on his sweet little head, jiggling it until it was just right. Then Private Martinez offered his cooing passengers a playful American-style salute, crunched the jeep into gear, and spun it back onto the road, the girls ambling through the gates and back to the reality of an RAF station at war.

"Isn't he just the cutest guy you have ever seen," one of the WAAFs swooned, all of them leaning merrily upon each other for support and bathing shamelessly in the afterglow of this most memorable night.

"WHAT'S ALL THIS BLOODY RACKET GOING ON HERE?"

Their idyll was rudely shattered by bellowing lungs that had surely been created for no higher purpose than striking terror into otherwise happy-go-lucky servicewomen. They straightened themselves up and hurriedly endeavoured to comport themselves like women under orders once more.

"And a good time was had by all, by the look of things," Sergeant Harris proceeded to sneer, striding purposefully over to size them up and down beneath the glow of a pale moon that was flitting in and out of the clouds. She flicked Nancy's loosened tie between her fingers, noting that "that's you on a charge for a start."

She carried on circling the chastened WAAFs to see if there were any other little shortcomings that might warrant censure. "You've all been out sniffing around those over-sexed Yanks again, haven't you." she then ventured.

"We were invited to attend a concert they were hosting, Sergeant," one of them replied warily.

Huh!" was the curt, dismissive response. "And I suppose *you* have been warbling for their delectation?" Harris opined, drawing up almost nose-to-nose with Eileen, who fought the urge to cringe at the odorous breath in her face.

"I had Group Captain Parker's express permission, Sergeant. He thinks it a good thing that we are helping to foster a cordial relationship with our American allies," she explained, staring dead ahead (though peripheral vision apprised her of the NCO's nostrils twitching in frustration that the station commander's continued indulgence acted as an effective brake upon Harris's determination to whip this budding songstress into line).

"Oh, I imagine those relationships have been washed down with plenty of 'cordial' alright," Harris sneered, sniffing Eileen's own breath before stepping out her face to address them collectively once more.

"But just remember: this is an operational air station. And when you bunch of reprobates can be bothered to grace it with your presence it is in my hands that you have been entrusted – not the grubby, wandering mits of those Yankee airmen. I will not tolerate my girls rolling in through those gates like drunken tarts. Therefore, I suggest you pipe down, get your slinky little arses into your beds, and make sure you report to me at 0-600 hours prompt for assignment to special cleaning duties. All of you!"

"Yes, sergeant," they snapped again, this time soberly aware of the lateness of the hour and how quickly the appointed time for making amends for their spontaneous outburst of hilarity would be upon them.

"…And if perchance you clap eyes upon that dopey lump of lard that goes by the name of Aircraftwoman Clarke you can instruct her to join you. She and I are long overdue for a little chat," Harris barked ominously in closing.

* * * * *

Contrary to Sergeant Harris's scurrilous accusation, their American hosts had plied them with nothing stronger than Coca-Cola. However, Eileen awoke in the small hours feeling a desperate need to wee, slipping into her dressing gown to sneak over to the ablutions block. Mission accomplished, she was about to slip back out again when she thought she heard a suppressed cry of pain coming from one of the other cubicles. Tiptoeing silently along to the one with the door closed, she bent over to spy a pair of stubby RAF Oxford shoes. She gingerly pushed the doors open. There was another sharp intake of breath as its startled occupant looked up and froze in terror.

"Cathy. What's the matter? Are you alright?"

Clearly not. The portly, tear-streaked WAAF cook was perspiring heavily, crouched on the toilet seat with her underwear in disarray. Eileen eased herself forward to make sense of what was happening. As she did so she caught a glimpse of the swirling mess of blood and yuck that had filled the toilet pan, some of which was splattered on Cathy's uniform. She quickly stepped back again, biting her knuckles and suppressing the urge to scream out in horror.

"No, don't!" Cathy wept, grabbing her arm. Then she winced and pulled her arm back to clutch at her abdomen as it cramped in agony.

"Wait there," Eileen insisted. A pointless instruction in the circumstances; but what else was there to say? She had not the faintest idea what was happening to Cathy, other than that it looked ominous.

She shuddered, turned, and raced out of the block, silently sneaking back to the billet, where she slithered up besides Nancy's bed and shook its slumbering occupant vigorously. Placing a hand over Nancy's mouth to hush her sudden surprise, in the dimness she gesticulated for her to likewise don her dressing gown and follow her over to the block.

"Oh my God!" Nancy hurried her own hand to her mouth as she beheld Cathy's blood-soaked uniform and underwear, the chubby lass palpitating in agony against the side of the cubicle.

"What's happening to her? Is she having some kind of heavy period?" Eileen was desperate to know.

"This is no period, Eileen," her more worldly-wise friend discerned, though she was loathed to verbalise precisely what it was. Instead, she leant forward to push Cathy's wiry fringe up off her forehead, gazing into her bleary eyes. "Cathy, you need to get to hospital straight away. Do you hear me?"

"No, you can't," the haemorrhaging Cockney spluttered. "Ar'll be in right big trouble if yer' do."

"Cathy, you are already in very serious trouble now. You must get medical attention without delay."

"What's happening?" Eileen demanded to know. "What has she done?"

"I might be wrong, but I think she has had… an abortion. And it looks like it has gone very badly wrong."

"What? How?"

Abortion: a loaded word that Eileen's strict Catholic upbringing had failed to prepare her to even think about, much less come face to face with the reality of – and in this most dire and insalubrious of settings.

"I 'ad to," Cathy groaned, clutching her belly as another spasm ripped without quarter through her shredded womb.

"Cathy, you've lost a lot of blood. And if infection has set in then you could die. Now I'm going to fetch the MO whether you want me to or not. All that matters right now is saving your life. Eileen will wait with you while I go and find him... and summon an ambulance to take you to hospital."

"No!" Cathy wailed.

Too late. Nancy had already disappeared. Meanwhile, attempting as best she could to shut out of her mind the horror of what she had stumbled upon during her chance nocturnal excursion, Eileen moved in to tend to the distraught teenager, squatting down to take hold of her hand. She too used her free hand to brush Cathy's fringe away and to wipe from her terrified face the perspiration now oozing from every pore.

"I 'ad to. Dad woulda' killed me. An' wiv' a blackie 'n awl'!"

"You mean Wilbur?" Eileen gasped, aware by now (as was probably most of the billet) that she had been seeing the Negro serviceman on the sly. Otherwise, she felt utterly out of her depth trying to piece together this concatenation of tales about miscegenation, a drunken ogre of a father, and a botched invasive procedure. She listened on aghast as Cathy elaborated.

"There's this woman I 'eard of. 'Er lives aht' Stepney way... 'Er 'as ways o' getting' rid of babies... Usin' knittin' needles an' fings'."

Eileen shook her headed appalled. "How can she possibly 'get rid' of babies? What does she do with these... 'knitting needles'?"

"Her puts 'em inside yer. Yer' know. Up yer'...."

Such unseemly frankness was simply too much for the naïve Catholic girl. Once more, unbearable grimaces contorted Cathy's face, presenting Eileen with the opportunity to press the poor girl's mouth tight to her chest and muffle any further gruesome revelations. However, Cathy thrust herself away to instead begin mouthing a more earnest petition.

"Tell Wilbur I love 'im. 'E's a real star geezer, 'e is – the best fing' that's ever 'appened to me. An' I ain't 'ad too many good fings' 'appen in my life, I can tell ya'...You like dancin', don't you, Eileen," she remembered, to which Eileen nodded – her own face now streaked with tears. "Well, Wilbur an' me used to dance too.... That's what were doin' when we used to sneak aht' to see each uvva'."

The desire to dance; the desire to sing; the desire to love and be loved – three of the most elemental forces by which human beings connect with each other. Yet what had these two lonely people ever done that was so wrong that they had been left with no choice but to conduct these joyous pleasures in secret – unlike Eileen and Nicky, never able to proudly parade both their talent and their love for each other? Eileen forced herself to gaze upwards at the flaking plasterwork of the ceiling and beg the Good Lord for an answer.

"Fank' you, Eileen... for bein' a friend to me," Cathy meanwhile whimpered, her breath growing shallower with each pained staccato utterance. "Ar' know I ain't too clevva'. An' I ain't much ter' look at, am I... I'm certainly not beautiful like you are... Perhaps that's why I ain't got too many friends. But you 'ave been a good friend to me, Eileen – you an' Nancy.... Neither of you ain't ever poked fun at me. Yer' mighta' pulled me' leg from time to time; but you ain't ever tried to make me feel stoopid'... like that 'orrible bleedin' Sergeant 'Arris does... I remember 'ow you invited me to that New Year's Eve dance' when yer' coulda' just invited someone else instead; someone prettier than wot' I am... I was right flattered, I tell ya'... An' if you 'adn't 'ave invited me I woulda' never met Wilbur, would I... Yeah, I love Wilbur. I always' will... 'E's a good un', Eileen.... An' there ain't too many good uns' in this world, is there..."

Cathy's simple observations rent Eileen's soul from top to bottom. What had she ever done to deserve such an accolade? When had she been a good friend? Was it really true that – even in her moments of greatest despair at the bumbling Cockney misfit – she had never bad-mouthed her or sought to draw attention to her many shortcomings in the brains and femininity stakes? Had she really followed the example of the Saviour by demonstrating love to the seemingly unlovely? Gripping the tiny crucifix around her neck, with every tear Eileen implored the Saviour to forgive this poor, humble child whose life was draining away with each cramping spasm and accompanying gush of blood. "Remember Cathy in Paradise, Lord," she paraphrased the dying words of the thief on the cross as she recalled them in Luke's Gospel... "In Your great mercy and love – remember her..."

Her frantic prayer was interrupted by the commotion of the MO charging into the block with Nancy and a posse of orderlies in tow.

"WHAT IN GOD'S NAME IS GOING ON IN HERE?" Sergeant Harris yelled, also bursting in to observe the grotesque scene of chaos.

Spotting the elusive Aircraftwoman Clarke, she was about to ejaculate a barrage of further blistering profanities until she spied the righteous anger etched upon Nancy's face, as well as the impotent shake of the MO's head. Then, mouth agape, the NCO glanced down in turn to watch Cathy splutter one last time before slumping to the toilet floor.

By now Eileen's nightdress was drenched a harrowing hue of scarlet from where she had clutched at the dying WAAF. Therefore, assisted by Nancy, the MO gently prised her away from Cathy's lifeless form. Whilst he searched and probed in vain for vital signs, Nancy lifted Eileen to her feet and slipped her lachrymose colleague into her own comforting embrace. It had turned out to be a memorable night alright – but not for reasons that any of these two appalled spectators could ever have imagined.

\* \* \* \* \*

They left camp at the crack of dawn on what had turned out to be a beautiful summer day, it being the first pass they could secure following the dressing down they had received from their section officer (as well as the punishment duties Sergeant Harris had dreamed up especially for them). Cycling to the appointed place, Eileen and Nancy met up with Wilbur waiting there in his trusty jeep. There was a solemn and laconic exchange of greetings before Nancy lovingly removed from the basket of her bicycle a small posy of pink and gold lilies. Then they permitted Wilbur to lead them to that peaceful clearing in the forest that was again graced with birdsong. There Nancy crouched to lay the flowers at the foot of the tall oak tree before joining Wilbur and Eileen to survey the simple tribute.

After a few moments spent in quiet contemplation, Wilbur reached into his tunic pocket and lifted out a small, dog-eared Book of Psalms. His devout mother had made it her parting gift to him when he had left his native Georgia for service overseas. His stubby fingers fumbled with its pages until he alighted upon the 130th Psalm, which he proceeded to read aloud in his gravelled Southern drawl…

> *"Out of the depths have I cried unto Thee, O Lord. Lord, hear my voice. Let Thine ears be attentive to the voice of my supplications. If Thou, Lord, shouldest mark iniquities, O Lord, who should stand? But there is forgiveness in Thee, that Thou mayest be feared. I wait for the Lord. My soul doth wait, and in His Word do I hope…"*

He closed the little book and put it away again, thereupon lifting his big bright eyes up to Heaven as Eileen's soaring voice pierced the stillness with the words of a hymn that she used to sing in church as a little girl – her own reminder to them of the Psalm's eternal truth…

> *"What wondrous love is this? O, my soul, O my soul.*
> *What wondrous love is this? O, my soul.*
> *What wondrous love is this?*
> *That caused the Lord of bliss,*
> *To bear the dreadful curse for my soul, for my soul.*
> *To bear the dreadful curse for my soul."*

Notwithstanding the beauty of both words and voice, it seemed such a meagre consolation for Wilbur having been cruelly excluded from attending the funeral of his beloved. And though conscious that it was not seemly for these two polite English ladies to be called upon to witness a grown man cry, the young black airman screwed up his face as tears welled up and trickled from those eyes closed tight in remorse. It fell to Nancy to reach up and lay an arm of comfort as best she could across his big broad shoulders.

"I did her wrong, Miss Nancy. This is all mah' fault," he shook his head and snuffled, hiding his face with his pudgy hand in shame.

She pressed her head against an upper arm rendered solid by the tensing of his muscular frame. "No, Wilbur. You did her right. You never showed her anything but love and kindness. And in the end, there is no greater gift that one human being can ever bestow upon another than to show love and kindness."

For a few more minutes they stood there savouring the birds calling sweetly from the trees: Nancy with her arm around Wilbur; and Eileen meditating upon a life that had passed – one small, insignificant life amongst millions that this war had claimed, either directly by bomb, bullet, shell or torpedo; or – like young Cathy – indirectly as a consequence of the titanic upheaval that it was churning in its wake. Then, realising that nothing more could be said, they each slowly edged away, retracing their steps to return to their respective duties.

No sooner had they left than the tranquillity of the forest was broken by the gathering drone of heavy bombers. Dozens of them suddenly roared low over the treetops, having taken off from nearby air stations on their way to help consolidate the Allied foothold in France. For several long moments their turbulent wake whipped through the trees, swaying their branches and rustling their leaves and blossoms.

Once the squadrons had passed, the peace and stillness returned. As it did so – and as the last blossoms tumbled to the forest floor – a small white feather could be observed dancing gracefully on the lingering breeze before gently descending to snag upon the petals of the posy, there to settle beside the hand-written card that had been set lovingly in its midst…

*In memory of Catherine Hilda Clarke,*
*Women's Auxiliary Air Force.*
*February 3rd 1925 – June 15th 1944.*

*"Dance for evermore."*

# *14*

It sure was one hell of a sight to behold: strung out across miles and miles of azure summer sky like a great swarm of marauding insects were over three hundred Boeing B17 Flying Fortress bombers cruising in tight defensive formations. Their silver metallic surfaces glinted in the sun, and lines of milk-white contrails were streaming from their wings.

They were flanked by almost as many North American P51 Mustangs and twin-engine Lockheed P38 Lightnings – two of the latest generation of US fighters capable of matching anything the *Luftwaffe* could put in the air. What's more, the provision of simple aluminium drop-tanks slung under their wings now afforded these potent flying machines the range to be able to escort the bombers deep into enemy airspace. This would be especially important on the long flight this particular mission had ahead of it to arrive over the Nazis' secret rocket plant on the distant Baltic Coast.

Very early in the morning on June 13th 1944 – precisely one week after D-Day – a fast-moving finger of flame had been reported racing across the sky over Kent, accompanied by a low-pitched grumbling noise that was described as resembling a motorbike with a broken silencer. Then the flame vanished and the grumbling ceased until a few seconds later the eerie silence was shattered by a colossal explosion that ripped apart Grove Road in London's East End. As well as badly damaging a busy railway bridge, six civilians lost their lives. The first of Hitler's new 'vengeance' weapons had been unleashed.

Few Allied planes possessed the speed to down the V1 flying bomb (or 'Doodlebug' as the terrorised citizens of the capital quickly nicknamed it). Therefore, the only hope of stopping this lethal device was to destroy its launch pads along the Channel coast, as well as its vital production facilities elsewhere across the Third Reich. This ongoing high-priority mission was code-named 'Operation Crossbow', and today – Tuesday, July 18th – the B17s of the 322nd Squadron had been detailed to attack the V1's special hydrogen-peroxide fuel production plant at Peenemunde.

Piloting LG-Z *"Lucky Little Lucy Mae"* of the 322nd Squadron (recognisable by the giant triangular letter 'A' of the 91st Bomb Group on its tail, as well as the cartoon of their kittenish, scantily-clad namesake painted on the bomber's nose), First Lieutenant Nicky Braschetti once again took a brief moment on this so-far uneventful flight to contemplate his own mortality. He guessed that over such a heavily-defended and strategically vital prize the Krauts could be relied upon to put up stiff opposition. He would not be proved wrong.

*"Hey, you guys. Looks like we got company,"* his starboard waist gunner alerted him over the interphone. *"Bandits at four o'clock high. There must be at least thirty of 'em – about two thousand yards out and closing."*

Nicky and his other crew members stared out across the wide expanse of blue sky and picked out the enemy fighters above them sizing up the combat box like a pack of carnivorous beasts on the prowl for easy kills.

*"Yeah, I see 'em too. They 109s?"*

*"Look like Focke-Wulf 190s to me."*

*"Hell, no, Anderton! They're 109s, I tell ya'."*

*"Pipe down, you lot."* Nicky felt it meet to caution them. *"Just keep your eyes peeled and only engage 'em if they get in close. Otherwise, save your ammo and leave 'em to the escorts to take care of."*

Sure enough, from their vantage point up in the 'greenhouse' Nicky and the co-pilot seated to his right stared up in unison to track the detachment of Mustangs that raced across high above them in order to break up the enemy attack. It enabled them instead to maintain the twenty-five ton bomber on a steady course now that the navigator had advised it was just ten minutes flight time till they would be over their target.

Even were the bandits that were now being scattered to get lucky, not for nothing did German fighter pilots refer to the mighty B17 as the *fliegendes Stachelschwein* (or 'flying porcupine'). *"Lucky Little Lucy Mae"* – one of the latest B17G variants – boasted no less than thirteen M2 Browning machine guns mounted in the Bendix chin turret, nose cheek turret, slung in the staggered waist portals, as well as in roof, belly and tail-mounted Sperry ball turrets. There was even a vertically-firing one located behind the bomb bay. All told, they afforded the 'Queen' an unprecedented arc of fire (unlike RAF Lancasters, which were notorious for their vulnerable blind-spot beneath the plane, the *Luftwaffe* even equipping its night fighters with an upward-facing machine gun – nicknamed *Schräge Musik* – specifically to exploit it).

Nicky continued to maintain course so that his bombardier would enjoy the best possible run. The huge bomb doors hinged open and in less than a minute the purpose of their gruelling eight hour flight was over, its four-and-a-half thousand pounds of payload hurtling through the broken cloud towards the target twenty-thousand feet below.

*"Nice work, Morales. Now I propose we get the hell outta' here before the Krauts come back for more."*

*"Sounds good to us, Lieutenant. Let's hope the folks in London remember our good deed on their behalf next time we're down there on R & R."*

*"Yeah. Especially all those young broads, eh Anderton!"*

*"Sure thing, buddy. I just can't wait to tell 'em!"* Anderton crowed.

Laughter coursed through the interphone. Nicky meanwhile banked the huge plane around so that it could join the rest of its cohort heading home. The 'Ragged Irregulars' had chalked up another successful mission. However, any notion that the return flight was going to be uneventful evaporated as soon as they approached the neck of the Jutland peninsula, where fresh enemy fighter squadrons could be seen massing off their flanks. With the Mustangs now having to work flat out to swat them away, it was inevitable that sooner or later lucky breaks would present themselves to the vengeful Germans.

*"Six o'clock high! Definitely 190s this time."*

*"I see 'em. The rounded cockpit is the give-away."*

*Look out! Look out! A pair of the little assholes is closing fast!"*

A furious exchange of fire rattled off as the Focke-Wulfs bore down without quarter and unleashed their cannons on the looming hulk of the *"Lucky Little Lucy Mae"*. Renowned as *the* most formidable fighter the *Luftwaffe* possessed, the 'Shrike' was fast and agile and this particular duo sped in to empty a flurry of lead into the bomber's wings and fuselage before climbing steeply to regroup for another run. A pitiful screech filled the interphone.

*"What's going on back there?"* Nicky called down in alarm.

*"They got Anderton, Lieutenant... He's taken it bad. Looks like that last volley almost sliced right through him!"*

*"Look out, boys. The Krauts are coming back! Seven o'clock high!"*

*"Where the hell have our Spam Cans disappeared to?"*

Another salvo of pitiless fire from the 190s was met by no less determined counter-fire. Every 'fifty' aboard the *"Lucky Little Lucy Mae"* that could be brought to bear was blazing away at them – gunners screaming excitedly that they could see the whites of the pilots' eyes. Meanwhile – and despite Nicky jinking the bomber this way and that – more cannon shot punched holes in its fuselage, this time severing vital electrical cables and thereby cutting all power to tail turret.

*"Hell, look! They got the* "Delta Dame"*!" the cry went up.*

Right before their very eyes the sun off the port side was momentary eclipsed by the flames and black smoke of a fearsome explosion. A rocket strike from a 190 had ripped the entire starboard wing clean off a neighbouring 'Fort'. What remained of the crippled plane thus commenced a furious spiralling descent, the macabre screaming of its two remaining engines trailing off as it plummeted. Nicky and his fellow crew members looked on appalled and could only imagine what thoughts must be gripping its own terrified crew as the sheer velocity of the spin made escape all but impossible. Within minutes the once gleaming *"Delta Dame"* had become just a fiery dot below them.

*"Oh my God... That was Tackaberry's plane, wasn't it?"*

*"Shit! Did anyone get out?"*

*"I didn't see any chutes."*

*"Poor bastards. Tackaberry's wife's just given birth to their first kid too!"*

While his co-pilot was distracted surveying the ominous splattering of shell holes in the starboard wing, Nicky squeezed his eyes tightly shut. The rubber indicator on his oxygen mask rasped in time as he mumbled rather too loudly to himself what he intended to be a silent prayer...

*"The Lord is shepherd. I shall not want... Yea, though I walk through the valley off the shadow of death, I will fear no evil... Surely goodness and mercy shall follow me all the days of my life..."*

*"We're all saying 'Amen' to that, Lieutenant,"* one of his crewmen replied.

The sober observation jolted Nicky to open his eyes again and stare across at the tiny picture of Eileen that he had taped in the corner of his instrument console. Her bonny smile, together with the timeless succour of King David's words, helped him grapple with his fraying nerves. After all, he was in command. Everyone was looking to him to do the right thing and get them safely back to England. Availing himself of a brief respite once the Mustangs reappeared and chased the enemy away, he took another deep breath and requested a situation report from his crew.

*"Seccombe."*

*"Check, Lieutenant."*

*"Woodward."*

*"Check."*

*"Lucado."*

*"Check."*

*"Johnson."*

*"Check... Lieutenant,"* a fricative, emotion-laden voice panted over the interphone. *"...But I'm afraid... I don't think there's much that can be done for Anderton... He's lost a lot of blood."*

Nicky exhaled volubly, shaking his head. *"Forrester."*

*"Check, Lieutenant. But I'm afraid the tail gun's FUBAR. I just can't get the ammunition feed to work."*

*"Okay. Forrester, get your ass out of there and man up Anderton's gun on the starboard waist. The rest of you try and cover our tail as best you can."*

Exiting the useless turret was easier said than done. The narrow confines of the tail were difficult enough to egress when on the ground. However, with his thick boots, sheepskin flying jacket and thirty-pound flak jacket on – and with his oxygen tank in his hand – negotiating the jagged metalwork rent apart by the 190s' handiwork was especially perilous. Meanwhile, a stiff wind howled through a huge gaping hole that had been punched open, adding to the biting sub-zero temperature inside the plane. Forrester's gloves and electrically-heated flying suit could mitigate the worst of the cold, but it could not prevent the ice accumulating on his eyelashes that he had to constantly brush away.

*"What the hell happened to him?"* he gawped in horror once he had stepped over the tool box to reach the waist portals.

Anderton lay slumped on the floor, whilst from his butchered remains the vermilion flow of blood that his traumatised colleague had been unable to staunch seeped in staccato bursts onto the gunner squatting inside the belly turret below. Meanwhile, Sergeant Johnson's juddering hand was fumbling with sulfa powder packets that he tried to sprinkle into a gaping thigh wound of his own that he had hastily tourniquetted.

*"I hate to be the bearer of bad news, Nick, but we got gasoline vapour pouring from the starboard wing,"* his co-pilot glanced over and pointed out. *"And no. 4 engine is belching out oil!"*

*"I confirm that, Lieutenant,"* his flight engineer added, having hurriedly scrambled back down from his battle station in the roof turret to interrogate his gauges. *"The starboard gas tanks are rapidly emptying."*

*"We can't afford to lose that stuff, Lucado. Shut off the valves to No. 4 engine and shift whatever gas is left as fast as you can to the other tanks."*

*"I'm doing that now, Lieutenant."*

Purposely starved of fuel to prevent fire, the propeller of No. 4 engine was left 'windmilling' uselessly. Despite 'feathering' it to reduce the drag, the resulting drop in airspeed now cast the plane's anxious skipper upon a dilemma. Unable to keep up with the combat box – and denuded of its mutual covering fire, as well as that of the escorts – they would be a sitting duck to any further enemy fighters they encountered. What's more, the escaping gas had cost them vital range that meant it was now touch-and-go whether they'd make it back anyway. Therefore, Nicky took the decision to put the plane into a dive that would take them down in a bank of low-lying cloud – safe from fighters, but further compounding the dire fuel situation. In order to save weight his men were therefore ordered to dump their guns and remaining ammunition out of the plane, along with any other superfluous equipment.

A ditching in the North Sea was now a very real possibility. The only question was how close to the English coast they could get before the remaining three engines died. Perhaps today would be the day that the *"Lucky Little Lucy Mae"* finally ran out of luck.

\* \* \* \* \*

That final mission had badly shaken up First Lieutenant Nicky Braschetti. Sure enough, he and his remaining crewmen had been forced to ditch when the *"Lucky Little Lucy Mae"* ran out of gas a hundred miles short of the Norfolk coast. Fortunately, their Mayday call had been picked up and a Royal Navy destroyer had been diverted to rescue them.

Alas, not counted amongst the survivors were Sergeants Anderton and Johnson (who had already perished from their wounds aboard the stricken plane), as well as Sergeant Seccombe (who had been badly injured during the ditching and had not survived a cold and miserable few hours in the life rafts). Three good men lost – not one of them a day over twenty-one.

However, at least the Peenemunde raid had edged Nicky closer to the magic tally of thirty-five missions, after which he had the option of returning to the States to help train up replacement pilots (this itself had been raised from the original figure of twenty-five due to the punishing losses amongst crews that the 'Mighty Eighth' had suffered during its two year-long campaign so far).

Therefore, with a heart brimming with thanksgiving, he determined that that little jeweller's shop in Cambridge would be his very first port of call. In its window display he had previously spied a beautiful three-stone diamond cross-over engagement ring. Sure, it was a pricey little treasure: but what was mere money when this was to be his gift of betrothal to the beautiful woman he adored! Besides, who could say whether continued flying operations would permit him the luxury of planning a more deliberative courtship!

Instead, he determined that he would surprise Eileen. He would seize the moment when they were next due to see each other again. It was this thought that animated him as he emerged from the shop with the sparkling jewel, taking a final peek at it in its black velvet box before safely tucking it away in the pocket of his brown 'Ike' jacket.

* * * * *

The warm August evening was just the tonic after the unsettled weather of the last few weeks. Here on England's south coast, at an impromptu outdoor auditorium draped with camouflage netting, several hundred guests were taking their seats for what promised to be a most memorable evening. Indeed, both the BBC and US armed force radio were present, their technicians working together to put the finishing touches to what was intended to be a live broadcast to the troops now that the bitter and costly slog that had marked the opening weeks of Normandy campaign had at last given way to a rapid war of movement.

Meanwhile, gracing this special morale-boosting extravaganza with his presence was none other that the Supreme Commander of the Allied Expeditionary Force himself, General Dwight D. Eisenhower. The audience of invited British and American officers and other ranks stood to attention as he was escorted in to take his place at their head. However, Ike was no fool. He knew it was not his attendance that had infused the gathering with such anticipation. Instead, once the introductory formalities were out of the way, their host for evening lost no time unveiling the real star of the show.

"Supreme Commander, ladies and gentlemen, assembled guests," he called out. "You are about to be entertained for the next hour by a man who needs absolutely no introduction from me. So please put your hands together for Major Glenn Miller and his orchestra!"

Though the applause was respectful as he strode onto the stage in his crisp army attire, it hinted at an excitement abroad that could not be entirely restrained by military protocol. Tall and elegant, the forty year-old Iowan trombonist and band leader was already a living legend back home, a string of his ground-breaking hits having introduced swing music to the masses. Then in

1942 he had forsaken an extremely lucrative touring and recording career to enlist with the US Army and offer his services entertaining the troops. Having gathered together some of the finest musician under arms (and who he now introduced), he had arrived in England a few days earlier to commence a hectic round of concerts at military bases and other venues. For as Miller put it simply, yet eloquently: "America means freedom; and there's no expression of freedom quite so sincere as music."

He wasn't kidding either. At first *adagio*, but soon unapologetically *accelerando*, from the moment his fifty-piece ensemble began mimicking the sound of a train gathering speed there was no way that bodies were going to be kept from swaying or feet from rhythmically tapping as *'Chattanooga Choo-Choo'* poured forth from their instruments. There followed a further selection of songs from Miller's extensive back catalogue – including *'Pennsylvania 6-5000'*, *'In The Mood'*, Hoagy Carmichael's lazily evocative *'Stardust'*, and Miller's own timeless signature tune, *'Moonlight Serenade'*. Eventually, Major Miller and the boys upped the tempo once more, this time joined on stage by a quartet of crooning a-cappella backing singers, who launched into the spritely opening bars of *'Don't Sit Under The Apple Tree'*.

Out on stage to join them there strode a lean figure suavely attired in the uniform of an army aviator, and who now took to the microphone to showcase a wonderful mellow voice. Duly reminding them all about 'the girl he met who just loves to pet', First Lieutenant Nicolino Francesco Braschetti USAAF responded to the libidinous stirring of his audience by firing off one of his heart-warming boyish grins.

By now the foot-tapping had spread to the sound technicians and the local dignitaries too. Even Ike himself looked as if he was itching for just one brief moment to join in, casting off the momentous responsibility for the fate of the Free World that now rested upon his shoulders. Surely rallying the vast Allied army in Europe couldn't get any better than this! They were all about to find out. For male eyes visibly lit up as out onto the stage with her hands coquettishly hidden behind her back strutted a gorgeous young broad with cute sable curls who some of more clued-up GIs thought they recognised. Yes, it was her: the sweet and adorable Leading Aircraftwoman Eileen Kathleen Kimberley GC. Only this time, gone were the stout RAF shoes and staid blue uniform. In their place were heeled white sandals and a knee-length chequered gingham dress with puffed shoulders. Drawn in at the waist, it revealed a pair of shapely hips that she placed her hands upon as she stepped up to the microphone, a scowl fixed upon Nicky as she wagged a finger at him in playful castigation. Truly, the transformation was complete. Goodbye, frustrated teenager from the mean streets of England's industrial Midlands. Hello, all-American bobbysoxer from the main streets of Illinois or Indiana.

By now fear of censure by 'The Chief' down on the front row was crumbling just as surely as was German resistance in France. The guys up the back were heartily whooping along to Eileen's mock instruction to Nicky not to dally with 'lots of girls on foreign shores.' For this humble WAAF telephonist to have been invited to accompany the illustrious Glenn Miller (and to perform in front of the loftiest brass-hat of them all!) was a most staggering accolade. Giving her performance everything, she was adamant she would not disappoint her admirers – both those drooling after her in the audience; and the hundreds of thousands of brave young men on the far side of the English Channel who were at that very moment pressing on towards Paris.

And so – perhaps blissfully unaware of the love that existed between these two idolised stars of the Allied war machine – the crowd swayed one final time as Nicky ambled across to join Eileen at her microphone, draping a possessive arm across her shoulders as together they triumphantly proclaimed...

> *"...I know the apple tree is reserved for you and me,*
> *And I'll be true till you come marching home!"*

\* \* \* \* \*

"Here, listen to this, girls," one of the WAAFs called out from her bed, lying sprawled out in her underwear whilst propping up her chin with her hands and lazily swaying one of her bare legs in the air behind her. *"'Glenn Miller concert: British WAAF gives 'thrilling' performance',"* she then scanned down the headline, reading the accompanying newspaper article out verbatim as the other young servicewomen looked up from sowing their uniforms, or polishing shoes and buttons.

> *"'A Women's Auxiliary Air Force telephonist serving with Bomber Command last night received a standing ovation from several hundred ecstatic troops when she sang for them at an open-air concert headlined by hot American band leader, Major Glenn Miller – who is currently in Britain touring with his orchestra. Performing in front of the Supreme Allied Commander, General Eisenhower, twenty-one year-old Leading Aircraftwoman Eileen Kimberley has lately been making a name for herself as an extremely gifted songstress, having put in several appearances at morale-raising events around the country. LACW Kimberley was last year awarded the George Cross for courageously rescuing an Australian gunner from a burning plane...' blah, blah, blah..."*

Just then, Eileen and Nancy breezed in after the end of their shift, only to find themselves suddenly confronted by a heady mixture of mock adoration and shameless leg-pulling, the other girls dropping what they were doing to crowd in and noisily enthuse over the starlet in their midst.

"So tell us, Eileen, what it's like to be the toast of every music reviewer this side of Broadway?"

"Yes. Is it right your 'manager' here has asked Vera Lynn if she'd like to be the support act on your next tour of the Far East?" another girl joked, moving in behind Nancy to swipe her cap and ruffle her flaxen mop.

Whilst Nancy gave as good as she got – pulling her assailant's bed apart by way of playful revenge – Eileen didn't know quite what to say. For all the glory that everyone seemed to want to bestow upon her, sometimes a part of her inwardly yearned to crawl back to the anonymity of being an ordinary serving airwoman again. For all that she loved singing – and for all that she especially craved to be singing alongside her beloved Nicky – it was becoming difficult to handle the way her friends and those around her seemed to treat her differently now; to either place her on a pedestal; or conversely let slip hints of jealously or resentment on account of her acclaim and her periodic absences from the more humdrum matter of answering telephones on a busy air station.

"You just be careful, love," an older and wiser colleague cautioned her from over in the corner of the billet – as if to hammer home the point. "The erks are getting right peeved about all this American 'bobby socks' pahlava. *'Peggy, the Pin-up Girl'*, they're calling you," she noted, apropos the popular GI ditty. "Of course, it doesn't help that you're going out with one of their more well-known pilots either. Some of them are even suggesting you don't care for the RAF any more, and that you've sold your soul to the Yanks instead."

"Oh, Gwen, that's nonsense," she gently protested, relaxing her shoulders at the absurdity of such talk. "I'm British. I love my country. And I'm proud to serve with the Royal Air Force."

"Anyway, never mind all that silliness," one of the radio telegraphers sidled up and nudged her excitedly. "Let's have a look at what he's bought you."

"Gosh! That is simply breath-taking!" another cooed, employing tender fingertips to raise Eileen's delicate left hand up so that the beautiful three-stone diamond cross-over engagement ring could be viewed by all those gathering around, who were transfixed with envy at its sheen and sparkle.

"It bet it must have cost the Earth."

"Yes, he really must love you something awful."

"Did he go down on one knee too?"

"That he did," Nancy smirked, certain her best friend wouldn't mind her sharing that particular touching and amusing confidence.

"Oh, Eileen, darling. How romantic!"

Quite. Though Nancy didn't say as much, the unsettled look in her china blue eyes alluded to something else her friend had once confided to her – and about which she had now backslidden: namely that having witnessed so many hasty engagements amongst people she had served with brought to a cruel demise by the caprices of war, she (like Nancy herself) had consistently proclaimed a desire to avoid the hostage to fortune implicit in such romantic commitment. Either she did indeed love her new fiancé with something approaching reckless insanity; or (Eileen maybe hoped) the newly-promoted Captain Nicky Braschetti would soon be safely ensconced in a less-hazardous training role. One that even so might mean a long, agonising period of separation as he returned to the United States to mentor the next cohort of draftees volunteering to fly missions with the 'Mighty Eighth'.

"GOOD GOD! IS THIS AN RAF ESTABLISHMENT? OR SOME TUPPENNY HA'PENNY WHOREHOUSE?" a thundering voice bellowed, its owner flinging open the door to gaze about at semi-naked women cavorting around each other's beds like giggling schoolgirls.

Too late to cover up, the WAAFs were reduced to snapping to attention where they were and in whatever state of disrobement they had been in. Either way, the almost tangible black storm cloud that hovered above Sergeant Harris as she fumed at the sight did not bode well for somebody.

"Well, I suppose we should be grateful for small mercies. At least the 'terrible twins' aren't parading about in their smalls," she observed, circling Eileen and Nancy. However, she had spotted that Nancy's dishevelled blonde locks were such that she might have been dragged through a hedge backwards. Ooops, the mischievous telephonist winced feebly. Jankers again!

Meanwhile, Eileen was just grateful that – with an up-ended bed and so much pasty feminine flesh on display to be appalled at – Sergeant Harris omitted for once to cast her usual aspersions upon her musical assignations. Instead, stooping purposefully to lift from the floor a pair of discarded pink frilly knickers, the fiery NCO squared up to their owner to dangle them at the end of her nose. Eyeballing the palpitating WAAF, she then flicked them in the air. Jankers for someone else too!

"What I am here to remind you of is that our station's new commanding officer is arriving tomorrow to take up his post. Therefore, you will all report for parade at 0-900 hours prompt. So if I were you I'd get back to polishing those buttons and shoes. Because if I spot even one of you letting the side down then my big toe will be up your arse so fast it will be out the other side of your pretty little faces before you can say 'What the hell was that, Sergeant'! Understood?"

"Yes, sergeant," they barked.

"That is all. As you were... or not, as the case may be," she concluded, looping her finger through the slipped strap of a bra and positioning it back on the shoulder of the blushing WAAF whose pert little bosom it was intended to support. Then she disappeared back outside and closed the door.

"Grief. Will I ever be shot of that woman?" Nancy finally exhaled, this time making sure Sergeant Harris was indisputably out of earshot.

"Are you entirely sure it's a woman?" somebody cracked.

"Yeah. I bet she had no trouble passing her FFI. No man in his right mind would want to dally with her!" added another, occasioning nervous snickers from the others.

Eileen shared the amusement. However, the tidings of which the wearisome NCO was the bearer had meantime sowed a seed of unease. Stereotypically-foppish, pipe-smoking public school type that he was, Group Captain Parker had been incredibly supportive of her talent for song. She just hoped that the new CO, whoever he was, would be equally forbearing.

# 15

There is nothing like a long train journey with which to sit back and plan the future with the man you love. And unlike the last time Eileen had made this journey – when she had been assailed by all kinds of doubts about committing herself to Gerald (and to the comfortable, if rather boring prospect of being the dutiful wife and receptionist of a provincial garage manager) – this time she was in no doubt about her feelings towards Nicky. Indeed, to these two people so madly love it really did seem like there were all manner of stirring vistas opening up before them. Their rumination was aided by the good fortune of being sat in a compartment all by themselves, the trains to the capital being so much quieter these days.

This was possibly on account of a sudden tailing off in London's popularity with sightseeing servicemen and women on leave now that V1 'doodlebug' attacks on the capital had been supplanted by a new terror. For at the moment when successful counter-measures (including deploying the new fast-flying Gloster Meteor jet fighter) had enabled four-fifths of all V1s to be destroyed in the air, the Nazis had unleashed their latest 'vengeance' weapon, which had impacted with warning upon Chiswick in west London on September 8th 1944. It was indicative of how chilling this new weapon was that, unlike the droning 'doodlebug', it would earn no grudging nickname from anxious Londoners. For unlike the V1 (which had been fired from fixed launch ramps along the Channel coast that the Allies had mostly destroyed or captured), the new supersonic V2 rockets were despatched from mobile launchers and could be upon their targets within minutes of take-off. With no opportunity for intercepting them, the Allies could only re-double the efforts of their air forces to locate and destroy the V2's production facilities, many of which the Germans had hidden in bomb-proof underground factories.

"So when this war is over and you go back to America, do you think you will return to teaching?"

"When 'you' go back? Uh-uh," Nicky shook his head and reminded her as together they idly gazed out at the countryside hurtling past. "When *we* go back," he corrected her. "Or have you forgotten already?"

She turned and briefly looked into his eyes before nestling herself even more securely into his embrace. The ensuing moment of bliss afforded her yet another opportunity to thrill at how things had transpired. Three years ago, when she had joined the Women's Auxiliary Air Force as a consolation prize for the frustrated dreams she once harboured of a career in show business, how could she have ever imagined that the chance failure to show up of a professional singer despatched to the Lincolnshire sticks – plus her initially hesitant consent to join her best friend on a paired date – would have resulted in the newspapers enthusing about how she was set to become the next "Forces' Sweetheart". Meanwhile, both Nicky and Eileen had been feted in a flattering article in 'Stars And Stripes' – the US armed forces magazine. To cap it all, the man who was the great love of her life was adamant that he would not be returning to the United States without her!

"Anyway," Nicky eventually responded, "the answer to your question is: no. I've been thinking a lot about things lately. You know, about how his war has changed us all. None of us are same people we were when we were first drafted. The world has changed; and so have we. So maybe I'll try something new; in a different place. You know I said I used to sing on the swing shift to help pay my way through college?"

From her safe and secure idyll resting her head upon his chest, Eileen nodded and her eyes fleetingly glanced up to acknowledge him.

"Well, my parents will probably go bananas, but I've thought about giving it a go professionally. You know, maybe moving out to somewhere like California – the place where it's all happening nowadays. Maybe even trying to make it in Hollywood. What d'ya say, honey?"

"So you are going be 'the next Frank Sinatra'. But how could I possibly deal with all those teenage girls swooning over you!" Eileen teased him.

However, the levity of her aside belied the lights illuminating inside her own head. California… Hollywood… dare she even imagine that the day might yet dawn when she too could reach out to seize hold that illusive, yet glittering star? Peggy Lee… Jeanette MacDonald… Lana Turner… Judy Garland… Eileen Kimberley!

No, that was simply too much to contemplate. What outrageous vanity had now befallen her that she could even think that way! What selfish cunning had overcome her that she had allowed her love for this man to be coloured (however subtly) by an awareness that he might just be her passport to a new and exciting life on the other side of an ocean, as well as maybe a career up there amongst all those illustrious names of the Hollywood dream factory!

Maybe the Waterbeach erks were right: she had sold her soul to some crazy notion that America was where her destiny lay – just like Granny O'Leary had also been right that she was a 'dreamer', forever 'chasing men' for what they might offer by way of social climbing or career advancement. Perhaps Gerald had been correct in his bitter judgement too: she was a 'tramp': a self-absorbed schemer who cold-shouldered, stamped on, or humiliated those men whose own modest dreams and ambitions had failed to match the expanse of her own. Finally, she guiltily recalled the other reason she had become a WAAF, accepting that she might indeed be her 'father's child'. After all, had he too not sought to erase history and start afresh when the old life he had known – as well as the little girl who loved him and looked up to him – had proved an inconvenient brake upon the ambition that consumed him. As she did so, there came rushing back into her consciousness the warning of Our Lord, of which Auntie Kathleen had oft reminded her – *"For what shall it profit a man, if he shall gain the whole world, and lose his own soul?"* The once-devout, working class Catholic girl from the backstreets of Birmingham bit her lip, appalled by the ravenous, insatiable monster she feared she had become.

"Hey, did I say something wrong?" Nicky rubbed her cheek softly with his knuckle, wiping away a tear that had fled her watery eyes.

By now the train was beginning to slow at the end of its journey. She lifted herself up and peered out of the carriage window to mask her self-reproach, feigning to survey the rooftops of suburban London that were now closing in around them.

"No, it's just me again. I'm asking for too much from you, I know."

"Hey, babe, don't think that way. You know I'd move Heaven and Earth to be with you. In fact, I've decided. I'm not going back to the States. Well, not yet," he qualified himself, squeezing her delicate hand as if to assure her that he was in no way renouncing their deliberations about marriage, California and (more fancifully) Hollywood stardom. She turned to him to hear him out.

"I've turned down that offer of a posting back home. Instead, I've requested to remain here in England with the 322nd. That way I can be with you until this thing is finally through. You know, they reckon that if the Allied armies can successfully cross the Rhine then this war could be over by Christmas."

Eileen should have been thrilled. However, that was not the emotion that was knotting her stomach as this armchair strategist offered his humble opinion that – with Paris and much of the Low Countries liberated, and the Russians at the gates of Warsaw – the much-vaunted 'Thousand Year Reich' would soon be history. And not before time!

"But that will mean more flying operations," she gasped, horror-struck that – the Allies' mounting air superior aside – missions over Germany were still taking a daunting toll upon the young aircrews of both Bomber Command and the 'Mighty Eighth'.

"Nicky, I have no right to ask you to put your life in danger that way," she angrily asserted. "Too many good men I have known have come back burned and mutilated. Too many never came back at all! I want you safely back in the States precisely because I love you and I couldn't bear to lose you!"

"And I love you too, honey. Can't you see that? I just want us to be together as much as we can. I've never felt this way about any other girl before. Do you really think I could bear to be apart from you for a single day unless I had to? Besides, the guys need me too. Just like the guys in your outfit need you ladies on the ground to keep 'em flying. Heck, there's a war still going on, Eileen. We can't just go around making selfish choices."

She had heard it again – this time from Nicky's lips: she was being 'selfish'; not considering 'the guys' who depended upon her, as well as her obligations to fellow WAAFs. Though stung, she forgave him and drew up to him. Her slender hands alighted upon his hot, rugged cheeks as she drew her lips to his. He responded by launching his arms tight around her as their tongues trailed each other with abandon.

"King's Cross! King's Cross! All change!" the stout little guard bawled as he wandered through the empty carriage.

"King's Cross, folks... Oops, I do beg your pardon, sir... miss," he blinked with embarrassment as he popped his head inside the compartment to behold this couple interrupt their courtship to acknowledge him. With a gentle, father-like voice, he smiled back and advised that "This train terminates here."

They say that déjà vu can be a spooky sensation. To tread as many revisited highways as Eileen was doing today was positively chilling. She rose to lift down from the rack above her head the musette bag that contained her tin hat and gas mask (as well as the make-up that she took out to hastily reapply!). Nicky waited for her to make herself presentable before offering her his arm so that they might make their way out onto the platform together. Though she was once more brimming with feverish longing, she again found that longing tinged with trepidation – so much so that (as when she had trod this particular path two year ago almost to the day) it caused her to want to straight away leap back on a train heading in the other direction.

Having mentioned that regrettable expedition (when her hopes of making contact again with her him had come to nothing), Nicky was most insistent that she not give up the search for her father. Maybe it had all been a misunderstanding – a mistake on the part of whoever this younger woman was that her father had taken under his wing. Nicky had been blessed with two doting parents who loved him and had always watched over him (too much so if tales of their clucking about what he might have gotten up to during his college years was to be believed!). As such, he found it inconceivable that Eileen's father could have entirely wiped all thought of her from his consciousness. More so as he had listened to her wax lyrical these last few months about all the happy moments she recalled spending with him during her childhood. What man could possibly turn his back on such beautiful memories? And upon the 'little girl' with whom he had shared them?

Therefore, it was at her fiancé's behest that she had reluctantly agreed to try one last time to put the record straight by calling upon him at the address in the capital where, to the best of her knowledge, he still resided. Maybe it is the mark of a true gentleman that Nicky's concern for his sweetheart was such that, of all the enchanted spots he could have chosen to pass his weekend leave with her (York, Oxford, Norwich, or even visiting her family in Birmingham – all places safely out of range of Hitler's awful V-weapons), he had instead chosen London.

Sure, the sights were still here – Leicester Square, the West End theatres; St Paul's Cathedral, Westminster Abbey, Big Ben and the Houses of Parliament, Buckingham Palace. Maybe if there was opportunity they would be able to spend time wandering around a few of these familiar repositories of history, marvelling at the English-speaking heritage of faith, law and liberty that their country's shared.

First however, there was the matter of making contact with her father to attend to. Therefore, availing themselves of both Eileen's recollections from her last visit and the continuing kindness and helpfulness of strangers along the way, they journeyed together by bus to that large terraced town house in Notting Hill that symbolised such painful, unfinished business in her life. Together they stood at the foot of its wide flight of white-washed stone steps and stared up, whilst further up the street children were playing, their excited screams drifting on the breeze. Summoning up the courage, and once again praying that she was doing the right thing, she let go of Nicky's hand and mounted the steps to ring the bell.

There was no response. As on the last occasion though, she rapped the knocker lustily and in due course was entreated to the sweet refrains of a prepubescent girl chortling nursery rhymes to herself from down the hallway – just as Eileen remembered she used to do. Finally, the door partially opened and that child's face appeared around it – that same young girl with freckles and pretty amber pig-tails, this time with her favourite dolly clutched to her chest. A lump lodged itself in Eileen's throat: the same young girl who was, in all probability, her half-sister!

"Hello. You're Maureen, aren't you," she announced, watching those same winsome eyes squinting in the September sun. "I guess you don't recognise me. It's been a while. I'm Eileen. I'm here to see your daddy."

The child took a moment to shield those eyes, the better to reacquaint herself with a visitor in a smart blue uniform that she did indeed remember. What's more, that visitor was now in the company of a bespectacled young man sporting the sharply-tailored tan-and-brown uniform of an American aviator, and who was waiting below in the street, his hands in his pockets, idly rolling stones in the gutter with his polished shoes.

"Hi," he smiled up warmly to the little girl before lifting one of those hand from a pocket to point. "Say, that's a cute little doll you got there."

Maureen disappeared back behind the door, her leaden feet clumping up the stairs again. Meanwhile, uttering those last few fateful words had left Eileen's heart feeling crushed within her chest. Everything within her had wanted to cry out 'he is *my* daddy too'. Why had God permitted things to turn out this way? Did He not know that she would willingly swap her beauty, her voice, her fame, her medals – indeed everything she had ever possessed – just to hear him whisper to her that *she* was his daughter too?

With her iron gaze almost boring holes in that imposing front door that had been momentary closed in her face, Nicky could not see the hurt in her eyes or the indignant mien upon her face as she suppressed the urge to shove it open and march straight in. Instead, she craned to overhear George Kimberley's other daughter mumbling "Mummy. That woman is here again – the one you told me not to tell Daddy about."

Older, wiser – and now exceedingly angrier – Eileen was not going to countenance the awful moment of truth being put off a moment longer. By the time that same tall, elegantly-attired woman finally deigned to come to the door and see, she had readied herself for this encounter.

"Hello, we've met before," she spat a superfluous reminder. "I'm Eileen Kimberley. I have come to see my father."

"Well you might," the woman leered once she had recovered from such an abrupt greeting. "But I'm afraid he is not in."

"Don't give me that…" Eileen spat again, fighting hard not to furnish her warning with a few of the more unladylike expletives she had picked up during her years in the RAF.

"But he is not in, I tell you. Look, I am not lying to you. Most weeks he is away on business, returning on Friday evenings."

"Today is Friday. In fact, it is Friday afternoon. Therefore, it is my intention to call again later today – when he is back."

From the stridency of the young airwoman's observation, it was plain that the secret past of George Wilfred Kimberley could not be kept a secret for much longer. Eileen carried on staring defiantly while his mistress (or whatever she was) let out a sigh of resignation, turning her head away and placing a knuckle beneath her nose as if to steel herself from crying. Meanwhile, hoping he would not have to wait too much longer to say 'hi' to Eileen's estranged father (and having only the haziest notion that something was amiss on the doorstep), Nicky could only stare up anxiously from the street. Finally, resolve having returned, George's paramour shifted her gaze back onto this unwanted visitor to confront both the awful truth and the bearer of it.

"Very well," she conceded. "Often he doesn't return until quite late though. He will be tired when he does. Therefore, can we make it tomorrow instead? Shall we say ten o'clock?"

Having fallen for that one before, Eileen was about to remonstrate that she would not broach being strung along a second time. However, as if conscious of this, her unsmiling rival moved quickly to assure her that "You have my word. He will be in when you call. He will see you."

Eileen sighed. "Ten o'clock tomorrow morning it will be then."

"Of course, you do realise this is going to cause an awful lot of trouble. What right do you think you have to just turn up here and do this to us?" Eileen was then surprised to hear the woman snap, having now been rejoined by her daughter, who huddled beneath her mother's trailing arm and from where she stared up at her half-sister with a child-like mixture of puzzlement and suspicion. However, Eileen had readied herself to counter this excuse too.

"What right have you had all these years to play such a cruel game upon me? And to deny a man the right to see his…"

Eileen suppressed the urge to append her curt reply with that familial, if emotionally-charged eight letter word. Instead, she glanced down at Maureen still surveying her with innocent eyes and hoped that by this time tomorrow they might have enjoyed the opportunity to discover so much more about each other than these curious doorstep encounters had so far permitted. Satisfied there was nothing further to add for now, she turned and headed back down the steps, aware that she needed to further beg Nicky's patient indulgence.

\* \* \* \* \*

"Well, if nothing else, at least now you know it was not your father's idea to avoid you."

Nicky's pertinent observation was only so much comfort to his troubled young fiancée as they sat together on the bench in the square. Meanwhile, dusk was gathering apace and stirring excited swifts to return to their nests in the rooftops above them. Nicky draped an arm upon her and tried to knead the tension from her drooping shoulders.

"She hates me with a passion," Eileen insisted through gritted teeth. "You can see it in her eyes. After all, here I am   her worst nightmare – crash-landing into the cosy little world she has created with my father. Terrified that now I am back on the scene, she won't have him all to herself anymore."

"Nor his money, eh! Say, how much would a guy have to pay over here to buy a swanky piece of real estate like that?"

Nicky's vain attempt to lighten proceedings only deepened Eileen's palpable despondency, as well as hinting at another reason why this 'other woman' in her father's life would never countenance him being reconciled with his eldest daughter if it was within her power to frustrate it.

"Look, quit beating yourself up over this. You said it yourself: she gave you her word. Short of going back there and sneaking in through a window, you've just gotta' trust her. I know it's hard. Here," he said, taking out a tiny little book of Psalms that he carried around in his breast pocket (and which this veteran flyer had often found himself dipping into ahead of difficult and dangerous missions). He thumbed the pages…

*"Delight yourself in the Lord; and He shall give thee the desires of thine heart. Commit thy way unto the Lord; trust Him also; and He shall bring it to pass."*

He looked up from the text to observe that she was having difficulty granting such assurance a place in her heart. Perhaps, after a lifetime of disappointment – and despite Auntie Kathleen's earnest prayers on her behalf – she was finally despairing of her childhood faith.

"Hey, wait, there's more…" he therefore continued…

*"Rest in the Lord, and wait patiently for Him; fret not thyself in any wise to do evil. For evildoers shall be cut off; but those that wait upon the Lord, they shall inherit the Earth."*

He moved in closer to her and squeezed her lovingly. "Don't be angry, honey. Look, I know you love your dad. I'm kinda' guessing too that it is reconciliation with your father – and not success in your singing career – that remains that 'unreachable' star you're always talking about. But there's no point trying to second-guess what might happen tomorrow. For now let's go find some little place where we can eat… and maybe unwind."

It was anxiety more than hunger that was churning Eileen's stomach at that moment. Otherwise, heading back out of the square they hopped on a bus heading up the West End, where after a further stroll they stumbled upon a cosy little restaurant where a pianist and a clarinettist were playing soft melodies in the background. It was almost as if it had been placed across their path for the express purpose of enabling them to cast aside their cares; and for Eileen to remind herself that amidst all the turmoil going on in her life she would no longer be called upon to face it alone

"I do so hope your parents won't mind that mine live apart," she gazed across at him, sipping from the brandy glass in her hand and still not convinced that the baggage from her past would not upset her hopes for the future.

"Baloney! Such things are no big deal in America any more. Maybe it's different over here. Say, didn't you British lose a king not so long back because he intended to marry a divorcee?"

"Yes, and an American one at that!" she ribbed him, to which he grinned.

"Eileen, come what may, I will take you back with me. You will be my wife. My mom with be your mother-in-law!" he opened his eyes wide at his sweetheart in mock dread on her behalf before softening them again. "And my dad will be your father-in-law. Which will be no big deal, because I kinda' reckon the old man always wanted a daughter anyway!"

She appreciated his humour. Then her face straightened and he watched an earnestness settle upon it that spoke from the very depth of her soul.

"Tomorrow, God willing, I will meet my father again for the first time in almost ten long years. I cannot express to you how much I am looking forward to it. And despite everything I might have been tempted to believe in the intervening years, I know he will be proud of me; of what I have achieved; and of who I have become. What's more, he will be proud of you too, Nicky – the outstanding young man who will one day soon become his son-in-law."

He was visibly humbled and slid a hand across the table to squeeze hers. Otherwise, like thousands of other couples across the capital that evening, they continued lazily making plans for what they would do when war was finally over and they could at last train their youth and their idealism upon the fashioning of a new world set free from the terrible legacy of the old. As they did, the pianist and his colleague on the clarinet were joined in due course by a dapper young man who discreetly drew up a bar stool alongside them, stubbing out his cigarette. Thereafter he proceeded to add verse to the beautiful laid-back ambience that his friends had coaxed from their instruments – and with a silky, seductive baritone voice that perfectly complemented the intimacy of this evening. It earned him gentle, yet grateful applause from the handful of other diners relaxing at their tables. The musicians nodded their appreciation and then began to tease from their instruments those introductory bars to perhaps *the* most iconic melody this war had so far produced, the singer joining them in an intimate rendition of *'A Nightingale Sang In Berkeley Square'*.

"Oh, Nicky. I absolutely adore this song," Eileen wept. "We simply must do our own version of it one day. Let it always *our* song to each other."

"Yeah, another time, eh," he lovingly rebuked her. "For now let someone else do the singing. Tonight, Eileen Kimberley, will you instead grant me the honour of joining me for this dance?"

Surprisingly, no one had yet ventured onto the small piece of polished floor that lay between musicians and diners. Eileen glanced across at it, then back again coyly at Nicky. Then she beheld him rise purposely from his seat and offer his outstretched fingertips across their table. Unspeakable awe gripped her as she too rose, accepted them, and permitted him to escort her out to where she might rest a hand upon the shoulder of her fiancé and he cast an arm around her waist. Swaying gently, they permitted the singer to tenderly express everything their hearts still yearned to share.

As the melody hinted, were ever two people 'so in love'? Now that other couples were joining them on the dance floor it seemed presumptuous in the extreme. And yet as guys in uniform and their young sweethearts also swayed slowly and wistfully all around them, Nicky and Eileen knew in their hearts that this was indeed *their* private moment. As long as they lived – and as long as their love endured – there would surely never be another one to surpass this. Two people whom God, Providence, fate, chance – call it what you will – had brought together from unremarkable and far distant places on either side of an immense ocean so that, with 'magic abroad in the air', they might know that, where ever fate had yet to take them, they would never be apart again – in their hearts at least, if regretfully not always in reality.

Alas, even so mellow a voice could not fully convey the profundity of 'such a romantic affair': the tall, bespectacled Chicago kid and his beautiful, adoring Brummie belle. And so as the final reprised stanza drew this fleeting moment in time to a close, they duly closed their eyes and fashioned their mouths for an intimate kiss. The magic was complete…

> *"…And like an echo far away,*
> *A nightingale sang in Berkeley Square."*

\* \* \* \* \*

They had turned up at the bus stop for Notting Hill in good time to make their appointed ten o'clock encounter. However, the traffic ahead of them seemed to be going nowhere. Eileen glanced down fretfully at the tiny watch on her wrist.

"Sorry, folks, this is as far as this bus is going, I'm afraid," the conductress popped her pretty little head up on the upper deck and called out.

Its passengers let rip with a collective groan before the renowned, if grudging 'spirit of the Blitz' kicked in and goaded them stoically to their feet to make alternative travel arrangements. Eileen and Nicky glanced at each other anxiously, but followed down the stairs after them

"Ar' s'pose yer' gonna' tell us we've awl' gotta' swap onto that bus behind, in't we," some old man grumbled, flopping his cloth cap back on his nobbled napper as he stepped down onto the pavement.

"No, love. That bus is also not going any further," the conductress warbled. "I'm afraid Ladbroke Grove is still closed to traffic after those German rocket strikes last night."

"Wot' rocket strikes wuz' they then?"

"Wot'? Din't yer' 'ear it?" a portly woman folded her matronly arms and marvelled at him. "Gawd' blimey, Mister. You must be an 'eavy sleeper. They must 'ave woke up 'arf of London."

By now, Eileen's darting eyes and half-open mouth informed Nicky that she was becoming exceedingly agitated. It was already 10.10 am. The residual pessimist in her had clearly surfaced. Therefore, he placed a comforting hand upon her shoulder and sought a more practical solution.

"Say, Miss," he purloined the conductress as she remounted the platform to ring the bell and signal her driver to turn around. "How far is it to walk from here to Rochester Terrace? Only my fiancée and I have an important appointment we must make."

"It's just under a mile, I think. About half an hour on foot. You might be able to do it quicker though if you head up some of the side streets instead."

"Thanks. I appreciate it."

With the deadline missed and at least another half-hour of walking ahead of them, he could only flash a smile of resignation, take hold of Eileen's hand, and bid them set off as indicated. They would just have to trust that, with parts of west London at a standstill in the aftermath of the strikes, her father would surely forgive his daughter turning up late for their long-awaited reunion.

Sure enough, the side streets proved both a quieter and quicker route. It therefore took less time than they had feared. Yet, ominously, as they drew closer they became more conscious of the smell of masonry dust and charred timber permeating the morning air. Eileen's gathering frown began to ooze pessimism once more, morphing into palpable dread as her pace quickened and that familiar corner came into view. Upon spotting it she could be restrained no longer. For there, straddling the entrance to Rochester Terrace, were barriers manned by civil defence workers in tin hats

"No...! No...!" she cried in disbelief, breaking free from Nicky's grip and accelerating to a sprint, halting at the barrier to briefly stare up the street in horror. Then she shoved both barrier and its startled sentinels aside.

"'Ere, Miss. You can't go through there. It's not safe!"

Nicky shot through after her, a civil defence workers tearing after them both in turn. However, with her powerful legs pounding away as fast as they could carry her she was already some considerable distance down the road before Nicky could launch his arms around her and halt her mere yards from a huge gaping hole in the phalanx of once-graceful terraced properties ahead of them.

It was a huge gaping hole where No. 139A had once stood – the adjoining properties reduced to shells of twisted beams and crumbling walls. Elsewhere, demolished brickwork and debris – and even human body parts – were scattered the length and breadth of this street where today no children were playing, and where the only sound to be heard was the subdued clinking and clonking of other volunteers painstakingly picking over what remained.

"No! No! My daddy... My daddy...!" she yelled hysterically, fighting to wriggle free of Nicky's embrace. The civil defence volunteer joined in the manhandling until eventually the distraught WAAF sank to her knees and settled into a fit of anguished wailing that was unbearable to behold.

"You live there?" the volunteer suggested rather fancifully to the American airman now straightening his twisted cap. Nicky stepped back from Eileen, looked him in the eye, and shook his head.

"Her father did. Were there any survivors?"

This time it was the volunteer's turn to regretfully shake his head.

If ever there was a more visceral reason Nicky needed to justify his decision to remain with his squadron in England, he cast his appalled gaze along the devastated street and found it. Angry and vengeful, he forgot the cautionary words of Psalm 37. Instead, he vowed to himself there and then to not rest until he had bombed every one of those V2 production facilities into a dust even finer than the faint coating that had now settled upon his uniform – along with the evil Nazi bastards whose wicked ideology that had spurred the design and use of these murderous and indiscriminate weapons.

Meanwhile, having spotted the drama that had taken place, a member of the search team broke from his depressing chore. Tiptoeing gingerly along the duckboards back onto the *terra firma*, he picked up a handful of small objects that had been collected together and strolled up the street. Respectfully, he then held out a small, shattered picture frame and a little girl's dolly. Observing that the WAAF at his feet was still too consumed by disconsolate sobbing, he reached out and handed them to her American companion instead.

Taking the dust-coated dolly in one hand and the frame in the other, Nicky tipped his head by way of gratitude. The dolly was instantly recognisable, and even this seasoned flyer who had witnessed carnage aplenty couldn't stem the shedding of an angry tear. Otherwise, he manoeuvred the frame in his hands so that he might study the family photograph it contained. Again, mother and daughter were instantly recognisable. However, undoubtedly older and wizened, the inscrutable face of the guy with the clipped moustache bore a less obvious likeness to the treasured image of George Kimberley that Eileen had often showed him. A flush of sadness overcame him as he continued to gaze down at the father-in-law he would never meet. Then, with mangled frame and dolly still in his hands, he slowly wandered over to the pavement on the opposite side of the street, where he knelt down to prop the dolly sat upright against a dwarf wall. Alongside it he placed the photograph. There he closed his eyes and offered up a quiet prayer for little Maureen, as well as for her parents. No less solemnly, he then returned to reach down with tender hands and try once more to coax George's desolate surviving daughter to her feet.

\* \* \* \* \*

On September 17th 1944 combined British, American, Canadian and Polish armoured and airborne forces embarked on 'Operation Market Garden' – a bold, if complex, multi-layered offensive aimed at seizing the bridges over the great rivers of Holland. This would enable Allied armies to roll across northern Germany and outflank Hitler's heavily-fortified Siegfried Line, as well as delivering them to Berlin. So bold, in fact, that it almost worked. However, after six days of intense street-by-street combat, the offensive stalled – undone by its own complexity, as well as by stiffer-than-expected German opposition at the bridge at Arnhem. Thereafter, the Allies withdrew to consolidate ahead of those bridges they had captured. Alas, the war – and all its terrible suffering – would not be over by Christmas after all.

# 16

It was the moment Sergeant Harris had been waiting for. And unfortunately, Leading Aircraftwoman Eileen Kimberley had handed her the excuse she needed on a plate. No wonder the stocky NCO was trying not to look pleased as punch as she stood at ease on the sideline watching proceedings from beneath the peak of her cap. Now, at last, she could finally bring this aspirant Hollywood starlet down a peg or two.

"I'm afraid being absent without leave is a very serious offence, Kimberley," the Squadron Officer reminded her. "Furthermore, you have led me to believe that absence was undertaken for the sole purpose of spending time with your fiancé – who the sergeant here informs me is a pilot with the American Eighth Air Force, as well as a sometime entertainer with their armed forces who you have performed alongside."

All the time, Eileen stared dead ahead and did not answer. With her heart on the floor and the bottom having dropped out of her world, she had simply been too distraught to face returning to camp after such a terrible loss. Now it was a perverse and paralysing cocktail of shame about her family's past and not wanting to be seen contriving convenient excuses that caused her to bear her fate in silence.

"You must understand that I'm not prepared to tolerate you using the Royal Air Force as some sort of convenient platform for your singing ambitions – and neither is new station commander. You may be good at what you do, and you may be popular in certain quarters. However, this country is at war, and this is an operational air station. As such, I will not have my WAAFs just breezing on and off camp when it suits them. Do you understand?"

"Yes, ma'am."

The Squadron Officer halted the reprimand, having sensed that something was amiss (though she could not make out what). Neither did LACW Kimberley seem in any hurry to enlighten her. Therefore, the officer sat back and looked up in earnest from her desk, trying to take the measure of the otherwise bright and personable young airwoman standing before her.

"Offset against all this is the fact that, up until now, you have had an exemplary record as a Royal Air Force telephonist. Therefore, I ask again, Kimberley, why have you suddenly acted out of character this way?"

Eileen's face twitched as if wrestling with an urge not to give too much away. "I have been upset about a few things lately. Personal family matters that I... I apologise, ma'am. It will not happen again," was all that she would say.

"I'm pleased to hear your contrition. However, I cannot take this offence lightly. Therefore, at your sergeant's recommendation, I feel it is important that you and Leading Aircraftwoman King be separated..."

"But, ma'am, I take full responsibility for my actions. Nancy had nothing to do with what happened." Eileen at last felt compelled to protest.

"Silence when the officer is speaking!" Sergeant Harris snapped.

"Be that as it may. However, I'm told there have been other little incidents of late – if not quite insubordination, then certainly of laxness on the part of you both in maintaining standards. Then there was that dreadful incident involving that colleague of yours and her black GI boyfriend. Therefore, you will both be reassigned to other postings within the next forty-eight hours."

From out of the corner of her eye, Eileen could just sense the glee abroad that Sergeant Harris had achieved her oft-stated goal of separating Waterbeach's 'terrible twins'. It left the distraught WAAF feeling so terribly guilty that she had let people down: Nicky, who had begged her to forsake his comforting arms and return to camp by the prescribed hour; and now Nancy too. Oh, that she had followed her first instinct and, instead of waiting until the following morning as instructed, had returned to see her father that very night. Then at least they would have been together when that evil rocket had scored a direct hit upon 139A Rochester Terrace – reunited in death, as it were. Now she had to face the future without him. What's more, by her culpable folly, it looked like she was going to have to face a long period apart from the other man she loved too. The story of her life, she despaired: one step forward, two steps back; joy one moment, only to be snatched away and replaced by sorrow again the next.

\* \* \* \* \*

*October 28th 1944*

*Dear Eileen,*

*I know things have been difficult for you of late, but please don't blame yourself. Terrible things happen all the time in war. God willing, by this time next year it really will all be over. Furthermore, let's not give up keeping in touch with each other – despite the distance between us.*

*I'm sorry to hear they've posted you so far from me – and from Nicky too. It seems excessive in the circumstances. I do wish you had come to see me first. I would certainly have spoken up for you. You do not deserve this. I think we both know why it has happened. And there was me rather foolishly assuming you would be posted to another East Anglian bomber base at least!*

*As I write this, it's raining almost as hard as it must be where you are. However, I have made good friends amongst the WAAFs at my new posting – including a jolly girl from Durham called Pippa West, who you once shared a posting with. She has such fond memories of you, and tells me it was her fault that you were launched on the road to a singing career in the first place, having pushed you to the front of the stage one night.*

*I hope Nicky is okay, and that – despite the distance between you both – you will get the chance to see each other soon. Just remember: when you need a bridesmaid at your wedding I want first refusal! Take care.*

*Your best friend always,*

*Nancy*

\* \* \* \* \*

RAF Ottercops Moss they called it. Set amidst desolate moorlands midway between Newcastle-upon-Tyne and the Scottish border, this tiny radar station had to rank as one of Royal Air Force's bleakest and most isolated outposts in mainland Britain – providing as it did surveillance cover for the great industrial cities of the north-east. Its principal claim to fame was that it was the Chain Home station that had tracked the incoming flight of Nazi Deputy Führer Rudolf Hess on his bizarre one-man negotiating mission in 1941. Meanwhile, Ottercops Moss was the source of perennial ridicule amongst scrambled fighter pilots on account of the uncanny ability of its operators to confuse enemy aircraft with thunderstorms!

Thankfully, the morning rain had passed and – if not exactly sunny – at least the weather was presenting a more benign face. Staring up at its tall masts, as well as out across the endless wilderness, Eileen drew up the collar of her greatcoat to shield herself from the cold wind blowing in from the North Sea, and which hurried the clouds along – some of which were dark enough to herald further squalls before the afternoon was through. They further added to the bleakness of this lonely spot. It was symbolic, Eileen thought, of the period of her life into which she had now entered – for to be assigned to Ottercops Moss was punishment indeed.

With only a handful of calls coming in and going out, Eileen despaired that being marooned here was such an absurd waste of her talents. What Ottercops Moss really needed was a clerk who could answer telephones. Thanks to the machinations of the malign Sergeant Harris, what it had ended up with was a skilled telephonist who was reduced to shuffling paperwork. Fortunately, her easy-going manner meant it was not long before Eileen had made friends again amongst the handful of WAAFs (and even fewer male personnel!) who also had the dubious fortune to serve here as radar operators or technicians. Indeed, apart from the sheep dotting the open fells, they were the only company for miles around. No cinemas; no dance halls; even the nearest pub was several miles away! She missed Nancy; she desperately missed Nicky; and she missed the opportunity to take to the stage and sing, fearing it would be a long time before she would have the opportunity to do so again.

\* \* \* \* \*

*November 25th 1944*

*My dearest Nicky,*

*Here I am writing to you again, feeling guilty that I am once more burdening you with my desolation. There's not much to do here, but at least on clear nights I can look up and see all the stars in their glory. That's when I find myself thinking of you – praying that God who created the heavens will keep you safe.*

*I find myself praying a lot lately. I pray for you and me. I pray for other people I know and love, like Mom and Auntie Kathleen. I pray for all the people who have suffered loss and are grieving as a result of this wicked war. I have found myself praying too for the person who has caused our separation, because does Our Lord not say "Love your enemies, bless them that curse you" and "pray for them which despitefully use you and persecute you." These last few weeks have shown me that I need to trust Him even more when the dark clouds circle. So perhaps some good has come out of what has happened.*

*Meanwhile, perhaps aware of my brief fame, Gloria and June – two of the new WAAF friends I have made – have roped me into performing in the station's Christmas concert. It won't be a lavish affair; but hopefully it will help lift the spirits of the poor souls who are stuck out here. And at least it keeps me singing! Indeed, I'm sometimes tempted to wonder whether being consigned to singing as part of a choir is God's way of teaching humility where once I was riddled with overweening pride.*

*Above all, I remain touched that you have chosen to return to England after your spell of well-deserved home leave – even though we look set to remain apart anyway. I am so sorry if your oft-expressed devotion to me will also put you in danger because of you resuming flying operations. I desperate pray God will keep you safe.*

*Anyway, I better go. Maybe soon we can be back together again. I yearn for that moment with everything that is within me.*

*Until then, all my love,*

*Eileen    xxx*

\* \* \* \* \*

"I say, Eileen. Be a love, will you, and get me the Air Ministry on the blower."

"The Air Ministry, ma'am?"

"That's right. It looks like once again those big-wigs in London have forgotten about us. I believe it was a chap called Sykes I spoke to last time – in the Works Department. He still hasn't returned my call."

"Yes, ma'am."

Watch out for the WAAF admin officer, they said. She's a disciplinarian – a right stickler for the rules, they added. While reaching for the telephone on the desk in front of her and scanning the list of contacts in her little notebook, Eileen briefly observed the woman in question retreat back into a perusing of the accounts. Whilst waiting for the call to be connected, she marvelled how her new chief was indeed a perfectionist. However, for all that she could be pedantic about uniforms and kit inspections, Eileen was beginning to appreciate that there was more to Section Officer Rachel Owen than all those dire warnings she had been plied with when she had first arrived.

"I have the Air Ministry on the line now, ma'am," she advised, turning to her address her. The WAAF officer picked up the phone on her own desk and permitted Eileen to transfer the call.

"Hello…" she hollered resolutely, pressing a finger to her free ear in order to better catch the voice at the other end. "Is that Mr Sykes…? Yes, it's Section Officer Rachel Owen here again – you remember, the admin officer at Ottercops Moss…? No, Ottercops Moss – the Chain Home station north of

Hadrian's Wall... How am I spelling it...? 'O' for Oscar, 'T' for Tango... Yes, that's us...What? You thought we'd been closed down..."

Eileen had turned around to fetch something from a filing cabinet, for a brief moment affording Owen the opportunity to glance up at her, roll her eyes, and shake her head in despair.

"...No, I'm afraid we're still here, Mr Sykes. In fact, that's why I'm calling you again. I just wondered if you have a date yet. You know, for when you *are* going to close us down... What? Can you get back to me? Well, I did phone two weeks ago and you haven't got back to me yet... Yes... Only with winter setting in, I'm sure you'll appreciate it's getting a bit nippy up here. So I just thought it would be nice to have a date when we can all finally pack up and head for more conducive climes... No, I said 'climes', not 'crimes'...! Oh, I see... Very well then. You'll call me back as soon as you have some news... That's if you don't hear from me again in the meantime, of course," she guffawed ironically. "Yes... Good day, Mr Sykes..."

"Ruddy Air Ministry wallahs! It seems we're stuck up here a bit longer by the look of things!" she muttered, slamming the phone down. It was the first time in the weeks she had been working with her that Eileen had heard this decorous woman swear.

One thing no one could fault their section officer for was an awareness of just how boring much of RAF life could be – especially for those hapless souls who happened to be posted to this forgotten place. Hence, it had been her idea that the personnel on the camp relieve their boredom with plays and concerts – of which she took an active part in writing and directing. She had also been responsible for procuring a wealth of edifying books for the camp's 'library' (which was actually two rather large bookshelves in the main mess hall!). By such means did she hope to maintain morale until such time as the Air Ministry deigned to finally close down Ottercops Moss – now that newer, more advanced radar facilities had rendered stations like it redundant.

Whilst Eileen missed the excitement of operating a fast-moving switchboard, if nothing else working in such close proximity to her formidable section officer had enabled her to discover that there was an incredible human side to the thirty year-old that not even the exigencies of maintaining discipline and good order on an isolated RAF camp could wholly disguise – as evidenced by her shocking (and, at first, slightly discombobulating) preference for addressing the women under her command by their Christian names. Indeed, she seemed to possess a genuine concern for them which even extended (or so Eileen had been told) to quietly helping one or two young WAAFs in distressing personal circumstances who might otherwise have found themselves at the mercy of the intransigence or incomprehension of the male-orientated mindset that riddled the Royal Air Force.

Meanwhile, as well as being the admin officer, Section Officer Owen was also the *de facto* catering officer for the station. One of the things she had tasked Eileen with was investigating the somewhat exorbitant cost of the booze allocation for the officers' mess. With closure on the cards, the numbers of officers could now be counted on the fingers of one hand. Hence it was becoming harder to justify the amount of spirits being ordered each month.

"I have recalculated those requisition figures that you asked for, ma'am," she therefore stood up and explained, presenting her findings so that her superior officer might scan them forensically with horrified eyes.

"Good grief, girl! The entirety of Fighter Command would be hard-pressed to down this much whiskey!" she then curled those eyes in alarm, comparing the revised estimates with what had been ordered up until now.

"It does seem rather excessive, ma'am."

"Excessive! If the Air Ministry could be bothered to despatch an auditor this far north they'd think us a right bunch of legless inebriants!"

She studied the revised figures again before signing off revised requisition forms with a hearty flourish of her pen. "Now be a love again: go take these forms to the CO and ask him to append his moniker to them as well."

"Yes, ma'am."

Having duly headed off to locate him, Eileen returned forthwith with the 'bumf' still in her hand and an anxious look on her face.

"You haven't any ideas where he might be, ma'am? He's not in his office. And I can't see him in the officers' mess either."

Owen rose wearily from her desk and huffed. "Second thoughts, Eileen, I'll go find him and get them signed. Our CO is the biggest single consumer of the drinks allocation. So I suspect he's probably squirreled away with it in his usual bolt hole. Maybe I better be the one to present him with the bad news. Sticking this drastically revised requisition in front of his nose should prove a pretty abrupt way of sobering him up!"

"Yes, ma'am."

It would appear that Section Officer Rachel Owen was not only the admin officer and the *de facto* catering officer, but also – given that the station commander was frequently *hors de combat* on account of being 'drunk and incapable' – the *de facto* person in charge at this windswept early warning station. Meanwhile, Eileen sat back down at her desk to gaze out at the hardy sheep mooching about outside, both their fodder and their fleeces rippling in the stiff breeze that also murmured through the gaps in the window panes. Aside from reading the complete works of William Shakespeare in the library, serious drinking was probably one of few other pastimes to be had on this godforsaken speck in the middle of nowhere.

Rumour had it that Owen's empathetic disposition towards her girls (as well as her determination that the CO would just have to get by on one bottle of whiskey a month!) owed much to her family background. Her mother had once been an active suffragette and temperance campaigner; whilst her father was a well-known Christian writer, pacifist and campaigner for Indian independence. Even someone of Eileen's political naivety could discern that this was a bizarre and unconventional pedigree for a commissioned officer in His Majesty's armed forces. And Section Officer Owen was nothing if not unconventional. Intelligent, witty and utterly unfazed by hierarchies of class or gender, after a spell of service doing hush-hush, top secret code-breaking work (from which she had been removed in circumstances that no one had yet fathomed) this chaste and well-travelled polymath had been assigned instead to mother the WAAFs of Ottercops Moss. This final titbit of rumour left the exiled young airwoman from Birmingham wondering whether she might not be the only person present on the station who was serving penance for a misdemeanour.

\* \* \* \* \*

*December 8th 1944*

*My beloved Eileen,*

> *After my recent furlough in Chicago, this is just a little 'sugar report' to tell you how lonely I am without you in my arms.*

> *However, while I was home I was approached by a famous music producer, who wants to sign me up to his recording label once I'm back in the States for good. I sure am flattered! What's more, I have put in a good word for you too. In fact, I remain determined that if I ever do achieve fame and success, then you will be right there sharing it with me. Perhaps we can even star in our own movies together!*

> *I really do hope we will be able to spend Christmas together. Let us resolve to make that time all the more special and make up for the many weeks we have been apart.*

> *I remain your ever loving all-American guy,*

*Nicky*

\* \* \* \* \*

Even though the cast almost outnumbered the audience, the attendees of the Christmas concert at RAF Ottercops Moss were having a whale of a time. It added to the Christmas feel that a cold front had dumped several inches of snow on the Northumberland moors overnight. Everyone was therefore in the mood for the light-hearted diversion provided by this witty Nativity sketch. It punctuated an earnest message of hope and redemption in a fallen world with glimmers of humour. Not that all the humour was intentional – as when Gloria, the batty WAAF detailed to play Mary, dropped the Baby Jesus, the doll's head promptly detaching and trundling across the stage. It prompted great hilarity amongst the erks rolling about in the aisles. Though shielding her eyes in dismay that her latest theatrical masterpiece might be coming undone, even Section Officer Owen couldn't mask a grin.

Fortunately, decorum was restored when Eileen and the rest of the choir reassembled to round off the evening with some good old-fashioned carols – again personally arranged and conducted by the irrepressible Section Officer Owen. Filling their lungs and singing heartily, it was moving to behold their officer's face aglow with pride that they had put on such a thoroughly professional performance. They took their bows at the end and looked on as she joined them on the stage of the small mess hall.

"Thank you, folks," she smiled at the audience ebulliently. "I thought you might like to know this will be our last Christmas at Ottercops Moss…"

There was a collective whoop of joy on the part of both audience and choir, as well as a smirk of relief on the part of their *de facto* entertainment officer.

"… Because I can today confirm that the Air Ministry have finally given me a date in the New Year when this station will close."

"Thank God. We're out of here at last!" someone cried, articulating the consensus amongst its close-knit service community that they had been keeping company with sheep and heather for far too long.

Eventually, the celebratory cheers subsided to permit Section Officer Owen to wind up her Christmas message to those present. Meanwhile, Eileen braced herself for the closing event of the evening: one she intended would bid Godspeed to those lucky enough to be boarding the bus that would be despatched up from Newcastle in a few days' time. This would then deliver them to the railway station and home leave with their families and loved ones.

Thus did Eileen behold the WAAF officer stretch out her hand and draw her forward. Meanwhile, a corporal on the piano located the appropriate sheet of music and started to play. For the first time in many months, Eileen now found herself left alone on a stage. Sensing the awe abroad amongst her small, but appreciative audience, she offered them a gentle smile and commenced her rendition of Bing Crosby's enchanting *'I'll Be Home For Christmas'*.

Maybe she couldn't entirely disguise her own disappointment that she wasn't going to be one of those lucky souls who had been allocated festive leave. She thought of all the soldiers, sailors and airmen still serving overseas, for whom this would be yet one more Christmas away from their families. Neither could she cast from her mind the terrible news that band leader Glenn Miller had been posted missing after the plane conveying him to a Christmas concert in France had been lost over the English Channel. Most of all though, she thought of Nicky – even though doing so rendered the words she was singing all the harder to bear.

* * * * *

If nothing else it was a day out: a relief from the tedium of the fells in winter. It was also the first time in months that Eileen had clapped eyes upon the welcome sight of a real working RAF station. Alas, RAF Brunton was only a training facility, so what limited flying was taking place today was solely to familiarise pilots with the handling qualities of the RAF's latest piston-engined fighters.

"Yes, Hawker Tempests, by the looks of it. Or are they Typhoons? I'm afraid aircraft recognition never was my strong point. Not that I ever got to see many planes in my line of work," Section Officer Rachel Owen joked, joining Eileen in shielding her eyes from the low winter sun to observe a pair of these otherwise formidable aircraft approach for a bumpy landing.

Excitement over, Rachel Owen jumped back in the car, prompting Eileen to do likewise. Then, with the items they had come to collect safely in the boot, they pulled away from the quartermaster's store and out past the guard house.

"Well, thank you, Eileen. It's been good to have your company this morning. I always have difficulty remembering the way – especially with all the direction signs removed. Although why they took them down around here I cannot imagine. I think we can safely say that had the Germans ever advanced this far north then – regardless of all that blabber about 'fighting them in the hills' – Mr Churchill and his government would have long since been packed aboard a ship bound for Canada!"

Eileen smiled. "I'm just sorry I'm not much good at map reading, ma'am. It was never my strong point."

It was Rachel's turn to appreciate self-deprecating humour. "Nonsense! You have been a godsend to me. And by the way, do stop calling me ma'am when we're on our own. It's Rachel, okay."

"Yes, ma'am. I mean... Rachel."

This was going to take some getting used to, Eileen fretted. Otherwise, there was definitely an interesting chemistry at work between the tall, demonstrative officer and her more diminutive and deferential clerk-cum-telephonist.

Truth to be told, Eileen had grown quite fond of her superior officer, who for a few weeks now had been letting slip little glimpses of herself – perhaps to subconsciously leaven the loneliness of managing an isolated radar station. Indeed, much of this morning spent motoring along the byways of Northumberland had passed with Rachel idly reminiscing about her childhood in India. She also jauntily let slip that she had been nicknamed 'Squiggle' at school on account of her appalling handwriting (to which the longsuffering clerk-cum-telephonist tasked with deciphering it had cheekily replied that nothing had changed since!). Rachel had further intimated how her pacifist father had been aghast at his eldest daughter's decision to join the Women's Auxiliary Air Force, although (as Rachel had explained) she considered standing by while Hitler ravaged Europe to be a far greater sin than taking up arms to stop him.

"You worked in intelligence and code-breaking, didn't you?" Eileen enquired, resuming their conversation.

"That's right. I loved it. Absolutely relished the challenge," she replied, though careful of necessity not to give too much away. Eileen understood.

"However, whilst I was there I received the dreadful news that my younger sister had attempted to commit suicide. Unfortunately, trying to wangle leave to be by her side during that dark moment led to me being reprimanded and transferred to radar reconnaissance duties instead. That's how I ended up marooned at Ottercops Moss. 'Bypassing the correct channels', my male superior termed what I had done. I suspect the truth was that he simply didn't like working with women; and he certainly never enjoyed working with an opinionated wench like me!"

"It looks like we've both been banished here for our sins then," her motoring companion chuckled impishly.

Yet perhaps Rachel was being a touch too forthcoming. There was a knowing look in her eye as she momentarily glanced sideways to share amusement at Eileen's remark – one more little clue that Section Officer Rachel Owen had taken a distinct shine to her. Why else, it seemed, had this erudite and conscionable officer elected to make the attractive young airwoman her earthly confessor? More intriguingly, why else during the morning's lengthy discourse had she barely made mention of boyfriends – of which she seemed to have passed her wartime years in the absence of?

"You're not in any hurry to get back, are you?" she glanced over at Eileen and asked.

It seemed a curious question. After all, surely anywhere was preferable to the bleakness of their posting. Besides which, Eileen was a woman under orders. She wasn't used to a superior officer offering her a choice about how and where to spend her day. She shrugged her shoulders, though continuing to worry about how today's little excursion was panning out.

"Good. Seahouses is not too far from here. We've still got time for a quick look at the sea before dusk draws in," she winked, removing her hand from the steering wheel to gently tap Eileen's reassuringly.

And with that they soon found themselves traversing the coast road, looking out of the car as it breezed past gaps in the dunes that offered glimpses of the rolling North Sea breakers. Drawing up in the little seaside town, Rachel yanked on the handbrake and bade Eileen join her for a short promenade along the wild and dramatic Northumberland coast.

"It's certainly impressive," Eileen noted once they had located a bench upon which to sit down and gaze across at the colossal medieval edifice of Bamburgh Castle that was looming in the distance.

"Yes. And that's Holy Island and the monastery of Lindisfarne over there," Rachel remarked, edging in closer to Eileen to lay one hand on her shoulder whilst pointing out to sea with the other. A fleeting tension prompted the young telephonist to cast a sideways glance at her before duly staring back out to sea at the shapes rising up through the haze.

Here it was – or so 'Squiggle' now enlightened her increasingly jittery companion – that Christianity had first flourished in England until Viking invaders had landed to plunder the monastery and subjugate the local inhabitants. Indeed, on this breezy winter's day it was not hard to observe the barbed wire, tank traps and pillboxes strewn out along the deserted beach and be struck by a different kind of symbolism: of their battered, yet unbeaten nation having fought so long and so hard to defend its proud Christian heritage from a similarly brutal and rapacious barbarism. The kind of symbolism that had driven the headstrong Rachel to pour her passion into service to her country and its air force – even to the exclusion of a man in her life.

"You seem quite knowledgeable about religious things," Eileen ventured to suggest, unsure of what else to say. "I mean you clearly put your heart and soul into writing and directing our Nativity play. And I've noticed the many religious books you've placed in the camp library."

"You could say that. It's not all a legacy of my parents. I'm a follower of Christ myself. Tell me, Eileen, do you believe in Him?"

Having feared that her senior officer was on the verge of indulging in the kind of unspeakable silliness that risked them both being slung out of the service, Eileen was relieved that her question felt like it was actually spoken in earnest. She made awkward eye contact once more before taking a deep breath and staring back out to sea.

"I'm a Roman Catholic, ma'am... I mean, Rachel," she corrected herself, trying to relax once more in her company "So yes, I do believe Jesus is our Saviour. Correct me if I am wrong however, but you're what they call an 'evangelical', aren't you? You believe in a different sort of Christianity to us."

"We don't believe in purgatory or penances, if that's what you mean. No, we believe that Christ, by his death and resurrection, has wiped away our sins for all time. If you have faith in Him then that is enough. 'Never will I leave you, never will I forsake you', Jesus promised. The rest of the New Testament is just good advice about how to avoid the pitfalls of sin and so live your life in a way that will enable the Holy Spirit to draw you closer to Him. That's why we don't believe in praying to saints or to the Virgin Mary. Christ is our 'all in all'. Nor do we confess our sins to priests. As believers, Jesus taught that we can confess our sins directly to God Himself, who – thanks to His sacrifice on the Cross – will always hear us and forgive us. After all, why confess to the monkey when you can confess to the Organ-Grinder!"

Her irreverent analogy teased a welcome grin on Eileen's part. Not only was such a witty observation so typical of her chief, but it reminded Eileen that she ought not feel too guilty that she had again been skipping Confession. Not that there were too many Catholic priests to be found roaming the windy moors of Northumberland! She chuckled to herself once more at the 'monkey' analogy.

"Tell me, Eileen, what's troubling you? I mean, I think I have known you long enough now to sense that something is tormenting you. You used to do quite a bit of singing, didn't you? Made quite a name for yourself, by all accounts. And I know you miss your fiancé. Forgive me that I wasn't able to grant you Christmas leave; but I hope you'll appreciate I have other personnel who have been waiting a long time to escape Ottercops Moss and spend time with their families."

Eileen broke from her introspection to acknowledge such concern. Otherwise, she still felt too ashamed to admit the truth – especially to an officer. Yet Rachel was different. A human being even! Therefore, she swallowed hard and looked across into her searching eyes.

"I lost my father recently. He was killed in a German rocket strike. You see, my parents separated when I was a little girl. I hadn't seen my father for almost ten years. However, my auntie had gotten hold of an address for him. And so I had travelled to London twice hoping to meet him. The first time without success; the second time on the very day that he was killed. Now all I have left are my memories of him. I will never know why he never made any attempt to get in touch with me – or indeed whether he even still loved me."

Rachel laid her hand upon Eileen's shoulder a second time in a gesture of quasi-maternal condolence. Indeed, perhaps that's what Eileen found so endearing about this remarkable officer. Despite her determination to prove her fortitude and independence – and to therefore break free from her often suffocating family circumstances – sometimes Eileen had looked up to Nicky to be the dashing and heroic absent father figure she subconsciously missed. If so, then was it imagining too much to admit too that she had maybe allowed Section Officer Rachel Owen to replace her own mother, whose attention had so often been elsewhere?

"Am I really such a bad person that even my own father couldn't love me? Maybe I am. Maybe I was selfish for wanting to travel from place to place singing when my calling in this war is to answer telephones. Maybe I was selfish wanting to be someone famous – and especially to be famous in America – when I ought to just be grateful for what I have. I'm afraid I have not conducted myself in a very Christian manner, have I, ma'am."

Eileen's sweet face screwed up with emotion and she began to weep. Rachel moved in to scoop her into her embrace and comfort her.

"Eileen, you mustn't blame yourself," she chided her softly. "Christianity isn't about being perfect; or even being 'good'. And you are not 'selfish'. Far from it! You see, there is a reason why I wanted you to accompany me today."

At that moment, Eileen broke from her tears to observe Rachel's intense brown eyes gazing into her own with something approaching awe.

"The name: 'Eileen Kimberley' – could it be, I wondered? Yes, it was, I now realise: the same Eileen Kimberley to whom I owe an immense debt of gratitude precisely because she acted unselfishly. To be precise, because once upon a time you chose to follow the example of our Saviour by showing love and compassion towards a member of my family."

Eileen was perplexed.

"But how? When did I ever show such compassion?" she snuffled, dabbing at her eyes. Rachel edged back over to her own side of the bench to elaborate.

"You remember your basic training at RAF Innsworth?" she hinted.

Eileen duly cast her mind back to all those arduous weeks of square-bashing that seemed so long ago now.

"Well, amongst your billet of recruits was a shy eighteen year-old girl who had joined the WAAF full of apprehension about whether she was up to it. She had joined because her big sister had already enlisted and was constantly prodding her to 'do her bit' for the war effort too. However, this shy young girl now found herself alone a long away from home. Never quite able to remember her right foot from her left, before long all her worst fears were confirmed. She had made a terrible mistake. She used to write home in tears telling her parents how harsh the corporal was, and how cruel some the other girls were to her because she simply couldn't get the hang of service life."

It was uncanny, but Eileen did indeed remember just such a girl. What was her name now? The one who eventually ran away; and who the MPs apprehended as she was about to board a train at Gloucester railway station?

"However," Rachel continued, instead gazing out to sea as if to suppress the urge herself to break down and cry. "In those letters she also mentioned another fellow recruit. Only this one was different. Where the others girls poked fun at her or shunned her in embarrassment, this particular WAAF elected to befriend her. With great patience, she even tried to help her master the things she needed to learn; always commending and encouraging her. Let me think: what were the exact words she used to say to her? 'You stick by me and *together* we will help *each other* to be strong'."

The cock crowed thrice upon Eileen's sudden realisation that *she* was the charitable WAAF in question. And that the girl she had befriended was called Ruth – Ruth Owen!

"Yes, Eileen. Ruth Owen is my little sister. Fortunately, her bid to end it all was rather half-hearted: a few pills – certainly not enough to do the job properly. But then maybe it was just a cry for help – and that she had not totally despaired of life after all. Maybe she was touched that there was still someone out there – a Christian, dare I say it; someone who cared enough to bequeath her at least one fond memory of a few weeks in her life that she might otherwise now prefer to forget. And you, Eileen, were that someone who befriended her. You were the one who cared."

Rachel was sufficiently knowledgeable about the Scriptures that, unlike Nicky or Wilbur, she had no need to resort to flicking the pages of a bible in order to eloquently recite some apposite words. This she now did, staring out at the long shadows both WAAFs were casting now that the pale sun had emerged again to beam low in the sky behind them…

> *"'For I was hungry, and ye gave me meat: I was thirsty, and ye gave me drink: I was a stranger, and ye took me in: Naked, and ye clothed me: I was sick, and ye visited me: I was in prison, and ye came unto me.' …And the King shall answer and say unto the righteous, '…inasmuch as ye have done it unto one of the least of these my brethren, ye have done it unto Me.'"*

Eileen remembered Ruth Owen and the friendship she had offered her. She recalled too Cathy Clarke's dying words that night on the floor of the WAAF ablutions block at Waterbeach. Now, as then, she suddenly found herself reduced to uncontrollable sobbing.

"Eileen, you were there for my sister at her lowest moment. I know losing your father and then being stuck in the middle of nowhere away from your fiancé has probably been your lowest moment. I just hope I have repaid your kindness to my family by being *your* friend during our time together – notwithstanding that I am also your section officer! I'm sorry that I wasn't able to sort Christmas out for you. However, I have pulled a few strings with people I know and managed to do this instead. God alone knows where they'll send me this time if my superior finds out about this bit of 'wangling'!" she sighed, unbuttoning her coat pocket, and taking something out, which she handed across to Eileen.

"What is it?" she responded, staring at the small brown envelope.

"Nothing personal, you understand, but with the place now winding down for closure I've decided I'd rather dispense with your services and sort out my own bumf. Therefore, I have managed to secure you a new posting: as a telephonist on the Bomber Command station at RAF Mildenhall – which I believe is a mere hop-skip-and-a-jump from where your fiancé is based."

"But ma'am," Eileen gasped, lifting the letter from out of the envelope and scanning its contents. "How can I ever repay you for this?"

"You already have, don't forget… And will you stop calling me 'ma'am'!"

\* \* \* \* \*

Having looked up from her desk and spotted the bus pulling to a halt on the lane down the hill, Section Officer Rachel Owen thought nothing more of it and returned to her paperwork; or more precisely to her latest theatrical masterpiece. For now that the transmitters had been switched off all that remained to be done over the next few weeks was to finally wind up activities at RAF Ottercops Moss. Just as well, she thanked the Lord, for the weather forecasters were predicting more heavy snow and sub-zero temperatures! Lest ennui set in, she had therefore resolved to make the most of the quiet time that remained to indulge her passion as an amateur playwright. She already had the basic plot in her head. Now she was eager to work on developing her characters. However, she had not been scribbling long before she heard a knock on her door. Miffed by the interruption, she put down her pencil.

"Come in."

To which a distinctly butch-looking WAAF NCO marched inside to arrive at her desk and salute stiffly. "Sergeant... I mean Corporal Harris, reporting for duty, ma'am."

"Ah, Corporal," Rachel sat back in her chair and folded her arms grandly. "Why, I've been expecting you. Who's been a naughty girl then!"

"I'm sorry, ma'am?"

Harris feigned to ignore the slight, though she had been smarting at her demotion during the long train journey up from Cambridge. Then from Newcastle railway station she had watched civilisation progressively give way to hoary uplands absent of any trace of humanity. Finally, she had clapped eyes on those distinctive (if now silent) radar masts that dominated the skyline, and which would be her new posting for the remainder of the winter.

"Just a bit of leg-pulling, Corporal. Anyway, don't be too put out by your demotion. Worse things can happen. Besides, the last poor girl who worked with me was sent up here as punishment too – so you're in good company. Or at least you would have been had she not been posted away this morning. Why, I'm surprised you didn't bump into her at the station."

"No, ma'am. I didn't," Harris grunted as impatiently as she thought officer-NCO propriety would permit. However, some grating sixth sense intimated who her new CO might be referring to.

"Anyway, with her departure I'm afraid there are no more girls left here for you to take charge of. In fact, there's not much of anything going on now apart from itemising and packing stores and equipment. By the way, Corporal, can you sing?"

"Sing, ma'am?"

"You know. *DO-RE-MI-FA-SO-LA-TI-DO* – that kind of singing. Only that dear girl had an absolutely fabulous voice. I was rather hoping you might like to step into the part I had cast for her in my latest production. You know it's so important at an isolated backwater like this to keep up the morale of the personnel. That's why I've sort of established this tradition of roping my charges into song and drama routines."

Had the tone-deaf Corporal Harris been able to sink her face into her hands in despair she would have done so. Instead, she faced the front and heard the section officer out as she waxed lyrical about the last WAAF from RAF Waterbeach who had found herself exiled to Ottercops Moss.

Once she had been dismissed, the seething NCO trudged over the frost-hardened ground to her quarters. Shoving the door open, she threw her kit bag down on the bed and paced over to the stove in the centre of the hut, where she squatted and held her stubby hands up to the meagre warmth radiating from its little glass door. Hissing at it, she rose and drifted over to the window in a barely suppressed rage, staring up accusingly at the stone grey skies. Why had she ended up at this godforsaken place where there was nothing around as far as the eye could see? Except bloody sheep!

# 17

With evening fast falling, the train finally pulled into the familiar environs of Cambridge station and drew to a halt alongside the platform. The engine hissed loudly and let out a billowing cloud of white steam that enveloped the handful of passengers steeping down onto that platform – including one very tired, yet relieved young airwoman. She thanked a soldier for helping to lift down her kit bag. Politely, she declined to take up his kind offer to carry it for her across the station. Meanwhile, waiting by the booking hall was one anxious young American aviator, impatient for the swathe of steam to clear so that at last he might spy out the beautiful girl he remembered so well.

Suddenly she was there. She spotted him too and advanced towards him. He did likewise, both of them quickening the pace until Eileen had hurried the final few yards into Nicky's outstretched arms, which closed tight around her. He then lifted her up bodily and their lips locked, her legs bent at the knees as she savoured the thrill of being airborne in his arms.

"I have missed you so much!" she wept as his grip eased and her feet alighted again upon the hard platform slabs.

"I've missed you too, honey!" he replied, releasing her so that they might step back and survey each other with thanksgiving in their hearts.

\* \* \* \* \*

The war and its attending tragedies continued. However, shafts of light were now streaming in from the end of what had been an exceedingly long, dark tunnel. Following a German counter-attack in the Belgian Ardennes over Christmas, Allied armies had eventually rallied and their air forces successfully polished off what few armoured resources Hitler had been able to marshal together for this last desperate throw of the dice. A crossing of the Rhine by the British and Americans was now only a matter of weeks away.

Meanwhile, in the East the Russians launched a massive offensive that drove the Germans out of Poland. Warsaw fell on January 17th 1945. The Oder river was crossed on February 5th, paving the way for a final Soviet assault on Berlin. On February 13th, Budapest fell; whilst on the same day over twelve hundred RAF and USAAF bombers obliterated the ancient city of Dresden, creating a firestorm in which over 25,000 Germans perished – many of them refugees fleeing west to escape the tender mercies of the vengeful Red Army.

It was Bomber Command's most controversial mission to date, with critics in the press and the House of Commons deploring what they saw as naked bloodlust perpetrated upon increasingly defenceless civilians. Even Churchill initially sought to distance himself from the attack. However, a defiant Air Chief Marshall Harris coldly reminded him that "Dresden was a mass of munitions works, an intact government centre, and a key transportation point to the East. It is now none of those things... Attacks on cities – like any other act of war – are strategically justified insofar as they tend to shorten the war and preserve the lives of Allied soldiers. Then, paraphrasing Bismarck's famous quip, he insisted that "I do not personally regard the whole of the remaining cities of Germany as worth the bones of one British grenadier!"

However, horror at the Dresden 'atrocity' was quickly eclipsed by revelations about a far more shocking atrocity. On January 27th Russian troops stumbled upon a little town called Auschwitz, where they liberated seven thousand emaciated survivors from a 'concentration camp' located nearby. It had become apparent that this was just one of many such camps into which the Nazis had been herding and slaughtering several million Jews and other minority groups that their racial theories deemed sub-human. Over a million such victims had perished in the now silent gas chambers of Auschwitz-Birkenau alone, their flesh recovered to manufacture soap and their hair to line the flying suits of German pilots! Meanwhile, at other camps bizarre and wicked medical experiments had been conducted upon unwitting human guinea pigs. Never before had human depravity manifested itself on such a systematic industrial scale – one final entreaty, if ever it was needed, for Allied aircrews to press on and finish the job they had started.

\* \* \* \* \*

It had been a cold and savage winter. And even though it was now late-March, the harsh weather was not finished yet. Almost a foot of snow had fallen overnight, and only after a herculean communal effort in which every available erk and WAAF had been handed a shovel had the runway at RAF Mildenhall been re-opened so that flying could be resumed.

Job done, there was just time for those girls assigned to dig out this particular extremity of the runway to engage in a brief snowball fight before tossing their shovels aboard the lorry despatched to retrieve them. Then, having helped each other aboard, they collapsed onto its bench seats, flapping arms or breathing into cupped hands to warm up their own numbed extremities.

"Oh, look, you lot. I shall have hair like Shirley Temple at this rate!" one of them clucked, brushing from it the dusting of powdery white snow.

"Don't worry, Phyllis. I'm sure that guy you're dating in the FMU will still fall over himself to buy you chocolates and flowers," someone assured her, ruffling Phyllis's damp frizzy locks

Eileen meanwhile scrunched her toes inside her cavernous wellington boots and hoped there was still enough circulation reaching them to stave off frostbite. Whatever the weather, it felt good to be back amongst a lively crowd of fellow WAAFs all gossiping about their sweethearts and what they were looking forward to doing together now that the end of the war (and their impending demobilisation) was finally in sight. She thought about Nicky and their forthcoming life together in the 'Land of the Free and the Home of the Brave'. They had already named a wedding date: Saturday, May 5th. As promised, Nancy would be her bridesmaid; Auntie Kathleen had booked the Catholic church in Selly Oak; and, as was a custom amongst British servicewomen, the girls on camp had each chipped in a few of their clothing coupons to help Eileen look immaculate in a white wedding dress.

All that remained for her to do was to navigate her way through the minefield that was US immigration procedure. Meanwhile, she had been busy practising for the day when trousers became 'pants', 'tom-ah-toes' became 'tom-ay-toes', biscuits 'cookies', and – in God's good time – she could put 'diapers' on the babies she and Nicky would make and nestle them into a 'stroller' for a trundle along the 'sidewalk' to the 'candy store'. That's assuming Nicky didn't just herd them all inside a big, chrome-plated 'automobile' and drive them there instead!

Still daydreaming about the sprawling, palm-shaded mansion in sunny California that she imagined them one day owning – with its swimming pool, air-conditioning, enormous refrigerator and sweeping views of the Pacific Ocean – she jumped down from the lorry, handed her shovel back in at the stores depot, and began the trudge back to her billet to warm up. As she did she spotted a pair of officers – male and female – heading her way. Though still clammy and bedraggled in the aftermath of the morning's exertions, she duly saluted as they passed by.

"Eileen!" she was startled to hear a male voice respond as they returned her salute. Both of them halted to survey the other in disbelief.

"Gerald!"

"Careful, girl," he chortled with that gentle, disarming grin she remembered so well. "It's Pilot Officer Graham now you know," he noted, laying a pointing finger across the solitary band on the shoulder strap of his greatcoat.

Eileen returned his smile, genuinely pleased that her former boyfriend had finally earned the commission that he so richly deserved. Even so, she couldn't help recalling Granny O'Leary's charge that 'she only chases officers'; and of how Gerald had once hurled that accusation at her too. Mercifully, bitterness and rancour were absent from his tone today. It quickly became apparent why.

"Do you two know each other?" enquired the well-spoken young officer at his side, her breath vaporising in the cold morning air as she spoke.

Eileen recognised her as one of the officers she had seen about the station – though until now they had never been introduced. Meanwhile, her eyes darted between Eileen and Gerald as if to enquire why this bedraggled WAAF with the nose glowing scarlet from the sub-zero chill was acquainted with her colleague.

"Yes," Gerald proffered, "Eileen, this is Assistant Section Officer Felicity Warren. Felicity, this is Eileen Kimberley. We were once very good friends."

"Ah, you're that WAAF with the wonderful voice who is billed to sing at the concert in the NAAFI this weekend," Felicity noted, having recognised the name – and from that she somehow picked up on the unspoken nature of the 'friendship' that had once existed between them.

"That's right, ma'am. Thank you for saying so."

"Felicity and I are engaged to be married shortly. We met a few months back at a dance. I'm afraid it really was love at first sight!" Gerald was eager to reveal, feeling at liberty to beam at Felicity proudly. His beloved in turn looked up as if to study once more his angular Roman nose and dark entrancing eyes – and in a manner that Eileen recalled she herself had once done. Once upon a time that now seemed like so long ago.

"I'm happy for you both. I'm engaged too – to an American airman. We shall be getting married in a few weeks' time," Eileen replied, also staring into those dark eyes as if to deduce how the revelation that she was hitching up with a 'Yank' might play upon his remembrance of the 'love at first sight' he had once professed for her. He smiled back graciously.

"So I guess you won't be sticking around in Britain once the war is finally over," he suggested.

"No, probably not. And you? Still looking forward to opening that little garage somewhere that you were always talking about?"

Though there was jest in her remark, it was spoken in earnest. She took a moment to study the homely Assistant Section Officer Warren and could readily imagine her slotting into the appointed role of garage receptionist. Again, Gerald was gracious enough to chuckle upon to hearing her recall his modest aspirations. However, his more deliberative reply was not what she was expecting at all.

"Alas, maybe not. You see, I've been approached and asked if I'll stand for Parliament. I've been thinking about it for a while now. You know, Eileen, things are going to be so different when this war is over. All the old divisions of class and means – that's finished now. There will be no going back to the bad old days – like our parents did after the last war. I want to help build a new country, a new society, and a new future: a future founded upon equality for all; one where it will no longer matter who your father was or which school he sent you too."

Though the announcement shocked her, the sentiments didn't. Over the last year or so she had frequently overheard the erks similarly talking about new beginnings and putting aside the 'bad old days'. Though Winston Churchill still rallied his people with his unquenchable bulldog spirit, the ground had been subtly shifting from beneath him and the party he led. The communitarian impulse that the war had done so much to foster had taken root in the hearts of millions of ordinary servicemen and women. They knew they were fighting for something more than king, country and a quaint old notion of imperial splendour that may not mean much now that it looked like the Americans and the Russians would be calling the shots in the post-war world. No, the fruits of victory that those ordinary citizen-soldiers, sailors and airmen were looking forward to sharing would be equal access to education to combat ignorance, a welfare state to end poverty and squalor, nationalisation to bring important industries into common ownership, and – last, but not least – a free health service to provide for those without the means to pay.

"I'm sure you'll make an excellent MP," she complimented him.

"Thank you. And one day I am confident Eileen Kimberley will have her name up in lights," he repaid the compliment.

"I say, airwoman. You look like you're absolutely perished," Felicity interjected, observing the shiver that Eileen was fighting to repress. "Now I suggest you get yourself out of those wet overalls, run a hot bath, and have a good soak before you're back on duty again."

"Thank you, ma'am. I will."

"She's right, Eileen. Anyway, I'm sure we'll bump into each other again. I've just been posted here with No. 15 Squadron. It rather helps with the wedding preparations if one can be near to one's prospective bride," he joked, casting Felicity another wistful glance to both thrill and placate her. "With Jerry on the ropes, hopefully flying operations will be a doddle from now on. You take care, Eileen. It's been good to see you again."

"Phew! You too," she chuckled nervously, drawing her hands to her mouth to breathe over them again and stimulate the circulation to her ungloved fingers.

It was as she did so, and then slowly rubbed her slender hands around in a ball, that Gerald caught sight of a most peculiar thing. He noticed the beautiful three-stone diamond cross-over engagement ring on her finger.

"Sir... Ma'am," Eileen meanwhile drew those frozen hands apart to salute. Gerald and Felicity saluted in return, watching as she stepped a few paces back, smiled, and headed on her way.

He couldn't be entirely sure from the fleeting sight he had caught of it, but that ring looks eerily familiar.

"You alright, darling? You look as if you've just seen a ghost," his fiancée fussed, observing the sudden troubled expression that he blinked to dispel.

"A ghost from the past, one might say. And that, my dear, is where it will stay," he assured her, banishing idle thoughts about what might have been; as well as about an idle prayer he had offered that that ring – or one very much like it – might one day bring luck in love to whoever would get to wear it.

\* \* \* \* \*

One by one the four Wright 'Cyclone' radial engines fired into life, the resulting propwash forcing puffs of exhaust smoke across the field. Major Nicky Braschetti and his co-pilot, First Lieutenant Dan Kovic, made a final check of their flight controls before the chocks were pulled and the mighty Flying Fortress taxied from its dispersal pad to halt and wait for the all-clear. It was while they were cooling their heels that Kovic took the opportunity to glance across and smile appreciatively at his newly-promoted buddy. Indeed, Nicky didn't have to fly with this mission. However, like all the best commanders, he was determined to set an example and lead from the front.

"One final milk run, let's hope," Nicky sighed back at him, staring into his dark brown eyes and reading his thoughts.

"Sure, Nick. Then we can all kiss goodbye to England and go home at last."

Once cleared for take-off, Nicky pressed the engine controls against the stops to send the plane thundering down the runway. Soon it was airborne, followed in rapid succession by a dozen similar B17s also lifting off into the bright, clear April sky.

"Sure is a mighty fine sight, eh Mitch?" the boyish private stared up, resting the baseball bat on his bony shoulder and cupping a hand to his brow to observe them.

"Abrahams, you'll find my boot up your 'mighty fine' ass if you don't keep your eyes on this damn game!" his pudgy colleague grunted, punching his fists into the chunky mitt and crouching back down to await the next pitch.

Otherwise, he rolled his eyes as Abrahams stole one last glance at the bombers disappearing over the horizon. This callow recruit had only shipped out from the States a week or two earlier. With news that the Red Army's final assault on Berlin had been launched and that Russian and American troops were on the cusp of linking up somewhere on the North German plain, he could be forgiven for wanting to savour what would probably be the last sight of the illustrious 322nd Squadron heading off on a combat mission over Europe.

* * * * *

*"Target approaching in five minutes, Skipper."*

*"Roger, Navigator. Bomb Aimer, did you hear that?"*

*"I heard that, Skipper."*

*"Good. I'll keep her steady for you. Thankfully, once again there's no flak; and no fighters either. Keep your eyes peeled though, chaps."*

Pilot Officer Gerald Graham checked his flight engineer's gauges one more time. Good, he thought too: let's keep it that way!

This would probably be his very last mission. No. 15 Squadron had earned itself an enviable record for precision bombing, the advanced 'G-H' airborne radar sets fitted to its Avro Lancasters enabling it to bomb through thick cloud with an impressive degree of accuracy. He offered up a quick prayer that this final mission might continue to pass uneventfully. Then, at last, his three years of often harrowing combat flying would be over.

*"Bomb doors open."*

*"Aye, Skipper… Approaching target… Damn you!"*

*"Is there a problem, Bomb Aimer?"* the pilot called out, perturbed that the intercom was filling with a sudden string of expletives.

*"Too bloody right, Skipper. I'm pressing the bomb release switches, but nothing's happening."*

*"Never mind, Trigger, old chap. Looks like we'll just have spare Jerry this parting present from us."* the pilot sighed. *"Engineer…"*

*"Aye, Skipper."*

*"You're a wizard with all things mechanical and electrical. Go take a look and see if you can sort out what's happened."*

*"Roger, Skipper. I suspect it may be that the bomb doors haven't fully opened – possibly due to icing around the hinges. If the doors are not fully opened then the release mechanism will not properly activate."*

*"Well, either way we can't risk landing with a bellyful of armed high explosive bombs. One jolt on the runway and we'll wipe out half of Suffolk! So, for all our sakes, just make sure you fix it before we arrive home!"*

*"Roger, Skipper,"* Gerald sighed. So much for an 'uneventful' last mission!

\* \* \* \* \*

One minute there was the usual in-flight banter; the next minute silence. Major Nicky Braschetti was therefore reduced to offering his bemused co-pilot hand signals to try and make himself understood. The gist of it was to get his ass down to the radio operator and find out what the hell had happened. This Lieutenant Kovic duly did, slithering through the belly of the Flying Fortress to tap the shoulder of Master Sergeant Monk, who was anxiously flicking switches and swivelling dials. Unclipping his oxygen mask, away from it he could only afford to yell into Monk's ear in brief bursts on account of the thin air prevalent at twenty thousand feet.

"The radio and the interphone, sir. They're out. Everything's FUBAR and I can't figure out why."

Kovic was trudging his way back to the greenhouse when he noticed the navigator also gesticulating to him. He brushed up close as another mask was momentarily unstrapped so that its wearer might yell at him above the roar of the engines.

"I don't know what's going on, Lieutenant, but the instruments are all over the place. I just don't think I can rely on what they're telling me."

What a way to end ones war: in radio silence and without a clue where they were. Wearily he slithered back to sidle up alongside his skipper, bodge his upper arm and shout into the ear Nicky then exposed, his countenance darkening as into it Kovic emptied each nugget of bad news.

"Okay, Dan," he hollered back at him, removing his own mask and likewise cussing at the erratic behaviour of the air speed indicator and other instruments on the panel in front of him. "We're just gonna' have to break and get the hell out of here. With no radio and no navigation systems if we stick around we'll just be a menace to the other guys in the box. Get Monk to flash off a message to Captain Haycock in the *"Mountain Eagle"* telling them we're heading home. Let him know that he's in charge of the mission from now on."

The makeshift messenger boy having done just that, Monk removed his Morse lamp from its box and, through the Plexiglas of the waist portal, flashed out the letters that told their wing mate that regrettably *"Crazy Maisie"* would not be accompanying the squadron any further. Message acknowledged, Nicky then gazed across at his opposite number blazing through the clear blue sky alongside him, raising his palms in a gesture of dismayed impotence. Then *"Crazy Maisie"* banked sharply to set a course for home.

"You know, Dan, I've often heard the guys say this plane is jinxed." Nicky bawled across once Kovic was seated back down alongside him.

"Yeah, me too, Nick. And now I believe them!"

"Anyway, if my calculations are correct, we should be back over the sea in about twenty minutes," Nicky advised. "Once we're safely clear of any flak I'll take her down below ten thousand feet. Then we can ditch the bombs. I'm just sorry our last mission looks like going out with a whimper rather than a bang!"

\* \* \* \* \*

By means of a bit of jiggery-pokery (including shutting and re-opening the bomb doors several times in succession), Gerald had managed to ensure there was no longer any impediment to eventual bomb release. However, despite unscrewing the facia and checking for disconnected wires, he was alarmed to discover that there was still no response from the release panel.

*"Sorry, Skipper,"* he sighed down the intercom once more. *"Looks like the Gremlins are well and truly having a party inside this old kite today. You're going to have manually jettison the bombs, I'm afraid."*

*"Okay, Engineer,"* the pilot conceded. *"I'll shut the bomb doors back up for now to reduce the drag and the draw on fuel. We should be over a designated release area shortly. Stay down where you are with Trigger and make sure that there are no 'hang-ups' left clinging inside the old girl's belly."*

*"Roger, Skipper."*

*"Oh... and Spanners."*

*"Yes, Skipper?"*

*"Thanks for giving it your best shot. You can service my car any time!"*

*"Thank you, Skipper."*

\* \* \* \* \*

"So let me get this straight, Wilson. You're telling me that, to all intents and purposes, you haven't got a clue where the hell we are?"

"Not with any degree of accuracy, sir. All I've been able to do is note the position of the sun and dead-reckon as best I can from our last confirmed positions. We may some distance off course one way or the other. But at least I'm confident we'll make landfall somewhere over eastern England. Without instruments it's best I can do, Major."

Through his thin-rimmed glasses Nicky stared down at his navigator standing alongside him and patted him on the shoulder paternally. "Yeah. Sure thing, Wilson. I guess 'somewhere over eastern England' is as good as it gets. Now the bombs have gone at least we won't be riding six thousand pounds of high explosive wherever I get to put her down."

Once Wilson had ducked back inside the plane Nicky glanced over at the little photograph of Eileen he had taped to his instrument panel and gave thanks for small mercies. The radio and navigation systems might be FUBAR. But, unlike the last time this highly experienced flyer had gotten into a spot of bother over the North Sea, at least *"Crazy Maisie"* had sufficient gas, her landing gear and flight controls were intact, and each member of her crew was alive and looking forward to the welcome sight of the English coast – and of a creditable fighting career that was hopefully now complete.

\* \* \* \* \*

The Lancaster's huge thirty-three foot bomb doors were opened for the last time. Having peered inside the inspection hatch to check for hang-ups, Gerald now watched as all her fourteen 1,000 pound fused bombs were manually jettisoned to drop harmlessly into the cold grey sea twelve thousand feet below.

He let out a sigh of relief, electing to linger so that he might savour the sight of them disappearing from view. As he did, out of the corner of his eye he thought he could just make out the red wing tips of an aircraft emerging through a fleeting break in the cloud. Then he spotted the distinctive star-and-bars on the port wing, as well as a triangular letter 'A' on the starboard. There was an American bomber cruising directly below them!

However, no sooner had he blinked in disbelief than there was a split second flash, followed by a puff of black smoke. Then the plane was gone – concealed by further cloud sweeping across to obscure the view below. Horror-struck, he hurriedly shuffled forward and unclipped his oxygen mask, tapping the bomb aimer on the shoulder excitedly.

"Did you see you that, Trigger?" he cried.

"See what, old chap?"

"That explosion. I could have sworn one of our bombs has just hit something. A plane… A Flying Fortress, if I wasn't mistaken."

"No, I didn't see anything."

"You must be mistaken, Spanners," the Skipper assured him when he raced up top to advise him in person. "Our boys have strict instructions not to loiter around this spot at low altitude. So have the Yanks."

Still Gerald was troubled. Might he indeed have imagined it? He was tired after all. By volunteering for these weeks of further missions he may have done right by his country. However, doing so had lately found him afflicted once more by all those recurring nightmares about 'losing it' – to which had been added increasing neuroses about the morality of the brass-hats purposely targeting German cities, even if it entailed incinerating women and children. Reluctant to argue over what he couldn't confirm, he sat back down amidst the familiar world of his gauges and instruments in the hope of mitigating the throbbing of his temples. Instead he found himself anxiously studying the little photograph of Felicity that he kept taped in the corner of the console. Soon this wretched war really would be over. Soon he would don a fresh, smartly-pressed uniform so that he might turn about at the front of the church and behold his beloved bride draw up alongside him. With those ruddy bombs gone and Blighty just a few more minutes flying time away, he lifted his eyes up to Heaven to give thanks that he had been spared – one of those fortunate members of RAF Bomber Command aircrew who had lived to tell the tale.

* * * * *

Eileen Kimberley bowed discreetly and basked in the applause of the hundreds of appreciative airmen and women who had crowded into RAF Mildenhall's NAAFI hall to hear her perform – including Gerald and Felicity, who she spied sitting with the officers at the front. She beamed a special smile for them both – her heart gladdened that her one-time boyfriend had found a true love of his own (and which had perhaps paved the way for this fine, outstanding young man – who she had once hurt so deeply – to respond with such impeccable magnanimity towards her).

Otherwise, they say all the best songs are sung from the heart. If nothing else, Eileen Kimberley now knew her own heart, and – apropos the lyrics of Vera Lynn's *'Yours'* that she had closed the show with – that she too had 'never loved anyone' the way she loved her gallant American sweetheart. Therefore, she guessed it was a small price to pay that she would not now get to see Nicky before their wedding day, which was barely a fortnight away.

The stars were now aligning at last. The war would soon be over. Hopefully, Nicky had by now flown his last mission. Soon she would become his wife. From there, who could say where their shared gift for song would one day take this acclaimed and iconic military couple – either 'here or on far distant shores'.

As often when she had given herself body and soul to a performance, she left the stage emotionally drained. It was therefore a relief to be able to retire for just a few minutes to the little store cupboard that had to double up as a dressing room. Maybe one day she might get to relax in one of those spacious Hollywood dressing rooms, with a big long mirror surrounded by lights, and around which there might be reflected the vivid colours and sweet perfume of flowers despatched from well-wishers. For now though, she contented herself with eyeing her own reflection in the prop-up vanity mirror the entertainment committee had provided for her, taking the opportunity to reapply her lipstick.

As she was doing so, she suddenly heard a knock on the door and in the mirror observed the outline of her squadron officer quietly slipping in. She dutifully turned about and rose to her feet to acknowledge her. Ominously, there was neither a return salute, nor congratulation, nor censure in her ashen face as she motioned for Eileen to sit back down. Meanwhile, the matronly officer placed her own ample posterior down upon a chest of stores that had been deposited next to the young airwoman's chair. Self-consciously, she then stared down at her feet for a split second before her eyes alighted again upon the anxious WAAF.

"It's Nicky, isn't it?" Eileen begged, staring down at the hand of comfort that the officer had now laid upon her delicate forearm. There was an agonising pause before the officer drew breath and replied.

"Lieutenant Colonel Sheeler called me from Bassingbourn. He thought you should know that – with their plane now well overdue and searches having thrown up no leads – he has had no choice but to formally post Major Braschetti and his crew as 'failed to return'.

There was another long, agonising silence during which time Eileen's warm brown eyes widened and then glazed over coldly. "He's dead, isn't he? He's dead." she crumpled her face.

The answer was self-evident, and her squadron officer didn't need to spell it out. Eileen had heard the term 'failed to return' banded about too often during her years in the Royal Air Force not to know that airmen who were chalked up 'FTR' seldom, if ever reappeared.

"I'm sorry, Kimberley. I truly am. Listen, I can arrange for a spell of compassionate leave; plus the necessary rail warrants for you to be at home with your family – where you belong at this unfortunate time."

Eileen was too dazed to respond, but the officer understood and would make the necessary arrangements anyway. Thereafter, there was nothing more she could do except permit that arm of comfort to linger for a few more moments, squeezing Eileen's tenderly before drawing it away. Then she rose to her feet and exited the room as solemnly and stealthily as she had crept in.

Eileen closed her eyes to permit the sobbing to start, opening them only fleetingly to stare down into the tiny mirror in front of her – time enough for sure to observe that her burnt-cork mascara had smudged, and that her carefully-crafted image of Hollywood starlet beauty was flawed once more by the unwelcome intrusion of a trail of tears.

# *18*

Tuesday, May 8th 1945: the news had come through overnight that the war in Europe was officially over. The first tangible signs of this on the streets of Birmingham were the hundreds of people monkeying up ladders to drape Union Jacks from their homes and string bunting between the lamp standards in the streets outside. One or two wizened souls noted that the last time they could recall the city being decked out this gaily had been for Queen Victoria's Diamond Jubilee almost half a century earlier.

The day had started off rainy and overcast before brightening up to culminate a fabulous, sunny afternoon. Soon everyone had grabbed their dining tables and chairs and lined them up in the street to commence the party to end all parties. Excited children played games whilst the relieved adults busied themselves hauling gramophone records and pianos out so that everyone could enjoy a right good knees-up. Meanwhile, in the city centre crowds thronged into Victoria Square ready to hear Winston Churchill's address to the nation being relayed on loudspeakers specially set up for the occasion. However, when a technical hitch prevented this, the Lord Mayor grabbed his radio set and placed it in the window of his parlour in the Council House, turning up the volume so that everyone could concur with the Prime Minister that "in all our long history we have never seen a greater day than this."

For those of a more spiritual persuasion, church services were held throughout the day – eight in Birmingham's St Philip's Cathedral alone, which over four thousand people attended. Meanwhile, with the city's licensees praying instead that they wouldn't run out of beer and spirits, those of a more earthly disposition could rejoice with the sign someone had placed in the window of their house in Bromsgrove Street, and which read "Please don't call for the rent – we've spent it celebrating the Victory!"

\* \* \* \* \*

*"I'll be seeing you in all the old familiar places"* the neighbours were all singing in the street outside. Its haunting lyrics drifted through the open window to where Eileen was lying on her bed, hugging her pillow. There she stared across at the wedding dress hung up on the inside of a wardrobe door that was ajar – a wedding dress for a 'wedding day' had come and gone without a wedding.

Now, like all those who had loved and lost in this war, the only way she would ever get to 'see' Nicky's unforgettable smile of again would be in things that sounded so poetic, yet cruelly intangible…

> *"I'll find you in the morning sun,*
> *And when the night is new.*
> *I'll be looking at the moon,*
> *But I'll be seeing you."*

Mouthing the words to herself, she closed her eyes and sobbed. Though still only twenty-one, she felt old before her time – burdened with trauma and heartache such as no young woman should ever have to endure. How could she ever love any man this much again? Where would she ever find the resolve to face the world without him?

Dusk was advancing by the time the door to her room was inched open so that an eye might peer at her lying there foetal-like and ossified in grief. The door was slowly edged open. Then the tall, graceful form of Auntie Kathleen appeared and sat down upon the foot of the bed. After pausing to contemplate her niece stricken with sorrow of the kind with which she too was tragically familiar, she reached out a hand to lay it tenderly upon her shoulder. Eileen looked up through reddened eyes. Lifting herself from her pillow she then flopped into Auntie Kathleen's embrace in a manner she had done on so many occasions during her often fraught childhood. Now as then, they were arms in which she felt at liberty to cry.

"Why, Auntie Kathleen…? Why?"

"I wish I could answer you, my child. But there are some things it is only for God to know."

"It all seems so senseless. Everything seems senseless. It's as if every time there is joy in my life it is snatched from me. Do you remember Flossy?" she asked as she permitted her aunt to gently rock her, infant-like.

"I do indeed. You would be all of six years-old, if my memory serves me correctly."

"I loved that little cat. I remember when Dad first brought her home as a kitten. She was a little ball of snowy white fur with a splash or two of black on her head and on her nose. We would play together for hours. And then one day we found she had a swelling on her neck – most likely a bite from a rat in the yard that Dad said had become infected. Next day she was dead. I remember at the time asking God why, when cats kill rats, my beautiful little Flossy had to be the one instance where it happened the other way around.

"And then when Mom and Dad split up, I found myself asking again: why? Why my parents? All the other boys and girls I knew had a daddy. Why was I the only one who was left without one? Why was I the one who had to endure cruel taunts in the playground about my 'wicked' mother and the 'heartless' father who had abandoned me? I loved my Dad, Auntie Kathleen. He was my hero, the man I looked up to. And now suddenly he was no longer there; and in his place there was a just a succession of other 'men' in Mum's life; some of whom were not very nice; some of whom even tried to…"

She descended into more voluble lamentation borne of trauma and unspoken resentment – goads against which she had all these years found herself constantly kicking; and in which she could see no other rhyme or reason than divine whim and intransigence.

"I was just a girl, Auntie Kathleen. Then as I grew older I took to thinking that maybe Granny O'Leary was right after all. Maybe my parents were 'children of the devil'; maybe I was too. Maybe that's the reason why all these terrible things keep happening to me. Is that why I seem destined to spend my whole life paying for my sins over and over again? Oh, Auntie Kathleen, when will my punishment ever end?" she wept again.

For once, this most devout and spiritual of all her close family members knew that the answer to Eileen's wrenching question would require something more than fumbling with a rosary or saying a few more Hail Marys. First though, there was something that she needed to put her straight about.

"You must never listen to Granny O'Leary, God rest her soul. Do you hear me!" she asserted, heaving Eileen out of her embrace to grip her by her upper arms and jolt her, her eyes glaring at her niece until she reluctantly made eye contact with her. "Granny O'Leary was an embittered old woman."

"That she was!" Eileen hissed, hinting at a vein of unforgiveness that still fuelled anger for the way her grandmother had constantly bad-mouthed her parents – and especially her father. "But why?"

Having chastened her, Auntie Kathleen withdrew all but a gentle hand still resting upon her shoulder.

"Do you remember all the stories she used to tell us about the 'old days'?" she recalled – to which Eileen nodded. "Well, when she married your grandfather she thought she had quite fallen on her feet. After all, her parents were just modest folk, whilst his family owned land in the west of Ireland. Any woman would have been glad to be marrying into that kind of security and prosperity. But then it all went wrong. Bad weather struck and the potato harvests failed. Disease afflicted their livestock. Prices slumped and Ireland was mired in an agricultural depression. Once again, the only way out was to emigrate; to leave behind everything that had been so painstakingly built up. And so Uncle Joseph left for America, whilst your grandfather and his new wife came to England – and to a lowly existence as a labourer. Birmingham must have been such a wrench after all the good things they'd enjoyed back in County Mayo. However, your grandfather was a godly man. He accepted that what the Lord gives He can also take away; but that if you work hard and have enough faith things can come right in His good time. And so they did. Grandpa was good at his job and was promoted to be an overseer – quite a respected one at that. And though he never regained the wealth he had to leave behind in Ireland, there was food on the table and the hope of better things to come.

"However, Granny never came to terms what had happened. She harboured bitterness in her heart; bitterness towards the British for what they did to Ireland; bitterness especially towards the 'officer class' for the way they had exploited your grandfather's difficulties; bitterness towards your mother for marrying a Protestant, who she warned would be no good for her; and bitterness towards me perhaps for turning to God – even as she was inwardly cursing Him for the disasters that He had allowed to befall them."

"And bitterness towards me for joining the Royal Air Force and mixing with that same 'officer class'; and for wanting to sing and dance and make something of my life?" Eileen surmised, things beginning to fall into place.

"Don't be angry, Eileen. And don't hate. It solves nothing. Haven't we all suffered too much because one man was so consumed with anger and hatred towards those he accused of humiliating Germany that he was willing to set the whole world on fire. Instead, remember Jesus on the Cross. If ever anyone had cause to be angry and full of hatred for the people who mocked Him and accused Him, then it was Our Lord. And yet what did He say as He hung there blooded and bruised on that cross, listening to them hurl their final insults and profanities at Him: 'Father, forgive them'."

As she always did, Auntie Kathleen spoke wisely. Eileen pondered what had been said. Outside meanwhile, darkness had fallen, whilst through the bedroom window the sound of revelry was continuing into the night. Together Eileen and Auntie Kathleen stood up and looked out to observe how these joyous sounds had been supplemented by the glow from street lights that had been switched on for the first time in almost six years. Likewise, thousands of other tiny lights across the city had also been purposely left unsheathed by black-out drapes in order to celebrate the end of both a literal and metaphorical reign of darkness. Even the trams were trundling up and down the Bristol Road with their cabin lights ablaze, whilst in the distance the searchlights around the Bournville chocolate factory had been similarly switched on to randomly roam back and forth across the heavens.

Closer to home, on the waste ground across from the brew house the vivid orange fingers of a roaring bonfire were dancing as merrily as the revellers from the street who were now hurrying around it to join in a hearty refrain of *'Land Of Hope And Glory'*. Fireworks that had been stashed away for the duration were also being unleashed into the night sky.

"You too must forgive, Eileen," her aunt counselled her. "Forgive Granny for her unkind words and how they often hurt you; forgive your mother for being human too – you know she loves you and would never knowingly have hurt you. Forgive your father – because he was a good man, and he too loved you and tried to do what he thought was best for you. And, last but not least, forgive yourself. I know it's hard. Sometimes I think so many of our priests talk too much about punishment, hellfire and damnation, and not enough about love, compassion and forgiveness. Remember though what Father Connolly once said about 'love', 'compassion' and 'forgiveness': that they were the three nails that pinned Our Lord to the Cross. And if, in His great love and compassion, Christ can forgive us poor, helpless sinners – even though we fail Him time after time – then we too must love and forgive. You must also resolve to put behind you the mistakes of the past – both those of others and your own too.

"Alas, my child, your love for Nicky was clearly not meant to be. Hard though it is to bear now, maybe God is trying to teach you something; and by so doing is preparing you for the moment when you will discover that missing man in your life that He is truly setting you up to meet."

\* \* \* \* \*

*June 2nd 1945*

*Dear Miss Kimberley,*

*You do not know me and I hope you will forgive me for making enquiries so that this letter might find you. I confess that neither do I know anything about you, other than little snippets I have unearthed. For example, I have read that you're a really fine singer; and that your fiancé was recently posted missing. Can I therefore offer my condolences and pray that God will comfort you. Having recently lost my husband of many years, I know from personal experience how painful such loss can be.*

*I know too that you were awarded the George Cross for gallantry. Indeed, it is in this capacity that I am writing to you – because the gallantry in question saved the life of someone very special to me. As such, though I apologise that this letter might appear somewhat belated, can I express my undying gratitude to you for rescuing my only son, Joey, from certain death aboard that burning plane – and a very horrible death at that!*

*Not long after he returned to Australia, Joey met and fell in love with a wonderful girl – Sam. Last year they were married. And yesterday Sam gave birth to their first child – a beautiful baby girl. At this time of great personal sadness for you I hope you will be encouraged by the knowledge that they have decided to name her 'Eileen' in honour of you.*

*One thing Joey did tell me was how fascinated he remembered you being to hear him describe Queensland, with its beaches, forests, and wide open spaces. I wish you every success with your singing career. Maybe one day when you're famous you will tour Australia and get to discover them for yourself. Maybe then I will also have the opportunity to thank you in person for your selfless bravery, without which I would never have experienced the indescribable joy of becoming a grandmother.*

*However, should things not work out for you in England, remember that Australia is still a great big land of opportunity. Right now, our government is keen to encourage more immigration – especially from the Mother Country. So should you ever want to experience a new life 'Down Under' – and need somewhere to stay until you can find your feet – please be assured that there is one humble abode in Queensland where you will always be assured of the most open-hearted welcome.*

*Eternally, gratefully yours,*

*Eleanor Abbott*

\* \* \* \* \*

"Okay, folks. Let's take it from the top."

Setting aside her mug of steaming tea, Eileen pounced back onto the stage. Though Flight Lieutenant Archie Wyndall's impatient and slightly effete order was followed obediently by the members of the band that he had gathered together, it was plain to any casual observer that the dapper Pickwickian officer was born to be an artist and not a warrior; to create and not destroy. It was just as well that the Royal Air Force had therefore graciously conceded that, in his own inimitable way, this talented young subaltern could make its own unique and important contribution to victory.

Comprised of serving RAF personnel, the Ad Astra Dance Band was one of several such outfits that had come together during the war to provide an invaluable boost to morale. These aircraft fitters, radio operators and clerks had been permitted to go ply their 'trade' as conscripted musicians – in which capacity they had provided concerts for service personnel, broadcasts for the BBC, and had even churned out the odd record or two. They may never have achieved the worldwide acclaim of Glenn Miller and the big American bands, but their music drew applause and appreciation wherever they played.

Archie was evidently satisfied that this afternoon's practice session had found them performing *'A Foggy Day In London Town'* to his exacting standards of musical excellent. Therefore, it remained only for Eileen to step up to the microphone and offer her own contribution on vocals and make the little number complete.

"That's it, chaps!" Wyndall enthused, also offering their sole female member a crafty wink. "Perfect! Just remember to play like this tomorrow. Meanwhile, 'squad' dismissed. It's anything but a 'foggy day' in 'London Town' this afternoon. So go out and enjoy what's left of it."

"And you, my love," he insisted, discreetly ambling over and sidling up to Eileen, wagging an avuncular finger at her. "You've been spending too much time singing with those Americans. Now they're all heading home I'm so glad you've decided to sing with the Ad Astrals instead. Have you any idea what a fillip having you onboard has made to our performances!"

She chuckled with mild embarrassment. Although her feminine sixth sense told her there was probably a frisson of romantic longing lurking somewhere behind his gushing words, the coquettish young airwoman accepted his compliment in good faith. The jovial band leader was genuinely chuffed at the contribution her voice had made to an already polished and professional sound. Meanwhile, playing with them had proved the perfect vehicle for extracting her from the trough of mournful gloom in which she had been wallowing.

"So we can't tempt you to join us tonight in the bar for a nightcap?" Archie petitioned her again as the musicians began to pack their instruments away for the evening, and Eileen grabbed her musette bag.

"Afraid not. I have an important errand I must undertake before I retire. But thanks anyway. And once again, thank you for taking me under your wing."

"My pleasure, Aircraftwoman Kimberley," he made light once more. "Just don't leave it so long next time."

"Yes, sir," she saluted, though with a similar hint that it was but a necessary formality of service life. One day soon, she and the other members of the Ad

Astra Dance Band would be out of uniform for good, free to feel unself-conscious about referring to each other by their Christian names, as well as to lap up the creative tension that marks all successful musical enterprises.

In one sense though, Archie Wyndall was right. Exiting the theatre by the stage door and merging in the crowded street on what promised to be a fabulous summer's evening, she accepted that she had perhaps spent far too much time in awe of Americans – both on account of her relationship with Nicky and because of all her latent hopes of Hollywood stardom. The Yanks were indeed now dismantling their many military outposts in Britain and heading home – their mission accomplished. And though again, Archie was right that the power of her amazing voice was undiminished, she had yet to hear from that music producer that Nicky had dangled her name in front of. With a surfeit of home-grown American talent to select from, she wondered whether she ever would.

However, just as letting go of Nicky was a painful, yet necessary part of putting her life back together again, likewise letting go of her dreams of dazzling transatlantic fame. She sensed (and Archie had counselled) that she needed to begin cultivating her own domestic audience here in Britain – and that she should begin by changing her previously rather staid musical repertoire. Meanwhile, of course, there was the not insignificant matter that she was still 'taking the King's shilling'.

Resigned to making the most of what time she had left in uniform, she hoped tomorrow's concert at the famous Astoria Ballroom on Charing Cross Road would be one more milestone on the road to raising her stage profile. For now though, there was another more painful act of 'letting go' that she felt she needed to perform now that fate had found her back in London once more. Stopping by at a florist's kiosk on Piccadilly, she perused, selected and paid for a beautiful spray of roses. Then it was a brisk stroll to Hyde Park Corner to hop aboard a No. 52 bus, followed by a further walk that would take her back to that fateful spot where another crazy dream of hers had died. Yet she knew this frustrated dream too now had to be let go of.

Symbolic of the advent of peace, walking down the street it seemed that normality had returned to Rochester Terrace. The sound of children playing on this warm, sunny evening could once again be heard. From those houses that were unscarred by war, neighbours too had emerged to scrub steps or engage in animated gossip around the colonnades that separated their terraced abodes. However, all that remained of No. 139A and its adjacent properties was a tidied-up patch of barren ground that was stark and mocking, like the gap in an old man's toothless smile.

There were so many things Eileen had wanted to tell her late father. For now, all she could do was lay her little spray of yellow and red roses at the foot of what was left of those wide, whitewashed steps and offer up a prayer that one day they would meet up again – somewhere on the other side. There they could have that precious conversation at last. Whatever faults and omissions she thought he might thereby have wanted to confess she now forgave him. Whatever part she thought she had played in putting off that conversation until it was tragically too late she likewise asked to be forgiven.

It was a more dignified farewell than the last occasion upon which she had shed tears at this spot. She determined to face whatever the future held knowing that – through some strange, yet indefinable presence – he would always watch over her, no matter where she went. She read the little card she had written one last time before turning and heading back up the street…

*George Wilfred Kimberley,*
*April 7ᵗʰ 1901 – September 22ⁿᵈ 1944.*
*"I will always love you, Dad."*

*Eileen.*

\* \* \* \* \*

The concert had indeed been a triumphant success, capped by a stirring encore of *'But Not For Me'* during which Eileen had left the audience spellbound. The applause and cheering was still ringing in the ears of the band members as made their way backstage, crowing and congratulating each other as they noisily made their way down the steps to crash out in their dressing rooms.

"If ever we need a reason to stay together after demob then just listen to them!" a band member enthused.

"Yes, how about you, Eileen? Are you going to stay around and carry on singing with us?" someone appealed to her.

"Yes, please do. With twenty superb musicians – and your radiant face and wonderful voice fronting us – where can we possibly go wrong?"

"Here, you lot. Just remember: *I* front this outfit!" Archie protested with mock dismay, pointedly bodging his broad chest with his forefinger.

"Oh, absolutely, Flight. Archie Wyndall and the Ad Astrals. Where would we be without you," one of his trombonists corrected them with equally mock deference before being bundled into the main dressing room by his colleagues.

"Seriously though, Eileen," Archie muttered to her as she was about to disappear inside her own dressing room, "I know there may come a day when you may want to branch out on your own. But I do so hope we can enjoy your company for a while longer.

"That you can, sir," she replied, hanging on the door portal and looking him in the eye. "They handed me my 'demob group number' this week. And because I'm young – and unmarried," she sighed (and as if she needed reminding), "it looks unlikely that I shall be released back into civilian life before the end of the year."

"Ooh, good… I mean, not so good. If you know what I mean," the twittering band leader smiled before replacing that smile with a more sympathetic puckering of his chops. "Still, at least you'll be with us for the summer. You see, I haven't told the lads yet; but it looks like we might be off to Germany next month."

"Germany?" she quizzed him excitedly.

"Germany, old girl. That's right. Now that war's over, we've been asked to do a tour of the bases in the British zone of occupation. A bit of a pick-me-up for all those other poor souls like you who will also have to wait around a while longer before they get to try on their demob suits."

"Wow! I've never been to… I mean I've never been abroad before."

The glow in her eyes told Archie that he might just have found the antidote to that idle conversation they had had the other night, during which his leading lady had hinted at maybe emigrating once she was released.

"Like I said, stick around, old girl. Keep in with your Uncle Archie – I mean Flight Lieutenant Wyndall – and you might get to see the world after all. Besides, you didn't seriously think I'd let you settle for pulling plugs in some lowly telephone exchange Down Under, did you?"

He gave her that crafty wink again. However, she politely inched the door to her dressing room closed lest her indulgence of his over-demonstrative chivalry invite presumption of other things

She collapsed into the chair that faced the dressing room table, upon which she gazed at her tired reflection in the mirror. There she loosened her tie, undid her top button and steeled herself to the task of removing the make-up that the stage girl had liberally applied. Then she removed her WAAF's cap and unclipped her hair, allowing her sable locks to be shaken free. Though still thankful for the looks God had given her (and which Archie and his band members were forever complimenting her), she frowned upon spotting the first sign of a wrinkle or two here and there.

Time had indeed caught up with her. She had been not quite eighteen when she had enlisted. During the ensuing four years she had blossomed from naïve teenager to a wiser and well-rounded young woman, having experienced so much along the way. She took a moment to study this earnest young woman who now gazed back at her. As she did, she found herself recalling a touching moment near the end of their time together when Section Officer Rachel Owen had unexpectedly opened up to her about the 'one true love' of her own life – a young naval lieutenant who had been killed at war's outbreak – and why she had felt unable to face romantic commitment ever since.

Like Rachel, Eileen too now appreciated why a time apart to herself was also going to be a prerequisite of putting the past behind her; to give herself the necessary space to finally settle in her own mind who she was and where she was heading. Should she carry on pursuing her love of song and seeking a professional outlet for this other great gift that God had blessed her with? Would she be able to bear the disappointment of discovering that this too might prove to be a dream frustrated? Was she therefore ready to kiss it goodbye and fall back instead upon the career the RAF had trained her to do (and at which she also excelled), whether that might entail 'pulling plugs' on a switchboard in Birmingham, or indeed maybe in some more favourable clime?

Just then there was a gentle tap on the dressing room door. Twisting her head to train an ear upon it – and with a concomitant curl of a wary eyebrow – for a moment she wondered whether she had acted with enough firmness to disabuse Archie Wyndall of any high hopes he might be entertaining. Flattered though she was, perhaps this time she would have to spell out more precisely that she was not interested in requiting his, or indeed any other man's priapic aspirations.

"Come in," she grudgingly huffed. She watched while the reflection of the door correspondingly opened with a tentative squeal.

"Miss Kimberley? Miss Eileen Kimberley?" she beheld a middle-aged man slope in and draw up behind her, removing his trilby and clutching it to his chest in supplication.

"Yes. I'm Eileen Kimberley. Do I know you?" she guardedly stared back at this reflection.

"I would hope so. You could say I'm your biggest fan," he shrugged his shoulders, again with the humility of a supplicant who felt culpably awkward intruding upon a lady's private space.

The face did indeed appear curiously familiar. It was perhaps this that led her to indulge this seedy looking character a tad longer than she knew she ought. Was he that music producer that Nicky had spoken about – finally turning up out of the blue to introduce himself and sign her up? If so, he was reticent in getting to the point? Besides, the accent placed him the wrong side of the Atlantic. Indeed, as he gazed across and addressed her from the comfort of clutching that hat, the voice was also uncannily familiar.

"You see, Eileen, I've been following you for a long time. Except, let's just say, I have suffered the pain of having to follow you from a distance, as it were. I read all about you in the newspapers. In fact, I kept every cutting I could find. I even saw you in a newsreel once. So I hope you'll forgive me; but I had to come tonight. My heart is aching, and I don't think I can wait a moment longer. I simply have to see for myself just how lovely you are; to behold the amazing woman you have become."

This was getting creepy. Not since she had unwittingly found herself alone in the presence of one of her mother's men 'friends' had she felt so desperately ill-at-ease in male company. The flip side of being famous, it seemed: to be drooled over by some slimy old man with a tobacco-stained moustache.

"And if I may be so bold," he continued, "performing that last song must have been so painful after losing your fiancé so close to your wedding day – what with its talk of 'the memory of his kiss' and 'happy plots' ending with 'marriage knots'. What's more, given all the terrible unhappiness I know you have experienced during your life it must take real courage to sing about 'lucky stars above – but not for me'. It is the mark of a true professional that you can handle a melody like that with such aplomb."

She blanched, aware that there may well have been a tear in her eye as she sang. Yet how did this guy know about the 'terrible unhappiness' in her life? And of her fixation with 'lucky stars above'? She swallowed hard.

"Thank you for your kind words. But I don't know who you are or what you want. However, if it's an autograph you're after then I'm happy to sign one for you. But please understand: I would feel more comfortable if you left."

"Autograph? Eileen, you would fob me off with an autograph?"

"Look. Please, just go!" she rose, turning about and gritting her teeth in the best impression she could muster of robustness in the face of a threat. Otherwise, she took comfort from the sound of muffled celebrations coming from the guys' dressing room just next door.

"Go? Eileen, please… don't you recognise me?" the stranger pleaded, raising his hands and backing away from her, horrified.

"No, I'm afraid..." she stuttered, even though she studied his face again and pondered his vague Midlands accent – her tongue curling around, but never quite ejaculating the words 'I don't'. Instead, as if a ghost had brushed her, this time it was her turn to take a step back, her mouth rigid and rictus and utterly unable to verbalise what she was too terrified to admit.

"Eileen," the stranger brushed his hand through his black, bryl-creemed hair and articulated it for her. "It's me: your father – your daddy!"

# *19*

"But I genuinely believed you were dead," she exclaimed. "The blast completely flattened several properties on that side of the street. No one could have survived that."

They carried on walking arm-in-arm together beneath the shade of the trees that lined Victoria Embankment. Occasionally they would halt to gaze across its long stone wall at the tugboats steaming up and down the Thames. To say Eileen was shocked that her misplaced assumption had been proved spectacularly wrong was an understatement. It was written in the manner in which she was rejoicing and hanging on his every word.

"Sadly, you're right. No one did survive – including Fiona and my little Maureen. And neither would I had my train not been delayed. The sight that greeted me when I returned home that night is one I shall never forget."

The pain in George Kimberley's soft brown eyes spoke of a man still grieving the loss of both his youngest daughter – Eileen's half-sister – and her mother. For just a moment it tempered his joy that the other daughter he had not seen in over ten years was by his side once more.

"You know, at the time I wished I had died with them. I kept asking myself why I had been spared. If only I had visited my client in the car instead of relying on hit-and-miss wartime train services. In fact, had that train arrived back in Paddington even an hour or two late I would have been at home. But the three hour delay at Reading? It spared my life."

Eileen exhaled a deep sigh to match. "An 'if only' spared my life too. I was adamant throughout that fateful Friday evening that I wanted to go round and see you there and then. It was Nicky who, against my every instinct, persuaded me to put off visiting until morning – as I had agreed with your wife. I somehow just didn't trust her not to contrive another excuse to get you out of the house so that you might avoid having to meet me."

Her father pursed his lips tight in an admission that such was his wife's probable intention, twitching his neat Clark Gable moustache as he did so.

"I'm sorry, Eileen. I genuinely had no idea you had been searching for me. Fiona never mentioned anything about your first visit. Had I known, I would have welcomed you with open arms. I never stopped loving you. Or wondering where you were; or whether you still thought about me."

She snuggled in close to him as if to banish such a preposterous notion, still amazed that here she was clinging to the beloved, Lazarus-like father she had given up for dead, cursing that in her own grief-stricken despair she had omitted to verify beyond all doubt whether he really had perished. She put it down to that abiding cynicism within her that, in the final analysis, happy endings seldom attended the 'wicked' Eileen. Even now, she was conscious she was perhaps clinging onto his arm too tightly, afraid he might somehow vanish before her very eyes, and that yesterday's magical and unexpected reunion would prove to have been just another cruel mirage.

"I can't say I didn't wish I had died with you too. I suppose that's why I was so blessed to have Nicky in my life at that time. I really don't think I could have pulled through without him. So perhaps God really does place special people in our lives – if only for a brief moment. Anyway, I guess I owe you an apology too, Dad: for not recognising you last night."

"I know. I've changed. Age catches up with us all," was the excuse he offered her, along with a warm, paternal smile, though she suspected the shock of losing his wife and child was the real reason that he appeared drawn, wizened and so unlike the more youthful photograph she still carried with her.

"Anyway," he frowned. "Who was that guy who burst in on us?"

"That was Archie – Flight Lieutenant Archie Wyndall – the leader of the Ad Astra Dance Band," she chuckled mischievously. "I think he has a bit of a soft spot for me – if you know what I mean!" she winked. "Anyway, he wouldn't really have punched you on the nose – though the look on his face when he saw you standing there was absolutely priceless."

"Even better the look on his face when you explained that the father of the girl he has his eye on wasn't dead after all!" George added.

Eileen chuckled again at the inference before reminding him of her resolution to give romantic entanglements a wide berth for a while yet. It gave George the opportunity to once more express his regret that he had never had the opportunity to meet the man who should by now have been his son-in-law.

"Anyway," he sighed again in self-reproach. "All the apologies are due on my part. I should have kept in touch with you. What I did was wrong. The only thing I can say in my defence is that I genuinely thought removing myself from your life was for the best – especially after the tongue-lashing your grandmother gave me that afternoon I last saw you."

Eileen's eyes darkened. Auntie Kathleen was right: Granny O'Leary had never approved of George marrying her mother. And even though, in their innocence, children only perceive their parents' relationship as if through a glass darkly, hindsight had since afforded her the ability to piece together the malign presence Granny must have exerted upon her parents' marriage – always nit-picking; always willing it to fail; always revelling in the perverse satisfaction of her dire predictions about its demise having come true. Worst of all, her father had believed all the horrible things the embittered old lady had said. But then had Eileen's too not lent undue credence to her grandmother's opinions about her own loves and ambitions? She could therefore empathise with the twisted logic that had led her father to assume that 'removing' himself from her life was actually in the best interests of his daughter.

"Make no mistake, Eileen, I never stopped loving your mother either. Even now, after all these years, I sometimes wonder whether she would say the same about me. The crazy thing was on that last occasion your mother and I had spent a lot of time together talking and apologising for all our stubbornness. At the end of it we had resolved to swallow our pride and give it another go."

"Yes, I remember Mom telling me at the time," her eyes glazed as she cast her memory back as if it was only yesterday. "I was so thrilled. At last, my daddy is back in my life, I told myself. I even ran down to the church to light a candle and say thank you to Our Lady!"

"Fools that we were, we had reckoned without your grandmother. Soon enough she fanned the flames of resentment again, and in no time at all we both ended up saying things we maybe wished we hadn't. As I recall, only your Auntie Kathleen spoke with anything resembling a voice of reason. She's a good woman, your Auntie Kathleen."

As they paused again to lean against the stone wall and stare out across the river, Eileen nodded obligingly. Her beloved aunt was indeed the best sort.

"Eileen, it tore me apart to leave you," he continued, surveying the bomb-ravaged skyline of Southwark and Lambeth. "Otherwise, I thought the least I could do was make sure you didn't have to suffer too much as a result of our break-up. Therefore, I put aside a little money each month and quietly posted it to Auntie Kathleen. I knew I could trust her to do the right thing by you."

"So that was how she came by the money to pay for my dance lessons," Eileen marvelled. "And how she managed to 'come by' your address when I approached her and told her I wanted to get in touch with you again."

"During those years I often thought aloud about getting in touch with you again – more so when I read that you had become one of the Royal Air Force's most celebrated WAAFs," he broke to tease her. Then his expression turned downcast again as he added, "However, Fiona wasn't happy. I had a new life with her now – and with Maureen. She would beg me: why go and turn the poor girl's life upside down again by reminding her of the past?"

Such a selfish and unfeeling response further fuelled Eileen's resentment towards this woman. However, she knew she should not speak ill of the dead – especially someone her father clearly loved deeply. Hence she bit her tongue and listened while he confessed the most heart-breaking thing of all about this desperately unhappy outcome.

"Besides, above all I felt ashamed that I had let you down so badly. And I guess as time went by that shame convinced me that you would be justified if you had come to hate me because of all that I had done to you. My shame then hardened into a sort of paralysis that kept me from making good the yearning in my heart to see you again."

She drew her arm up and hugged him close, as if to gently castigate him for ever having allowed himself to think so disparagingly of his qualities as a father – and when all her memories of him were so positive. He was the man whose love and forbearance had instilled in his daughter a lasting legacy of respect for herself as a woman, and which had spurred her on to prize that same self-sacrificial chivalry in the other men in her life too: qualities that will always attend a true gentleman; qualities that had first drawn her to Nicky, for sure – but also, she conceded, to Frank and Gerald before him.

"So what led you to walk back into my life the way that you did?"

He stared back out across the river and spent time pondering a reply.

"I had lost two people who meant the world to me. I therefore came to the conclusion that the only reason why my life had been spared that night was so that I might be reconciled at last with the only other person who also meant the world to me. By chance I spotted an advert for the Ad Astra Dance Band, and that they were scheduled to appear at the Astoria. Then I spotted your name up there with them. I thought it really is now or never. I hope I didn't frighten or embarrass you."

She hugged him again. How ridiculous! But then George Wilfred Kimberley wasn't the only person strolling along the river bank on that beautiful summer morning who had spent the best part of their life feeling crushed by the weight of all their shortcomings – real or imaginary. Nor for thinking that they were a 'bad' person who thoroughly deserved all the bad things that fate had heaped upon them.

"Do you still go to church?" he then sprang a question upon her, out of the blue. She blinked for a second, then shrugged her shoulders as if in shame – unsure whether to nod or shake her head.

"I still believe – if that's what you mean. As for going to Mass and Confession, well... I once got talking to a WAAF officer – quite an unusual one at that. She said we don't need to confess our sins to priests. We can talk to God Himself – the 'Organ-Grinder' she called him! I guess it's what I have found myself doing lately. Why do you ask?"

It was her father's turn to be embarrassed to articulate what was on his heart.

"I was going to ask you to say a prayer or light a candle for me. If ever a man is in need of forgiveness then you're looking at him. If ever a man is so undeserving to have such a beautiful and understanding daughter as you, then again: you're looking at him."

There was another warm embrace between father and long-lost daughter – this time to show that ten long years of misunderstanding and misapprehension on both their parts was indeed forgiven.

* * * * *

Heading back into the West End, they found themselves mingling idly with the tourists and the pigeons enjoying each other's company in Trafalgar Square, the swarming birds tame enough to take morsels from the hand or alight in a line along a shoulder and an outstretched arm. In like manner, Eileen quickly found herself accosted by American and Commonwealth servicemen in uniform, who offered her their little box cameras so that she might capture them posing at the foot of Nelson's Column – the quintessential backdrop with which to maybe remember the England that had been their home for the last few years, and from which they would shortly be departing.

"That's Canada House, isn't it?" Eileen pointed out once she had shaken herself free of both pigeons and sightseers.

"I believe so," George replied, though the huge Canadian ensign unfurling in the warm breeze was a giveaway – the same breeze that also despatched lazy droplets upon them from the flumes of the fountains nearby.

"I wrote a letter there the other day," Eileen enlightened him, a curious glow on her bonny face.

"Enquiring about emigrating once you're demobbed, perchance?"

Eileen nodded excitedly. "If not Canada, then I might try my luck in Australia or New Zealand instead. You know, being in the Women's Auxiliary Air Force has taught me so much. It has given me the chance to meet so many amazing people from all over the world, and to learn things about their countries. There is indeed a big wide world out there. I wonder whether I could ever settle down in Birmingham and be content with the narrow horizons I once knew. Does that sound fancy or pretentious?" she asked hopefully.

"Not at all. I've thought about such things myself. After all, there's nothing to keep me in England any more – present company excepted, of course!" he felt obliged to grin by way of qualification. Eileen returned him a knowing smile. What's more, it had been quite amusing to learn that, by virtue of her father having passed the war years running a sheet music distribution company, they had both unwittingly ended up working in show business – well, sort of!

"No, nowadays the popularity of the cinema and the gramophone record means it's becoming increasingly difficult to earn a living in that line of work. Therefore, I was thinking of striking out into something new," he informed her.

Eileen was content to just listen as he bounced tantalising ideas around. Despite the tragedy that he had endured, George Kimberley remained the same bright, personable and enterprising individual he always was. A handsome charmer with it! He was truly the sort of man who could apply himself to anything and succeed – at home or overseas.

"Of course, you do realise that one day when I'm famous I might have need of a manager," she teased him.

"Yes. You probably will," he looked into her eyes, availing himself of that same fanciful flippancy to avoid committing himself. "Otherwise, I'm sorry you never heard anything more from that American guy who wanted to sign Nicky up with his recording label."

"I still haven't given up hope. Maybe I realise now though that perhaps I wanted it for the wrong reasons. I accept that there were times too when – for all that I loved him – I was maybe using Nicky to those ends too."

"Yes, sometimes we all guilty of projecting our hopes and aspirations onto the ones we love. I certainly did with your mother. I had such big dreams about what I wanted to achieve and where I wanted to be. I must have left her wondering whether I really did love her for who she was – or whether I just wanted her as an attractive-looking accompaniment to my towering ambitions. In the end, that was one of the factors that caused us to drift apart – and for your grandmother to wag her finger and huff 'I told you so'."

"Gosh, I really am my father's child then," Eileen gasped, another piece of the intriguing mosaic that was her life slotting itself into place.

* * * * *

It was well past five o'clock by the time this last leg of their odyssey in the capital had come to an end – one remarkable day given over completely to father and daughter strolling leisurely around its many landmarks whilst reminiscing and reacquainting themselves with each other. Now here they were at last in the busy and familiar environs of King's Cross station.

"I'm so sorry I have to go, Dad. I wish I could stay with you forever," she pined, turning to him so that he might proudly behold her one last time looking so smart in her RAF uniform.

"I know. That's life. But you know you are always welcome to stay with me any time. And next time the Ad Astra Dance Band is back in town you know I will come and watch you perform."

"Archie has been really understanding with me," his benediction reminded her. "When he knew you were my father – the father I hadn't seen in years; the father I had given up for dead – he very kindly wrote out another twenty-four hour pass and told me to catch up with band at our next performance up north. Dad, this has been the most magical twenty-four hours I have ever spent."

As she began to weep he moved in to comfort her and to dry the eyes of his 'little girl'. Meanwhile, over the tannoy the station announcer's dulcet tones informed the passengers milling about the booking hall that the six o'clock departure for York was boarding on Platform Seven.

"That's your train, isn't it?" he noted, nudging away a stray tear of his own – to which she nodded reluctantly.

He purchased a platform ticket and joined her locating the train. Dumping Eileen's kit bag aboard, her father then stepped back down on the platform and closed the door for her. Eileen poked her head and shoulders out of its open window to pass the final few moments with him before the fingers on the station clock inched around to the appointed time.

"You know I'm not an especially religious man, Eileen. However, I do believe there is something or someone greater than ourselves up there," he smiled as he cast his gaze up at the sun still streaming through the station's arched glass roof. "I also believe that when we dream – and when we yearn for those dreams to come true – that something or someone often has to bid us wait. Sometimes we can be left waiting a very long time. So we grow impatient and try to hurry things along. However, that waiting makes us stronger; it teaches us things we need to accept to be complete as human beings: patience, humility, forgiveness even. Then, when we are finally ready, that something or somebody allows our dreams to come true."

He watched Eileen's mouth form a most serene smile. "You've been talking to my Auntie Kathleen again! She told me exactly the same thing." she then chuckled.

"Then you have this on better authority than just me," he smiled too.

The guard's whistle trilled at one end of the platform, followed by the locomotive's own whistle whooping from the other.

"So long, Leading Aircraftwoman Kimberley," her father waved to her discreetly. "I'll write to you soon."

"So long, Dad. I will too," she returned his wave.

"Don't forget. Learn to forgive yourself. That's what I never did."

With the train clanking along and gathering speed, they were the last words she caught. There remained just a few more precious moments while she watched him standing there. Then they waved their last farewell and the train rocked its way across a set of points and out of the station. He was gone. Out of her life again – though, thankfully, it would not be forever.

\* \* \* \* \*

It would prove to be a summer of surprises. It has been ten long years since the British people had last gone to the polls. Suffice to say, a lot of water had flowed under the proverbial bridge since then. Mindful of this, the Labour Party declined Winston Churchill's offer to remain in the wartime coalition. Parliament was dissolved on Friday, June 15th and a general election called for Thursday, July 5th. However, because of the logistics of counting the votes of millions of servicemen still stationed overseas it would not be until Thursday, July 26th that the result would finally be announced.

A political earthquake had taken place. Though Churchill remained a hugely respected war leader, the Conservative Party had entered the election poorly prepared and with a record of peacetime government that was now out of step with the times. Conversely – and having demonstrated their competence in the wartime coalition – the message of 'Let us face the future' that Labour ministers expounded struck a chord with the millions of the ordinary voters who had spent the last six years working and fighting to secure a fairer and more just society. Returned with a colossal 393 seats and an unassailable parliamentary majority, it was the mild-mannered Labour leader Clement Attlee that the King invited to form a new government – one that was about to embark upon the greatest social transformation Britain had yet witnessed.

On the day the result was announced, Churchill himself had been meeting with fellow Allied leaders at Potsdam to agree upon the shape of the new post-war world. First though, there was unfinished business to resolve. On Monday, August 6th a lone American B29 Super Fortress bomber flying high over the Japanese city of Hiroshima released a single large device. A few minutes later it detonated with such explosive force that virtually the entire city was obliterated in a blinding flash – along with eighty thousand of its inhabitants. Three days later, hundreds of thousands of Russian troops swarmed into Japanese-controlled Manchuria. While Japanese ministers were contending with each other over the import of these dramatic new developments, the United States demonstrated its resolve again by dropping a second 'atomic' bomb, this time on Nagasaki. So it was that at midday on Wednesday, August 15th 1945 the Japanese people listened in stunned silence as their Emperor announced over the radio his ministers' acceptance of the Allies' terms of unconditional surrender.

The war was over at last.

# *20*

"Guten Tag, Mein Fraulein. Would you like coffee?"

It had all the making of the most surreal dream – one blessed with white tablecloths, polished silver cutlery and lovingly-folded cloth napkins. Once upon a time, Bückeberg might have been another German town upon which the Royal Air Force dropped bombs. Yet it was here that Eileen now found herself a guest in one of its top-class hotels, being attended to by a handsome young waiter who looked truly magnificent in his liveried uniform.

"Yes, thank you. That would be nice."

She watched while his white-gloved hand poured the strong-smelling brown brew from the pot to the cup beside her place at the table. As he drew the pot back, he chanced a glance at her.

"You are Fraulein Kimberley, yes?" he smiled as their eyes met.

"That's right," she marvelled. "But how do you know?"

He smiled again and admitted that "I have heard that you are the very beautiful singer with a dance orchestra that is popular amongst British soldiers and airmen. Maybe I too will one day hear you sing," he suggested coyly.

"That is very kind of you to say so," she simpered, allowing her head to rest upon one shoulder as if touched by his sweetness. "What's your name?"

"My name is Hans, Mein Fraulein."

"Danke schoen, Hans. Maybe one day you will."

He bowed, clicked his heels, and withdrew, leaving her to savour the coffee and the ambience – as well as to feel pleased with herself for having mastered some phrases she had picked up during her stay in Germany so far. Otherwise, she watched Hans drift across the room to attend to some of the other guests attired in air force blue, studying him more closely as he did so. She tried to imagine what this attractive young man might have been up to barely a few months previously. Perhaps he had been a soldier or a sailor; or maybe even an erk with the *Luftwaffe* – undertaking the kind of airfield chores that she had watched young men on her own side perform a thousand times. Yet here he was, waiting on tables at this plush hotel that had meantime been commandeered by his country's victorious enemy.

Undoubtedly, his near-perfect command of the English language had helped him land this job whereby he might scrape together enough in foreign currency tips with which to support himself – and maybe his family if he had one. Just as well, really. For those Germans Eileen had encountered on this tour so far were clearly paying a daunting price for having thrown in their lot with that mad Austrian corporal: their cities flattened; their homes destroyed; their loved ones missing or dead; their *heimat* carved up into 'zones of occupation' by its vanquishers. Meanwhile, in the shame of their defeat, the only means that many had left with which to eke out an existence was by bartering for life's necessities with those Allied soldiers who were now their ever-present overlords – offering a shoe shine in exchange for a cigarette; or carrying a kit bag in exchange for a fistful of candy; or maybe a young *fraulein* having to perform a more intimate service in exchange for food on the table.

But then to ponder how Hans might have come by his linguistic skill was only to be left with the intriguing thought that he might once have employed it to more sinister ends – interrogating downed Allied airmen, for example. Or was it really supposing too much to imagine that this superficially polite and gentle soul had been a brutal orderly working at that notorious Bergen-Belsen concentration camp that British soldiers had stumbled upon just a few miles from this very spot? After all, SS troops were rumoured to have discarded their uniforms, stashed their weapons, and taken refuge in the surrounding forests (which was why British service personnel seldom ventured beyond the confines of the town without armed RAF policemen to escort them). Hence, in the time it took Hans to briefly glance her way again and offer that ambiguous smile, her thoughts flashed back to unforgettable newsreel footage she had seen of Belsen's gaunt and listless survivors – as well as the skeletal remains of those who had perished being bull-dozed into mass graves. It had forever seared upon her consciousness the sheer inhumanity of the regime she had played her part in defeating. Surreal dream indeed!

"Ah, there you are, Eileen," she looked up from her daydreaming to spot Flight Lieutenant Archie Wyndall ambling in, Hans breezing over to draw out a chair so that her 'CO' might join her – the usually exuberant band leader distinctly hung-over from the VJ Day celebrations of the night before.

"Coffee, Mein Herr?" Hans enquired.

"Love one."

"Or should that be 'need' one?" Eileen suggested cheekily.

"Does it show? That's the last time I toast the King's good health with schnapps!" he shook his head repentantly.

"I assume the rest of the band members stayed up toasting with you?" she chirruped, her eyes roaming around the room to observe that only now were they beginning to saunter in looking the worse for wear. It was just as well that the flight to their next engagement was not scheduled to depart until later that afternoon.

"Gosh, Eileen. How do you manage to look so spritely this early in the day," one of them marvelled as he sat down and joined them. No sooner had he reached into his tunic pocket for a resuscitating smoke than the ever-obliging Hans had swooped in with a lighter to hand with which he proceeded to light the cigarette for him.

"Such service! German efficiency, eh!"

"It is a pleasure, Mein Herr," the young waiter clicked his heels, flashing another, this time more barbed smile at Eileen before discreetly breezing back out of earshot.

"It's because I stayed off the schnapps," she continued. "And retired to my room before the serious drinking got underway… Or so it would seem."

"Very wise, my dear" Archie groaned.

"So I take it you won't be going on the sightseeing tour this morning?" she enquired, donning a regretful frown. From the further groans of her colleagues she took that to be a negative.

Last night had certainly been the mother of all parties – as befitted both the final cessation of hostilities and the penultimate concert on their successful German tour. Celle, Fassberg, Gatow, Gutersloh, Laarbruk, Wunstorf – more places that Bomber Command might once have targeted, but which during this memorable summer of 1945 had become instead a network of bases in the British sector of occupied Germany. This past month the Ad Astra Dance Band had played to packed houses there – including last night's shindig in Bückeberg, this sleepy little Saxon town on a 'Y'-shaped road junction west of Hannover. Here it was that the RAF had chosen to set up its British Air Forces of Occupation headquarters.

What a plum posting it was too. Once a *Luftwaffe* HQ, it was now RAF air staff who found themselves billeted in this five-star hotel. Meanwhile, the accompanying cohort of WAAF typists, telephonists and administrators could enjoy having their barnets coiffured by the nice German lady who managed the hairdressing salon across the road. Even the NAAFI in the commandeered shop next door boasted an array of pastries and other goodies the likes of which Eileen had not seen in years. It made her sad to think she would be here for all of one night. Instead, she contented herself with the thought that their whistle-stop tour had further cemented her place in the affections of service personnel throughout the Occupation Zone. And if the inscrutable Hans was to be believed, then she could now boast a circle of fans amongst the locals too!

\* \* \* \* \*

It was magnificent. A true fairy tale palace set amidst beautiful parkland that boasted an impressive, granite-arched entrance; tall, shading trees; and stylishly-trimmed hedges. Meanwhile, ducks meandering idly amongst the wide lily pads that floated atop the moat that enveloped it.

"Schloss-Bückeburg has been the ancestral seat of the princes of Schaumburg-Lippe since 1601. One of their descendants still lives here today. Then, following a fire in 1732, the castle was restored in the baroque and rococo styles that you see before you."

Fascinating! Through the medium of a flying officer who spoke German, their guide elaborated upon the history of this enchanted place, Eileen's gaze swivelling here and there to soak up the wonder of it all.

"...Now, if we're all together, he will take us to see the forty-two metre-tall mausoleum that is modelled on the Pantheon in Rome... He says the gold mosaic on its cupola ceiling is one of the largest such features in the world... Then if there is time he will also take us to visit the famous Bückeberg Stadtkirche, where one of Johann Sebastian Bach's sons once worked as the *Konzertmeister*..." the guide informed them through the interpreter, the little group of WAAFs and male subalterns falling in behind him as he moved off.

Eileen lifted her gaze to take in a few more glimpses of the exterior of the palace before bringing up the rear. This delightful overseas jaunt was the first occasion that she had ever set foot outside of England. That it was being undertaken in such agreeable company and at His Majesty's government's expense was icing on the cake, so to speak. Besides, if nothing else, sights like this awesome royal abode were once again reawakening her urge to travel the world and take in all its wonders.

\* \* \* \* \*

With Eileen and the Ad Astra Dance Band safely aboard the late afternoon flight, the C47 Dakota transport plane took off from the nearby airfield in the same glorious sunshine that had enabled the palace of Schloss-Bückeburg to be shown off at its best. Something else it enabled was for the pilot to route their flight so as to pass low over what remained of the once-vibrant sea port of Hamburg.

As he did so, his passengers each craned over to stare out of the windows in silent awe at the devastated city below – the unwilling recipient of the 22,580 tons of bombs that the RAF alone had dropped on it in an effort to destroy docks, U-boat pens, oil refineries and other industrial facilities. As a consequence, there was hardly a building that had not been levelled or reduced to macabre skeletal hulks, around which rubble had been cleared so that the ant-like inhabitants they could pick out in the streets below might go about the business of somehow rebuilding their lives.

"Poor souls," someone muttered in remorse at the handiwork that the aircrews of Bomber Command had wrought upon their fellow human beings.

There was a further long contemplative silence before someone at the back yelled out "Serves the bastards right. Just remember Coventry, lads."

"An' Plymouth," the drummer added in his distinctive West Country accent.

"And Belfast," the double bass player from Antrim piped up.

"And Cardiff," Taffy the trumpeter threw in for good measure.

"And London. Never forget what those swines did to London!" the Cockney pianist across the aisle reminded them.

"Come on, chaps," Archie reluctantly waded in, clearly moved by having witnessed what remained of Germany's second city from out of the window next to Eileen, where he was sat. "Two wrongs can't make a right. Besides, not even London looked like this. Let's just say our boys did what they had to do to put an end to a monstrous tyranny. Better still, let us all pray that they never have to do anything like this again – especially now the politicians have these new 'atom' bombs to play with."

It was an appalling prospect, and filled Eileen with dread – especially having overheard some of the lads discussing how initial rejoicing and mutual backslapping by Soviet and American troops was giving way to hardening suspicion amongst their leaders about the intentions of the other side.

"'Then the Lord rained brimstone and fire on Sodom and Gomorrah'," Archie meanwhile muttered to her.

"I'm sorry," she replied.

"It's from the Old Testament. Genesis chapter nineteen, verse twenty-four."

"Oh," she proffered.

"It was one of Bomber Command's most devastating raids of the entire war: Operation Gomorrah in July 1943. I was working in signals intelligence at the time. We were tasked with evaluating the aftermath of the raid," he edged closer to her to elaborate.

"It was the first occasion that our chaps dropped 'window', or 'chaff' – millions of pieces of silver foil that completely blinded German radar. It meant that our boys had a clear run at the city. Apparently, by the third day of the operation the fires our bombers had started had combined with the dry weather to whip up a scorching one-hundred-and-fifty-mile-an-hour firestorm that blazed across the city – incinerating everything in its path. Even those civilians who had take refuge underground weren't spared because the firestorm sucked all the oxygen out of the air raid shelters. By the end of the mission over forty thousand people had perished. Over half of Hamburg's dwellings had been destroyed and over a million of its inhabitants forced to flee the city.

"I can't say too much. But what I can tell you is that we pieced together enough information to know how profoundly this raid shocked the Nazi hierarchy. It was probably the closest we ever came to Air Chief Marshall Harris's objective of shattering German civilian morale."

Eileen offered him a wan smile and then gazed back out of the window, where the sun in the western sky was illuminating just what 'shattering civilian morale' looked like in tangible form. The *Luftwaffe*, together with Hitler's V-weapons, had claimed the lives of over sixty thousand British civilians. Yet the Allied air forces had wiped out over ten times as many German civilians. Maybe Archie was correct: two wrongs can never make a right. But then she recalled again the names of ravaged British cities that his band members had ejaculated with such righteous indignation. Furthermore, she could well imagine what manner of barbaric indignities ideologically-driven young Germans like Hans might have perpetrated upon her prostrate island nation had they ever set foot on her side of the English Channel.

* * * * *

Maybe it was respect for her as their talented female vocalist, or belated recognition that WAAFs in general had earned their place in the roll call of heroic service to their country. However, as the only woman in the band Eileen had been shown nothing but kindness throughout this tour. In addition, though Archie could be draconian when demanding excellence from his musicians, in matters of general service discipline he had proved as benign as that sun that was to be observed nestling on the horizon out to sea when their plane touched down at its destination. This evening was no exception. Employing his usual sardonic tones, he bade them each turn in and get a good night's rest ready for practice tomorrow at 0-900 hours sharp, followed by the concert itself that evening.

Still manifesting his 'soft spot' for her, he personally accompanied Eileen to her quarters. This turned out to be in a billet overlooking a becalmed North Sea that was bathed in the amber glow of a romantic sunset, gentle waves lapping hypnotically upon the shore. Shame it wasn't his leading lady with whom he would be contemplating the romance of it all, she could see his mind working as he heaved her kit bag inside before allowing her to politely, but firmly bid him goodnight.

That Archie was a gentleman at heart had allayed her initial anxieties. She had so enjoyed the camaraderie of performing with him and the boys – not least because they were all so refreshingly free of the stuffiness that usually infused officer-ranks relations. How could it be otherwise? With the war over, most of this otherwise laid-back gaggle of bohemians were itching to play professionally again on the lucrative club circuit that they had left behind when call-up notices had been served on them.

Tomorrow would be the last night of their triumphant German tour before they returned to England and a spell of well-earned leave. Who could say whether progressive demobilisation would thereafter thin their ranks such that it risked depriving Archie of his most talented musicians, effectively calling time on the Ad Astra Dance Band.

Once she had unpacked her kit and had faithfully placed beside her bed the treasured photograph of her father, she drifted over to stare out of the window at those dying rays of sunlight. There she pondered what her own eventual return to civvy street might have in store. To be sure, she had learned a valuable trade as a telephonist which would stand her in good stead, whether she chose to exercise it at home or maybe in Australia or New Zealand. In his letters to her, her father was meanwhile brimming with ideas for business ventures. He also promised to take his 'little girl' under his wing and teach her how to manage them alongside him – or maybe even help her set up one of her own. However, having always maintained that she lacked the ruthlessness to make a good NCO, she failed to see how she would fare much better having to bang heads together in the world of commerce and enterprise.

No, music was still her first love. Neither had she lost hope that by the time her turn came to hang up her uniform for the last time some record producer somewhere might have signed her up and set her on the still elusive road to fame and fortune.

* * * * *

With the morning practice session out of the way (and Archie satisfied that they were playing to their usual high standard), the afternoon was free for the band members to do as they pleased. For Eileen, this entailed a welcome opportunity to grab the gaily-coloured swimsuit she had purchased at one of the spa towns they had visited and head off to the beach to make the most of another gorgeous summer's day. Having enjoyed the almost forgotten pleasure of strolling barefoot on the sand and of dipping her toes in the sea, by-and-by she located a quiet spot in the dunes upon which to lay down her towel and soak up the sun.

Renowned for its mile-upon-mile of sandy beaches, Sylt was a T-shaped island off the west coast of Schleswig-Holstein in the far north of the country. Connected to the mainland by the narrow *Hindenburgdamm* causeway upon which a railway had been laid, it had become established as a popular holiday destination amongst Germans. The site of a Nazi seaplane base during the war, the RAF had also taken a shine to it and had now established a base of their own for the purposes of air-sea rescue and weapons trials. Although it was something of a lonely outpost, on a day like today its benign climate and spectacular beauty more than compensated for this, only the periodic coming and going of planes from the nearby airfield disturbing the pristine tranquillity of its golden shoreline.

It seemed like an eternity since Eileen had enjoyed the opportunity to doze off in solitude with the sun soaking into her exposed limbs – time enough to treasure recollections of all the wonderful friends and exciting adventures her four years in the Royal Air Force had blessed her with. It made her rather sad to think that in a few months' time it would all be consigned to fading memories. Perhaps a return to civvy street was not so inviting after all.

She flipped herself over to lie face down and settle her head upon the cushion she had formed with her folded arms, perchance to doze some more. It was then that a rustling in the grass disturbed her ruminations and prompted her to lift her head and scan her surroundings. Aware that local men frequented this beach, she sat up more fully to survey the shoreline and the dunes, though all she could spot were odd souls in the distance also out enjoying the wonderful beach-walking weather. Hence she spread herself back out on her towel, this time face up to tan the front of her body, squeezing fine grains of sand between her fingertips as somnolence beckoned once more.

There she could again be in the arms of her dashing Major Nicky Braschetti, his kisses exciting her and his powerful hands racing up and down her body as together they poured out their passion upon the warm, powdery sand. Half in this dream world, she reached down her own hand to find it fleetingly brushing against something warm and wet. Invitingly warm and wet, in fact! Casting restraint to the gentle breeze, she lingered to fondle it lazily, though flitting back into lucidity just long enough to sense it pulling away from her grasp.

Then, without so much as a by-your-leave, she felt it trailing up her leg to plunge determinedly somewhere where it shouldn't!

She awoke and sat up with a start to behold a huge great Alsation staring back at her, its bushy tail, bright eyes and moist, twitching nose communicating playfulness.

"No. Go away. Go on..." she tried to shoo aside the excited mutt. "Nein... Geh weg," she continued, jabbering something that had worked when warding off the importuning of the black-marketeers and teenage waifs in other German towns. After all, it was a 'German' shepherd dog!

Then, before she could snatch them back, the hound had spotted and grabbed her slinky shorts and made off over the dunes with them.

"Buster...! Buster...! Here, boy...!" she then heard a more familiar tongue call out from the beach. Seconds later, she was shielding her eyes to behold a sun-bronzed young man emerge over the dunes to loom over her.

"Ah, Buster, there you are... I'm so sorry, miss..." he spread the palm of his hand upon his smooth, rippling torso, catching his breath to gaze down at her beseechingly. "Entschuldigen Sie bitte."

"It's okay. I'm English," Eileen explained, having drawn up her towel up to mask her cleavage.

This curious young man chided his dog to circuit around his legs and deposit Eileen's shorts in his hand. "These must be yours, I assume," he then smiled cheekiily, handing them back to her.

"They are indeed!" she huffed, trying not make her annoyance too obvious.

"If you're English, then I guess you must be one of the new WAAFs that arrived last week."

"Actually, I arrived last night. I'm Eileen Kimberley – the singer with the Ad Astra Dance Band. We're performing a concert here tonight.

"So you're the famous Eileen Kimberley. Well, I never," he enthused, reaching down to offer her his hand. "I'm Harry. Harry Ewell. I'm a sergeant with the RAF Police. And this is Buster, my dog."

"Yes, we are well acquainted by now. Little thief!" Eileen rested her arms upon her knees and offered the animal a jesting scowl. Otherwise, the dog was content to gaze up at its master with its big, panting tongue dangling rhythmically from the side of its mouth.

"I do apologise. I hope he didn't frighten you. He's daft as a brush really. Mind you, one word from me and he wouldn't hesitate to rip your throat out!"

"Charming!"

"Well, he is a trained guard dog."

Buster glanced up for his master's approval before ambling over so that Eileen could run her outstretched hand along his coat and scratch behind his ears. Meanwhile, Harry sat himself down on the sloping flank of the dune in order to better make the acquaintance of this gifted starlet, whose impending arrival had been the talk of the station. It was a task momentarily interrupted when a banking Spitfire zoomed in low alongside them, the pilot waving.

"Wow! Isn't that plane still such an awesome sight to behold!" Eileen swooned, cupping her hand to her eyes again and waving back. As it raced out to sea, the pilot wiggled its wings in a parting salute that complemented the evocative fading drone of its Rolls Royce Merlin engine.

"Not the only awesome sight around here to behold. Don't you know this beach is also frequented by naturists?"

"Naturists?"

"You know: young *frauleins* who prefer to sunbathe with no clothes on," Harry chuckled at her naivety. "Why else do you think those fighter boys enjoy practising their low flying skills along these sands?"

This time they both chuckled nervously. Eileen watched while Harry reclined back to rest upon elbows that he had dug into the sand for support, a tattoo on his muscular arm proudly announcing his undying love for his mother.

"Anyway, I'm glad you didn't decide to sunbathe further along the dunes," he opined nudging their nascent conversation along. "The bomb disposal lads can't be entirely certain they've located all the ordnance the RAF must have dropped on this place over the years."

"Yes, I saw the warning signs."

"That's why I was worried when I thought I'd lost Buster. Stick to the beach though and you should be okay."

"It's certainly a lovely spot to be posted."

"A bit bleak in the winter, I would imagine," Harry surmised, gazing out to sea and sucking on a hardy strand of grass that he had plucked. "Buster loves it here though, don't you boy. I take him a walk most days when we're off duty."

"How long are you posted here for?"

He shrugged his shoulders. "Until 'demob', I guess. Maybe the end of the year. And yourself?

"I'm here for tonight's concert; and then we have the weekend to unwind before we fly back to England on Monday."

"You engaged? Have a boyfriend?" he enquired, though from the matter-of-fact way he tossed the question her way she assumed he didn't intend it to sound forward. She dipped her gaze and shook her head obligingly.

"Me neither. A girlfriend, I mean. There was someone once. She was driver with the ATS. We were engaged to be married. But then she was killed in a road accident a few months back. So out went all my hopes of wedded bliss."

"I'm sorry to hear that," Eileen dipped her gaze a second time. "I was engaged too; to an American airman. He was posted missing earlier this year."

This time it was Harry's turn to offer condolence. Meanwhile, having accepted that his afternoon constitutional was on hold for the duration, Buster wandered back over to lie down beside his master, who ran his fingers lazily along the huge, bony shoulders of his canine companion. Buster then spread his head upon his crossed paws and fixed his doleful eyes upon Eileen.

"I do a bit of singing myself, mind," the handsome police sergeant then confessed.

"Oh really," she replied, returning Buster's searching gaze as if to mask the memory of the last occasion upon which she had been thrilled to discover that the alluring young man she was sat opposite could sing. Could her still tender heart ever afford to have its hopes dashed like that again?

"Only in the station choir, mind you. Some of us lads here who are Christians get together each week to sing a few hymns and choruses. I'm sure your show will garner far more applause than we'll ever get," he grinned self-effacingly.

"It doesn't matter," she smiled back and assured him. "It's the joy that you put into what you sing that matters. And did I hear you say you were 'Christians'? I thought most people in our country were Christians," she added in a touching, if different manifestation of naivety.

"Are you a Christian then," he turned to her, intrigued.

What she was loathed to admit was that, what with the pressure of touring, she was lapsing again in her obligation to attend Confession and Mass. It had left her once more labouring under a cloud of guilt that she was not a good enough 'Christian' – and that by her omission she might again risk inviting God's wrath down upon her. Therefore, she shrugged defiantly.

"Of course, I am. I'm a Roman Catholic. I pray and I go to… well, I try to do good things – just like Jesus tells us to do. And when I fail, well… Look, I know I'm not perfect…"

Harry evinced a smile of his own: warm and forbearing whilst uncannily reaffirming what Rachel Owen had been keen to emphasise to her.

"Eileen, Christianity isn't about being 'perfect'; or even about doing 'good things'. You can't earn God's love and forgiveness. It is a free gift that He graciously gives you. If you believe that Jesus died on that cross for you, and accept His gift of salvation, then your sins are forgiven – for all time. No, it doesn't mean you're perfect. But it does mean you no longer have to doubt whether or not you are His child."

"But I do believe," she asserted.

"Then believe too that He has forgiven you – for all time. No more struggling to be 'perfect'. Do good not to beg His forgiveness; but in recognition and gratitude that He already has forgiven you."

There followed a few moments of awkward silence. Time enough for Eileen to contemplate that was now twice that she had heard that tantalising message of hope. Had she really spent her whole life striving to 'earn' something that her Saviour had freely granted her from the bounty of His measureless love? No need for priests; nor the ritual of confessions; nor constantly beating herself up because she feared she was not a 'good enough' person?

"Anyway, Miss RAF Singing Sensation: are you up for a paddle? Or even a swim maybe," Harry suggested, changing the subject lest she thought he might be 'preaching' at her. Meanwhile, he cheekily fired off in her direction the stalk of grass he had been chewing.

"Swimming? Not likely. I can't risk my hair blossoming into a fuzzball this close to tonight's performance. However, I'll happily join you for a paddle."

"In which case – lead the way, Buster."

This the huge black-and-tan hound duly did, excitedly bounding ahead of Harry, who had clapped eyes on a piece of driftwood that he then hurled across the sand for Buster to give chase. Eileen gathered up her things and trailed after them, laying them down again at the water's edge and venturing out to join her new friend knee deep in the gentle waves.

"Gosh! This is wonderful. And the water isn't even cold either. You know, I haven't had a paddle in the sea since I was a little girl."

"Make the most of it. The weather round here can change. When the storms roll in it's a different place altogether. Anyway," he nudged her arm playfully, "if you're around tomorrow afternoon there's a holiday retreat further up the island that once belonged to Hermann Goering – Hitler's head of the *Luftwaffe*. I can take you to see it, if you like. We can borrow some bikes. Apparently, inside there's this huge bed that was made especially to bear the weight of the corpulent old *Reichsmarschall*."

"Let me get this straight: you want to take me out tomorrow to a holiday 'retreat' where you intend to show me a huge great bed. Harry Ewell! My Auntie Kathleen warned me about boys like you!" she nudged him back under the pretence of being utterly scandalised.

They both fell about in a fit of youthful giggles. However, his clumsy offer had now well and truly broken the ice. So while Harry and Eileen took turns to throw the driftwood out to sea for Buster to swim after and retrieve (and Buster's underwhelmed expression told the truth that women can't throw!), they continued to deepen their acquaintance, flitting from topic to topic – family, friends, service life, and occasionally onto their respective faiths once more. To his pleasant surprise, Eileen was in no way fazed that he was sharing his beliefs.

"Oh, Buster. You didn't remind me," he suddenly exclaimed, glancing down at his watch. "Sorry about this, Eileen. But I'm on duty at four. So I'd better dash," he then insisted as he waded back onto the sand, poked his feet in his sandals, and summoned Buster to join him.

"So you're not coming to the concert tonight at eight?" she fretted, taking a last opportunity to admire his physique being draped in sunshine.

"I'm off again at ten. So I should be able to sneak in late… if that's okay. Anyway, it's been nice meeting you. And I hope Buster didn't give you too much of a fright back there."

She chuckled and returned the farewell wave he offered her as he began to jog back towards the camp with Buster trotting ahead of him.

"Oh, and listen," he turned around to add. "If I don't get chance to speak to you after the concert – and if you're still around on Sunday morning – we hold a little church service of our own in the mess hall at ten thirty. You're more than welcome to come along and join us."

"Will you be singing?" she casually enquired.

"I might."

"Then I might just take you up on that," she chortled, offering both Harry and Buster a final wave as they made their way back along the beach.

Love, compassion, and forgiveness – the three nails that pinned Our Lord to the Cross, she recalled Auntie Kathleen had said. As she recalled too all those statues and stained-glass images of Christ's suffering that loomed so large in her experience of 'church', all of sudden they didn't seem so abstract after all. Could it really be that, just as she was proud to consider herself 'her father's child', so she could step up and confess to being her Heavenly Father's 'ransomed' child also? Could this 'salvation by faith' that Harry chatted about really be that simple?


\* \* \* \* \*


The Friday night concert at air station B170 Westerland (or 'RAF Sylt' as those stationed here had taken to calling it) was just what its officers, men and handful of WAAFs had been waiting for. And Flight Lieutenant Archie Wyndall made sure they got it: all two hours (plus interlude) of popular swing melodies like *'Jersey Bounce'*, *'Moonglow'*, *'La Paloma'*, *'Ziguener'*, *'Frenesi'* and *'Fascinating Rhythm'* that had everyone in the house finger-drumming, foot-tapping and – towards the end of the show – dancing too.

As always, the highlight of the evening was the magical voice and entrancing stage presence of Leading Aircraftwoman Eileen Kimberley, who indulged her enthralled listeners with a collection of hot numbers that Archie had put together especially for her: *'I've Got My Love To Keep Me Warm'*, *'Sentimental Journey'*, *'A Room With A View'*, *'How High The Moon'* and rounded off with Billie Holiday's haunting *'That Old Devil Called Love'*.

She joined Archie and the bandsmen to take a gratifying bow before they all disappeared off stage to catch their breaths before the wild applause and foot-stomping ringing in their ears drew them back onstage to offer their audience a final encore. It was during her performance of this – a smouldering, evocative rendition of George and Ira Gershwin's *'The Man I Love'* – that through the dazzling glow of the stage lights above her Eileen made out Sergeant Harry Ewell sneaking into the back of the room as promised. He looked immaculate in his white belt and gaiters and white peaked cap, which he removed to brush back his hair and to flash an apologetic smile.

Seeing him standing there, mouth agape in wonderment, spurred her to once more put her heart and soul into what she was singing, offering her listeners a truly spine-tingling triumphant finale that left everyone in the house on their feet applauding and cheering.

"There you go, Eileen. Aren't you glad your good old Uncle Archie persuaded you put aside the mawkish stuff and launch yourself into jazz and swing!" their leader gloated as he and his musicians gathered in the dressing room afterwards. There they helped themselves to a well-earned nightcap of scotch, schnapps or whatever else their leader had managed to raid from the officers' mess during the preceding afternoon.

"I'll say!" one of the trombonists enthused. "They absolutely adore you, girl. You really are destined for greater things. Surely there must be a record producer out there somewhere who can see that!"

Though Eileen was, by disposition, inclined to affect modesty in the face of such effusive compliments, she could not gainsay the sensation that they were right. Maybe if this isolated air station had instead been New York's legendary Cotton Club, then tonight could have been the start of something big. However, the war was over, the Yanks had gone home; and, alas, there was still no word from any American music impresario with which to gladden her heart.

"You know, lads, I shall miss you all once we're demobbed," Archie meanwhile felt moved to open up his heart, Eileen sure she spotted a glimmer of a tear in his big soft eyes as he said it.

"We'll miss you too, Skipper," one of his clarinettists spoke for them all.

"Yes, I do hope we can all keep in touch. Who knows – maybe we will all play together again one day," someone else opined.

"We'll especially miss you, Eileen," one of the handsome saxophonists assured her. "If ever you find yourself at a loose end, you call me and I'll come and play alongside you."

From their hearty murmurs, she was again left in no doubt that this was the consensus amongst her companions. She was moved upon observing the sincerity in the faces of these men who had so encouraged her.

"Guys, you're so sweet. I shall miss you too. Good luck with whatever you each decide to do. In the meantime, enjoy your leave."

"And how about you, Eileen?" one of them addressed her hopefully. "How are you planning to spend yours?"

"Oh, first I shall spend it with my family in Birmingham. And then I will visit my father in London. He has promised to take me away for a week by the seaside. I'm hoping we can once again catch up on all the many things we still have to share with each other."

"Anyway, chaps," cried Archie, gathering them all round, "if we don't get to tour again in the autumn, let's all drink a toast right now to the future – whatever it may hold."

"TO THE FUTURE!" they all raised their glasses.

\* \* \* \* \*

The contrast could not have been greater. After the lively Friday night concert, the little Sunday morning assembly looked to set to be a rather downbeat affair. No cheering crowds, no jubilant encores, no free-flowing spirits. Instead there were all of a dozen souls gathered round in the mess hall while everyone else who was not on duty was at one of the two denominational church services being held elsewhere on the camp.

Eileen crept in and sat down at the back, quickly becoming aware that there was a different 'spirit' abroad at this gathering of Sylt's 'non-conformists' – one that she felt stirring her own heart from the moment an officer present rose to his feet and opened his bible to read from St Paul's epistle to the Roman church. She glanced across at Harry, who offered her a reassuring smile.

"'Therefore, there is now no condemnation for those who are in Christ Jesus'…"

She listened with interest, even if not always picking up the gist of what was being quoted. Aside from the more memorable Gospel stories she had been taught as a child, she had never read the Bible properly. Yet she understood only too clearly from her own life that "those who are in the realm of the flesh cannot please God". Oh brother, she feared: more sermons issuing judgement and condemnation! Yet she could not have been more wrong.

"… 'For those who are led by the Spirit of God are the children of God. The Spirit you received does not make you slaves, so that you live in fear again; rather, the Spirit you received brought about your adoption to sonship. And by Him, we cry *Abba*,'… which means Father – Daddy!" the officer looked up and glanced around at the small congregation – Eileen included – as he sought to expound upon the Aramaic transliteration.

A shudder convulsed her body. She had never before heard the connection between earthly and heavenly fathers being phrased quite so intimately. Yet it chimed with a scripture that she recalled Rachel Owen had put to her that day they had motored along the wild Northumberland coast – the words of Our Lord in which he asked those of his listeners who were earthly fathers which of them, if his son asked for bread, would hand him a stone; or if he asked for a fish, would toss him a snake.

Eileen had spent ten years of her life as a 'lost' child, desperately searching for her earthly father. Throughout she had remained convinced in her heart – despite all the discouragement and everything his detractors had scoffed – that he was out there somewhere just waiting to love her and to wrap his arms around his 'little girl' once more. So why, oh why, she interrogated herself, had she ever allowed herself to believe that her Heavenly Father didn't also love her? Or that he didn't yearn to wrap his arms around her in like manner – not wanting to 'punish' her or cruelly frustrate her dreams, but rather waiting patiently for her to surrender herself to a life-changing encounter with Him?

She became aware of the tears in her eyes, dabbing at them as they dripped onto her uniform. Then she became aware too of a beautiful solo baritone voice gently offering up a hymn of worship…

> *"When I survey the wondrous cross.*
> *On which the Prince of Glory died.*
> *My richest gain I count but loss,*
> *And pour contempt on all my pride…"*

It was Harry. This time it was Eileen's turn to glance across a spellbound room in awe, observing him look up to Heaven and put his heart, soul and voice into the timeless truths he was expressing – truths that now granted her a peace in her heart at that moment that knew no bounds. She closed her eyes and sought forgiveness – most graciously given – for all the times she had ever doubted that her Heavenly Father loved her too; or that He would in His own good time also 'freely give her all things'.

> *"…Were the whole realm of nature mine,*
> *That were an offering far too small.*
> *Love so amazing, so divine,*
> *Demands my soul, my life, my all."*

Eileen too now sank her head back and looked up to Heaven. She sensed for the first time that the journey she had set out upon all those years ago was strangely complete. She had found her earthly father. Now she had found her Heavenly Father too. Or, more tellingly, *they* had each found her.

# *21*

*"O say can you see, by the dawn's early light,*
*What so proudly we hailed at the twilight's last gleaming..."*

On and on, the crowded train rattled southwards. However, Eileen noticed out of the window that the bomb-scarred suburbs of Southampton were now flitting past. Just as well, she thought, because the passengers in the neighbouring compartments of the carriage were getting mighty agitated by the girls' jolly singing. She, however, found herself surprisingly relaxed about it all; and was even tempted to join in. Maybe it was just that the week by the sea in Brighton that she had spent with her father recently had helped to further heal the memory of what could have been. And the party atmosphere in the compartment next door certainly reminded her of that.

*"...O say does that Star-Spangled Banner yet wave,*
*O'er the land of the free and the home of the brave!"*

"Oye, keep it down, girls!" one of the soldiers standing in the corridor yelled. "We're not all off to make babies with a Yank, yer' know!"

His snide observation halted their song, but it was quickly replaced by a fit of giggles amongst the sextet of happy young girls. Meanwhile, Eileen stood to lift down her case before drifting out into the corridor, brushing past the agitated squaddie, who was puffing on a diminished cigarette and gazing out of the window with a look of glum resignation on his face.

"Bloody GI brides!" he grunted, hauling up his kit bag and making for the door. "If they were shipping out to the Far East like me they wouldn't be laughing quite so loud!"

"Oh, don't be so miserable, you horrible spoilsport!" one of the girls leant out of the compartment and called after him.

"Yeah, look on the bright side, mate," her friend added. "At least you won't have all those Japs chasing you around the jungle with their bayonets!"

"I take it you ladies are all heading for docks," Eileen enquired as the girls also motioned to haul down bulky suitcases that clearly contained what few treasured possessions they were taking with them from the Old World.

"We most certainly are," a jolly little blonde lass beamed. "Our ship sails this evening bound for New York – and a brand new life. What say you, girls?"

"Statue of Liberty, here we come," her friend hollered, showing off her glittering wedding ring. "Then I'm boarding a train for Springfield, Illinois to join my new husband. He's a sergeant in the US Rangers, you know."

"And I'm off to Portland, Oregon," another enthused – and a very long train journey ahead of her when their ship docked!

"This time next month we'll both be in California," her friends roared, barely able to contain their excitement as they heaved their bulging luggage down onto the platform. The news raised a poignant smile on Eileen's face.

"Meanwhile, Yours Truly 'ere is off ter' Lost Cabin, Wyoming – where ever the bleedin' 'ell that is!" said another in her delightful Cockney accent, hauling hers after them, having probably still not fully taken in what exile to the great American wilderness might entail for a lass from London's East End.

These girls were lucky ones, Eileen sighed as she observed them skipping down the platform in their pretty dresses, arm-in-arm and singing as they went. Meanwhile, a diminutive old porter was hurrying after them with those worldly possessions piled high on his trolley. They were indeed sailing off to an exciting new life in the United States. If their luck held, they would bond anew with their GI husbands in the vastly different milieu of peace time, adapt to their new country, raise children, and never look back at the life they now were leaving behind. Pity instead those girls she knew whose dreams lay shattered upon discovering that the American servicemen they had looked forward to marrying had wives and sweethearts already waiting for them back home. Pity even more those girls who had gotten pregnant, only to find that the fathers of their children had returned without them, having wiped the slate clean of whatever youthful 'mistakes' they had made while based in England.

Eileen's idle ruminating soon gave way to the more pressing matter of why she had stepped aboard the ten o'clock train from Waterloo that morning. She therefore headed out onto the station concourse, glancing about to spy out the people she had travelled down to meet. Sure enough, across the way the door of beautiful big silver-grey MG saloon car opened. A familiar face emerged upon which was painted a huge cheesy grin, her bobbed blonde crown instantly recognisable. Then from the other side of the car another familiar face emerged, this time the hints of her gorgeous red mane tucked in her RAF cap rekindling memories of another treasured friendship. Together, these two young women now raced over to greet her.

"Nancy!" Eileen screamed, those golden locks dancing on excited shoulders as her 'best friend' launched her arms tight around the tear-filled arrival.

"And Pippa!" she then gasped, released from Nancy's grip to instead hurl herself into the embrace of her other 'best friend' – the one from her Lincolnshire days, who she hadn't seen in two long years.

"Oh, look: you're making me cry now, yer' great hinny!" Pippa snuffled, squeezing her tight.

Demonstrative greetings complete, Nancy picked up Eileen's case and hurried her over to the car, where it was placed in the boot. Then the girls all piled in together on the back seat, Eileen squashed into the middle so that she might be introduced to Nancy's parents sitting in the front.

"Pleased to meet you, Mr and Mrs King," she smiled, reaching the hand of greeting through the gap between them.

"We're pleased to meet you too, my dear" her mother turned to observe her and to enthuse in her delectably polite tones. "Nancy has told us so much about you. I do so hope you can fulfil your dream of a singing career."

"So do I, Mrs King," she sighed, noting how Nancy's father seemed overwhelmed and subdued by the presence in his car of four excitable females. Instead, he dutifully thrust the car into gear and out onto the city streets.

"Anyway," Nancy insisted, "the first thing you two are going to do when we get back is get out of these confounded uniforms. Then you simply must try on the dresses that mother has had made especially for you. Trust me, girls; you will look a million dollars in them."

"Don't be so eager, my dear. I'm sure your friends here are quite exhausted after their long journeys," Nancy's mother light-heartedly fussed.

She was not wrong. Pippa had travelled up from Devon that morning. For Eileen too, it had been a long train journey into London from her new posting in Norfolk (though with time for an overnight stop-off to visit her father), and then the onward journey down to Hampshire. Right up until the last minute she was convinced that RAF bureaucracy would conspire to frustrate her request for leave to attend this eagerly-awaited special occasion.

Yet here she was, gazing out of the window excitedly as the tall cranes and mighty ships of Southampton Water were left behind. Instead, they were motoring off towards the rustic splendour of the New Forest, thereby fulfilling Eileen's long-standing promise to accept the open invitation Nancy had extended to stay at her family home. Furthermore, she was doing so at a most important moment in her best friend's life. For in two days' time Mr King would be escorting his daughter up the aisle of their local parish church to be given away in marriage to one Squadron Leader Peter Knowles, a dashing young fighter pilot she had met and fallen in love with. Once upon a time, in one of the many letters by which they had kept in touch, Nancy had jovially demanded that she be granted first refusal to be the bridesmaid at Eileen's wedding. Yet in barely forty-eight hours' time it would be Eileen – and Pippa too – who would instead play bridesmaids for what promised to be a most memorable weekend indeed.

\* \* \* \* \*

Eventually, the car drew up outside an enchanted old country house situated in a tiny village that boasted a pub, a chapel and a scattering of dwellings, the chimneys of which were idly puffing trails of smoke into the dusky October sky. Sure enough – as Eileen remembered Nancy recounting – its inhabitants also kept company with a herd of wild horses that grazed on the common.

On lazy summer afternoons Eileen imagined this central piece of greenery playing host to the village cricket match. Therefore, it was perhaps appropriate that in one corner of it, beneath the shade of an old oak tree, there stood a simple cenotaph that bore a handful of names – there as if to proclaim an idyll of Merry England that had stood firm against the despoiling march of progress, as well as the malign machinations of Napoleon Bonaparte, Kaiser Bill and (more recently) Adolf Hitler.

After a hearty evening meal prepared by her mother (and which demonstrated why wartime rationing in the countryside – with its ready access to fresh produce – was always a different affair to the sparser wartime rationing experienced in the cities), all three of them retired to share gossip in the guest bedroom that had been made ready for Pippa and Eileen. There too, they could at last try on those beautiful white chiffon bridesmaids' dresses with daisy-chain neckline and puffed sleeve detail.

"This is absolutely fabulous, pet!" Pippa swooned, twisting herself in front of the full-length mirror so that she might observe what a gorgeous woman it had transformed her into.

"Girls, I won't tell you how many clothing coupons Mother had to stash away in order to acquire the material for your dresses," Nancy rolled her eyes, relieved that the finished products not only made her friends look like 'a million dollars', but needed very little by way of alteration.

"I feel like I'm a princess," Eileen insisted, busily swishing about in hers in front of the mirror.

"We are princesses!" Pippa assured her, nudging her out of the way to do likewise for one final time.

"So you are. But just wait until you get to see my dress," Nancy teased them. "I am going to upstage you both!"

That they didn't doubt, helping each other step out of their dresses and hang them up ready for the big day before throwing over themselves the less eye-catching garb of the nighties they had each brought with them in their cases.

"So is there no wedding in prospect for you yet, Pippa," Eileen enquired.

"Oh, there is a young man I have my eye on. Trouble is, pet, I can't seem to coax him to notice me."

"What? With your breathtaking good looks! Then he must be blind, Pippa, that's all I can say," Nancy chortled, making herself at home on the huge iron-framed bed by squatting on legs that now she tucked beneath her.

She looked across at Eileen, who had joined them on the bed. However, Nancy halted herself before she risked clumsily asking her the same question. Pippa picked up on this and knew that they could not pass the weekend subdued by awkwardness about their friend's cruel bereavement.

"We were so sorry for you when we heard what happened to Nicky. You didn't deserve to lose him – and so close to the end of hostilities too."

Eileen shrugged dolefully. "None of the many people we have known who have lost loved ones 'deserved' it. But that's just war, I guess: no discriminator of who we are or where we come from. Thank God it's all over now."

Pippa reached over and squeezed her hand, whilst Nancy rested an arm upon her shoulder. There followed a moment of quiet thanksgiving that – whatever the vagaries of war and its often tragically brief romantic affairs – they would always have each other. Hopefully, they would always keep in touch too – as they had promised. However, with the advent of peace they probably sensed that the gathering distractions of new lives, new loves, and new friendships would work to frustrate that assurance.

"Anyway, it has not all been doom and gloom," Eileen countered, looking at each of them with wistful reflection in her eye. "I have found my father at last. Or – can you believe it – he found me! I cannot even begin to tell you how amazing that is. Maybe my father was that special someone I was looking for all along. The special someone with whom I know I will always be able to share my crazy dreams."

There was another episode of hand squeezing and shoulder hugging before Nancy and Pippa watched her don a guarded, yet revealing look to suggest that "And as for the kind of 'man in my life' that you're thinking about, well…"

"Really?" Nancy's eye lit up, anticipating what that look might portent.

"It's nothing serious, you understand," Eileen sought to moderate their excitement. "His name is Harry. He's a sergeant with the RAF Police. I met him recently when I was in Germany. We're just friends, that's all."

"Tell us about him," Pippa begged.

"Yes, is he big, tall and handsome?" Nancy bounced on the mattress at the thrill of the news.

"Yes," Eileen chuckled, "he's all of those things. But, more importantly, he is just a very good friend. Alas, I was only with him a day or so; but he asked if he could write to me. So we have kept up a correspondence ever since. He is musically-minded; and he has a marvellous singing voice. However, I guess I like him because he is, well…different. We talk about lots of things, but mostly about life and well... you know, spiritual things."

"I don't believe you, Eileen Kimberley! You're not about to start carrying on with a bloody vicar, are you!" Nancy shook her head and cussed, grabbing a pillow and beating her with it.

"Like I said, he's just a friend!" Eileen repeated again in mock outrage. "Besides, you once told me you weren't the marrying and settling-down kind. So what has this 'Peter' fellow done to make you change your mind, Little Miss Wild Child?" she grabbed a pillow and bopped the bride-to-be across the face in like manner.

"At least my guy can fly a Spitfire. This Harry fellow probably preaches windy sermons! So take that, you silly old fruitcake!" Nancy countered, slamming her pillow down on her by-now dishevelled Brummie bridesmaid.

"And I don't know what you think is so funny," Eileen recovered her poise, glaring at Nancy's Geordie bridesmaid, who had meanwhile dissolved into a fit of giggles. Therefore, she promptly beat her about the head with the pillow as well, thoroughly dishevelling Pippa's bushy red mane as she did.

"Yes, fancy that! Pippa West can't get her man. He must be one of those 'funny' sort," Nancy charged for good measure, winking at Eileen and ganging up with her in conspiratorial relish.

"Yes," her friend crooned, "the kind that 'fancies' men instead!"

Pippa had barely motioned to register outrage at such an aspersion before both Nancy and Eileen had gripped their pillows anew to deliver a volley of well-aimed blows that sent the redhead somersaulting clean off the bed to land with thud on the bare floor boards, cackling hysterically.

Meanwhile, downstairs in the sitting room, Mr King looked up from his pipe and newspaper, and Mrs King from the thousand-piece jigsaw that was her evening relaxation. With the chandelier above them shuddering from all that girlish tomfoolery, each parent glanced across at the other with weary resignation. Wild child indeed!

* * * * *

Once the autumnal mist had lifted, the sun broke through to reveal a lovely sunny day. Therefore, after lunch Nancy suggested they partake of an afternoon stroll through the tranquil forest glades that stretched out beyond the village green.

"Now you can see why I love this place," she explained as the three of them marched through the shady woodland, a lively breeze swaying the branches above them and hurrying along those leaves that had already fallen.

"Aye, so does Holly, by the look of it!" Pippa huffed, the family's bounding golden Labrador tugging her along with such vigour that the amber-crowned WAAF was unsure whether she was taking Holly for a walk or Holly was taking her.

"Yes, apologies," Nancy bellowed. "However, I usually keep her on the lead lest she dive off into the undergrowth, where there might be adders lurking."

"What? Poisonous snakes?" Eileen's eyes popped with alarm.

"Oh, don't worry. It's probably too late in the season for them now anyway. Mind you, there are wild boars about. But if we make enough noise then, like the snakes, they will probably keep themselves to themselves."

Even the thought of snakes left Eileen shuddering. Perhaps that posting to Malaya (with all its jungle creepy-crawlies) she had recently missed out on wasn't such a loss after all!

"This is one of the things I missed most when I was away in the RAF: going for long walk through the forest with Holly," Nancy asserted. "It's always so invigorating. And it affords one time to ponder ones life and give thanks for all the good things one has been blessed with."

"You're certainly lucky to have grown up in such a magical setting," noted Pippa in between Holly still pulling her this way and that. "And now you've secured your demob and are all set to marry a decorated war hero."

"Don't worry, girls. Your turn will come," Nancy consoled them, reaching down to grab a handful of dead leaves with which to playfully shower Eileen.

"It's alright for you," Pippa groaned. "They've been packing all us remaining WAAFs off on these so-called 'vocational' courses. To 'prepare' us for the big wide world of civvy street."

"Preparing us for a life to domesticity, more like. What's 'vocational' about learning to cook, sew and change babies' nappies? Do they not think I haven't learned enough about that already, having helped raise my cousin Monica?" Eileen huffed – one more reminder of why she was adamant she would not meekly accept a return to the world the Women's Auxiliary Air Force had otherwise enabled her to escape.

"All the more reason to get your arse on that boat to Australia. See the world – like you've always promised you would," Nancy counselled her.

"What about you, pet? What are you planning to do once that ring's safely on your finger?" Pippa then enquired of their host.

"Well, Peter has applied to continue with his commission. So I may end up seeing the world too – albeit this time in MQs as an air force wife. Otherwise, I've thought about writing a book about my time with the Women's Auxiliary Air Force. I've always fancied being an author."

Eventually the trees gave way to open heathland, upon which they could spy more wild horses grazing. With even Holly now panting furiously, all three of them elected to sit down upon a rough-cut wooden bench from which they could catch their breaths and admire the view. It fell to Nancy to be sat in the middle, in due course casting her sisterly arms around them both as they savoured the peacefulness.

"I'll buy it."

"I'm sorry."

"Your book, pet," Pippa repeated, reaching up a hand to tug Nancy's woolly bobble hat over her eyes. "I'll buy it."

"Yes, especially if *we* get a mention!" Eileen teased her.

Nancy shoved her hat back out of her bright blue eyes and offered them both a faintly lachrymose smile, as well as hug from those arms draped around the two very best friends she had ever had.

"Believe me, girls. Had I not been blessed to have had you two remarkable souls in my life, then I would only ever have had half a story to tell!"

* * * * *

"Big day for you tomorrow, eh, pet."

Having bid Nancy goodnight, Pippa and her fellow bridesmaid drifted off to their room. The bride-to-be did likewise, aware that tomorrow she would wake up in her family home for the last time as Miss Nancy King.

As soon as she had closed the door to the guest bedroom, Pippa noticed Eileen exhale volubly before sitting herself down in the window sill to rest her arms and her chin upon her folded knees. There she lingered to admire the bright albino moon that was illuminating the meadows that spread out in the distance towards Salisbury. Meanwhile, the slightly ajar window permitted the evocative hoot of an owl stirring in the woodland to carry into their room.

"Pippa," she sighed.

"Aye, pet," her friend replied, whilst readying herself for bed.

"Can I tell you a secret?"

Pippa was momentarily taken aback. "Of course you can. That's what best mates are for," she assured her even so.

"A long time ago I once betrayed Nancy. I mean, I had an affair with a man she was dating."

Pippa really was taken aback now. Though Eileen didn't glance away from gazing up at the moon, she knew it was possible that indignation, if not outrage, might yet be contorting the face of the one in whom she was venturing to lift from her soul something that had been troubling her throughout their stay. However, in the absence of such an outburst she pressed on.

"He was a Canadian pilot at Scampton. Nancy and I had run into him a few weeks earlier when his plane had been diverted to our station because of bad weather. He was a much older man; rugged with it, and a bit of a maverick. Nancy fell for him straight away – as I guessed she would. But then, unbeknown to her, so did I. Alas, he was killed shortly afterwards. Nancy never did find out about us.

"I can't explain why I did it. I felt so desperately guilty afterwards. Maybe I still do. I would never do anything that would ever hurt her," Eileen turned to look up at her friend, a faint glistening in her eyes. "But I just felt I had to tell someone; maybe to finally show how sorry I am for being, well... human."

The surprise revelation prompted Pippa to hiss down her nostrils, though not in a condemnatory way. Instead, she moved in to join her friend over by the window and to gaze up at the huge, rotund light in the heavens that Eileen's own gaze was once more trained upon.

"We were all 'human' during the war, Eileen. It's what war does to people: brings out the best and worst in them.

"Besides, I have a secret too," she continued. "I've never told anyone else about this... but I once had an affair with an older man too – a married one at that. In fact, he was the station commander, no less; and I was assigned to clean and tidy his quarters. Yet I couldn't even think straight whenever he was in the room – though God alone knows why. Yes, he was handsome. Realistically though, a public school-educated senior officer was never going to leave his wife and bairns to marry the likes of me – a young lass from a northern pit village with an accent to match. I was just his little distraction 'for the duration'. Thank God no one ever found out. Yet even now I feel such a fool just thinking about it. But... well, you live and you learn, eh, pet."

You live and you learn: It was Geordie wisdom at its most succinct. Thereupon, Pippa rested her head tenderly upon Eileen's. There together they pondered how much they had indeed lived and learned; and having thus let go of these regrettable chapters in their lives they sought from Heaven the only forgiveness that now mattered.

\* \* \* \* \*

The wedding of Squadron Leader Peter Knowles DFC (Bar) and Miss Nancy King took place on Saturday, October 6th 1945 in the parish church on the edge of the New Forest where her family worshipped. It was a truly glittering affair, attended by folks from her village and beyond. It was also amply supplemented by many RAF and WAAF personnel with whom Peter and Nancy had served (a welcome touch of relief from air force blue nonetheless provided by Nancy's older brother looking resplendent in his naval commander's uniform). A Royal Air Force guard of honour saw Nancy and her father into the church. As promised, the bride looked magnificent in the beautiful wedding dress her mother had scrimped and saved to have made (as did Eileen and Pippa holding its train). The groom and best man looked immaculate too in their uniforms and medals. Sure enough, both bridesmaids could be glimpsed nursing stray tears when the moment arrived for the groom to lift the veil and exchange vows with his beautiful bride.

The service was followed by a reception with family and friends, at which a band played, Eileen sang, and everyone danced. At the end of this magical evening, Peter and Nancy set off together with the best wishes of their guests ringing in their ears (as was the clanging of the cans that the pilots of Peter's squadron had tied with string to the bumper of his little Triumph sports car!).

* * * * *

Alas, like all big days, Nancy's big day was over much too soon, and Eileen and Pippa found themselves back in uniform on the concourse of Southampton railway station – a little bit hung over, but otherwise content that they had played their part in making that big day such an enchanted memory.

"You know, in a funny old way I'm going to sad now it's all over,"

"Me too," Pippa concurred, sensing there was something more profound than yesterday's wedding that Eileen was alluding to.

Indeed they suspected that Nancy had spoken truer than she knew that afternoon on the bench. Of all the wonderful memories that the quarter of a million young women who had served in the Women's Auxiliary Air Force would look back on in the years to come (and about which Nancy might yet write), it would be the friendships they had made that they would always treasure the most. Likewise, Pippa and Eileen knew it would be that incredible camaraderie that they would miss the most. How else would a girl from a broken home in Birmingham have ever come to have shared such a close and defining relationship with a well-to-do lawyer's daughter from Hampshire and a colliery overseer's offspring from Durham? And during their time together how else would they have ever come to have shared fun, laughter and adventure (as well as romance) with amazing young men from every corner of the English-speaking world?

If Nancy was true to her calling as a globe-trotting air force wife, and Eileen could yet bag that elusive recording contract in the United States, then this wedding might just have been the last occasion in a very long time that they would enjoy the opportunity to bask in their enduring friendship. Three beautiful young women; three different, yet compelling stories; one Royal Air Force in which they had proudly served; one long and bitter war in which they had done their duty; and which had bequeathed them more than enough tales of courage and fortitude; of mischief and hilarity; and, yes, of  tragedy and heartache too. Enough indeed to fill Nancy's book – and of which, as long as they lived, they would never forget.

* * * * *

*"Assisted passages to Australia,"* read the large advertisement hoarding that had caught her eye, with its endearing cartoon of a kangaroo beckoning newcomers from the Mother Country.

Having waved Pippa off aboard her train – and with a while to wait before the arrival of her own delayed train to Waterloo – Eileen had made a passage instead to the refreshment hall. There she could sip piping hot tea and wryly look back on just how much of her service life had been spent waiting for trains. She could also continue studying that evocative poster across the way and the possibilities of the new life Down Under that could be hers once the RAF finally got round to releasing her.

It was while lost in such musing that she became aware of a handsome army officer in a kilt staring at her through the window of the canteen. At first she feigned to ignore him; but then she didn't quite withdraw her eyes fast enough when she caught him smiling at her. She felt obliged to return his smile, albeit grudgingly. As she feared, it was all the excuse he needed to open the door and breeze up to her table. Then, without thought of asking, he slid into the seat opposite and removed his Glengarry. Damn cheek, she thought.

"I hope you don't mind," he softened his features to apologise. "But you're Eileen Kimberley, aren't you?"

She had been here before. "That's right," she therefore drew breath and eyed him up warily, thereby hoping she had not fuelled his hopes. An autograph she would kindly oblige. Anything else, forget it.

"I thought you were. I've heard you sing... At a concert you performed recently. You have a marvellous voice, if I may say so."

"Thank you, sir" she replied, grateful for the compliment, but wishing that one day a fawning remark like that might just be accompanied by the unfolding of a contract for her to sign, as well as cheque book and pen poised to write out a sizeable advance.

"It's fortunate you are here. I hope you can spare me a moment."

Eileen had barely motioned to reply that there was a train she needed to catch (even if it was running fifty minutes late!) when he lifted a hand to halt her.

"My name is Lieutenant Harold Mackenzie – of the Argyll & Sutherland Highlanders. I'm in charge of the reception party looking after those of my regiment's prisoners of war who are arriving back from the Far East. In fact, I am currently processing a group that arrived on a ship that docked this very morning."

"I'm so glad they're home. I've heard the Japanese did terrible things to our boys whilst they were in captivity."

"You heard right then. Half-starved and forced to build a wretched railway through the jungle, many succumbed to disease or appalling mistreatment. Those that survived were then transported in the suffocating holds of 'hell ships' to do forced labour in Japan. Sadly, many of them would never get to see the glens again."

"Like I said, it was truly terrible," she shook her head in righteous anger.

"Alas, stepping off a ship to cheering crowds and jostling reporters has probably been a bit overwhelming; which is why I have ushered them into a room by themselves. At least that way they can gather their thoughts before the final train journey home. That's why I was wondering if... well..." the officer prevaricated, searching for the appropriate form of words with which to beg from her what he knew would be a daunting favour.

"Look, these chaps haven't set eyes on a white woman in over three years, let alone heard one sing. Therefore, I was wondering if you would be kind enough to accompany me and perhaps say hello to them. I can't promise they will have heard of you. But I know they will appreciate such a gesture all the same."

She was unsure what to say. Or even what she could conceivably say that would leaven the trauma of long years spent in such dismal captivity. However, if she had any pretentions to be a professional artiste then surely she could not begrudge these potential new fans a few minutes of her time.

"Okay, if you think I can cheer them up," she agreed, finishing her tea, grabbing her case and following the tall, stocky officer off to a waiting room that had been set aside especially for these new arrivals.

To be sure, Eileen had seen the newsreel footage of the POW camps and the disbelief upon the faces of their skeletal inmates that liberation had dawned at last. Yet whilst the lads that Lieutenant Mackenzie had marshalled together had clearly put on weight since then (and been kitted out with new uniforms – including red-and-white chequered Glengarries), it was possible to discern in their gaunt faces that what they had experienced would remain with them for a very long time to come. Firstly though, to a man they rose to their feet and stood to attention as their reception officer strode in and introduced their surprise guest.

"As you were, men. Now listen hear. You won't have heard of this young lady. But this is Eileen Kimberley. She's served with distinction in the Women's Auxiliary Air Force. Whilst you've all been away she has also earned a reputation as a popular singer."

"Hello, Eileen. It's good ta' meet ye," one of the lads held out his hands and offered her his crooked smile, to general concurrence all round.

"Yes, thank you for coming to say hello to us," another of them enthused, almost as if he was the first Adam marvelling with thanksgiving that into his presence had been ushered his newly-fashioned Eve.

Eileen was moved. Then she offered them a smile of her own and spoke from the heart, saying "I want you to know we are all so glad you are home at last,"

"Aye, love. So are we!" someone gushed ironically, prompting mirth from his comrades

"If tha' lassies back home are all as beautiful as ye, then methinks we've got some catchin' up ta' doo'!" another chuckled in his thick Glaswegian drawl.

"Aye, an' for once we're thinkin' why canni' we not have joined tha' air force instead!" someone else added to a further burst of laughter.

"So ye can sing then, lass?"

"I can sing." she shrugged, biting her bottom lip and twisting on her heels coyly. "What do you want to hear?"

The thought suddenly struck her: the last time these boys had probably listened to the wireless was the winter of 1941/42. A whole swathe of soul-stirring music had since come and gone of which they knew nothing.

"How about something by Gracie Fields," someone up the back called out

"Why not. Do you remember *'Wish Me Luck As You Wave Me Goodbye'*?" Eileen enquired, jauntily warbling the opening lines as a prompt.

"'Wave me goodbye'? Steady on, lassie. We've only just got back!" the Glaswegian rasped. Cue more heartfelt laughter all round.

"I used ta' love George Formby. I remember how he really used ta' make people laugh," someone else proffered.

"Are you trying to suggest I look like George Formby!" Eileen dug her hands into her hips in faux outrage, prompting more hearty guffaws.

"Campbell here, he's been overseas a long time, ya' know," his mate suggested, "He's fair forgotten what a lassie looks like."

It was good to see them in such high spirits after what they had endured. Therefore, wishing to oblige, Eileen straightened her back and reasserted herself in their midst.

"Let me see," she quizzed them playfully. "Who's seen the film *'Turned Out Nice Again'*?"

Straight away a forest of hands stood erect. For some of them it was possible that this 1941 comedy was the last British film they had watched.

"Well, how about this little number from the movie – if I can remember the lyrics. But I think they go something like this…"

Then, without accompaniment – and with the abiding memory of a night out that she had enjoyed at the time – she launched into an impromptu performance of *'Auntie Maggie's Remedy'*. With its risqué references to 'a pain in the Robert E. Lee', 'getting windy' and 'a girl whose putting on weight in a spot where it just shouldn't be' – to all of which the antidote was the old girl's eponymous potion – she soon had them belly-laughing, supplemented by hearty Caledonian cheers at appropriate points in the song..

It was as she was drawing her witty rendition to a close that from out of the adjoining toilet there emerged a Highlander supporting with his shoulder a young man whose ill-fitting sailor's uniform and drawn, listless demeanour immediately set him apart. This young man the soldier now eased into a vacant chair. The applause suddenly faded. To the instinctive frown of silent pity that Eileen donned was added a gathering realisation that the face was achingly familiar – even after all these years.

"Frank?" she felt herself moved to verbalise such a shocking epiphany.

"Ye know this guy?" one of the lads frowned too, staring across at her.

"I think so… I mean… Yes, I do."

"Some of the lads also know him as Frank. They think he may be one of the survivors from the sinking of Force Z during the opening days of the Japanese attack," Lieutenant Mackenzie interjected as Eileen moved in closer to the man who had been her childhood playmate, squatting down to gaze into vacant eyes that stared past her as if she was not even there.

"In the weeks before Singapore surrendered many of the sailors and marines from the two battleships were handed rifles and ordered to make good the losses in our ranks: 'Plymouth Argylls' the lads used to call them – after the football team. Frank here was liberated from a prison camp in Siam, where we found him in a pitiful condition. We've cared for him since; but I'm afraid…"

Afraid? Afraid of what? The answer to that question came when Eileen shot a leftward glance at the Highlander who had been assisting Frank with his ablutions, and who now stared back at her with pained regret and circled his forefinger about in the vicinity of his right temple.

"Frank… Frank… It's Eileen," she fought off the urge to weep. "You remember me. I used to live in the next street to you – in Selly Oak. You were my first boyfriend. We used to go everywhere together…"

For a moment he lifted his vacant stare, his watery eyes alighting upon her soft, blanching face. It raised the hope within her that those memories might just prevail of the two of them strolling arm-in-arm in Cannon Hill Park, or canoodling on the back row of the Gaumont picture house. However, she watched helplessly as instead the vacant stare returned and he sniffled fearfully, like an infant that had spotted the approach of the bogeyman.

"Frank… Frank… What have they done to you, Frank?"

Sensing her distress, the officer lifted Eileen back to her feet and slowly escorted her out of the room. However, her anguished sobbing crowded out what brief merriment there had been amongst the Highlanders, miens of hardened sobriety returning to their care-worn faces. Meanwhile, the faithful comrade of the hollow shell of skin and bone that had once been Able Seaman Frank Rossiter moved in to tenderly cradle his trembling frame, aware from bitter experience just what three-and-a-half years of malnutrition, abuse and torture can do to the mind of a man.

# 22

The buzzer on the switchboard jolted Eileen out of her daydream. She hauled a lead across to connect and answer the call.

"Thetford 782, which number please... Go ahead, caller, you're connected," she replied, just a hint of world-weariness creeping into the clipped and punctiliousness manner with which she handled the call.

The switchboard went quiet again, permitting the bored telephonist to retrace her train of thought, staring up at the clock on the wall to see if the hands might have moved since she had last glanced at it.

Witnessing the void that had been Frank's broken expression had brought things more clearly into perspective during her final few weeks with the Royal Air Force – not the least being the mocking disparity between the wars these two childhood sweethearts had experienced; hers pock-marked by tragedy for sure, but also by dancing, romancing and happy memories aplenty; his by the unrelenting horror and mind-shattering degradation of his incarceration in that jungle prison camp.

Eileen's final posting was to RAF Methwold in Norfolk – a satellite station for her old stomping ground of Feltwell. The proximity of so many familiar haunts associated with her first operational posting back in 1942 made wistful reminiscing all the more poignant. Perhaps it was just the case that, with no more ops over Germany and more and more personnel being demobbed, those that remained had time on their hands with which to reflect upon a tumultuous chapter in their lives that had now closed. Even the dances and the concerts that the station organised seemed to be overshadowed by this curious sensation of *la recherché du temps perdu*.

In such spirit, Eileen remembered the day she and Nancy had first stepped into their billet at Feltwell – "Bloody hell, this place is draughty," Nancy had trumpeted with her trademark brassiness. She recalled too its little stove roaring away in the middle of the billet, and which attempted without much success to banish the seasonal nip in the air. Remembering the hoary frost she had woken up to this morning, nothing much had changed on that score! She recalled their scrape with the two local boys who had accosted them down a dark country lane not far from here. Her recollection of ramming her bike into her assailant and then both of them legging it back to camp occasioned another chuckle. "Bloody good show," she remembered their section officer had commended them (though only after she had given them the obligatory dressing down for mislaying their bicycles!).

It had been at Feltwell that she had first encountered those raucous New Zealanders of No. 75 Squadron – doing their bit for the Mother Country twelve thousands miles from home. To her surprise though, it was Gerald into whose arms she had drifted, the chivalrous Herefordshire flight engineer whose hopes of eventual marriage she had felt unable to reciprocate. Now an up-and-coming Labour MP, she had read reports recently about the rousing maiden speech he had delivered in the House of Commons. She recalled too the day Alastair Manley had arrived unexpectedly at Feltwell when his plane had been diverted – as well as the unforgettable (and unsanctioned!) flight aboard that plane that he had secreted she and Nancy aboard.

Sadly – along with many fine men that night – this larger-than-life Canadian had surrendered his life during the famous 'Dambusters' mission that had set off from RAF Scampton in May 1943. It had been a mission in which Eileen had been privileged to play a modest, yet memorable part (wryly she wondered if Air Chief Marshall 'Bomber' Harris still remembered that part!). Healing had been effected by her subsequent transfer to RAF Dunholme Lodge – home of those riotous Rhodesians of No. 44 Squadron. It was here that she had been befriended by Pippa – whose enthusiastic endorsement (along with that of Polly the Hen!) had unwittingly helped launch Eileen's remarkable singing career with the Royal Air Force. It was at Dunholme too that she had rescued that impish young Joey Abbott from his burning plane – an act of instinctive heroism that had forever endeared her to the tail gunner's fellow Australians.

By 1944 she was back in Nancy's company, this time stationed together at RAF Waterbeach – still her most fondly remembered posting of all. Here it was that Eileen had first experienced the thrill of jiving and jitterbugging with the Yanks – and of that magical first date with the most awesome Yank of them all: Nicky Braschetti. In the interludes between the handful of calls she was answering, she quietly shed a tear of thanksgiving that God had granted her the bittersweet privilege of having loved, and been loved by, this most promising young man, who – like so many other gallant Americans – had offered up his life for a just cause (and offered it a long, long way from home).

The memory of other amazing characters that she had known flitted into her thoughts: that cheeky Cockney WAAF, Cathy Clarke, and her adoring Wilbur; Section Officer Rachel Owen, who had first awakened her to the awesome truth that forgiveness was the free gift of grace alone; and the ever-genial Archie Wyndall, who had offered her the opportunity to join an unforgettable tour with his dazzling Ad Astra Dance Band. She was even given to idly musing what Sergeant Muriel Harris might be doing with herself now – someone who had spitefully sought to foil her dreams, yet towards whom this charitable young WAAF had learned to bear no ill will.

And now – in the time that remained – Eileen passed this final afternoon pondering the letters she continued to receive; for tomorrow she would return to her native Birmingham for Christmas and New Year leave, thereafter to be demobbed at last. The letters her father had been busy penning her were bubbling with the latest schemes he was mulling over for pursuing promising avenues of business (as well as offering advice regarding Eileen's own thinking aloud about the future). Meanwhile, the seed that Rachel Owen had planted was being tenderly watered by the ongoing correspondence she was engaged in with Harry Ewell (who was also on the cusp of being demobbed).

"Switchboard, which number please… Thank you, caller. I'm trying that number for you now… Go ahead, caller, you're connected."

And that was that. Eileen had just handled her very last call as a WAAF telephonist. With the clock having inched its laborious way to four o'clock, the relief shift had already breezed into the exchange. Unhooking her headset, she handed her seat to the newly-arrived operator and exchanged a few pleasantries whilst donning her greatcoat. Then she ventured outside on a crisp December afternoon upon which the sun was already setting, its vibrant streaks of amber and ochre leeching through the darkening clouds.

Carrying on her way took her past one of the station's huge, cavernous hangars, where she decided to stop and stare inside. A handful of fitters were working away in one corner, one of them intermittently whistling a tune which echoed in the stillness. Therefore, she felt at liberty to wander inside to say a final farewell to another remarkable companion from her years with the RAF.

It was only when one was stood next an Avro Lancaster Mark III heavy bomber that one truly appreciated what a colossal beast it was. Eileen felt quite insignificant standing alone admiring the aircraft that (alongside the Spitfire and the Hurricane) had won the war in skies for Britain. With its four mighty engines, one-hundred-and-two foot wing span, sixty-nine foot fuselage – and weighing in at thirty-six tons with its payload of bombs aboard – it must have taken both skill and nerves of steel to pilot one. Clad in its camouflage livery, this particular example belonged to No. 207 Squadron, which had been based at Methwold since plans to send it to the Far East had been abandoned following the surrender of Japan.

The story of 207 Squadron was typical. During the war its aircrew flew 540 operations, by both day and night, losing 154 aircraft. Almost a thousand of its aircrew were either killed or posted missing, and 171 of them served time as POWs of the Germans. Again, mirroring the epic story of Bomber Command, one fifth of those brave young men who had perished hailed from the Empire or Dominions. The squadron's most costly mission was the attack on the Wesseling synthetic fuel plant on the night of June 21st/22nd 1944, when five aircraft and thirty-two men were lost. In all, its aircrew were the recipients of seven Distinguished Service Orders, 115 Distinguished Flying Crosses, 92 Distinguished Flying Medals, and ten mentions in despatches.

Eileen stepped beneath the shadow of its wing to run a delicate and incongruous little hand upon one of the chunky tyres of its undercarriage. There she closed her eyes and offered up a silent prayer for the 55,573 courageous young men of RAF Bomber Command who had made the ultimate sacrifice – almost half of those who had served – as well as for the thousands more still nursing grievous wounds to bodies and minds that would require years of plastic surgery and other painful medical interventions in order to fit them for something resembling a normal life. Only German U-boat crews suffered a higher rate of casualties.

Sadly, now that war was over it seemed that a sense of shame and embarrassment about what had happened to places like Hamburg and Dresden would mean there would be scant recognition of their sacrifice. Indeed, Churchill had pointedly omitted any reference to the men of Bomber Command in his victory speech. Yet the achievements these brave lads had wrought were manifest – not the least being the substantial resources the *Luftwaffe* had been compelled to divert defending the skies over Germany. This in turn had denied the Nazis air superiority over the fronts in France, Italy and Russia – thus paving the way for the victory of Allied armies there.

To Eileen, such cold, strategic considerations were abstract. More than a few of those lads had been gallant friends she had known; friends she would never dance with again. Making her way back outside she turned to stare back at the enormous plane and take in the eerie tranquillity of the hangar for a final time. As she lingered, it was almost as if she could see their faces and hear their laughter. It was the way she would always remember them.

\* \* \* \*

Christmas at home was a welcome, yet strangely melancholic affair. Eileen put this down her own curious situation of being effectively-out-yet-not-officially-out of the Royal Air Force; but also to her mother having finished with one 'boyfriend', but having not yet stumbled upon whoever the next dubious character might be.

This meant that for the first time in a long while Mary seemed to want to draw close to her daughter. Maybe she was aware that in the intervening years Eileen had grown up and that it would not be long before she would leave home for good – maybe for America, Australia or wherever that the unquenchable wanderlust that service in the RAF had aroused might yet take her. What price now the mother's reckless chasing of younger men (and the promise of happiness thereby that had always proved delusional)?

Perhaps conscious of this – and to demonstrate that, wherever in the world she went, she would always love her mother – Eileen decided to take her up town to see New Street and Corporation Street gaily lit up with Christmas lights for the first time in seven years. Although what was on display in shop windows was still limited by rationing, it felt good for mother and daughter to be doing something together again – just the two of them.

After catching their breath at the Lyons tea shop, they decided to watch an early evening showing of *'Brief Encounter'* at the Odeon Cinema. By the time the scene arrived where Alec and Laura have their final platform farewell gate-crashed by the loquacious Dolly Messiter both mother and daughter were sobbing and sharing handkerchiefs.

"Were you and Dad ever madly in love – I mean like Alec and Laura were obviously in love?" Eileen enquired as they queued for the tram afterwards.

It seemed a strange question. For a moment Mary was reticent about recalling things that had happened a long time ago. So much water had passed under the bridge since then. The world was a different place now.

"As I recall, bab, we were," she eventually smiled, the glow from the gas lamps catching a wistful glaze in her eye as she spoke. Then her countenance darkened as she opened her heart and, for the first time in Eileen's hearing, admitted that "Now you ask, if I am honest then it was the one and only time I have ever been in love."

Eileen winced to behold the evident pain in her voice.

"Dad still remembers the time when you were both planning to get back together again. But… well, it didn't happen, did it."

There was a vague shake of the head that Mary had allowed another missed opportunity to be snatched from her hands. Though their nascent conversation was interrupted by the drawing up of the trundling blue-and-cream tramcar, something had stirred in her mother's soul that she was not going to shrug off. Once they had sat themselves down and paid for their fares, she sighed heavily and offered the wisdom of bitter experience.

"We were both fools. Instead of following our hearts, we listened to the wrong people filling our heads with all manner of nonsense. If I could have my life back again and do one thing differently, it would be to always, always listen to what my heart is saying and follow it. Maybe if I had followed my heart I would have still been with your father now. He was a good man, despite what others have said about him. I often think about him. I guess the truth is that I still love him even now. And were he to walk back into my life and ask me to marry him all over again, you know what, our Eileen: I probably would!

But I suspect it may never happen. I have missed my only chance of real happiness. Maybe I was unworthy of him."

"You can't tell yourself that, Mum. I have spent too long thinking I was unworthy of someone's love," her daughter counselled. Otherwise, she passed no comment on the other plaintive admission. From her many conversations with him over these last six months, Eileen knew that – for all that her mother still held a special place in George's affections – it was probably too late in the day for such wishful thinking to conceivably come to pass.

"Bab, I messed up your life. I'm sorry for that. Had we stayed together you could have had two parents to care for you – instead of just me. Had we stayed together we could have all lived together in one of those nice big houses in Quinton, and with a motor car and lots of holidays by the sea. Had we stayed together those horrible children at school wouldn't have called you spiteful names. Had we stayed together you could have stuck at those dance classes and maybe gone on to star in movies."

Eileen rested her head against her mother's shoulder, recalling that parting admonition that Frank had once offered her: *"Just remember, Eileen. This war may take you to unfamiliar places. You may meet and befriend many different people – in all kinds of bizarre circumstances. But never forget where you come from; nor the people in your life who have been there for you. In the end, they are the only ones who will really care about you. They are the only ones who will be there for you when this war is over and all the others have moved on."* Sage words indeed!

"Mum," she lifted her head and turned to address her in earnest. "You did the best you could. Besides, I will never forget that day you marched up to the school, grabbed hold of those boys by their collars and threatened to bang their heads together if they ever again called me... a 'bastard'!" she lowered her voice, the better to whisper the offending word on a saloon deck packed with respectable-looking passengers. "And as for dancing, well: what the dance classes couldn't teach me, hopefully Flight Officer Parkinson has."

"Who?"

"Flight Officer Cecilia Parkinson. She was one of the WAAF officers at Methwold. Believe it or not, she used to be a professional dance teacher before the war. Therefore, to keep her hand in – and God forbid that we remaining station personnel ever found ourselves at a loose end – she gave us dance lessons. She was always telling me I was a graceful mover! And what's more, she's promised to put in a good word for me if ever I need one."

Mary smiled. "Yes, you always did love singing and dancing. I do hope things work out for you in the end – even if it means that one day it may take you away from this city that I know you have always loved... to Hollywood."

"Oh, Mum. If only!" Eileen nudged her. "I rather fear that particular star crashed from the sky when I lost Nicky. For now I am just content to trust God and pray that He will reveal the right opening for me at just the right time – whatever that opening might be."

They continued to swap mother-daughter tales right up to the point where the tram arrived in Selly Oak, as well as on the lazy walk back from the stop to their humble abode. Once inside, Mary put the kettle on and scuttled about the kitchen to put together a hearty supper with which to round off a memorable evening together.

"Oh, by the way; there's a letter for you on the fireplace. It came this morning," she broke to call over to her daughter as she did so.

"It's probably from Harry – that boy I told you about that I met in Germany," Eileen surmised, returning from hanging up their coats.

"I don't think so. It says it's come all the way from Australia. I am sorry, bab. I completely forgot to tell you."

All of a sudden, her daughter's eyes were ablaze. Racing over she picked up the letter in a flurry of excitement and sliced open the envelope. Unfolding the pages, she then flashed her eyes across the pertinent details and let out one almighty gasp, closing those eyes in thanksgiving.

"Is it...?" her mother half-rejoiced, yet half-feared. Eileen bit her lip and nodded. Her mother looked her up and down askance, but could not bring herself to verbalise what it now meant.

"Yes. It's from Eleanor Abbott in Queensland – Joey's mother. I simply must tell Dad the good news," she wept.

Eileen drew forward to hug her mother excitedly. By so doing, at that seminal moment she had no way of discerning that the complexion was visibly draining from her mother's cheeks. It was as if the only residual beacon of light in Mary's life was about to be snuffed out. The one glimmer of hope she had clung to since learning of Eileen's remarkable reconciliation with her father would soon be leaving for the other side of the world.

Before that happened though, Eileen's thoughts turned to one further concluding formality that needed attending to before she would be free to face the future.

\* \* \* \* \*

"Next."

"Leading Aircraftwoman 2090088 Kimberley, Eileen K."

There was brief moment during which Eileen was left hanging while the assistant quartermaster scanned for her name on the list. Then – having recognised it from somewhere – she looked up from her paperwork and a beady eye alighted upon the WAAF now waiting patiently in line.

"Yes, *the* Eileen Kimberley!" Eileen flashed her eyebrows before lifting up onto the table her kit bag and its contents for the woman to check.

Everything was ticked off as present and correct. As it was cleared from the table Eileen caught her last sight of the bag she had hauled around with her for the last four years before it disappeared to be booked back into the stores.

"No weapons or other explosive devices to be handed in?"

It was Eileen's turn to look askance.

"No," she declared with a hint of amusement.

"And I take it you're keeping your uniform," the clerk grunted, eyes once more scanning over the plethora of bumf in her hand.

"Yes."

"In which case, sign for these – the clothing vouchers you are entitled to in lieu of a demob outfit."

Eileen duly signed. The clerk's eyes meanwhile raced over the paperwork a final time.

"That's everything then. Here's your RAF Form 2783 – 'Notification of Final Payment of Pay and Allowances Due for War Gratuity and Post War Credit'," she observed, stamping a few more papers and handing Eileen an envelope containing the said document.

And with that mouthful of official verbiage – and in the absence of a 'goodbye', 'so long' or 'kiss my arse' – it was all over. She was no longer a rank or a serial number, but just a name again: Miss Eileen Kathleen Kimberley.

\* \* \* \* \*

It was fortunate that No. 105 Personnel Despatch Centre (WAAF) just happened to be the old barrage balloon station at RAF Wythall in the Worcestershire countryside, just a few miles south of Birmingham. Therefore, with demobilisation complete, two short bus journeys would see her safely back home in Selly Oak. In addition, before she left a WAAF officer did make a point of shaking her hand and wishing her all the best for the future.

The journey home gave her time to open the envelope and scan through the particulars of her return to normal life. Dated January 4th 1946, her final pay packet was three pounds, fifteen shillings and eleven pence. In addition, she was entitled to a payment for War Gratuity and Post War Credit in order to tide her over until she could find a job (although – true to the bumbling reputation of officialdom – she had been forewarned that it might be two months before this would be credited to her Post Office savings account!). With fifty-one months service in total that worked out to be just shy of eighteen pounds for War Gratuity and twenty-five pounds for Post War Credit. Interestingly, Labour's 1945 election manifesto had warned that "a short boom period after the war, when savings, gratuities and Post War Credits are there to be spent, can make a profiteer's paradise". Therefore, in a sign of things to come, the Attlee government had promptly hiked the rate of Income Tax to make sure these so-called 'profiteers' wouldn't be getting their hands on Eileen's money!

At last, with just her handbag and the uniform she was stood up in, she arrived home and could head upstairs to undertake one more poignant act that would complete the transformation from airwoman to civilian. With clothes laid out on the bed ready, she wandered over to her dressing table.

First to go was the cap. Watching herself in the mirror – and with calm and purposeful resolve – she gently lifted it from her head, unclipped her hair, and shook her dark, silky locks free, brushing her hands through them to add body. Then she unbuttoned her tunic and removed it. The skirt too was undone and laid aside. The tie was loosened; and finally the blouse removed.

She spent a few moments standing there in her underwear, admiring her still curvaceous figure before slipping on a petal-patterned dress and hooking a belt around it with which to show off those commendable curves anew. Then she gathered up the discarded uniform, draped it all together on a hanger, and placed it inside her wardrobe. One day it would emerge again, she hoped: something to show off in years to come, and to tell her children and grandchildren the story behind it.

Finally, having sat down at the dressing table, she took from the drawer a small presentation box. Opening it she lingered to study the George Cross and ribbon inside – 'For Gallantry', read the inscription upon it. Placing the box upon the dresser, she then carefully slid from the finger of her left hand her beautiful three-stone diamond cross-over engagement ring. This she placed alongside the cross in the presentation box. Lifting up the box and staring wistfully at both medal and ring – respectively symbolic of her service to her country and of the love of a very special man that she had known whilst performing that service – she recalled lines of a famous poem by A E Housman that she had memorised from her schooldays, and which seemed appropriate for this final act of closure...

*"Into my heart on air that kills,*
*From yon far country blows.*
*What are those blue remembered hills?*
*What spires, what farms are those?*

*That is the land of lost content,*
*I see it shining plain.*
*The happy highways where I went,*
*And cannot come again."*

She closed the box and lovingly placed it back inside the drawer of the dressing table – two more incredible tales of 'lost content' that she would one day bore her grandchildren with! Then she looked up at her reflection in the mirror and observed a smile dawning for the first time. One long, happy highway had come and gone. A new highway was beckoning.

# *23*

*"Waltzing Matilda, waltzing Matilda,*
*You'll come a-waltzing Matilda with me.*
*And he sang as he watched and waited till his billy boiled,*
*'You'll come a-waltzing Matilda, with me'..."*

There was no mistaking the carnival atmosphere abroad on this bright spring afternoon – even if it was tinged with a note of maudlin farewell. The crowds lining Liverpool's waterfront were enthusiastically waving up at the decks of the converted troopship, from where this refrain was ringing out – so evocative of the thrilling new land where its passengers were bound.

"So. This is it, I guess," said Eileen, mesmerised by the sea of happy faces lining the decks and waving back.

"Yes. This it is. No turning back now," she heard her father insist. There was equally no mistaking the resolve in his tone as he stood erect beside her, his gaze also transfixed by those heaving decks.

"They say Australia is the place that all aspiring young people should be heading for nowadays," she then noted.

"Then these Aussies should feel privileged that a 'youngster' called Kimberley is about to head their way!" her father asserted. It was an esoteric joke which Eileen appreciated, joining him in a melancholic chuckle.

To be sure, those passengers who were already aboard were clearly animated to be embarking upon the four week voyage around the Cape of Good Hope – to say nothing of the new life that awaited them when the ship progressively disgorged them in Fremantle, Melbourne and Sydney. And yet there was the inevitable awareness that in order to pursue their dreams of a better life these emigrants were leaving everything behind – most pertinently, families and friends they might never see again. Indeed, amongst those passengers still milling about on the dockside there were tears aplenty as they savoured a last embrace with loved ones before trudging up the gangplank with a suitcase or two that contained all they would be taking with them.

Even though Japan had been defeated, Australians remained acutely aware of the vulnerability of their wide open spaces – just over seven million people in a country the size of continental Europe. Therefore, desperate to boost the country's population, the government in Canberra had begun promoting itself as *the* most exciting destination for ambitious young men and women looking to escape the gloom of post-war Britain. This particular sailing for Down Under would therefore be amongst the first of many in the coming years – from Britain as well as other war-ravaged nations of Europe.

However, at such a moment infused with emotion these geopolitical imperatives meant little to the twenty-two year-old girl from Birmingham who now turned to face her father and to bury her head into the breast of his suit. It was in these last few moments within his comforting embrace that she too now wept for all she was worth.

"Hey... Hey... Whatever happened to Daddy's big strong girl – the one who served four years in the air force, rescuing people from aeroplanes?"

George rested his head upon hers tenderly.

"I know... I'm sorry," she emerged, hurrying away lingering tears.

She felt so desperately guilty that, having searched so diligently to find him, here she was: about to be parted from him again. And it was all her doing! Yes, there was airmail – and maybe in time those airline companies now buying up the veritable surfeit of military transport planes would shrink the world still further. Yet realistically, who could say when Kimberley father and daughter would see each other again.

"You know I will always think about you," she trembled. "And pray for you too. Above all, I want you to know that – wherever I go and whatever I do – there will never be another man in my life who will ever replace you."

George grinned warmly.

"Oh, I wouldn't be too sure about that! But I know what you're trying to say. And you know too that you will always be my little girl," he assured her, humbled that the father-daughter bond would remain strong enough to survive the ten thousand miles that would soon lie between them.

Just at the point when George could sense tears welling in his own dark, winsome eyes, their heartfelt goodbyes were interrupted by a long blast of the ship's horn that filled the air and echoed off the surrounding buildings.

"Looks like they're about to cast off," he snuffled. "Better go then."

"Yes. Time to go," was all she could add laconically, fighting to hold back the urge to cry some more.

There was time for one last hug with which to cement that unbreakable bond, as well as to bid Godspeed for the voyage ahead. Then Eileen released her father and watched him stoop down to grasp hold of his own two suitcases.

With one in each hand, he then set his face towards the gangplank and commenced an ascent that would transport him to a new life across the ocean. Once arrived at its summit, he turned, placed a case down, and waved a final farewell to the beloved daughter he was leaving behind. Then he was gone.

Thereafter, the dockhands manoeuvred the gangplank back onto the edge of the quay, whilst along the ship's length ropes were being untied and cast off. Imperceptibly at first, but then with gathering pace, the mighty vessel edged away from the quayside.

Eileen had meanwhile drifted back over to the spot where Harry Ewell was waiting, Buster issuing a touching wail as she approached. His reward was for her to rub his coat and a caress his ears before she nestled herself beneath the arm of his master. There the three of them watched in contemplative awe as the tugs hauled the ship about upon the Mersey's timeless grey-green waters.

"Don't you think he'll find it strange?" Harry enquired. "I mean having to start out all over again in another country. And at his time of life too."

Eileen looked up to observe him qualify his words. However, her smile informed him that she was confident on that score.

"This is my father you're talking about. He has had to rebuild his life from scratch before," she assured him, in no doubt at all that George Wilfred Kimberley was still capable of turning his agile mind and his undeniable talents to any new challenge that came his way. Managing a sugar plantation in Queensland would be no different.

"It was clear from Eleanor Abbott's letters that she has been struggling to run the plantation since her husband's passing – even though her son is obviously doing his best. Alas, Joey might have been a courageous tail gunner; but he is not a businessman. Therefore, it was becoming essential that she recruit someone who could oversee the workers and manage the plantation – especially now that mechanisation is offering the prospect of growing the business."

"And your father just happens to be the right man for such a demanding job. Of course, I dare say it smoothed the way with Australian immigration authorities that his daughter just happens to be a war heroine who famously rescued one of their airmen from a burning plane."

"Undoubtedly!" she fired back tongue-in-cheek. It might also have helped when confronted with the awkward fact that her father was just teetering on the forty-five year age limit that applied to assisted passages. 'Youngster' indeed!

"Anyway," she continued, "Joey's mum did promise that there would always be an 'open-hearted welcome' in her home for me. I just enquired whether she would mind if my father called in the favour instead!"

"Talking of which, I suppose we should be grateful that your father has not been averse to calling in some favours of his own," Harry alluded.

Eileen smiled serenely. For just when she had been on the cusp of accepting a telephonist's job with the GPO in Birmingham, her mother had pointed out another letter that had arrived on the mantelpiece – this time informing her daughter that she had been successful following her audition to play the leading lady in a brand new musical opening at London's Adelphi Theatre. Together with her training in dance (which Flight Officer Parkinson's classes at Methwold had recently sharpened up), thus had her time as a celebrated songstress with the Royal Air Force helped land her the starring role in a production that was now playing to packed houses and rave reviews, placing the name of *"EILEEN KIMBERLEY"* up in lights at last.

Otherwise, Cecilia Parkinson was not the only person who had put in a good word on her behalf. Ever the incorrigible charmer, her father's career in the music business (modest though it was) had not left him without contacts amongst West End theatre impresarios! Meanwhile, Harry squeezed her proudly, thankful on a more personal level that George Kimberley's 'good word' had thereby helped land her boyfriend a role in the show too – employing his fine voice as a supporting member of the production's cast.

"You know, if the success of the show continues, the director is hoping we can transfer it to Broadway. Imagine that, Harry. I might get sing and dance in front of an audience of Americans again."

Eileen's head was still in a whirl at the mere thought of it when she suddenly felt Harry take hold of her shoulders and gently turn her about to face him. There she gazed up into expectant eyes that even so hoped they had correctly gauged her likely response to what he was about to ask. Nervously, he took from his pocket a small velvet box, opening it in her presence.

"Eileen. Will you marry me?"

For a second or two this strapping ex-military policeman feared he might have indeed made a wrong move. Even Buster's doleful eyes conveyed apprehension – the panting Alsation alternately staring up at them both, aware in his canine mind that something momentous was afoot.

"Oh, Harry," she sighed heavily, staring at the gem. "What can I say? It's absolutely beautiful! But look, it's going to be such a hectic life for us both from now on, what with the busy schedule of rehearsals and performances – plus there's the possibility of the show playing in New York. I don't know if I have the right to expect you to..."

"I know all that," he cut her short. "But, trust me: I have prayed long and hard about this. I have never been so sure about anything before. I knew I was in love with you that magical night in Sylt when I first heard you sing. Besides which, when you sloped off to the ladies' room earlier I rather craftily took the opportunity of asking your father's permission to..."

"You did!" she gulped, her eyes breaking briefly to glance up from the magnificent solitaire engagement ring that had so enthralled her.

"I think I persuaded him that I am able and trustworthy to look after his precious 'little girl' in his absence!" he grinned cockily. Then he donned that earnest demeanour once more.

"So I ask you again: Eileen Kimberley, will you marry me?"

There was a pregnant pause. Buster could hardly bear the tension – let alone his love-struck master! Then Eileen's mischievous brown eyes lit up and she flung her arms around Harry to permit him to lift her clean off the ground and be swung around.

"Yes! Yes! Yes!" she squealed, the heads of bystanders around about turning to observe him place her back down, undraping those arms from around his neck so that he might grasp her left hand and slide the ring onto her finger.

There was only the briefest moment during which she could admire the fit – and the women amongst the bystanders could coo joyfully – before the ship's siren fired off one final deafening blast. It prompted all those folks still lingering on the quayside to break out into an equally deafening cheer, launching themselves lustily into a chorus of *'Auld Lang Syng'*.

"Look, there's your father!" cried Harry, excitedly pointing out the figure in the trilby waving at them from the stern, where the ship's passengers were now congregating to take one last long look at dear old Blighty.

"So long, Dad! I will always love you!" she yelled out as she clung to the handsome young man into whose hands her father had now entrusted his most precious treasure. Together Eileen and Harry now joined in the singing, waving furiously at the departing ship as its propellers began to churn.

For all that Eileen Kimberley had spent her years striving for such things, in the end God had indeed granted her 'the desires of her heart' – in life, in love, and in a career in song – just as the Psalmist had promised. And though whenever they looked up at the night sky from now on, she and her earthly father would each see different stars shimmering in a different hemisphere, she nonetheless gave thanks that henceforth there was one bright Morning Star that would forever illuminate the thrilling highway that her Heavenly Father had now set her upon; as well as reminding her of the long and exceedingly memorable one she had already travelled.

# *I hope you have enjoyed 'To Reach For The Stars'.*

Many of the tales in this novel are based around stories and anecdotes that my late mother recounted to me from her own wartime years as a WAAF telephonist serving with RAF Bomber Command. To fill in the gaps I remain indebted to other personal recollections that many former WAAFs have kindly uploaded onto the BBC's 'People's War' project:-

*http://www.bbc.co.uk/history/ww2peopleswar/*

In addition, for readers who would like to know more about what life was like for Britain's legion of women-in-air-force-blue, I recommend:-

*"Keeping Watch: A WAAF in Bomber Command"*
*by Pip Beck (Goodall Publications, 1989)*

*"We All Wore Blue: Experiences in the WAAF"*
*by Muriel Gane Pushman (The History Press, 2006)*

Meanwhile, for a comprehensive account of the war as the aircrew of RAF Bomber Command experienced it, I recommend:-

*"Bomber Boys: Fighting Back, 1940-1945"*
*by Patrick Bishop (Harper Press, 2011)*

And likewise, as the aviators of the US Eighth Air Force experienced it:-

*"The Mighty Eighth: A History of the Units, Men and Machines of the*
*US Eighth Air Force"*
*by Roger A Freeman (Orion, re-issued 2000)*

\* \* \* \* \*

Although the principal characters in this book are fictitious, their stories are interwoven with real squadrons, real air stations, real air battles, and real incidents that took place involving the war's key protagonists.

For example, the famous opening address by Wing Commander Guy Gibson VC DSO (Bar) DFC (Bar) to the newly-assembled aircrews of No. 617 Squadron – like much else about the unforgettable 'Operation Chastise' that he led – is taken from the accounts gathered together in Max Arthur's superb *"Dambusters: A Landmark Oral History" (Virgin Books, 2008).*

There are also accounts of a WAAF telephonist on duty at RAF Scampton on the night of the 'Dambusters' Raid, who misdirected Air Chief Marshall Harris's momentous call to the White House in Washington DC through to the 'White House' public house in Grantham instead.

Likewise, on the eve of the raid Gibson's beloved black Labrador, Nigger, was indeed run over outside the guard house of RAF Scampton by a speeding car. The culprit was never found.

Although Flight Lieutenant Alastair Manley and his Avro Lancaster *'Y Yellow'* are creations of my own, their collision with a high-tension pylon over Holland mirrors the tragic fate of Flight Lieutenant Bill Astell DFC and his crew, who were flying *'B Baker'* on the night the dams were attacked. Otherwise, Manley would not have been the only '617' crew member to have had his trousers summarily removed as a right-of-passage into this remarkable squadron!

With his swept-back hair, thin-rimmed glasses and film star good looks, I confess that Major Nicky Braschetti bears a striking resemblance to a real flyer with the US 'Mighty Eighth' who my late mother was engaged to be married to, but who was tragically posted missing at the war's end. However, there is nothing fictitious about the 322<sup>nd</sup> Squadron and its mission to bomb the Nazi rocket facilities at Peenemunde on July 18<sup>th</sup> 1944. I am indebted to the 91<sup>st</sup> Bomb Group Memorial Association for the wealth of research material it has placed online – including the daily flight logs of the missions they flew.

Major Glenn Miller and his orchestra did indeed perform in front of General Dwight D. Eisenhower at a special concert on August 4<sup>th</sup> 1944 that was staged beneath camouflage netting at the Supreme Headquarters Allied Expeditionary Force at Thorney Island on England's south coast.

The character of the 'unconventional' Section Officer Rachel Owen was inspired by Felicity Ashbee – the real (and equally unconventional) admin officer who served at the Ottercops Moss radar station in late 1944. This witty, code-breaking aesthete later wrote a book about her service – including her banishment to Ottercops Moss – entitled *"For The Duration: A Light-hearted WAAF Memoir" (Syracuse University Press, 2012)*

The Ad Astra Dance Band was very much inspired by the great RAF dance bands of the era – including the Squadronaires (in which the legendary trombonist George Chisholm and jazz pianist Ronnie Aldrich played) and the Skyrockets (whose WAAF lead singer, Doreen Lundy, eventually married band leader and trombonist Paul Fenoulhet).

\* \* \* \* \*

I know my late mother would have found much to warm to in the character of Eileen Kimberley – even though (unlike Eileen) she never realised the career on the stage that she dreamed of as a teenager. However, wartime service in the Royal Air Force was to provide the launch-pad for many famous names in British entertainment – including Richard Attenborough, Richard Burton, Roald Dahl, Denholm Elliott, Bill Frazer, Tony Hancock, Christopher Lee, Warren Mitchell, Patrick Moore, Frank Muir and Peter Sellers.

In addition, Denis Norden and Eric Sykes were both patrons of the RAF Sylt Association, having served there together in 1945. They also organised a food collection for survivors of the Bergen-Belsen concentration camp after visiting it whilst performing a concert for RAF personnel at nearby Bückeberg.

* * * * *

The most famous WAAF of the Second World War remains Section Officer Daphne Pearson GC, who was awarded the George Cross in recognition of her daring rescue of a pilot from a burning bomber in May 1940 – the first woman ever to receive the award (and one of only thirteen female recipients to date). Daphne moved to Australia after the war. However, fifty-five years later – at a reunion of the Victoria Cross & George Cross Association – she would finally get to meet the man whose life she saved that day.

* * * * *

In conclusion, I trust you will join me in saluting all those British, American and Commonwealth service personnel who helped take the war in the skies to the enemy by day and by night – often at such staggering cost in their own lives. I hope I have been faithful to their memory, and that those dauntless veterans who are still alive will forgive the occasional literary licence on my part, as well as any (hopefully rare) minor factual errors.

If you have enjoyed reading this, why not delve into another tale chronicling the caprices of love, war and human frailty…

France 1954: two officers – one a dashing professional soldier and aristocrat, and one a low-born reservist – celebrate the rekindling of a curious friendship that was once fashioned in the crucible of war.

Seven years later, and that friendship has unravelled amidst the bitterness and recrimination of another brutal war that is now tearing France apart.

This is the story of that friendship; a story where moments of heroism and idealism alternate with moments when raw and unthinking passion sweeps all before it; a story of love and betrayal, and of a friendship that has all along been conducted unknowingly in the shadow of a cruel and most terrible secret.

17782354R00165

Printed in Great Britain
by Amazon